[Foxtrot Mike Lima]

Veronica Tracey Spy/PI
Book Five

[Cat Connor]

For information regarding permission email the publisher at 9mmPressNZ@gmail.com,
subject line: Permission.

Editor: Nicky Hurle
Chief nonsense wrangler: Margot Kinberg
Proofreader and saviour: Chrissy Gordon
Formatting: 9mm Press
Publisher: 9mm Press, New Zealand
Publication date: June 2024
Country of first publication: New Zealand.

ISBN: D2D paperback: 978-1-7386219-0-3
ISBN: 978-1-7386219-1-0
ISBN: ePub: 978-1-7386219-2-7
ISBN: 978-1-7386219-3-4
ISBN: 978-1-7386219-4-1

[Foxtrot Mike Lima]:

A bombshell in the newspaper causes Veronica Tracey to scramble for a plan to deal with potential fallout. Then out of the blue, she steps into a minefield created by her Nana and her on-again off-again boyfriend Ben Reynolds. The blast radius touches all aspects of her life permanently changing the trajectory.

Before Ronnie can fully process that stunner she gets word from *Genesis* that Ben is missing while working an intelligence gig. Finding Ben proves challenging even with her special skill set. With lies and half-truths mounting up, an illegal arms deal, incoming bad actors, and surprising revelations, life seemingly spins out of control.

Concurrently, Crockett grapples with a request to shield an old friend from the CIA and FBI, presenting both a challenge and an unforeseen advantage for the team.

The convergence of all factors sets fires that the team aren't sure they can extinguish as they hurtle ever closer to the brink of world war.

[Foxtrot Mike Lima] is dedicated to the memory of Ellie Conway.

9mm Press

Chapter One:
[Ronnie: Caught.]

I turned into Tawai Street and cruised to the end. Nothing of note. I checked my rearview mirror then my watch. My potential target backed out of a driveway and drove towards me. Here we go. Right on time.

Was he going to work or was he going to play?

"Time to leave," I whispered to myself. I flicked the right indicator then turned into Ararino Street.

The car followed. I could see the driver in my rearview mirror, and confirmed it was my target. Perfect. I indicated left at the railway station carpark entry and pulled in as if I was going to park my car and jump on a train. Not much choice when it came to parking spots in the northern end, so I went down to *The Tote* end of the parking area.

Two spaces from the end was a familiar car. I'd seen the target get in it several times but never clearly clocked the driver. This was my chance. I parked close enough, but not right next to the car. Sure enough, my target parked on the passenger side of the other car. It looked like there was a space between the cars from where I was. I pretended to be on my phone while keeping an eye on the situation.

The target and a woman exited their cars at the same time. Moments later he had his tongue down her throat, and I had some pretty pictures. I don't know if they didn't care, or thought they were being clever, as they walked arm in arm through the car park and into the subway. Both carried laptop cases. I had a feeling they were for show. Especially as he usually drove into the city during the week.

I had everything I needed to write a report for his spouse. I told myself it would be easier to just flick him the photos, but that's not how we operate.

My name is Veronica Tracey, everyone but Nana calls me Ronnie. I'm a mostly reformed espionage officer for NZSIS, but I occasionally do a bit of espionage work for various agencies. The pay is good. Technically, I co-own a private investigation company with my two best friends, Steph and Jenn, and am not in the intelligence game. *Wherefore Art Thou* is doing quite nicely thank you.

I have a few pet dislikes; one of them is cheaters, but I would never put anyone in danger from a jealous spouse attack. So, the photos we take of cheating spouses are for our use only. We see, so the client doesn't have to. It's a good policy. No names. No photos. No problems.

Once out of the car, I walked briskly to the platform. From the Upper Hutt side, I snapped a few more photos of the couple hugging on platform one. I can take a photo, and no one knows I've done it. It's a skill. I waited for a train. Two minutes later the Wellington bound train arrived and departed. The couple vanished with it.

My job was done so I drove back to the office to download the photos into the client file and write a report. Case wrapped up before nine in the morning. Excellent.

Five minutes after sitting down at my desk, my cell phone rang. No caller ID.

"Unknown caller," Siri said.

I watched the screen as the phone rang on and on.

"Are you going to get that?" Steph asked from her desk.

"Thinking about it." I wiped my finger across the screen. "Ronnie Tracey speaking. And you are?"

"Ronnie ..."

I recognised that poncy British accent. "Jackson."

"Long time, no hear. What you up to these days?"

"Not long enough."

He ignored my comment. Steph mouthed, "Who is it?" Guess my face wasn't expressing joy. I beckoned her to me and wrote a note: Jackson, knew him when I was stationed in London. I gave it to her.

She nodded.

"What's it been? Six years since you were in London?"

"All of that."

"I was surprised when I heard you'd left the service. What do you do now?"

"I'm a private investigator. I have my own business." My brain was racing to grasp why he was calling. And it kept coming up blank.

"Catching thieves and cheaters. Good honest work."

"Something like that. And you?"

"Still with the firm."

"And this phone call?"

"Was thinking about some travel. Wondered if New

4

Zealand was somewhere I should visit."

And he thought I'd want to know? We did not part on good terms. And strange gets stranger.

"I can't make that decision for you, Jackson." You might have to use your own brain this time. "It's lovely here. Depends what you want when it comes to a holiday, doesn't it?"

I wasn't selling it. I'd never be a travel agent.

"Perhaps I'll come over. Buy you a beer?"

"Sure." I will definitely be busy that day. "You've got my number."

"Which island are you on?"

"North."

"Near the capital?"

"Sort of."

"You're a mine of information. Cheers."

I hung up.

Steph came back over. "What's happening here?" she asked, waving a finger in a circle near my face.

"That's what I'd like to know."

"Something to do with your friend?"

"Oh, we're not friends. He's MI6 and the kind of officer that takes all the credit instead of doing all the work."

"Ah, that explains your less than delighted expression. I take it he's coming to New Zealand?"

"So he said. I'll be sick that day."

Steph laughed and went back to work. I watched her sit down at her desk while I thought about Jackson Frost. His parents should've called him Richard.

Why was he coming here? Now?

"You right there?" Steph asked. "Staring at me for a reason?"

"Sorry, zoned out." I smiled. "Hey, I got the photos this morning to seal the latest cheating spouse on my list. I'll write up the report and send you my hours. Let's invoice him and get shot of this case."

"Proved then?"

"Yeah, and I don't think our client is going to expect his husband to be cheating with a woman."

Steph nodded. "Poor bugger."

The frown was hard to shake, and I didn't need extra help to create wrinkles. I opened the file and added the finishing touches to my report. Jackson didn't stray far from my thoughts, and it irked me. Why now? What did he really want? I shuffled his call into a recess in my mind. He'd taken up enough brain real estate and he was nowhere near important enough to spend another minute on.

I fired the report to Steph for a read through and then updated my expenses and sent her that as well. The report came back with no changes. I attached it to an email and sent it to the client. We make no recommendations when it's a spousal case (unless violence is involved). It's up to each client how they proceed.

I flicked through my recent messages and texted Ben.

Me: Dinner?

Three dots appeared then disappeared.

Ben: Your Nana wants us to have lunch with her.

I puffed air from my mouth.

Me: And she asked you, not me. It's a trap.

Ben: Definitely a trap. I'll be at the office to pick you up at one.

Me: Fine. Okay.

Ben: We're stronger together. It'll be okay.

Me: If you say so. Do not underestimate that sneaky old woman.

Far from fine and okay. Nana managed to marry Donald off to Enzo, but that wedded bliss stoked her marriage fire instead of quelling it. She had Ben and I in her crosshairs, again. It was going to take some finesse to sidestep her conniving marriage trap.

Chapter Two:
[Mitch: We're all okay.]

The warm sun made seeing the screen in front of me difficult. Closing the curtains on a sunny day made me claustrophobic but having them open meant I couldn't see. There I was again in a catch-22 with myself, squinting at the screen. Wasn't the first time and it wouldn't be the last.

Sounds of laughter floated up the stairs. The girls were playing in the living room with their Barbies. I tried to settle myself noting the restlessness building wasn't connected to my inability to read the screen without squinting.

I picked up a pair of sunglasses from my desk and put them on, and then logged into *Genesis*. There were sixteen intelligence reports from Oceania and Southeast Asia. My domain. I thought being co-director of Iverson Industries and holder of many US Government military tech contracts was enough, and I never expected to be involved in the intelligence field, so I didn't see the baton coming. MacKinnon passed it to me via back channels after his death. My involvement was to remain confidential forever. No one knew who controlled *Genesis* or what regions were anyone's sphere of operation. That information got out once and resulted in the deaths of MacKinnon and his son. *Genesis* was a global agency that must be protected at all costs. The weight of that knowledge sat heavily on my shoulders.

I stood up and looked over the banister of the mezzanine floor when I heard the girls' voices coming closer. They were making their way up from the living area. I could see them on the stairs.

"Girls, Daddy has some work to do. Go back downstairs and play. I'll be down before lunch."

Grace responded, "Okay, Daddy. Can we have a snack please?"

I looked at the time. An hour until their usual lunch time. "Sure, but a piece of fruit, not cookies."

"Yes, Daddy," Isabella said.

The footfalls retreated.

Grace's voice rang out, "I have a banana!"

And started reading the reports. They'd been filtered through the analysts attached to my group. Eight of the reports indicated an arms deal fell over in Thailand. Good work. *Genesis* did that. Word was the players were moving the location of the deal from Thailand to New Zealand. Those behind the arms deal were still shadowy figures. Disruption is one thing, capturing the main instigators is another. Prior to Thailand we'd been crucial to the disruption of a deal going down in Poland. It was believed to be the same dealers.

I opened another report while giving the information thought. "Why would they move the operation to New Zealand?" I whispered at the screen. "It has to be virtual. They can't have moved the weapons themselves, surely?"

There was talk that it was a weapons system they were selling. It was unverified, but chatter suggested some form of long-range system.

By the time I'd read the whole report I knew as much as anyone else. The recommendation was to put at least one intelligence officer into the space to uncover who the kingpin was and prevent the deal going down. There was a link to the Thai Embassy in Wellington, albeit a loose link. Another report popped up on the screen. I clicked on it and started to read.

Air whistled through my teeth on an exhale. Just like that the stakes ramped up. Shit. I scanned the report for the names of the officers involved. One in particular popped up. I hadn't seen Jonathon Tierney's name in years, but there it was. He wasn't *Genesis* but had passed information to a *Genesis* operator, unwittingly? I hoped it was unwittingly, but I knew Tierney and he was one smart cookie.

Fishy. Very fishy.

If Tierney was involved, then it was a CIA operation. CIA were after the same players and result. Tierney as a source did not sit well with me. I clicked back to the previous report. There was another name: Jackson Frost, British citizen, disavowed MI6 operative, running amok with the Russians. He's thought to have had involvement in an illegal arms deal in Europe that went bad and led to the deaths of two MI6 officers. I stood and paced the mezzanine floor while I thought. I walked back to the computer and read the report again. My stomach twisted.

There was nothing to suggest Jackson Frost had travelled to New Zealand. He'd been added to the 'No Fly' list. I wasn't green enough to think that would ever stop someone determined to travel, but it certainly made it more difficult for them.

Who could I put into the operation? Now I had confirmation that the deals were headed to New Zealand and were no longer the purview of Europe or Asia.

Ben Reynolds was the logical choice. He was both CIA and *Genesis*. There was a good chance he'd already been given the assignment by his own people. To my knowledge Tierney was not in country running ops. No one had reported seeing him travelling. Of course, he could've flown with the US Air Force.

I paced some more. Wearing a track in the carpet used to be something Ellie was good at. Guess it was my turn now.

My computer dinged. I strode back to my chair and sat down. A message request hung on the screen. Incoming from the United States. As soon as I saw the name Jonathon Tierney, I wondered if it was actually incoming from the Unites States, or if he was here. It wasn't coming through *Genesis* but another secure message system, Signal.

I blew out more air and clicked on the request. No wonder my stomach twisted, I thought.

Tierney: Reaching out to see how you are?
Me: We're good. Life in New Zealand is good.

Tierney: Do you see anyone from home?

Me: I live in New Zealand, Tierney. The country was locked down for some time due to COVID. No one could travel to or from here, remember. For the best part of two years we stayed safe. Not much of that back home, was there?

Tierney: No. There wasn't. I meant recent visitors or contacts.

Me: No. Is there someone you think has visited me way out here in the Marlborough Sounds?

Three dots moved on the screen. I waited. I had no clue why Tierney was reaching out with questions. But having just seen his name in a report and now with proper contact, hinted that there was something he wanted.

Tierney: Anyone from the United Kingdom reach out or visit?

Me: No. What's this about?

Tierney: Your wife had a few friends in the UK and Russia. I wondered if anyone had reached out to you extending their condolences.

Me: I think we are way past condolences.

Tierney: People often keep in touch. I was just asking.

Me: Why?

Tierney: Don't worry about it, Mitch. Love to the girls. They must be quite big by now.

Me: Is there someone I should be looking out for?

Could someone mean us harm?

Tierney: No, I was wondering, that's all.

The chat window closed. All content turned to nothing but scattered remnants of pixels.

I stood and stretched. Tierney was not a person to make contact without a very good reason. He lurked in shadows. I knew that Tierney and my wife, Ellie, had an interesting relationship over the years. Comparatively friendly most of the time until it wasn't. He'd sent flowers when she died. That gave me an idea. Tierney said she had friends in the UK and Russia; I knew of a couple of them but not all.

In the spare room, at the back of the closet was a box of cards and letters that arrived after the deaths of Ellie and Delta A. I switched the screensaver on and went into the spare room to search out the box. It was easy to find. It was a bright yellow document storage box. I sat on the bed before taking off the lid. It was full. Ellie was a popular person. One short pep talk later I lifted the first five cards from the box. I opened each one and put it down after reading who sent it. Memories flooded back as I read more cards. The call. The gut punch that told me my wife was dead. Crockett arriving with the letter from Ellie. The end of life as we knew it. The beginning of solo-parenthood and a vastly different way of life. And now her old life was knocking on the door. But why? Had to be something to do with the illegal arms sale.

I sat reading and adding cards to the pile next to me.

Nothing screamed importance. Nothing caused me to pause. The pile grew until it toppled, cards cascading onto the floor. I hadn't kept in touch with anyone except Crockett on a regular basis. Crockett kept his ear to the gossip mill for me. There was talk that Ellie was alive. I'd heard gossip insinuating she survived the drone strike. Talk like that was dangerous and gave false hope. I couldn't afford to let myself go down that path; the girls needed a functioning parent. As far as I knew the two survivors were Crockett and Wesson. It looked like Davenport would pull through, but he didn't. That man was a fighter but that was a helluva losing battle.

I shook the thoughts away and opened another card. Jackpot. It was from Timothy Jones. He was a US Air Force pilot once upon a time. I let Jones' name trigger memories. He was a part of what Ellie called the Quasi-UN. They were a group of four who spent their days rescuing hostages, kidnap victims, and delivering a special brand of justice. Seamus Kennedy ARW. Colin Holmes SAS. Misha Praskovya FSB. Timothy Jones USAF. I placed the card from Jones on the other side of me from the discard pile. It wasn't long before I found another name from the group. This time Colin Holmes. I put that card on top of the other and continued looking. There was nothing that told me what to look for, so I went with my gut feeling when reading the names. There was a card from Rowan Grange. I threw that to the discard heap on the floor. Rock stars aren't a lot of use.

A card from Mike Davenport made the cut to the potentially useful pile. Mostly because I liked Lee Davenport's brother. He was ex-military and currently an actor. There were many letters and cards from Sandra Sinclair. She was the Delta A liaison and resident tech expert. She also took charge of our German Shepherd, Argo, when we left. Sandra needed her own pile. Some of her cards were recent and seeing them reminded me how hopeless I was at keeping in touch. I'd dropped them into the box to keep them for reasons unknown. More cards of no interest followed and then one other card stood out. It was from Ethan James, the husband of the former Director of the FBI, Cait O'Hare. He was a private security specialist after years of law enforcement. A reformed detective. He worked with Sean O'Hare.

I took the card through to the computer. Ethan worked with Sean O'Hare. He was one of the few people that would've known about the clandestine labs Delta A were investigating and what happened next. I placed the card next to my keyboard and went back to searching for whatever it was that I thought I would find. Then I found cards from two FBI SWAT members, Kris and Jerry Dixon. I added their cards to the helpful pile. The next card was from someone I vaguely remembered, a guy Ellie called, Andrews. He was also SWAT. His card needed to go on the 'of interest' pile. I knew Ellie was close to Andrews, and they'd worked and trained together. Cards from the rest of the Grange rock band were thrown to the heap on the floor. Leon Kapowski's card went on the helpful pile. He was Ellie's neurologist. There was a card from someone called Tony. It took a bit to find the connection, but I found it. Tony was bomb-squad. His card went in the helpful pile. A card from someone called Caps caused a smile to linger on my face. Caps was a gangbanger from D.C., someone that Ellie had a lot of time for. I flipped the card and watched it float down to the huge discard pile.

Then I saw it. A card from Jackson Frost. I didn't have any context for him to send a card. He was disavowed recently. Maybe Ellie had dealings with him when he was still MI6. Maybe Tierney expected Frost to reach out. I kept the card with the useful pile simply because I didn't know where else to put it. Maybe I should start a bad guy pile. It was a connection I hadn't known about. It could be important. It could be nothing. It could be the reason for Tierney's messages.

Then there was one card left. I lifted it from the bottom of the box. Noel Gerrard, former NCIS now retired. His card went onto the useful pile. It was a small collection. I took them through to my desk and stacked them up. Back in the spare room, I shovelled the remaining cards back into the box and put the lid on, then slid the box back into its usual position on the shelf at the back of the closet. I put the letters and cards from Sandra in a drawer in the spare room. I'd go through them later and maybe call her. Maybe I'd get a chance to see Argo even if it was via FaceTime. It didn't matter that time had marched on; I missed the dog. I missed my wife. I missed our life. The black hole that opened in my chest the day of the drone strike hadn't closed.

Back at my desk I looked at the time. The girls needed lunch. It wouldn't hurt to take a break from whatever was going on in the world for half an hour. I hoped I'd get some clarity with the pause for lunch and a much-needed coffee.

I walked quietly down the stairs and observed the girls playing together. Grace was so like her mother. It struck me as a funny thing to think when they are identical twins. They looked like Ellie, the bluest of dark blue eyes, blonde hair, fine features, but Grace had her temperament. She took charge, she problem-solved, she looked after Isabella, always. I didn't really see myself in the girls. I thought it was because I missed Ellie so much and seeing her in them kept her close. Seemed like a good reason.

My mind wandered back to before the twins arrived. We'd agreed to tell them about Ellie's job by making it no big deal and always telling the truth, but in a way small people could understand. Now they were older they asked questions. Sometimes the questions weren't ones I wanted to answer.

Grace shook my arm, pulling me back to reality. "You looked sad," she said.

"I'm not. I promise," I replied. "I was thinking about your mom."

"Did Mommy love us as much as you?" Grace asked with a cheeky smile.

"Of course." I winked at her. "You were our little miracles and she loved you to the stars and back."

"Then why isn't she here?" Isabella said.

"Mommy died. Remember we've talked about it."

"She was working ...," Isabella said.

"That's right."

"And she saved everyone," Grace added.

"Yes, she did." Except the people she was with. Except her team.

"Can we hear Mommy's voice again?" Isabella asked.

"Yes. But not right now."

I kept Ellie's personal phone charged and still paid her phone bill so I could hear her voice mail message and other voice memo's she'd made. The girls liked to hear her voice. Another reason was to maintain her iCloud storage and all the photos she'd taken over the years.

"Did Crockett know Mommy?" Grace asked.

"Yes, he did know your mommy. He worked with her."

"Does it make you sad when we ask about Mommy?" Isabella asked with a frown on her face.

Telling the truth isn't always easy. "Sometimes it does but I like telling you stories about your mom. And I promised her I would tell you all about her."

"Can you show us the pictures in her phone again?"

"Yes. Later, okay?"

Grace nodded.

"What was Mommy's job?" Isabella asked.

"I'm pretty sure you know the answer, Isabella."

"I like it when you tell us," she replied.

Fair enough. "She was a Special Agent in Charge of a

very special unit within the criminal division of the FBI. Mom was in charge of the Delta teams. She was with Delta A for a long time as a special agent and then a supervisory special agent." I looked at their faces as they tried to take it all in. "She was a like a police officer, that's what that means."

"She caught bad guys," Grace said with a smile.

"Was mommy important?" Isabella asked.

"Yes, to us. And to the FBI. She got a lot of commendations."

"What's a com ... commend ... commend nation?"

Grace's attempts brought a smile to my face.

"Com-men-day-tion," I said slowly. "Medals and framed pieces of paper that mean mommy did a good job."

"Can we see them?"

"Yes. Come on." I walked down the hall and into my bedroom with the girls in tow. I got a box out of the closet and put it on the bed. One by one I showed the girls all the commendations that Ellie had shoved in drawers of our home rather than hang anywhere. There were a couple that had hung in her office at work but mostly they were hidden from view. She never felt comfortable being singled out for what she always said was a team effort. Grace picked up Ellie's badge and looked at it.

"I like this," she said. "I will have one like this."

"Who is that?" Isabella asked pointing to a large German Shepherd in a photo with Ellie. He wore an FBI vest and a medal. "He looks like he's smiling."

"That is Argo. He loved you two very much. He was our dog, but he was also an FBI dog."

"What did Argo do?"

"He helped people who were sad and hurt. And he protected people like mom."

"He didn't protect her when she died."

"No, Isabella. He wasn't there." Even if he was there Argo couldn't have stopped the explosion that killed their mother.

"Where does he live now?"

"He lives in Virginia with Special Agent Sandra Sinclair. She was on mom's team, and she was mom's friend. She took Argo so he wouldn't get lonely without us."

"He's not alone?"

"No, he's not alone. He has Sandra and other people to care for him."

"Daddy, where did mommy go?"

"To heaven, that's where good people go, Grace. To heaven. So she can watch over us."

"Is Mommy all by herself in heaven?"

I shook my head. "Mommy is with people who loved her."

"I hope they love her a whole lot." Grace sat on my knee and wrapped her arms around my neck, still clutching her mother's FBI badge in her hand. "I'm going to be just like her and catch bad people."

Isabella twirled in front of us. "I'm going to be a ballet dancer," she said. "Mommy can watch me from heaven."

"I think mommy is very proud of both of you and

wants you to be happy whatever you end up doing."

"And she is proud of you as well, Daddy." Isabella stopped twirling.

"I hope so, Isabella."

The little girl nodded. "I know she is. She tells me in my dreams." The seriousness on Isabella's face brought a smile to my lips. "She told me."

"What did she say?" Grace asked. She turned on my knee so she could see her sister.

"She said, Daddy does important things, and he looks after people and makes bad people stop being bad."

I looked at my earnest child. Her big blue eyes and serious expression; sometimes there was a sudden flash of her mother in Isabella's expressions, and this was one of those times.

"What do you do, Daddy?" Grace asked.

"I make drones. You've seen some of them."

Grace nodded. Strands of her hair stuck to my face. "In the workshop downstairs."

"That's right."

"Do they keep people safe?" she asked.

"Some of them do."

"Are we the people you look after?"

"Well, you are the most important two people that I look after," I replied, and planted a kiss on her forehead. Isabella clambered across the bed and onto my spare knee. I kissed her on the forehead as she leaned against me. "We should put all mommy's things away."

"Can we hang them up?" Grace asked.

"We can do that." I put an arm around each child. "You two can find the best places and I'll hang them for you."

My grip tightened on the girls and stood, lifting them higher until their feet dangled way above the floor. They giggled as I spun around and then gently let them go over the bed. They fell, laughing.

"Again, Daddy, again!" They chorused, clambering to their feet and bouncing.

Chapter Three:
[Ronnie: Lunch with Nana.]

Ben arrived exactly when he said he would. He smiled at me as he opened the office door and announced himself. "I'm here, let's go."

I rose from my chair, hooked my handbag over my shoulder, and shot a grimace at Steph who was grinning from ear to ear.

"Less grinning, unless you'd like to join?" I said. "I'm sure Nana would love to plan a wedding for you and Jenn."

The grin slid right off her face. "I'm good. You kids have fun."

Ben held the door open for me.

He planted a quick kiss on my lips and whispered, "Stronger together. Don't look so worried. She can't actually make us do anything."

That has not been my experience with Nana. If he's honest, it's not been his experience with Nana either. We were fish in a barrel.

The drive was short. Too short. Ben parked down the street from the retirement home and we entered Nana's apartment from the garden door. The scent from her room freshener reeds hung heavy in the warm air. It was hard to place; something akin to aniseed, rosemary, and a subtle whiff of creeping death.

"Hi Nana," I called. She was in the kitchenette fussing

with something.

"Hello, Veronica, Benjamin. Thank you for the lunch visit."

That was way too formal. I turned and there were the *Cronies of Doom* situated on the couch. Nana's best friends, Ester the former policewoman and Frankie once a school principal. Great. The whole Scooby gang.

"Can I help Nana?" I made my way across the room to her. Ben headed towards the *Cronies of Doom*.

"Yes, dear, take the tray to the table please." I kissed her papery cheek and did as I was told. Once I'd placed the plates of luncheon meats and salad bowls on the table, I returned the tray for the next load. Nana stretched her thin old lips into a smile. "It's lovely having you both available for lunch." She patted my hand as I lifted the tray of plates and cutlery.

I made no comment but set the table and returned the tray.

Nana took the tray and placed it on the now clear bench.

"Luncheon is ready," she announced. No hint of frailty in her voice. That would come later when we didn't do what she wanted or when she broached whatever subject she had us here for. I knew exactly what the subject was. I knew my Nana.

Ben helped Ester and Frankie to their feet and escorted them to the dining table. I caught his eye as he went around the table making sure everyone was seated. Too helpful. That would just spur them on. He needed to be more inconsiderate. His eyes met mine. He knew. His fate was sealed. He took the seat next to me.

"Thank you for having us, June," he said.

I kicked him under the table. No, that was definitely the wrong way to play this lunch. As much as I love Nana, and I truly did give up my career to be closer to her, I knew she was about to spring a trap or push us in the direction she wanted us going, and Ben was playing right into her boney hands.

"We don't get to see you together very often," Nana said, the frailty creeping into her voice. "I'm not getting any younger ..."

None of us are. The lunch had potential to age me exponentially.

Ben passed the plates of food around. I kicked him again. He had to stop being helpful. All he was doing was sealing our fate. Nana's faded blue eyes missed nothing. She sat there smiling like the cat that got the canary. I caught Frankie giving a slight nod in her direction. Ester remained focused on the food in front of her until Nana spoke again. All eyes on Nana.

"Isn't it about time you two made things official?"

No preamble. Just straight to it. She wasn't getting any younger. I stifled a sigh.

"We're happy the way we are," I replied, shoving a forkful of salad into my mouth and hoping I choked on it. I chewed and swallowed. I was still alive.

Ben nudged me with his foot. I looked at him and my blood ran cold. He didn't look like he agreed with me.

No. Nope. Yeah. Nah. Was he in on this?

I leaned close to his ear and kept my voice low enough that Nana couldn't hear me. "Am I missing something?"

His answer was to fork food into his mouth and chew.

Buggery bollocks.

Nana tapped her plate with her fork to get my attention. "It's time, don't you think Veronica?"

I could feel blood draining from my head. If I hadn't been sitting down, I'd probably have fallen over.

Stronger together. That's what he meant? Not ganging up on Nana, but *stronger together*.

"Time for what Nana?"

She didn't answer because Ben moved. He stood and pushed his chair into the table. For a split second I thought he was going to tell Nana off and leave.

Nana clapped her old hands with glee as Ben took my hand and encouraged me to turn around in my chair. There was a small box in his other hand as he took a knee in front of me.

"Veronica, Ronnie, Tracey will you do me the honour of marrying me?" He opened the box and there was a stunning diamond ring. Three stones. The one in the middle looked to be about a carat. I tried to recover my composure, but all I was doing was staring like an idiot at the opened box. "Ronnie?"

I dragged my eyes up to Ben's. For the first time ever, I saw fear on his face.

I took a breath.

Time stood still.

Blood rushed away from my brain so fast I thought I was going to pass out.

I inhaled. Surprisingly, I was still breathing.

Then I said the word that would change our lives. "Yes."

He started to smile, then the smile paused before reaching his eyes. "Yes, you will or yes, you're Ronnie?"

"Yes. I am Ronnie." A thrill moved through me. Blood began to flow again. "Yes, I will."

His hand shook as he took the ring from the box and slipped it onto my finger. He stood and pulled me to my feet and into his arms.

I said, yes.

I said, yes?

Nana and the *Cronies of Doom* cheered.

What had I done?

Chapter Four:
[Mitch: Gone but never forgotten.]

Lunch was a jovial affair in Mahau Sound. Sandwiches and giggling. Nothing made me happier than hearing my girls laugh. I almost succeeded at pushing all thoughts of arms deals from my mind. Almost.

I still didn't completely understand why MacKinnon had given me *Genesis*. I'd work hard at being what MacKinnon needed me to be for the sake of *Genesis*, because I believed in what they were trying to achieve. I understood the need for independent clandestine activity and for secrecy when it came to *Genesis*. It was one helluva operation. Worldwide, not country specific; no one country had any sway. Everyone involved with Genesis was there because they believed they were doing good for the world, not just their country.

Isabella pushed her plate away knocking her glass in the process. The sloshing water caught my attention. The glass didn't fall.

"Be careful Isabella," I cautioned gently.

She nodded. Her blue eyes were wide. "It didn't fall."

It didn't fall. No harm, no foul.

Grace left crusts on her plate. She never did like the crusts.

"Take your crusts out to the deck, Grace. Feed the birds."

"Come on, Isabella," Grace said, standing and picking

up the plate with two hands. "Open the door for me."

Isabella ran ahead and opened the door. Moments later they were back. Grace put the plate on the table.

"Who wants a cookie?" I asked.

"Us!" chorused the girls.

"Go get one each from the cookie jar. I'll clean up, then Dad needs to go back to work. You two play down here, please."

"Yes, Daddy," they chorused again.

I cleared the table, did the dishes, put everything away, then went back upstairs. It was time to tell Reynolds I wanted him to work the arms deal situation. Another report was waiting for me. There were two more names. Sandra King was a Canadian espionage officer reportedly cosy with the Ukrainians. Her movements had led to an airport in Poland, more specifically, Chopin Airport in Warsaw. She was suspected to be making her way to New Zealand. And Steven Sadler, MI6. He was seen at Heathrow. Intel suggested he was also on the way to New Zealand. I added both names to an email update that would go out to all operatives, so everyone knew we had people incoming. Jackson Frost's name went on a watch list I released to the SE Asia and Oceania *Genesis* group. Frost's name was red flagged. It was necessary to know exactly where he was and what he was doing. A new piece of information had come to light. An informant said they'd heard Frost talk about a Polish Embassy and a dance. I found everything I could surrounding that piece of intel and then reached out to Ben Reynolds.

As usual, I employed voice changing software to make the call to Reynolds and leave a message. Technology works in our favour more often than not. I took a small black book from my desk drawer and looked up the required words.

Then I called Ben and left him a message, "Friends are coming to town. Not the movie type. Maybe brunch? One likes syrup with everything, and the other is into mushy peas."

Once the call was made, I hung up the phone, settled into my seat, and sent an encrypted email to Reynolds. Time to hide my email address like always. It wasn't just a hidden email address; everything from my computer went via VPN. Safer that way. In the email, I told Reynolds that I understood he was working a job for Joe. There was also a missionary aspect which would require a Bible. And then I told him to pick up a cake. The next sentence made me smile, sometimes using code words was amusing. It was about a sausage sizzle and a circus, information from the last intelligence I'd received.

It was more coded communication. Wouldn't be long before I would be able to type coded comms without checking the book. The email and the voice message told Reynolds that he was required to work a *Genesis* job alongside the CIA one. He also needed to set up a meet for two incoming friendlies, one Canadian and one Brit. And finally, there was an unfriendly. The sausage and circus comment meant Ben needed to look for an event that was linked to the Polish Embassy. I then sent one final email asking for frequent check-ins and telling Reynolds to be careful. It was a bit of a reminder for him that this operation was running covertly alongside the CIA operation. If he needed more info, I told him to reply to the email. Even though the email address was hidden behind one that looked like it belonged to a teenager, I would still get any replies sent.

I considered mentioning that I'd heard from Tierney but didn't. Reynolds didn't need to know that. Tierney wasn't his case officer. Or was he?

Another report arrived. Breath caught in my throat as I read it.

The advice was to lift the *Genesis* terror threat level to orange, as it was believed that the arms deal venues overseas were disrupted by terrorists. That wasn't entirely true. *Genesis* played a big role in the disrupting and we're not terrorists. I got busy and contacted everyone I worked with within my theatre of operations. The alert level: high. I had two names that I sent along with the rise in the alert level. A terror threat lift within New Zealand was a big deal. It wasn't the first time, and it wouldn't be the last, but they needed to squash it before something happened. I looked at the names provided again.

Fucking bargain basement Bin Ladens coming out of Indonesia.

Using my back-channel resources, I provided a clean piece of intel to be shared within the intelligence communities of New Zealand, Australia, and the US. They should already be aware, but we have often gathered intel and actioned it before other parties had heard of it. There was also a high probability that my email alerts would be buried.

Chapter Five:
[Ben: My fun life.]

We told Steph our big news when we arrived at Ronnie's office. She looked as shocked as Ronnie had when I proposed. For a long beat I thought Ronnie was going to say no. I can't believe she didn't. My mind was wandering by the time I left her at the office in Steph's capable hands and drove back to the city. We had a little while before her Nana would start wanting dates and venues. I walked into my apartment and realised I was smiling.

She said yes.

My phone buzzed. There was voice mail. Must've happened while I was driving. Our phones switched alerts and ringers off while they were in a moving vehicle unless we overrode it manually. Clever and safe. I listened to the message, which appeared to be a female voice. If it was a woman? It was hard to know these days with the technology out there to change a voice into whatever you wanted.

The message was clear: there were incoming friendlies. A Canadian and a Brit. There was also a troublemaker inbound, and something linked to Poland. I switched the coffee maker on. And then the bad news. The terror alert level hiked to high. An event was possible. It's the world we live in now, it's always possible. I didn't let the hike bother me.

Email pinged on my phone. An insane looking email address told me it was from *Genesis*. I read the email while I poured coffee. A requirement of this mission was frequent checking in with *Genesis*. All of it added up to make the new job interesting. Or fun for a masochist. I'd already had word that Jonathon Tierney was planning to show his face. It had been a long while since I'd laid eyes on him. The last time was during a job in Paris. I was there filming a movie while attending big dinners and wooing backers for another production. It's amazing what people divulge when they get an actor in their sights.

Late one night, I met with Tierney. I'd come across information that required action. It was either him or State Department, but someone had to act. Turned out it was me and Tierney. He was okay in the field back then. That was ten years ago and he wasn't on the right side of sixty then.

I was interested to see what the backstop would be like with this mission. Potentially, Tierney would be the boss and *Genesis* would be receiving intel directly from me. No problem there. I'd worked with him before and it all worked out. *Genesis* was always there somewhere and even deeper in the shadows than Tierney. But any backstopping would be handled by the CIA and not *Genesis*.

I deleted the email and the voice message and took my coffee and phone into the dining room. At the dining table I looked over the newspaper. There was nothing much to read. Looked like a slow news day. Our *news* would be carefully released by my agent when I told her. Then we'd brighten up the dull news days. I flipped the paper over and saw a write up about an upcoming ball. Guess COVID was over now, and life was coming back with vengeance. Except COVID wasn't over. It was still, and always would be, a part of our lives. There was no escaping that reality.

Reading about the ball caused a smile. It was at The Event Space in Lower Hutt and sponsored by the Embassy of Poland. A ball to celebrate what it means to be Polish in New Zealand. Wouldn't a ball be a great place to meet potential buyers? That was the moment I realised that *Genesis* was ahead of the game again. It was a ticket holder only affair, everyone dressed up, banqueting, and dancing. People would enjoy themselves and let their guard down.

Hadn't been to a ball in years. Paris was probably the last place I attended a formal dance. It wouldn't be a bad place to ferret out some information especially in light of the intel that had come my way.

I left my cup on the table and went into my bedroom. From the closet I took a suit bag that was shoved way in the back. I unzipped it and looked at the black tuxedo. I knew it fitted. I'd worn it filming an episode of my series and got to keep it. Ronnie liked it a lot - something to do with the fit and satin lapels. It could probably do with being dry cleaned. I found the white shirt that I wore with it and my bowtie. I might as well get it all cleaned. I put the shirt and bowtie in the suit bag and zipped it up. Next, I made a phone call to secure tickets to the ball. I contacted my agent and asked her to get me three tickets.

"It's this coming Friday night, two days away. Why do you suddenly want to go to a ball?"

"I just found out about it. And because I want to go."

"A Polish ball?"

"Yep. I've got Polish blood. My great grandfather was from Poland."

"Three tickets?"

"Yes."

"All right. I'll get back to you."

"Make it happen Taylor, this is important to me."

"I hope you can dance," she said and hung up.

One more call and then I'd take my suit to the dry cleaner. I rang Ginny.

"Hey, it's me," I said.

"Hellaire, Ben, how are you?"

"Ringing with an invitation. I've got my agent working on getting tickets to a Polish ball this Friday. How would you and Tom like to come along? I know it's short notice."

Silence.

"Ginny?"

"We'd love to, you know that. We haven't been out to anything formal in years."

"Get your dress out of mothballs. We dance on Friday night."

"Where is it?"

"Lower Hutt Event Centre."

"That's the newish building by the Town Hall, isn't it?"

"I think so, yes." I folded the newspaper up and put it

in the recycling.

"How exciting."

"I'll be in touch and let you know what time the car will pick you up."

"Thanks very much for inviting us, Ben. See you Friday night."

I hung up.

All I needed now was my agent to come through with the tickets. I was going stag, but I would've loved to see Ronnie in a ball gown. Maybe next time. Something tweaked inside me. Terror alert high. I didn't want Ronnie there. Just in case.

Taylor called me back within half an hour saying I had three tickets and asking if I was interested in the ball the following Saturday night as well. I grabbed the newspaper out of the recycling and did a fast search for the event. How'd I miss it? Another embassy ball, but this time it was being held at the Upper Hutt Town Hall. It was sponsored by the Thai Embassy. It was a masked charity ball raising money for the Wellington Children's Hospital.

I called Taylor back. "Yes, I wanna go. Thank you. See if you can get four tickets for that one."

"Okay. Who knew you liked to dance that much."

"I wouldn't want to waste of all those ballroom dancing lessons I had so I looked good on the dance floor while we were filming."

She said nothing about my dancing. "I'll get back to you."

I shoved my phone in my pocket and left the house with the suit bag over my arm. Didn't take me long to walk to the nearest dry cleaner. The suit would be ready for pick-up the next day. Considering I needed to wear it Friday night, that worked well. I went for coffee, then made my way down to the American Embassy. I had a meeting with Kirsten. She wasn't my favourite person, but she was my immediate superior. I was no stranger to the embassy guards and staff. Americans visit the embassy for all sorts of reasons so no one would care that I was visiting the embassy today. I walked up the hill and said hello to everyone I saw on the way. I loved New Zealand. No one cared if you were on television every week. No one chased anyone with cameras. Politicians went to Saturday markets to get their groceries just like everyone else. I pushed the button on the crosswalk. The man on the other side looked familiar as did the two men behind him. The lights changed. The buzzer buzzed. As he stepped onto the crosswalk, I recognised him and his protection detail.

"Morning, Prime Minister."

"Hi, Ben. Call me Chris. Good show this week."

"Thanks, Sir." He shook his head slightly. "Thanks Chris."

"Looking forward to the episode next week."

I walked up the sidewalk until I came to the embassy entrance. The guard beckoned me through.

"Identification," he said.

I pulled my passport out of my jacket pocket and

handed it to him. He looked at it carefully, like he'd never seen it before.

"Go on in, Mr Reynolds."

"Thanks, Sergeant."

Every time I went up there, he scrutinised my passport like it was a forgery. I shoved it into my inside pocket as I walked towards the embassy building.

Before I got to the door, the sergeant called out, "Good show this week."

I waved without turning around.

Once inside, through the metal detectors, and all signed in, I asked if Tierney was around.

"No, Sir."

"Kirsten?"

The woman typed on her keyboard. "I've sent her a message. She'll be down in a few minutes. You can wait over there." She pointed to a couch.

"Thanks." I sat on the couch and waited.

Fifteen minutes slipped by while I read lines on my phone. Waiting isn't wasted as long as you have something to occupy the time. A door opened. I looked up and there was Kirsten.

"Come on," she said, holding the door open.

I pushed my phone into my pocket, followed her through the door into the interior, and then through a series of corridors. She opened her office door and invited me in.

"Have a seat, Ben," Kirsten said as she circled the desk and sat in her chair.

There was a chair in front of her desk, I was pleased that it wasn't at the end of her desk. That would put me too close to her for my comfort.

"I've got tickets to a ball Friday night. It might be a good place to gather intel," I said. "Balls have worked for me before."

"Where is it?"

"Lower Hutt."

"What makes you think a ball is going to net intelligence?"

"It's hosted by the Polish Embassy. The original arms deal was going down in Poland before it was disrupted."

"Good word, disrupted. Intelligence officers were lost during that disruption." She batted her eyelashes. "That's a flimsy excuse. But clever way to have a night off dancing and get us to pay for it."

"I am aware people died." I paused for a beat. "It's a good place to pick up info. We need information. People at balls are having a good time. You know, people talk to me."

She pursed her lips. For a second, I thought she was going to blow me a kiss and felt my balls retreat. The crisis was averted as she relaxed her mouth.

"Sounds like a fun night. Need a date?"

No, thanks. "Going stag. It's easier to get people talking when I'm alone." She did not need to know I was taking Tom and Ginny with me. And the last thing I wanted was to take Kirsten ball-breaking Knight on something that looked like a date. Common knowledge around the campfire was that she batted for whichever team would have her. She's not my type. I prefer women who know their worth and Kirsten sold out on the first low bid. An image of Ronnie danced across my mind.

"Anything else?" Kirsten flicked her tongue around her lips.

"Not at this point."

I decided to withhold the potential of another dance next weekend and the terror threat. Why didn't she know about it? Or did she? That reminded me I needed to polish my shoes.

Kirsten opened a drawer and then passed me a cheap cell phone. "It's a burner," she said. "The techs added contacts for you. We want you checking in at least four times a day. This situation might move fast or could move slow. Either way, you're in the field, so maintain check-ins."

The office door opened. I turned my head to see who it was.

An old man walked in leaning on a cane. His beady dark eyes were shadowed by his thick brows. The hooked beak-like nose was unmistakable. It was Jonathon Tierney.

"Jonathon," I said, standing. I reached for his hand.

"Good to see you, my boy," he replied, shaking my hand with a strong sinewy grip.

Kirsten's smile wasn't the fakest thing on her face, but it was close to it. "I'll get you a chair," she said.

"No need. I'll take yours and let you know when we are

41

done."

I stifled a smirk. Kirsten was kicked out of her own office.

She stood and brushed past the desk as she tried to control the annoyance in her expression. She lost and she was pissed.

Tierney moved around the expansive desk and sat in the chair, leaning his cane against a bookcase behind him. He saw the phone. "Did she give you that?"

"Yes."

He picked it up, took the battery out of it, and snapped the phone in half, stuffing it in his pocket. He might be old, but he wasn't lacking strength. "She would've bugged it. It's too dangerous. All we need is someone to operate a bug detection app, or an actual RF detector, or wonder why someone like you would have a cheap nasty phone."

Tierney took another phone from his pocket and passed it to me. "It's clean. I cannot afford to lose you to sloppiness."

I picked the phone up and looked at Tierney. "Passcode?"

"Your birthday. I advise you to change it to something less obvious."

I entered the date into the lock screen. The iPhone 14 unlocked. I scrolled through the installed apps and noted Signal was there. The other apps were regular apps that iPhones came with. It took me moments to set facial recognition and a new pin code.

"What do I need to know?" I asked.

"We'll get to that, my boy. I take it you saw the Polish ball story and have managed to get tickets."

"Of course."

"Tickets for the Thai ball as well next weekend?"

"Hope so, sir. Let me just check." I looked at my own phone. There was a message from Taylor. She'd secured four tickets for the Thai ball. "Yes, sir. I have tickets."

"Do what you do best, Ben. Find out who is selling those arms and have a wonderful time, while getting yourself invited into the arms dealers' inner sanctum."

"Looking forward to it."

"Be careful out there. They're running out of places to hold this auction, or deal, or whatever it is they're doing. That makes me jumpy."

And there was still nothing about the intelligence regarding a heightened threat alert.

"Who do I liaise with?"

"Kirsten is to be kept out of this situation."

A frown edged in. "Why?"

"You don't need to know why. Just know that you should keep that to yourself. Me, Ben. Keep me informed. My number is in your new phone under Grandad."

"Got it."

"I want you to check in regularly with me. Much easier to check up on an elderly grandfather than anyone else. We're prone to falls and illness."

"Text messages?"

"Yes. I want a trail. If anyone sees you using your phone, I want them to see a text conversation with your poor old grandad. Let's start that this afternoon."

"All right."

"There is a robust backstop in place. You are yourself and you are bidding on behalf of an organisation that must keep their hands clean."

"And the organisation is?"

"Leviticus."

"And they are?" I doubted he was talking about the third book of the Torah, and of the Old Testament, also known as the Third book of Moses.

He almost smiled. "They're a global entity trading in intelligence and problem solving."

"Global," I repeated, keeping my expression neutral. Being a working actor comes in handy in this business. "And it's all fictitious? Why would they need weapons?"

"I believe the problem-solving part of the business has a use for weapons."

"All right. I am Ben Reynolds bidding on behalf of the global entity, Leviticus. How backstopped is this?"

"Very. We set up the company and its website some years ago now. It's carefully crafted to give the appearance that the company is a private military contractor, and we installed people who brought that to life. The company can answer any query regarding you."

"Okay. It's solid?"

"Naturally. It's one of the companies we've used several times for various things. It's even had a name change or two."

"Not as many times as Blackwater?"

"No," Tierney said. "But it's been around long enough to give credibility. Our operatives have worked in several countries and undertaken several missions as a PMC would."

"How long have they been Leviticus?"

"Not long, a matter of weeks. There was an upheaval in the company and a rebranding. Prior to becoming Leviticus, the company was Exodus."

"Nice. Do I need anything else apart from the phone?"

"No. You can access the company website via an application on the phone so you can familiarise yourself with their work. Off you go." Tierney didn't stand. He pointed to the door. "I saw your show this week. You're very good at what you do."

I didn't expect that.

"Thank you, Sir." I opened the door and found Kirsten sitting on a chair in the hallway. "See ya, Kirsten."

She glared at me. "Make sure you check in with me."

"Sure."

Nope. The big boss is here now. I had a feeling Kirsten might be out of a job soon. She certainly would not be happy when I didn't check in with her and she couldn't track me. Tierney was right, she would've bugged the phone and enabled tracking. She was nothing if not predictable.

I had a fancy burner phone in my pocket which fitted with the whole tuxedo ball scenario. A crappy little burner looked like something someone on the fringe of society would use. An iPhone 14 gave a whole different vibe.

Classier. Someone who likes quality. As I walked back home, I thought about the job and whether there was anything to find at the Polish ball. If not, it was an expensive night with nothing to show. It didn't feel like it would be a no gain event. Either way, I'd enjoy the atmosphere and the chance to use my dance skills.

The Leviticus situation was interesting. Tierney watched me closely when he said the name. I wondered if he'd heard something about *Genesis*. No doubt he would've, secret or not. We know enough got out to kill the founder and his son. Did he suspect I was working for *Genesis*? Is that why he watched me when he said Leviticus?

My pocket vibrated. I pulled my real phone out and saw a message from Ronnie.

Ronnie: Plans for the weekend?

Me: Sadly yes, work, work, work. I'll see you Sunday night?

Ronnie: Sounds good to me. I'll wrangle Nana myself this weekend then, or maybe I'll lie low.

Me: We're doing this, right?

Ronnie: We are.

Me: Okay, fiancée. See you Sunday evening.

Just as I walked in the door of my apartment there was another text. This time it wasn't Ronnie. It was *Uncle* asking if she was going to the ball with me.

I was better going stag when it came to invitations and

46

intelligence. Next time, perhaps.

Me: Not this time Uncle.
Uncle: Is that a mistake?
Me: No

I wanted to ask about Leviticus and see what the real *Genesis* knew, but not via text and not out in the open.

Chapter Six:
[Ben: Dance with me? Friday night.]

Tuxedo, pocket square, military shine on my shoes: I was ready for an evening of chitchat, dancing, and hopefully, I'd hook myself into an arms deal.

It was just a run-of-the-mill night out. My personal phone was safely off and in a Faraday cage in my closet. I grinned what I thought was a charming grin at my reflection on my way out the door.

Here we go.

I dropped a weekender on the back seat of the Mustang. It'd be easier to stay out in the Hutt with both dances out that way. Would've been great to stay at Ronnie's, but that wasn't the best idea considering I was working and didn't invite her to tonight's event or tell her about it. I didn't know if she'd heard about the terror level hike. But she was *Genesis* like me, so, she would eventually hear about it if she hadn't already. I was planning on catching up with her on Sunday. No doubt Donald and Enzo would know all about my proposal by then.

I'd familiarised myself with the names of the two suspected terrorists; Amir Faheem and Omar Al-Fasil. I had their photographs burned into my memory. If they showed up, I'd know it. Two things about being an actor; it made me very good with faces and very good with names.

Should I stay at Ginny and Tom's or a hotel?

By the time I'd hit the highway I knew I was going to Ginny and Tom's. I'm not sure what changed my mind about checking into that new hotel in the Hutt, but I didn't give it too much thought.

Ginny was still getting ready when I arrived. I grabbed Tom and we stashed my car in Ronnie's garage down in Naenae.

When we got back, Ginny was having a cigarette on the back steps, dressed in a long white dress, with a frosted fur-trimmed white leather coat draped around her shoulders. Nice. Looked like it came from Josef Baranov's shop in the city.

"Is that a Baranov?" I asked from the bottom step.

Ginny flashed a bright smile. "Of course."

"Perfect for tonight. There's a bit of a chill in the air."

Ginny put her cigarette out and retreated into the house. Tom and I followed. I made a call and ordered a car. Not a cab, but a town car. Tonight we would arrive in style. There was an image to keep up. An actor/spy and two "friends" go to a ball ... I wondered briefly what the punch line was. I checked the phone Tierney had given me and texted him.

Me: Hope you're having a good evening, Grandad.

Three dots moved on the screen.

Grandad: All good here Grandson. Hope you have many dance partners. If I was a younger man, I'd be there with you.

There was still nothing about Faheem and Al-Fasil from Tierney. How could he ignore intelligence that I'm sure he would have received from *Genesis*? Or how was the intelligence missing from all his channels? I imagined that was why *Genesis* existed. I sat at the dining table as I thought about the lack of information. Names and faces, but no clue as to how the two men would go about their goal. I thought about the venue and that led to pulling up a street view on my phone. There were some bollards. Maybe enough to deter a car bomb.

"Why so serious?" Ginny asked from the kitchen.

"Just looking at the venue," I said with a smile. "The car will be here in half an hour. Hope you have dancing shoes on, and an appetite."

"Looking forward to all of it. What a wonderful treat a night out like this is."

"Cocktail before the car arrives?" Tom asked, walking into the kitchen.

"A small one," Ginny replied.

"Sounds good," I said. "Vodka please."

"Done."

I stood up and put the phone in my pocket. Checked I had my wallet. Wished I had a Glock, but knew I was going to have to go without a firearm.

* * *

Tom and Ginny entered the venue ahead of me. I scoped

out the foyer looking for familiar faces. No one stood out. I caught up to Ginny and Tom inside. A hostess was showing people to their tables. The tables were round and located at one end of the vast room. The other end was devoted to a dance floor with a small group of classical musicians in one corner.

The hostesses smile became a scowl when she approached me. "I've watched your show," she said.

"Thank you."

"Didn't say I liked it," she replied.

Jesus.

She motioned to a table. "You are there." There was a hard edge to her voice. Maybe I'd offended her in some way with the show. It's not as stupid as it sounds. People are easily offended these days.

"Thank you." I remained polite. One thing you can't do when you're a so-called public figure is to be rude or dismissive. Nothing gets into the gossip column faster than a rude celebrity. Reality whacked me. I was hardly a celebrity. I have an action-based television series that a lot of people like. Ratings were high enough to get another season - six and counting. I've also been in a few movies that people liked.

Ginny winked at me from two tables away. I guess deciding to go to a ball last minute, means not sitting together. Tom was with Ginny, so she wasn't alone.

I introduced myself to my table mates. There was still no sign of the potential terrorists. Maybe it was a false alarm. Sometimes it was. Occasionally we heard about something just because some faction or other wanted us on edge and chasing our tails. That could be happening here. Did I believe that? It wasn't worth the risk of letting that thought cement. I heard my phone. A nice reminder to put it on silent. I checked the message.

Grandad: I can't get my bluetooth to work.
Me: Sorry Grandad, I'm out. I'll come over tomorrow and show you.

I opened settings and made sure bluetooth was on and my phone was discoverable, then turned it to silent and made sure vibration was on. Grandad was on form. He must've gotten intel saying the target was using bluetooth to make contact.

And now there was nothing to do but wait and enjoy the night. The host introduced himself and gave a little information about the purpose of the dance. He smiled in my direction, and that was when I realised I was about to be singled out.

"New Zealand's most eligible bachelor is in the house. Ladies get your dance cards ready for Ben Reynolds." He pointed me out. I waved. Here I am. Just your friendly neighbourhood actor looking to make an arms deal.

I *was* a bachelor. Now I am a fiancé. And nobody knew yet. A big chunk of me wished they did, but the other part squashed that, because if I needed to be single for the night to get info then that was what had to happen. There was no information that told us the arms deals were perpetuated by a male. It could just as easily be a woman. I scanned the room without being too obvious. It could be anyone.

Before the music started two women at my table asked for dances. One was nearly a hundred and the other looked about fifty. Perfect.

I smiled at each of them. "I'd be honoured ladies."

The oldest of them introduced herself. "I'm Nancy." She offered her gloved hand.

We shook hands.

The other woman said, "I'm Laura, pleased to meet you, Ben."

No handshake.

"It's a pleasure, ladies." I saw Tom take Ginny's hand and lead her to the dance floor. Their ears would be open just because they always were. "Who would like this dance?"

Nancy leaned back slightly. "Go ahead, Laura. I need to build up to dancing."

With Laura's hand clasped onto the crook of my arm, I escorted her to the dance floor. The band played a waltz. I took Laura in my arms and led her around the floor. As we neared Tom and Ginny, my phone buzzed. I couldn't check until the dance finished, and Laura was back in her seat. I excused myself and joined Tom and Ginny who were back at their table.

"I need some cover to check my phone," I said to Tom. He stood as I took my phone from my pocket.

Grandad: Are you sure you can't help tonight.

Me: I'm out Grandad. I'll see you tomorrow.

When I sent the reply an alert popped up. Nancy had found my phone and sent a picture via bluetooth. I accepted and then opened the image. Old people using tech.

It was a photo of Nancy sitting at the table. It wasn't a selfie as someone else took the photo. Maybe that was her way of saying she had the next dance?

I looked over and nodded.

"I better get back over there. The older woman at the table I'm at just sent me a pic," I said to Tom.

"Sexy?"

"No."

"Have fun, Ben," Ginny said, with a cheeky smile on her face. "Older women have more experience."

I laughed and walked away.

At the table, Nancy was on her feet waiting.

"Technology is wonderful," she said.

"Sure is," I replied, offering her my elbow. "Shall we?"

Halfway through a foxtrot, she clung to me like I was a life buoy, and she was drowning in heavy seas.

"Are you alright?" I asked.

"Yes, yes, I am. Just remembering my youth."

I took note of the other dancers and wondered who of the throng on the dance floor or seated at the tables, was looking to make a deal. From the corner of my eye, I glimpsed a man and he vanished. Was it one of the potential terrorists? The song ended. I didn't see him as we

54

walked back to the table, nor did I see where he went. I excused myself and went looking for the bathrooms. If he wasn't visible, that was a likely place or maybe the kitchen.

I opened the men's room door. No stalls were closed. No one was in there.

I opened the disabled bathroom door. No one there either. I exited the men's room.

Two women came out of the ladies talking in a recognisable accent. They saw me and stopped.

"You're Ben Reynolds," one said.

"All my life," I replied. "Kentucky?"

"Yes. Eastern Kentucky."

Coal mining country.

"Can I have a dance?" the other one said. "I'm Hazel, this is my sister Willa."

"Don't think they'll be playing any bluegrass, but sure you can."

"We're not all flat-foot all the time," Hazel said. "Sometimes we square dance."

Willa chuckled.

"I'll see you ladies safely inside," I replied, and hooked one on each side of me. At the doorway I asked where their table was. Willa pointed towards the back. We wound our way through the tables to theirs. "I'll be back soon."

On my way back to the door, I was swamped by dance invitations and shook hands with at least forty men.

Back at my table I sat for a moment. Took stock and

wondered how to get to the kitchen without causing a scene to see if our friendly neighbourhood terrorists were out there. Ginny appeared at my elbow like I'd summoned her somehow.

"Hellaire Ben, darling, I think this is my dance." The band played another waltz.

I caught Tom in my periphery as he asked Nancy to dance.

Off we went again to the dance floor.

"What's wrong?" Ginny asked. "Who are you looking for?"

"Was I that obvious?"

"No. I know you that well. Who is it?"

"A couple of men, think they're Indonesian. Maybe Muslim. Maybe big trouble."

"Could they be part of the kitchen crew?"

"Yes."

"Have you been into the kitchen?"

"No. I was intercepted by a couple of Eastern Kentucky belles."

"Shall we go now?"

We were at the edge of the dance floor quite close to the main entrance. Ginny broke away and fanned her face with her hand. Her bracelet clad arm jingled. "Some air, I think?" she said.

I ushered her off the floor and through the door. Hopefully no one took much notice. Together we found the kitchen.

"I'll ask about allergy free canapés, and you look

around," Ginny said. She swung the door open, and we stepped into hustle and bustle. "Excuse me!" Ginny called. "Who do I speak with about a food allergy?"

A man in white stepped away from a stainless-steel bench and towards Ginny. My eyes darted around the busy kitchen.

"That would be me," the man said to Ginny. I didn't hear the rest of the conversation as I was taking in what appeared to be chaos and looking for one or both men. A door opened on the other side of the room. It was a walk-in cool room. Al-Fasil came out carrying a tray of something.

Were they working for the catering company?

He looked up as I stared straight at him.

He didn't attempt to run. He carried on with whatever he was doing. Behind me someone cleared their throat. I spun around to see Faheem.

"Excuse me," he said.

I stepped aside. Ginny moved closer to me and took my arm. "That's all settled. The chef will prepare a dairy-free option for our table."

"Good. Let's go back."

I took her back to the dance floor. The waltz was still playing. We danced.

"Are the people here?" Ginny asked.

"Yes."

"Now what?"

"We dance."

Servers with trays of canapés walked around the edge

of the dance floor to place plates on various tables. Other servers refilled champagne and wine glasses. My phone buzzed in my pocket again. Ginny felt it.

"Are you pleased to see me or is your phone saying hel-laire?"

I chuckled. "Always pleased to see you, but I think Tom would have a problem if I was *that* pleased."

The dance wound down and I took Ginny back to her seat before quickly checking my phone. It was another photo from Nancy. I accepted the image. It wasn't of her at the table; it was of me walking through the foyer with Willa and Hazel. Odd. I looked over at Nancy, but she wasn't looking at me. Perhaps she was the jealous type.

I made my way over to Willa and Hazel as the band struck up another song.

"Ladies, who wants this dance?"

Willa smiled. "I believe I do."

Hazel watched us go.

By the time the dance was over I had another phone alert, and I wasn't getting anywhere near anyone who smelled of an arms deal. I took Willa back to her table and gathered Hazel for a dance.

My phone would have to wait.

By the time I checked it again there were four photos; airdropped and waiting for acceptance. All from Nancy.

I accepted and looked over at her from where I'd land-ed by Ginny and Tom. She was engrossed in a conversa-tion with an older gentleman. The photos were of me dancing. The angle said they weren't taken from Nancy's position at the table but from someone walking the outside of the dance floor. How did I not notice someone taking photos? How are they coming from Nancy's phone?

Willa and Hazel told me they were in New Zealand on vacation and had heard about the ball from the friends they were staying with. Nice. I mentally filed that until I could make actual notes. Nancy and her friend Laura were at the ball because they belonged to the Polish Association. I kept an eye on the main doors, wondering what the supposed terrorists were up to, because they looked like they were there to work the event.

I excused myself and joined Tom and Ginny's table sitting in a vacant seat next to Tom.

"I'm working here," I said keeping my voice low and steady. "If you see anything at all out of the ordinary, tell me."

He nodded. "The wine's great. This is a good night," he said. "I've got your back."

I patted his shoulder and wove my way around people to get to my table. Nancy was in a flap.

"What's the matter?" I asked. "How can I help?"

"I've misplaced my phone."

"I'm sure it can't have gone far. You sent me a photo. Who took it?"

Laura piped up. "That was me. How forward of us."

"Give me a few minutes and I'll see if I can find that phone." I walked over to the nearest solid wall. With my back to it, I took my phone from my pocket and searched the metadata from the photos. Found an attached phone number and made a call.

The phone rang in my ear. I scanned as many people as I could hoping to see someone answer a phone. And at the far end of the room, I saw someone look at a phone. I hung up. They put the phone away. I rang back. They took the phone out and looked at it again. This time they answered.

"What?"

"I think you accidentally have my friend's phone," I said. The person was looking around and noticed me. I waved. "I'm coming to you. Don't move."

I shoved my phone in my pocket and made my way to the dark-haired man at the back of the room. Kept him in sight the whole way. The last thing I wanted was to lose him. I stepped in front of him making sure I was in his personal space.

"Why did you take the phone?"

"Don't know what you're talking about. Bloody actors think they own the world," he growled.

"Phone." I held my hand out.

He shook his head. "Get fucked."

"Pal, this is not going to go your way. You stole a phone from an elderly woman."

"She gave it to me."

"Right, okay, she gave it to you. And why would she do that?"

"I don't know."

"And you decided to take photos of me dancing with

various women and send them to me from her phone." I lowered my voice. "This doesn't end well for you."

My phone buzzed. I took a quick peek. It was a message. An AirDropped note.

"Don't move," I said to the thief and accepted the message. It said there was a deal and asked if I was interested. Was I just a vacuous actor or was I really with Leviticus?

"Give me that fucking phone," I snarled, and snatched it from his hands. "You keep your hands off other people's property."

"Leviticus," he said.

With a menacing look, I spun on my heels and returned the phone to its rightful owner, then went to Tom.

"What was that?"

"He stole a phone and sent me a bunch of pictures. Some fuckwit who has some kind of mental issues. Guess they sell tickets to anyone." He knew about Leviticus. He was involved.

At least I got the phone back for Nancy.

I glanced at the message I'd received again. It came from a number not a name. I crafted a response in Notes saying I was working for Leviticus and sent it via Air-Drop.

A few minutes later I had an answer. I was about to be vetted for an arms deal. I hoped Tierney's backstop for me was as good as he said it was. If I get the invite, then we'd know. If I get shot, we'll also know. At that moment all I knew was that we were in far enough to be vetted.

Another AirDropped note arrived. There was a string of letters. Underneath the string it said: Pass phrase. You'll know why in a few days. That'll give you time to break the code.

Being vetted for the deal didn't allay my concerns regarding the two men that *Genesis* flagged as terrorists. So far, no move from them. I didn't want them to make a move, but I wanted to know what they were planning. The host of the evening wandered through the dancers and made his way to us.

"Mr Reynolds, I'm Jakub. Thank you for coming to our dance," Jakub shook my hand. A photographer stood behind him. "It's a pleasure to have you here. I did some research and found out you have Polish blood. A great-grandfather?" He beckoned to the guy with the camera. "Is it all right if we get some photos?"

"Of course. And yes, a Polish great-grandfather is correct."

Jakub looked pleased. "Shall we?"

I stood next to him, shook his hand, slung my arm around his shoulders. Photos were taken. The man was happy. When the photographer moved off, I took the chance to introduce my friends.

"Let me introduce my friends, Tom and Ginny."

Everyone shook hands. Jakub was a friendly guy. That might be helpful. We chatted for a few minutes then I made my move. "I couldn't get a list of guests, could I?"

"I don't know why you would want that."

Thinking on my feet and being charming that's what I

do. "It seems a strange request, but I do it all the time. I collect names. It helps my acting process." Spinning shit might be my superpower. "It's all right if you can't let me have a list."

He wanted to help. I could see it. "I can do that," he said. "For you, Mr Reynolds."

"Call me Ben. My friends all me Ben."

We shook hands again. "If you meet me in the foyer in a few minutes, I can give you a list."

"Thank you." I meant it; I honestly thought he'd turn me down.

Jakub shuffled through a group of people then disappeared.

Tom shook his head slowly. "I did not think that would work."

"Nor did I." I slapped his back and rejoined my table.

Nancy beamed at me. "Thank you for getting my phone back."

"My pleasure. Hang on to it this time."

She nodded.

My phone buzzed again. This time I looked quickly.

Grandad.

"My Grandad has been having phone trouble all evening," I said to Nancy, shaking my head. "I better answer him."

Grandad: Are you sure you can't come tonight?
Me: Tomorrow. I'll fix it tomorrow.

"Is he alright?" Nancy asked.

"Yes. I'll see him tomorrow and sort out his phone issue," I tucked my phone back into my inside pocket.

"What a good grandson you are."

I took a canapé and ate it then washed the remnants down with half a glass of champagne. This job made me thirsty.

Watching people, wondering about the terrorists, waiting to go meet with Jakub and get myself a guest list. Thirsty work. A server topped up my glass and touched my arm lightly.

"Sir, Mr Jakub is waiting for you."

"Thank you."

I excused myself from the ladies and joined Jakub outside the door.

"I have a flash drive for you," he said, holding a tiny drive in his fingers and dropping it into my outstretched hand.

"Thank you. That's very kind of you to indulge someone like me."

"We are friends," he replied, slapping my back. "Next All Black's game. We go together."

"Sounds good to me!" I pocketed the drive.

Jakub went back into the dance. I took the opportunity to go to the bathroom. Once in there, I chose a stall. With the door securely locked behind me, I sat down, and from my inside pocket I took the phone and a tiny adapter. I plugged the flash drive into the phone using the adapter and checked the list. Nothing popped out right away.

I added notes about what I'd seen, including the phone thief, and Al-Fasil and Faheem. Then I added a new note about the AirDrop, and that I was in. Now we had to wait for vetting. Plus, I had a code to break that would allow me access to the application once I was vetted. I checked that I'd added the string of letters to the flash drive. It was good of Jakub to give me a means of saving my notes and getting them off my phone.

I had no idea who else was involved in the bidding or interested in an arms deal. I hadn't seen the Canadian, or the MI6 guy, even though they were supposed to be incoming. Were they incoming friendlies, or not so friendly? There wasn't a lot of intel around that.

I knew Frost was not a friendly, but he wasn't on the guest list either.

A door swung closed. Footsteps echoed in the bathroom. It was a good time to put everything away and flush. Mid-flush I opened the door and walked out to find Faheem and Al-Fasil. Unbelievable.

"Excuse me," I said, moving towards a basin. I could see them in the mirror. I turned on a faucet and washed my hands keeping an eye on them.

They were close together and talking with bowed heads.

I dried my hands and walked past them. One shoved his foot in front of me. I sidestepped.

The other grabbed my arm. I spun around and smacked him in the face with my elbow.

He let go. I shoved them both, escaped out the door,

and hustled back to the main room. At the ballroom doorway, I took a breath and stepped calmly onto the dance floor. A few moments later I was with Ginny and Tom.

"The men I am looking for tried to grab me," I said, crouching down between them because there was no spare chair.

What I didn't know was why they would try to grab me. I'm an actor. Unless, I guess, they thought I was worth money. Funny move for so-called terrorists. Not funny ha-ha, funny strange. Or they knew I was working for Leviticus, and Leviticus was a target.

"What now?" Tom asked.

"We wait until the ball is officially ended then leave quickly using the crowd as cover. I'll have a car waiting," I replied. Then stood, made a call, and asked for a pickup from an old friend of Crockett's. The only time I made calls like that was when trouble was going down. I knew Art would get us home safely.

"How much longer?"

"Half an hour. People are starting to drift away." And I didn't want anyone making a play for me with Ginny there. The last thing anyone wanted was Ginny knocked to the ground or injured. Mind you her bracelet encrusted wrists/forearms could do some damage if she swung them at anyone. And she would swing at someone if challenged. And she'd connect. Best not to risk it.

Nancy caught my attention with a small wave.

"I'll see what Nancy wants, then I'll be back," I said,

and joined Nancy and Laura at our table. I crouched between them.

"I thought we could have one last dance," Nancy said with a small smile.

"Of course." I rose to my feet and offered her my elbow. "One last dance it is."

Chapter Seven:
[Ben: This will end badly.]

Art drove us to Ginny and Tom's and said goodnight.

Once inside, Tom got the coffee going and Ginny went down the hall to get ready for bed. I sat at the dining room table and looked at the little flash drive. People amazed me. So willing to do something they shouldn't do when asked by someone with a little bit of celebrity status.

"What you got there?" Tom asked.

"That guest list for the ball," I replied, and put the flash drive back into my pocket.

"That was some fancy footwork back there, getting Jakub to play your game," Tom said.

I leaned back and looked at Tom. "How long have you been in the service?"

"Pardon?"

"How long have you been in the service?" I waited to see if he'd deny it or pretend he didn't know what I was talking about.

A small smile crossed his lips. "Drink your coffee."

"It's a pretty good secret but I've finally tumbled to it." I shook my head slowly. "It's both of you, isn't it?"

"Drink your coffee. Go to bed. You did good. No one died."

"Because they're not terrorists like we think of terrorists. They're not about to blow up a ball room full of peo-

people." I took a sip of coffee. "Their activity isn't geared towards mass casualties, yet. I think they're looking to make a buy, but they haven't been included. And maybe they've figured out who some of the players are or think they can kidnap their way inside." Or maybe they think I'm worth cashing in?

Once they got hold of whatever arms were included in the deal, then, they might become terrorists. So far, they were two men who'd failed. Not very impressive.

"That's a big conclusion to draw from two kitchen hands attacking you at a dance."

I shrugged one shoulder. "But I might be right. I might be right about a few things."

There was always room for being wrong.

I texted Grandad.

Me: Home safe

Took a few minutes before I got a reply.

Grandad: Good. No car trouble I take it.
Me: No car trouble. Sleep well.

"Who are you texting?" Tom asked.

"Grandad," I replied.

"Thought he died some years ago."

"Apparently not."

I looked at my phone screen as it lit up with an incoming call. Nancy. I showed Tom.

"The woman from the ball?"

"Yeah."

I answered the call on speaker.

It wasn't Nancy.

"You will come, or we will kill the old lady," the male voice said.

"Why would I do that?"

"The old lady will die if you do not."

"And again, why would I do that?"

His voice rose slightly. He was getting agitated. "She will die. She does not want to die."

"Not my problem."

I hung up.

Tom and I stared at each other. Did they have her or have her phone? Was it the same kitchen hands from the ball or someone else? Questions and no answers. That's life.

The phone rang again. Nancy.

I answered and put it straight onto speaker again. This time it was a woman. "Please, Ben, do as they say."

"Hang in there," I replied. I couldn't verify if it was Nancy or not. "Give the phone to the person I talked to before."

He came on the line. "Now you do what I say."

"No. Now you send a photo and prove to me you have the lady."

I hung up.

Tom placed his cup on the table. "You're a cool customer, Ben."

I shrugged. "I don't like people who make threats."

The phone buzzed. I opened messages and there was a photo of Nancy and one of the men from the kitchen. She was seated on a dining room chair, and he had a knife to her throat.

"Okay, they do have her." I showed Tom. "Guess I'll be going to get her."

"Or not," Tom replied. "You know it's a trap and they want you for whatever reason."

"I do."

The phone rang again. Again, I put the phone on speaker.

"Thanks for the photo," I said, before he could speak.

Flustered the man tripped over his words, "You come. She will ... she will die."

"I'm not going to come if that means she'll die."

"I said she will die if you don't come."

"We all know she's going to die anyway," I replied and yawned. "I'm tired. We can do this tomorrow."

"No! You come now!"

"What do you want from me?"

"She will die. Come!" He sounded stressed. Another voice in the background sounded calmer.

"Who else is there? Put that person on the phone."

"You come!"

"I want to talk to the other person." It was easy for me to remain calm. I wasn't holding anyone at knife point.

A discussion ensued in the background. Then the other voice had the phone.

"You are not a good man," the person said.

"Are you Al-Fasil or Faheem?" I asked, winking at Tom.

"Come or she dies."

"She's old, she's going to die anyway. She's not my problem."

"You spend a lot of time with her at the dance. She is your problem."

"Faheem?"

"How do you know me?"

I don't asshole. But I do know you're stupid.

"Where do I meet you?"

"You come now!"

I suppressed laughter. He didn't expect me to change tack.

"Where?"

"First go to Fergusson Drive. Then I call you back."

"Which direction on Fergusson Drive?"

There was a long pause. Maybe he didn't know?

"North."

"You sure?"

"North!"

"Okay. It's going to take me a bit of time to get there."

I hung up. Tom was shaking his head at me. "This is not a good idea."

"I imagine Nancy begs to differ."

"I'll drop you on Fergie, otherwise it will take you too long, and Dumb and Dumber will be ringing, and you won't be ready." Tom grabbed his keys from the sideboard. "Come on."

I looked at my tuxedo. I might as well stay in it. I didn't imagine I'd be that long, and it was a week until the next ball. Plenty of time to get it cleaned.

Tom said a quick goodbye to Ginny then followed me out the back door. "Can I grab a screwdriver?" I asked and stepped aside to let him past. As weapons go a screwdriver is easy to conceal and not illegal to carry.

"Sure," Tom unlocked the shed door and let me in.

I walked across the concrete floor in the semi-dark. Security lighting outside sent small rivers of light through the open door. Enough to see by. I grabbed a screwdriver. My hand brushed against something and stung. There was more light at the bench, so I could see I'd cut my hand. Blood dripped on the work bench. Shit. There was a box of microfibre cloths under the bench. I tugged one out and held it against my hand. I'd splashed a bit of blood around.

"Sticking plaster?" I asked, shoving the screwdriver into my inside pocket. It'd be an okay weapon.

Tom stepped into the shed and took a first-aid kit from a shelf. He opened a fabric plaster. "Where?"

Unwrapping the cut caused more bleeding. He stuck the plaster in place. Then wrapped some micropore around it.

"Might need a stitch or two."

"Thanks, the tape should hold it until I get back." There was blood on my shirt cuff. I probably needed a new shirt anyway.

"Let's get you to Fergie Drive then."

Chapter Eight:
[Ronnie: What on earth?]

Sunlight hit me square in the eyes when I pulled back the curtains in the lounge. Blue sky and sunshine, always welcome on a Sunday. That felt like a good start to the day. The three-stone diamond ring on my finger sparkled in the sunlight. Ben did well choosing my ring.

Habit had me check the the house across the road for signs of life. All was quiet. It'd been that way since the murders. No new neighbours and it was a good thing, considering the terrible people that had plagued our street for over a year.

A noise behind me caused me to tear my eyes off the quiet road and spin around. It was Donald. He held up the French press and waggled it.

I nodded and he disappeared. By the time I crossed the room and walked into the kitchen, coffee was brewing, and Donald was making toast.

"You having brekkie?" he asked, flapping a butter knife towards the toast.

"Later. I need coffee." I sat in my usual chair at the kitchen table.

"You don't seem your usual morning self," Donald commented.

"I'm fine. It's just Sunday." A sigh escaped. "Where's Enzo?"

Enzo was Donald's gorgeous husband.

Donald rolled his eyes at me. "Working."

"He was home last night?"

"Yes, he left at silly o'clock this morning after a phone call."

"Don't suppose you ..."

"No. He doesn't tell me." The toast popped. Donald leapt, a strangled squeak popped out of his mouth.

Every time a coconut. I don't recall him ever making toast without getting a fright when the toaster popped.

He recovered his composure. "He doesn't tell me about work. It's for my own protection."

Donald's words caused a smile to tweak my lips. Yes, it was for his own protection. Our beloved Enzo was an active espionage officer with some special interrogation skills. I'd used his skills more than a few times since he came into our lives. Once upon a time, they made me squeamish. That's not the case now. But I prefer not to know exactly how he comes by his information.

I poured the coffee. Donald sat down with his plate of toast and opened the newspaper.

My mind wandered to thoughts of Ben as I sipped my coffee. We had a Sunday dinner date and that pleased me. I knew he was working but I didn't know details. I did, however, get a security alert saying the terrorism level went up a notch. There was a good chance that had something to do with whatever he was working. Ben is skilled at gathering intelligence and I was pretty sure he was on an intelligence job rather than an acting gig. I have a special skill of my own. I can find almost anyone and anything. Paper rustled. Donald's head popped over the top of the open newspaper.

"WHAT IS ON YOUR FINGER?"

Took him long enough to notice. Four days! That's got to be a record. Perhaps married life has dulled his bling senses.

"What, this?" I held my hand up and wiggled my fingers. "These gorgeous rocks?"

His eyes almost popped out of their sockets.

"O.M.G. Oh. My. God. Ben finally did it!" He threw the newspaper backward over his head. It sailed to the floor. Donald reached across the table and grabbed my left hand. Within seconds the man had a jeweller's loupe in his hand and was inspecting my engagement ring.

"Do you carry a freaking jeweller's loupe on your person?"

"Yes, and it's a good thing." He looked up. Placed the loupe on the table and smiled widely. "They are beautiful diamonds. That ring set him back a pretty penny. He's not tight."

"So glad you approve," I said taking my hand back.

"When's the big day? Is there a date? Is there a colour scheme? Or a theme?"

"Slow down." I held my hand up to stop his questions. "Buggery bollocks, Donald. You're worse than Nana." I chuckled at him. "I know what the theme will not be."

Donald wrinkled his nose. "When will you admit that our theme was fabulous?"

I shook my head at him. "I don't know, Donald, maybe

never!"

But I would be getting a bit of revenge for the tangerine and purple monstrosity of a best-woman dress that Donald and Enzo insisted I wore at their sixties themed 'Spy who shagged me' wedding. Donald retrieved the newspaper and shook it, as he settled back into his seat.

I gave him my sweetest smile. "I'm sure you'll love our wedding, Donald."

Donald laughed. I drank my coffee thinking of ways to make his life a living hell.

A few minutes later he crinkled the paper. "Ronnie, you should read this," he said, and handed me the folded paper and tapped a story. "How did we miss this?"

"Shit," I muttered as I read the headline and saw the photo. "The mystery solving dynamic trio." The story beneath was just as bad as the headline. I skimmed over the blah blah. Some intrepid reporter had done a story on Nana and the *Cronies of Doom*. Seriously, fuck my life. I checked the byline, Tamati Anderson. It was worse than I originally thought. It'd gone national. I recognised the journalist's name and knew he worked for Fairfax Media. Why would a journalist like Tamati Anderson write a story about Nana? Slow news day? He'd really gone low after reporting on that 'scandal' involving the bookshop owner who was a secret best-selling author.

"That's the worst start to a day in the history of shitty starts," I muttered and handed Donald back the paper.

"At least it's not front page. Page eight. Who reads that far into the newspaper?" It was a good try on his part, but we both knew how this little story would affect our lives. "The photo could've been better." Donald made pfft noises. "If she'd said, I could've made sure they looked fabulous, but no. Now the world will see her like that."

"I don't see how we can get in front of this." I chewed my lip and looked at the time. "They'll be up and reading it by now."

Donald chomped into a piece of toast, hurriedly swallowed, and asked, "What's the worst that could happen?"

"I don't know, Donald. What do you think? Nana just got publicity. She didn't tell us she'd been interviewed probably because I would've stomped the little fire out before it took hold. But here we are." There would be no stopping her now. "We thought it was bad with the whole not-neighbour saga and the eventual murders of those unfortunates."

I thought it was horrific when she discovered the internet and began emailing me her theories on anything that even smelt like a twinge of mystery.

That was all forgotten now.

This was nuclear. They were right about the terror level hike.

"Nothing could be as bad as that," Donald replied, a shudder punctuated his words.

"Mark my words, Donald. This is going to be bad, bad."

They'll have all the relics from the retirement home asking them to investigate all manner of things. Nana had a way of inserting herself into difficult situations. Keeping her safe and out of harm's way was a full-time job on its own, never mind trying to wrangle the three old ducks as a group. Donald knew first-hand how tricky they were. He could no longer deny anything about their behaviour.

"What are we going to do?"

"Pretend we haven't seen the story," I said. "We're going to do nothing."

"You think that will work?"

"Absolutely not, but it's worth a shot."

Donald drank his coffee without another word.

By the time I'd finished two coffees, Donald was gone. It was his turn to do the grocery shopping. Romeo ambled into the kitchen and looked at me.

"Time for a walk old boy," I said.

He danced from foot to foot. I put his harness on him utilising his 'dancing feet' to get him to step into it without any hassle. He was getting on in years. His muzzle was all grey now, instead of white and black. Romeo was the best greyhound in the world. Smart, kind, and easy to train. He no longer enjoyed tearing up the park doing massive circles at high speed, those days were well behind him. He still loved a long walk and even longer naps.

We walked at a leisurely pace around Trentham Memorial Park and met plenty of regulars on our way. Right before we left the park an elderly woman hurried into our path.

"I thought that was you Ronnie," she said, as she moved her little dog out of Romeo's way. "I see your Nana made the paper."

My heart sank. Great. Nana was about to be world famous in Upper Hutt.

"Oh, did she, Mrs G?" I mustered as much innocence as I could. Didn't want it getting back to Nana that I'd seen that story.

"Yes, Ronnie, she did. A marvellous story about her, Ester, and Frankie and how they solve mysteries all over town."

My mind spun out. Of course they solve mysteries all over town. What else would they do? Knit? Scrapbook? Play canasta? Not cause mischief?

None of those things. Nana and *the Cronies of Doom* cause mayhem. That's hardly mystery solving.

I managed to say none of my thoughts out loud.

"Nana will love that story," I said. Romeo moved sideways. The small dog was getting too close, and he didn't like little dogs under his feet. "I best get this guy home and myself off to work." I wasn't going to work to do any work. I was going to work to hide.

"You obviously get your detective skills from your Nana and your late Grandfather," Mrs G said, with delight. "Working on a Sunday, that's dedication."

Yep, that's where I get them. Nothing to do with years of training.

"Bye Mrs G. Have a lovely day."

Romeo and I walked away.

I dropped him home, grabbed my car keys, and drove to the office. Steph and Jenn were in the office when I arrived.

"Hi," I called, and plonked my laptop bag on my desk. "Are we all hiding or are you two working on a Sunday?"

"That depends ..." Steph replied.

"On?"

"You seen it?" Jenn asked.

"Yep." Ah, that was what it depended on.

"Is there a plan?" Steph asked.

"I'm ignoring it."

"Excellent plan," Jenn and Steph replied in unison, "What could go wrong?" They high-fived each other.

"What's on today? You two aren't here to hide, so?" I sat at my desk and ignored their obvious delight with themselves.

"I'm finishing up notes on the last spousal surveillance," Jenn said. "Steph said a new job came in overnight."

"Interesting one?"

Steph nodded. "Some potential corporate espionage."

"Oh, juicy," I replied. "Reach out and let them know we can help."

"Bags me!" Jenn said, thrusting her arm in the air.

"Isn't it usually bags not me?"

Jenn nodded. "I'm just over these cheating buggers and need something to sink my teeth into."

"Bags you it is then," I replied. "Might be just as boring though."

"I'll take my chances."

"All right then, have at it." I took my laptop from my bag and opened it up. "I've got a couple of reports to write before I send you the expenses to add to the two invoices we're sending early this week," I said to Steph. So, I was hiding *and* working. My engagement ring sparkled under the office lights and momentarily mesmerised me. I wondered how long it would take to become used to it.

"Good," Steph replied without looking up from her keyboard. "I suppose I will sanction overtime this weekend due to extenuating circumstances."

Steph disliked allowing overtime. It went against every bone in her accountant body. She liked money coming in, not going out.

And then my cell phone rang.

"Nana and possibly one other calling," my phone announced. "Nana and possibly one other calling."

Always amused me when it did the 'possibly one other' thing. Usually, it was because there were two saved contacts with the same number. In this case, Nana and then her real name, June. The phone kept announcing the call until I touched the screen to decline it. I was not ready for famous Nana. I could barely cope with regular Nana. I concentrated on the job at hand and finished the reports. Nana rang back twice over the course of an hour. Both times I declined the call. Then the office phone rang.

Steph coughed and looked at me. "We all know who that is." She pointed to the phone.

"Could be anyone," I replied. "Could be a new case."

"You get it then," she said.

I shook my head. "I need to proofread this last report."

Jenn was off meeting the new client after reaching out

to the company and discovering the head honcho was in their offices. So, either Steph or I had to answer the call, or let it kick to the answer service. We stared at each other as the ringing stopped and a message began. It was definitely Nana. "Veronica dear, the girls and I were wondering if you could call in later this morning?" There was a pause. "We've got a few cases and need some advice."

Steph roared with laughter.

"That was fast," I muttered as Steph's laughter flowed.

Steph attempted words but they came out as choked gibberish.

The phone rang again. Her laughter hit another high. No way was I answering a call with Steph almost in hysterics. It wouldn't appear professional for any potential client. Best not to answer. Just in case. A little voice in my head reminded me it was Sunday and very few clients phoned us on a Sunday.

I scanned the document on my screen for anything that required fixing. The answer service kicked in. I held my breath and exhaled when I heard a male voice that I didn't recognise. "Might have the wrong number, but my friend Joe said to give you a call because you have a good selection of red roses. It's a broken heart situation. Was hoping you could help."

My stomach dropped.

Steph's laughter died. "That was a weird message. We've never been confused with a florist before." She rose from her chair.

"There's a first for everything," I replied. I was fairly sure that it wasn't a wrong number.

Steph turned to look at me, her blue eyes brightened. "It's a you thing, isn't it?"

I nodded. "Sounds like a me thing."

Steph sat back down.

I sent the reports to the clients and then sent Steph the spreadsheets before packing my laptop away. I had no idea who made the call, but I'd bet on Nana's life that it wasn't good.

"I'm going home," I said. "I'm keeping my phone on me. You can track me if I don't check-in regularly."

She nodded.

I played the message again, wrote it in my notebook, then deleted the message. I ran down the stairs with my laptop bag hitting my hip on each stair.

On the drive home, I tried to remember what the parts of the message meant. The only part I did remember seeing in the *Genesis* code book was Joe. Joe equalled American. The only American I knew that was part of *Genesis* here in New Zealand, and would generate a message to me, was Benjamin Reynolds. He was hard not to like so we always got along regardless of our boyfriend/girlfriend status. It was just a matter of time before Nana wore him down and he proposed. He could just about get anyone to tell him anything with his charm, blue eyes, and dimples, but he was no match for my Nana.

Nana told me when she first met Ben that he was perfect for me. She's worried I'd be past my prime by the time I got around to marriage. And until Ben proposed the other day, I thought I'd be well past my prime by the time a wedding ring slipped onto my finger.

I swallowed the fear that something awful had happened to Ben. It wasn't helpful. Get the facts, then make a plan.

Chapter Nine:
[Ronnie: Red Roses for Joe.]

Romeo greeted me at the front door and kept pace with me as I climbed the stairs. He ambled back to his bed in the lounge, and I hurried to my bedroom and the bat cave.

I closed my bedroom door, opened the wardrobe, pushed aside shirts on hangers, and pressed my hand onto an electronic plate next to a hidden door. The door lock popped. I opened the door and lights flicked on as a computer spun into life. I closed the door and sat at my desk. There were two screens in front of me and a keyboard. I took a code book and a flash drive from a hidden safe at the back of a drawer under my desk and plugged the flash drive into one of the screens and then navigated to the Genesis link. While the link opened, I checked the book. Red roses for a broken heart and something to do with Joe.

Red Roses = urgent.

Joe = American.

Heart = missing officer.

A message window popped up on the screen with a ding. Three dots appeared in the window. I waited.

Genesis: There is a problem.

Me: Red roses for a broken heart and it was you that rang my office?

Genesis: Affirmative.

Me: Joe is Ben Reynolds?

Genesis: Affirmative.

I stared as three dots moved. Ben was missing? That was bad.

Genesis: Radio silence since just before midnight Friday.

Me: Where was he?

Genesis: Working an operation in the Hutt.

Me: And?

Genesis: Find him, Ronnie. Bring him home.

Me: What do I need to know? Is this about the hiked terror alert?

Genesis: Potentially. He was working on intel around an illegal arms sale for *Genesis* and his usual company. Ben had/has tickets to two black-tie events that our sources flagged as live-drops or some sort of staging area for displaced arms deals.

Me: Did he confirm the terror threat?

Genesis: Not before he disappeared. At least not to us.

Genesis: You have the authority to bring in anyone required to get the job done.

Genesis: Set timers. Check-in via text at the following number every three hours.

A cell phone number appeared on the screen. I added it to my phone contacts and named it *Uncle* then changed my mind and gave it a proper name. And added alarms for every three hours.

Me: Thank you, you are now Uncle George
Genesis: Stay Frosty Oscar Mike
Me: Did he make contact with the arms dealers?
Me: How much trouble is he in?

The chat window vanished. The link closed. Don't answer me then. I'll work it out for myself. I put everything away and left the bat cave. Before I shut the wardrobe, I took a black leather backpack from the shelf above the rail. I packed a few items of essential clothing, some toiletries, and sneakers. Just in case. I slung the bag over one shoulder.

Back in the lounge, I gave Romeo a quick head rub and told him he was in charge until Donald came home. He gave me a look that implied he was in charge regardless. Smart dog.

I scrawled a note on the kitchen blackboard saying I was out working, and left. Sitting in my car I sent two texts to Ben. They turned from blue to green. That told me his phone was off. If he was working, then he probably left his personal phone at home. So, it could well be off and at home.

I emailed him.

Then I checked something else. We've worked together for a number of years, and we've dated a lot over that time. Ages ago we set up ways to communicate in case something happened. Shit happens. Best to be prepared.

I checked an author website. We both liked her books and had in the past left coded messages inside comments on her blog. Crime writer *Margot Kinberg* blogged regularly and that worked in our favour. It stopped a communication thread being discovered by accident. We would leave a comment on one post and the answer on another. I checked all posts over the last week. Just in case. There was nothing from Ben's alias. I pulled up an email account using Safari. It was an account that Ben created, and I could access. There was no draft email waiting for me.

I scrolled through mutual acquaintances in my contacts and fired off a few text messages. They were short and sweet: Seen Reynolds in the last 48?

They all came back negative.

I leaned my head on the head rest. Usually if someone is missing, I get pulled in by whatever agency and given a full brief, or at least given the information whoever asked wanted me to have.

But this was Ben. I know all the things. Or do I?

But this was Ben.

That was the point where I wondered how clouded my judgment was because this was Ben.

I knew what I had to do.

Genesis knew he was missing, but it wasn't just a *Genesis* job. Who did I know over at Ben's usual place of work? Kirsten Knight. I knew he wasn't her biggest fan, but she was a starting point. I found her number and gave her a ring. She answered surprisingly fast. I could hear phones ringing and the hum of talking in the background.

"It's Ronnie Tracey, Kirsten."

"Wow, it's been a while." Background noise disappeared as a door closed. "How can I help?"

"Don't suppose you've heard from Ben Reynolds in the last few days?"

Silence for a beat. "No. I haven't."

"Is he on a job?"

"Maybe. How about we meet up for a coffee?"

"Sounds good, where?"

"Petone foreshore. Sea air is always refreshing."

I glanced at my watch. "When?"

"Five."

It was only midday.

"Which side of the wharf?"

"Dog side."

Right, Romeo would love nothing more than to play in the sea.

"See you then." I hung up.

I needed to know who he talked to and if they were involved in his disappearance. I suspected the call I got was made with voice changing software and probably from whoever ran *Genesis* here. And whoever I spoke to via the Genesis chat application, said it was them who'd rung me. I phoned Steph. I was curious. I needed to find Ben, but also wanted to find out some more about who rang me at work.

"Hey, Ronnie," she said when she answered her cell

phone. "How can I help?"

"See if you can find the phone number that rang."

"Ah, the guy looking for a florist. Give me a sec."

I waited. Tapping my fingers on the armrest in the car and willing Steph to hurry up. Time seemed to slow down to excruciatingly small increments that move slower than sludge on a cold day.

"Okay, I got it. The call came from a cell phone. The phone is now off, but its last location pinged in near Linkwater, in Marlborough."

What the hell? Marlborough. That felt quite random, but it couldn't be. Why would someone from Marlborough ring me and say Ben was missing? Because that is effectively what they said. Linkwater? I pulled a map of Marlborough up on my phone. Linkwater was between Havelock and Picton. That really helped. Not.

"Could the phone's location be wrong?" I asked.

"It could. It's an unregistered phone by the way."

Of course, it would be a burner. Why would someone make a call from a phone we could trace?

"Thanks Steph."

"Be careful. Hey, Crockett is at his office. He checked in before."

"Thanks. Definitely the person I need to talk with."

At least I didn't have to go looking for him. Who knew we'd all be in our offices on a Sunday? We're obviously all rubbish at weekends.

I hung up and headed for Crockett's office. Halfway there I remembered that Crockett had a mate down in the

Marlborough Sounds. Nah. That felt like an actual coincidence.

Chapter Ten:
[Crockett: Charlie India Alpha.]

"What makes you think our mates at Charlie India are involved?"

"We're in New Zealand and they operate overseas."

I couldn't argue with that, but it still seemed like a poke in the dark with a floppy hotdog.

I leaned back in my chair. The fingers of my right hand beat a tattoo on the coffee table next to me. A minute crept past as I waited for something, anything, to happen. Just because I didn't have plans for my Sunday didn't mean I wanted to waste it.

"Knock it off," Ronnie grumbled. "That's really annoying."

"Why were the old Charlie India noddies your first thought?"

She sighed. "Because it's Ben who is missing. Because he was working a job. Because Ben is Charlie Indigo on most days that end in Y." And because he's working for two agencies this time around.

"Hang on a minute, did you just say indigo instead of India?"

"I've always said indigo instead of India. I like the colour. Is that a problem?"

"Not at all. You do you, Ronnie." Glad that was clarified. "How do you know he's missing?"

"He told me." She rolled her eyes at me. "How do you think I know?"

"I asked because I don't know."

"They sent out a newsletter with a list of missing persons."

Ronnie can be a pain in the bum sometimes.

"You done?"

She nodded.

"How do you know?"

"He hasn't answered his texts, phone, or email in at least twenty-four hours."

"Anything else?" Because I know her and there's always more.

"No answer on our other means of communication either. No one I've reached out to has heard from him this weekend. That means, Crockett, that he is missing." She sighed. "He's not just Ben anymore, Crockett. He's my Ben." She lifted her left hand and wriggled her fingers. "We're ..."

"Engaged," I finished for her. "That's fantastic news."

She nodded. "Thanks. I'd like him home."

"Understood."

"I was told he missed his check-ins. That's pretty much all I know."

"Do you know what the job was?"

"No. But it was Hutt based and sounded fancy. Some sort of black-tie affair."

"That narrows it down." Worry edged into her expression. Not like her to physically show concern. The jobs we do have the potential to go very wrong and I imagined that would weigh on her. "Can we find out what he was working?"

"Maybe, but they tell so many porkies, can we believe what we're told?"

She wasn't wrong.

"Do your woo-woo thing. See if you can locate him."

"Every time a coconut," Ronnie said with a well-placed scowl. "You *trying* to piss me off?"

I shrugged. "Did it work?"

A smile flashed across her lips then vanished. The scowl returned.

"I'll try it. Coming with?"

"Sure. Where?"

"My offices."

"I'll follow you."

We arrived at *'Wherefore Art Thou'* fifteen minutes after leaving my office. Not bad going. Traffic was light and the traffic light gods worked in our favour for a change.

I followed Ronnie up the stairs and down the hallway to a room I knew she liked using for her woo-woo. She spun on me as soon as I crossed the threshold.

"Keep your opinion and comments to yourself."

"Yes, ma'am." I threw a salute in her direction. "Can I ask questions, ma'am?"

"Relevant ones, yes."

I grabbed a chair from near the big table, moved it closer to the door and sat on it. Ronnie did her thing.

There was a ritual when she had the space for it and today, she did.

And then she surprised me.

"Hey Siri, play *Goodbye Stranger* by Supertramp."

I'd failed to notice the HomePod mini until it lit up on the bookcase behind Ronnie. That was a new addition to her space. She carried on spreading a map across the table. Moments later after some quiet reflection, I assumed, she let a pendulum chain run through her fingers and caught the last ten centimetres. With the crystal hanging motionless over the map, she began. Didn't matter how many times I saw that crystal swing on the chain, it always fascinated me. I watched. Ronnie worked her woo-woo magic, trying to get a bead on the places our mate Ben had been, or still was.

The crystal spun in big wide clockwise circles as Ronnie moved her hand above the map. It suddenly stopped then swung in a north-south line.

"That's different. What's that?" I asked.

"Movement." She moved her hand back to where the movement began. The circles spun tighter and tighter then stopped. The stone hung. "Ben's apartment." She moved again and the direction of the swing changed. A line. She moved to the end of the line and the circles returned.

"What's that then?"

"The American Embassy. This is showing more movement. I think he drove out of town. Or maybe he took the train."

A new song began. *Patience* by Guns N' Roses.

She followed the circles. I followed her hand waiting to see what would happen next. Didn't take long before there was another indication of either Ben stopping somewhere or residual energy from places he'd been. I didn't know which and it didn't matter how many times I saw Ronnie do this; I didn't fully understand how it worked. It's true when they say the universe works in mysterious ways.

At the edge of the map the pendulum stopped dead.

"Can you turn the map over for me?" Ronnie asked.

I did. She kept her hand where it stopped. A few seconds later there was more movement. Her fingers never moved, not even micro muscle movements. The pendulum moved by itself as it searched and reacted to various energies. Hence, I termed her gift woo-woo. I knew it freaked Ben out a bit. He never wanted to try his hand at it, but I did. The concept of being able to tune into the universe, and energy, and the power that they held, that was too much for me to resist.

"Lower Hutt, near the CBD," she said. The pendulum swung in tight circles over something.

"What's that?"

"The Event Centre, I think. If that was where the event was held then it should be easy to find out what it was." The pendulum moved again.

"Now where?"

"Naenae," she said. "The garage where I store my cars."

Her hand began following the direction of the swinging pendulum as it moved away from that area. It suddenly stopped and hung.

"Is that something?" I asked, leaning forward to see where the pendulum stopped.

"Pinehaven," she replied. "He could've been at Ginny and Tom's, but he's been there a lot so maybe it's not recent."

The pendulum started its journey again. It paused on Fergusson Drive near St Pat's College. I watched as it led Ronnie to Trentham. It paused over Ronnie's home, then moved into Upper Hutt City.

"Where's that?" I asked as it paused again. I couldn't see exactly where.

"My offices and the supermarket," she replied. Her hand then came back towards Trentham. More rapid swinging followed.

I saw the crystal drop suddenly. From circles to a dead hang.

"What's that?"

Tequila Sunrise started on the HomePod.

She was quiet for a beat. She let the chain go. The crystal rolled in a circle then stopped. Point inward.

"What is it, Ronnie?" I hopped to my feet and moved closer. I stared at the place the point indicated. "That's down the road from me. What the hell?"

She nodded.

"Okay, so this is what I saw. He went to the embassy. That would follow suit if he was working a Charlie Indigo job. But he often mentions he's called into the embassy. So, it might be me wishing it was significant."

"I'd say it is significant, Ronnie."

She nodded. "After that he's in Lower Hutt then jumps to Naenae. Then he went to Pinehaven." She looked up at me. "I don't know if he was at Ginny and Tom's before he vanished, or if it's residual energy. Same with the movement out to the Hutt, really. He trained and drove in and out of Wellington all the time."

"And?"

"After Ginny's the next pause is Fergusson Drive somewhere around Silverstream. And then it showed me my offices and came back to Trentham. And it looks like he's down your street. The intermediate school end where the mosque is. And it doesn't make sense. I was told he was working a black-tie affair, so maybe that was in Lower Hutt. He wouldn't catch the train to that or drive himself. He'd have a town car of some sort. A driver. And why would he be there?" She pointed at the place on the map at the end of my street. "Hardly the venue for a ball or a fancy schmancy anything. That was more likely to be in Lower Hutt."

"You're saying that he's missing, but he's close."

She nodded. "Looks that way." Ronnie sighed. "Or he was close. The other thing is, I can't tell the order of his stops/pauses. I don't know where he went first. I don't know how many times he traveled Fergusson Drive for example, or how many times he's visited his embassy. Or how often he went to Ginny and Tom's. Or my place or the bloody supermarket."

"Have you spoken to Ginny?"

"No."

"Any word come down the *Genesis* pipeline?"

Her head snapped up and eyes met mine. "Pardon?"

"Listen Ronnie, I'm not an idiot. I know you know things. I know you have a way inside."

"As if," she said, tossing her hair over her shoulder. "I don't know what you're talking about."

"Okay." Best to leave that line alone. "Perhaps we should talk to Ginny?"

She nodded.

"First, we should go for a wander down the end of your street with Romeo. Because it's a bit suss that I picked up Ben's energy there, and if he's there and can't reach out then ..."

Neil Young's *Like a Hurricane* played.

"I know, Ronnie. We'll check it out first. I'll go see who is still in the office while you pack up."

I let myself out and strode down the hall to the door to the main office. I swung it open and saw Steph at her desk. "Hey."

"Hi, Crockett. What brings you in?"

"Had a meeting with Ronnie." I glanced around the room. "Jenn out?"

"She's writing up reports downstairs in the bookshop. Emily wanted to start stocktake today, so she decided to open the shop while she did that."

Everyone is in on a Sunday. Must be something in the

air. It was good that Jenn spent time downstairs. She was about as jumpy as I was after a loser and his harassment of Emily some months back. We outfitted the bookshop with state-of-the-art security cameras. I had access and so did Ronnie, Jenn, and Steph. The best thing was we could hear what was said and respond. We scared the shit out of a few idiots doing that. A loud disembodied voice is enough to scare most people and it's funny as hell.

I had a thought and ran back to Ronnie, almost colliding with her in the hallway.

"Walking feet," she said putting her hands out to brace for impact. Luckily my brakes work.

"Can't you track his phone?"

She shook her head.

"He doesn't have one of my phones. He's probably using a phone supplied by his agency that no one can access."

Except his case officer, whoever that was, might have access. I knew it was occasionally Kirsten Knight because we'd talked about her in general terms. I also knew Ben had a fairly low opinion of the woman.

Hmm. "When you do ..." she gave me a warning look. "The thing." I circled my hand in the air as if I was holding a pendulum by the chain. "That's similar to satellite tracking on a phone?"

"Yeah, I guess it is."

"The signal still shows where you went even if there's a delay."

She nodded. "Yes."

"I think we should go now. Do we need Romeo?"

She nodded.

Ronnie popped her head into the main office and told Steph we were off out.

Chapter Eleven:
[Ronnie: Romeo knows best.]

Romeo was happy to see us when we got home. It was tricky to put his harness on with his prancing on the spot and tail wagging. Two walks in one day made for a very happy hound. Crockett gave him a pat on his boney head which settled him enough for me to get his harness clipped together.

"We walking?"

"I think that'd be a better idea than driving. Let this guy stretch his legs before we put him to work."

"Do you have something of Ben's for the dog to scent?"

"I don't think I'll need it. He knows who Ben is."

"And if he doesn't?"

Fair point. "I'll be right back. Might have one of his tee-shirts." I glanced at the diamonds on my hand. Probably not them.

It was quiet and peaceful at home. Donald was still shopping, and Enzo was working. The lack of neighbours across the street made the whole area feel lighter. I hurried up the hallway and into my room. The wardrobe seemed to beckon me. I quietly closed my bedroom door. Wouldn't hurt to check and see if anything more had filtered through to *Genesis.* I opened the wardrobe and moved my clothes aside, then pressed my palm on the lock next to the revealed door.

Crockett called out. "Hurry up!"

Bugger. I stopped, moved the hangers back then grabbed a tee shirt of Ben's that was folded on my dresser. *Genesis* would have to wait. They'd figure out I was meeting with a Charlie Indigo source later, anyway. Some days it felt like *Genesis* was all seeing and all knowing.

I moved a little quicker on the way back to the kitchen with Ben's shirt in my hands.

"Sorry. Pit stop," I said with a smile and waved the folded shirt. "Ben's"

Crockett nodded. "Let's go."

It didn't take much longer than seven minutes to get to the mosque. I looked through the side gate to Fergusson Intermediate. He could be anywhere here. Romeo stepped sideways moving towards the mosque. He sniffed the air, then whined.

"Okay, we're going in the gate," I told him.

There were no signs of life as we approached the building. I cupped my hand on the window and leant into it, trying to see inside. Nothing moved. I tried the door. It was locked.

"You alright?" Crockett asked.

"Funny that it's locked during the day. I thought it was like a church. Open all the time."

Crockett cupped his hand on the glass and peered inside. "There's an alarm."

"Probably shouldn't break the door down then."

Romeo turned and led me around the side of the building. Crockett followed. We found a back door. It was locked.

"We're sure he was here?"

"Romeo is. The universe is sure he was at some stage."

I turned around with Romeo to walk back.

Crockett grabbed my arm, "And you want to leave without finding out if he still is?"

"Nope. But I also don't want to get in the midst of his op."

"Then why are we looking for him in the first place?"

I sighed. "Because he didn't check-in and something smells off." And I was asked to bring him home. And it's Ben. My Ben.

"Okay, follow my lead." Crockett took Romeo's leash and walked up to the front door. He knocked firmly and carefully unclipped the leash, holding Romeo by a single finger looped under his harness. "Play along Romeo. If the door opens you get in and find Ben," Crockett whispered. Romeo looked at him and appeared to nod.

A shadow moved on the other side of the door. It wasn't deserted. The door opened. A bearded man who was about six feet tall, wearing white, including a white turban, smiled at Crockett.

"Sorry to bother you but could we trouble you for a bowl of water?" Romeo slipped past the man and into the dim building. The man gave an unsure laugh as Romeo vanished from sight.

"He must be very thirsty. Of course. Come in. The kitchen is this way." He led the way.

I pushed my hair up under my cap and rolled my sleeves down. Then checked I was buttoned up and respectable. All good. Now I just had to keep my mouth in check. The nice man didn't need nonsense from my mouth, and we needed to find Ben.

"Your dog has found the kitchen. I am Mohammad," he said, and pointed at Romeo sitting beautifully on the kitchen floor.

This greyhound can sit.

"Good boy, Romeo," I said quietly.

"Did he race?" Mohammad asked.

"Yes." I kept my eyes on the dog. "He loved to race. He loved to win." Romeo wasn't just sitting in the kitchen. He was sitting in front of a closed internal door.

"What's through there?" Crockett asked, pointing at the door.

Romeo whined then yapped softly, moving his front feet in a bit of a shuffle. I placed my hand on his head and whispered, "I hear you, Ro. I hear you. Good boy."

"What does that mean?" Mohammad asked.

Crockett sidestepped the question and he asked again. Crockett answered, "He thinks someone he knows is here." Crockett's voice remained measured and calm.

Mohammad frowned and stroked his beard. "I am the only one in the mosque today." He placed a bowl of water on the floor near Romeo. The dog took the hint and had a drink. At least he didn't make us liars. "I am the only one here."

"You haven't seen a six-foot American, blue eyes, light brown hair, thinks he's famous?" Crockett asked.

I rolled my eyes.

"No American."

"Why is it so quiet?" I asked.

"Most Muslims go down to the other mosque in Lower Hutt. Ours is unfortunately underused."

"I'm sorry. It seems like a nice place." There was good energy in the building.

I knew it wasn't always a mosque. The building started out as a school for intellectually handicapped kids. I'm sure there were a few other uses as well. I did know that in one incarnation it was a Nanny school.

"Thank you for your kind words," Mohammad said.

Romeo sat directly in front of the closed door.

"Oh dear," I said. "I don't suppose you could let him see what's in there. Would that be all right?" I jammed as much innocence as I could into my words. Just a woman with a nosy greyhound.

Mohammad nodded. "I don't see why not," he said, and reached for the door handle. Romeo whined and stepped closer to the door. His nails tapping on the Lino with his excitement and inability to keep still. Mohammad tried to turn the handle then stopped and frowned some more. "It's locked." He seemed genuinely surprised.

"Is it not usually?" I asked.

"No, not at all." He hurried over to the bench and pulled open a drawer. "Here we are. The key."

Mohammad shoved the key into the lock and turned it. He then used the door handle and swung the door wide. There was darkness and stairs. He turned a light on. Romeo flew down the stairs barking.

We all followed. Mohammad seemed quite confused. "I don't know who would lock the door."

At the bottom of the stairs Romeo was pawing at another door. "May I?" Crockett asked with his hand on the doorknob.

"Of course," Mohammad nodded.

Crockett opened the door. More darkness. Crockett found a light switch near the door. The light flickered on. In the middle of the room was a chair. Romeo was sniffing it for all he was worth. On the floor was a chain and a screwdriver. One end of the chain was attached to a bolt in the wall, the other to a pair of handcuffs.

I swallowed hard. If he was in here at any point, I doubted it was for fun.

"What is this?" Mohammad seemed horrified. "Why would this be in our mosque?" He waved his arm about the room.

"I don't know," I said. "You've not seen this set up before?"

He shook his head. "Never. This is disturbing."

I scanned the floor for anything that might indicate Ben was there and picked up the screwdriver. Over by one wall, there was something small up against the skirting. It could be nothing. It could be a cockroach. Crockett had Mohammad's attention, so I used that to my advantage and picked up the thing. It was a flash drive. I shoved it in my pocket before anyone noticed and breathed a sigh of relief that it wasn't a cockroach.

"Who has access here?" Crockett said.

"Everyone who comes to the mosque. I've never seen *anyone* go down here."

"Are you always here?" Crockett asked.

"No. Most days, but not always."

"In the last two days?" Crockett queried.

"I was not here."

Convenient.

"Can you think of anyone attached to the mosque who would be down here with a prisoner? With someone they needed to chain to a wall?"

The man shook his head. "This is very bad."

"Yes, it is," I replied. "Things like this ..." I swept my arm towards the chair and chain. "Don't help alleviate distrust."

He nodded. "What do you want me to do?"

I pulled a business card from my pocket. It was a generic card for '*Wherefore Art Thou*' without an investigator's name attached. "If you see anyone or hear that anyone has been using this room, please call my office."

He read the card then looked at me. "Yes. I will."

"Thank you. And thank you for the water," I replied, tapping my thigh so Romeo knew we were moving again.

We walked back to my place in silence. There were too many people out gardening and so forth, to talk about what we'd seen.

Once we were safely indoors, I made coffee.

"You are sure he was working for Charlie Indigo, right?"

"Now you're saying indigo." Felt like a very small win.

"And I am sure that he's working for Charlie Indigo." *Genesis* told me and Kirsten wants to meet in person. I glanced at the clock on the kitchen wall. It was nearly three. To make the meeting in Petone, I'd have to leave about twenty-to-five. "Let's have our coffee in the lounge."

Crockett led the way, and I palmed the flash drive I'd hidden in my pocket.

Chapter Twelve:
[Ronnie: The Murk Deepens.]

I sipped my coffee while keeping an eye on the time.

"Some place you need to be?" Crockett asked, putting his mug on a coaster on the coffee table. "You've checked your watch three times in the last ten minutes."

"Is it a crime to look at my watch?"

"No, but you're withholding something." He picked his cup up again and took a sip. "You make good coffee. What is it?"

"Robert Harris's Italian roast." I was trying to decide if I should tell him about Kirsten or not. I opted for not. At least not yet.

"Have they appointed a new head for NZSIS?" Crockett asked. "After that whole Chandler debacle, I expected an announcement by now. Guess I could've missed it."

"Not formally. I saw something buried in the newspaper a week or so ago that said who the acting head was."

"Do we know the person?"

"Chur bro," I replied with a grin. "He's everybody's bro."

"Peter Piper?" Crockett queried and for good reason, because Peter Piper picked a peck of absolutely nothing. His parents clearly had a sense of humour.

"That's him."

"Couldn't find anyone more average?"

"Guess not. At least he's not an arsehole."

"Yet. It could still happen. Power does that to some blokes."

"And Russia could still nuke us," I replied.

"They could."

The timer went off on my phone. I picked it up and sent a quick text to Uncle George.

Me: Working
Three dots moved.
Uncle George: Take care

"Anything to report?" Crockett asked as I put my phone face down on the coffee table.

"No. Family stuff."

"You set an alarm for family stuff?"

"Sometimes." It was time to get off that subject. "Is this a good time to tell you I found something at the mosque?"

"The screwdriver?"

I shook my head. "As well as."

He froze for a beat then slowly made eye contact with me as I opened my hand and revealed a small flash drive.

"That's not nothing," he said, picking it up. "You're pretty good with the sleight of hand."

"We need to see what's on it and for that I need to use one of the computers at the office."

"The shielded one, right?"

"That would be smart. We don't know who left it there or why."

"Drink up, then we'll head back to your office." He dropped the flash drive back into my outstretched hand. "Let's hope it's helpful. And let's get cracking, it's creeping towards beer o'clock."

I had a feeling it was helpful. The fact that the flash drive was dropped or thrown into its resting place, and overlooked by whomever had Ben, was interesting. Who had Ben? The question spun endlessly in my mind as I rinsed the mugs after we'd finished our coffees, and while we drove back to the office. When we got there, Steph was gone, and Jenn was in residence.

"You're back," she said, looking over her laptop at me.

"I am. Or I'm a figment of your imagination. Up to you what you believe,' I replied with a smile in my voice. "Where's Steph?"

"I'm not sure. She got a phone call and vanished."

"Like up in a puff of smoke or she walked down the stairs?"

"Strangely, she walked down the stairs," Jenn replied, deadpan. "Much more fun when she goes up in a puff of smoke."

I pointed to a chair and motioned to Crockett to bring it closer to the desk on the back wall. On the desk was a secure computer. Not internet capable at all. It was a vault that stored all manner of sensitive things, including various Trojan horses and viruses. Just in case.

Our files were moved to the vault once cases were completed, and payment made. Then whichever device held them during the job was scrubbed of all data pertaining to the finished case. It was nice and clean, with no residue for someone to come across. Hackers are always a concern, so we protected our client's information using military grade encryption and stored all data in the vault.

Crockett watched as I accessed the computer with my fingerprint. I plugged the flash drive into the USB-C port and opened it to reveal its contents. There were several numbered folders. I chose the lowest number to start the ball rolling. The folder opened to reveal a few files. I opened the first one. Crockett and I read the screen in silence. It was notes on an event. It said who was spoken with and what they said.

"Is this from Ben?" Crockett asked.

"I think so." I didn't know for sure, but someone left it for us, and he was supposedly attending a couple of black-tie events, but I thought he'd only got to one so far. "Do you recognise any of the names?" I saw Frost and rolled my mind back to his weird phone call.

Crockett pointed at the list. "Third down is someone. Pretty sure he was on the last alert I received from my crowd."

I wrote the name of my wannabe mate, Jackson Frost, onto a piece of paper on my desk. I read what Ben had written. "He said he wasn't there, or he didn't see him." Interesting. What the hell had Frost done?

"Yep, Sandra King." He pointed to a name in the middle of the list. "And that bloke, Steven Sadler."

"They weren't alerts?"

"No. Sadler works for the UK and King is cosy with the

Ukraine."

"Doesn't sound like a Ukraine name," I said, adding their names to the piece of paper.

"As far as I know she's Canadian but freelances, and lately she's been linked to the Ukrainians."

"So, those two," I pointed at names on my piece of paper. "Are they intelligence community?" It said they weren't seen at the event. Maybe they were supposed to be there.

"Yes."

"And this one?" I underlined Jackson Frost's name. I knew what he used to be, but I had suspicions.

"British, disillusioned, running with some Russians. Or so I heard. I think he was disavowed. He was into some bad shit. Caused the death of two MI6 operatives during an operation."

Screw Frost, what a splash of seagull shit he was. Still with MI6. Pfft. I moved on. It felt like I'd missed a couple of reports from *Genesis*. Crockett knew about the three people Ben had noted, but I didn't. With a mental shrug I moved that thought aside. We didn't all get told everything, for good reason. Or I missed a report.

"So, whatever Ben was hoping to gather, would've involved Frost at some stage judging by the way his name is underlined."

"I'd say so."

"Any other names pop out?"

Crockett leaned in and read the list carefully before shaking his head.

I closed the file and opened the next.

Jackson Frost's name was at the top of the page. Underneath it was a series of letters and a note that said 'What has this got to do with Nancy?' Below that he'd written 'memorised'.

"Got to be a cipher," Crockett said.

"Could be. It's coded something. Weird that it doesn't say why, unless he thought someone might get hold of this note." I copied the string of letters to the piece of paper, taking care to make sure I wrote them exactly as they were. "The plot thickens."

The next five files all contained observations. There was nothing that leapt off the screen yelling that it was the key to the whole thing. We moved on to the next folder. And that contained files like the first. No more notes containing numbers or anything, but plenty about various people and who they were speaking to.

At the bottom it said: Contact made. Vetting process started.

I touched the screen. My finger rested on the last note on the page.

"He made contact," Crockett said quietly.

"This is all from his phone," I said, leaning back in my chair and looking at the screen. He'd taken all the notes on his phone then saved them in folders.

"How do you know?"

"The format. There's not much info on each page. Also, I've seen Ben do it before."

"And it got onto a flash drive how?"

"Directly from his phone. He would've copied it encrypted, straight to the drive."

"What do you think happened next?"

"If he had time, he would've wiped the phone before anyone could get anything off it and hidden the flash drive."

"The clue to finding Ben is in all these notes?"

"Maybe." I hoped so. "Nancy is a good starting point."

I scanned a list of names on the screen. Nancy Frost-Andrews.

Crockett pointed at the name. "There was only one Nancy. This Nancy Frost-Andrews woman."

I skim read the list of names. It looked like a guest list. Wondered how Ben got hold of that.

Then I saw two first names I recognised, along with Ben's name. I committed the two names to memory. Virginia and Thomas. Surely not? I cleared the screen and cleaned the computer.

Crockett watched, but didn't comment on the names that felt familiar to me. I thought about the names. That was the first time I'd seen their surname. We weren't told when we met Ginny and Tom. Maybe Crockett didn't notice? Virginia and Thomas Smith.

Mr and Mrs Smith? That couldn't be right. Brad Pitt and Angeline Jolie popped into focus. I pushed that aside. I doubted Ginny and Tom were assassins.

Crockett's voice helped me move past the assassin situation. "Before I forget, did you see the Herald this morning?"

"I saw the Dom. You talking about the story about my Nana?"

"June has reach."

"I'm ignoring it."

"That's a definite plan."

"We'll see if it's a good one or not." I laughed. "It's better than acknowledging her new-found fame status."

"She's going to lap it up."

"Like a pig in muck."

"I'll try and avoid the subject at our weekly poker game."

I looked at him. "And they never mentioned the story to you?"

"Not a word."

"Those crones are sneaky." I stood up. "I'll take this flash drive out to the tech room." Once in the tech room, I decided the drive would be best stored in the safe and that's where I put it. We had enough scrawled notes to carry on with for the moment. As I locked the tech room door a thought burrowed into my mind. Sleeper agents. I gave it a second to see if anything else wanted to join. It was hardly a sleeper situation, was it?

Jenn yelled out she was leaving. "See you tomorrow."

"Bye," I said.

Crockett and I locked up before we left.

"Where to?" Crockett asked as he held the door for me at the bottom of the stairs.

"Remember the stories about the cold war?"

"Which ones in particular?" he said, letting the door

close and lock behind me.

"Sleeper agents."

"Talk and walk, let's go to the car," he said. We were parked in the supermarket car park. "What about sleeper agents?"

"Just that ..." I looked at Crockett over the car roof.

"Who is it that you think is hiding in plain sight?"

He unlocked the car with the fob.

"I'm not sure anyone is ..."

"Ronnie ..."

"Crockett?" I opened the passenger door and got in the car. I buckled up while Crockett settled himself in the drivers seat.

"It's me, talk." He shot a smile at me. "This isn't the eighties."

"Yeah well, sleeper agents weren't just a seventies/eighties phenomenon."

"I'm aware."

"Not just Russian either."

"Ronnie, come on. What's going on here?"

"I'm not sure."

"Okay."

He started the car and drove without saying another word. He turned into his driveway seven minutes later and parked in front of his garage.

Chapter Thirteen:
[Ronnie: What now?]

I followed Crockett inside. He walked to the fridge, grabbed two beers, then set them on the bench. He popped the tops, slid one into a stubby holder, then handed it to me. He put his in a matching stubby holder and tapped the neck of his bottle on the one in my hand. "Cheers."

Crockett led the way to the lounge.

"Take a pew and start talking."

I sat down on the couch and took a sip of the beer in my hand. Fruity. Quite nice. I was over coffee for the day. My phone buzzed. A quick look showed me a text from Kirsten.

Kirsten: Can't make it today.

"Something wrong?" Crockett asked.

"No. Just a friend blowing me off."

Me: Get back to me when you can make it.

I turned my attention to the beer in my hand. "This is nice."

"Yeah, it's Panhead. Upper Hutt makes great beer." He took a swig of his. "Talk."

"I can't prove anything."

"Okay, who do you suspect is an intelligence operative?"

"Tom."

Crockett put his bottle on the coffee table and took a deep breath. His exhale sounded like a sigh.

"Tom? Ginny and Tom?"

"Yes."

"And who does Tom work for?"

"I don't know."

"Does Ben know?"

"No idea."

"Would they confide in him? Do you think it's possible?"

"I don't know anything." I took another long sip of cold beer. "Just this feeling that Tom isn't who we think he is."

He drank a few good pulls of beer while he considered what I'd said.

"People always have Faraday cages in their shed ..."

"Exactly. Makes me wonder what else he does that's familiar to us?"

"We should probably find out. We've got some questions. How do you want to get the answers, and what does this have to do with Ben?" Crockett hadn't shot me down in flames so maybe I wasn't a million miles off with my thoughts.

"The last file I closed; did you scan the names?"

He nodded. "I did."

"Did you see Thomas and Virginia?"

He nodded again. "That's what this is about? You saw

their names on a list? Was it their names, Tom and Ginny? Is their surname Smith?"

"Yes. I feel like it's them. No idea about the surname. There's a lot of Smiths in the world but it feels a bit fakey-fakey." I'm not big on coincidence. Synchronicity yes, coincidence no.

"I think we're going visiting. Finish your beer, we'll grab some tucker, and drop in."

"What about the line of letters that said memorised after them? What's that about?" I wasn't sure if I was dragging my feet on purpose, or if it was smart to look into the string of letters before tackling Ginny and Tom.

"You want to play with ideas before we move?"

I nodded. "Might be important."

Maybe. Might be. Perhaps. Not the greatest investigative language. Crockett hauled himself to his feet, disappeared, then came back with a pen and notebook.

"You wrote them down?" He held the pen poised over the paper.

I pulled a piece of paper from my pocket, unfolded it and gave it to him. He looked at it then at me. "Can you read them out, please?"

"Sure. They were all lowercase. Not sure if that's important." I took a breath, picked up the piece of paper and followed the letters with my finger as I said each one. "c q y v p z y c q k r b d l c." I took another breath. "s v z s k r y c q m v c k x c c s j n." And another breath. "m c b w m p j m b x s x i."

"Some spaces would've been handy. Easier to read,"

Crockett mumbled. "Starting with the easiest cipher code. A Caesar cipher."

He spaced the letters on the page, leaving enough room to work with them.

I watched him. "Seven you think?"

"I'll try and see. As good a place to start as any." He wrote the alphabet underneath the string and tried moving the letters seven places to the right and then the left.

"It's not seven."

Crockett worked his way through the most common Caesar keys. Nothing made sense. He finished his beer and sat back. Thoughts gathered like clouds on his face.

"What if ... it's Vigenère."

"Then we really need a key."

We grinned at each other. "Surely not!" Crockett said. He picked the pen back up and wrote the word K E Y at the bottom of the page, then the entire alphabet. He tried four times to make it make sense, then he potentially had it: K=10 E=4 Y=24. "If I'm right then they could've shifted the letters in alphabetical order." He shook his head. "That'd be too fucking easy."

"Even with a potential key, it's still going to take a bit of brain effort," I said, smiling. "Especially if it's not a straightforward alphabetic/numerical shift."

"Yeah. Be nicer if it was a longer potential key. This string of letters is going to take time, especially if this is a proper Vigenère and every letter has a different Caesar Cipher attached to it. We know they didn't start with A = any of the numbers before seven. Even though we think

E=4."

"It's going to take too long. We need to brute-force it," I said.

"What software do you need?"

"Something an old friend gave me." Just in case. Justin Case.

"Your place or the office?"

If we went to my place, then I'd be introducing him to my bat cave, because the software was on my bat cave computer. I guess Crockett was about to get my trust, big time. Welcome to the inner circle. Never thought an Aussie would be part of that.

"If we want to go ask questions of Ginny and Tom, do we do it now or later?" I wasn't trying to put off going home; it was a legitimate question.

"Later. We know where to find them," Crockett said. "Let's see how far we get with this."

"Home then," I said. "We'd better get going."

Chapter Fourteen:
[Ronnie: Just in Case.]

I unlocked the front door and ushered Crockett up the stairs. Donald was still out. No doubt he'd gone visiting after his grocery trip. That was Donald's usual Sunday.

At the top of the stairs, I turned to Crockett. "I'm going to show you something. This is a big deal on my part. No questions. Just accept what you see. Can you do that?"

"Jesus! What are you going to show me?"

"Just follow me." I walked down the hallway and opened my bedroom door. I heard Crockett suck air into his lungs. "Chill out. This is just the beginning." I might've been enjoying his discomfort a bit much.

"What are we doing in here?" His voice was barely a hoarse croak.

"Not what you think." I pointed to my bed. "Stand over there."

He did as he was told and I opened my wardrobe, pushed aside clothing hanging from hangers, and revealed a door. I pressed my hand against the lock then entered a code. I'd upgraded security recently. The door slid across as I touched it. Lights flicked on; the computer hummed as it woke.

"What the hell?" Crockett muttered.

"Come on," I said. "You might need to duck a bit." He joined me inside the bat cave. "There's a chair for you. Have a seat."

"This is incredible," He pulled up a chair. "I was right, wasn't I?"

"About?" I asked innocently.

"*Genesis*," he half-whispered.

I shrugged and opened a program disguised as a calculator. "Your turn to read the letters out."

He did as I asked. I typed. Once we had the string of letters in the program, I tapped the add code button.

A timer came up. The estimated time until the code was cracked was two hours.

"Do we wait or go visiting?" It was more a thought out loud than a question.

"May as well go visiting." He stood and put the chair back where it came from. "Unless you want to unburden yourself of all the secrets you hold."

I stood and considered his comment. "I think you've had enough of my secrets for one day."

All of a sudden, I did not feel like 'going visiting'. I knew we needed to talk to Tom and Ginny, but I didn't want to. Not yet. I needed to think. I wanted to know why Kirsten pulled out of our meeting.

"What's going on?" Crockett asked, touching my arm to get my attention as we walked down the hallway.

"I think we should pick this up tomorrow."

"Ben is missing. You want to take the night off?" Incredulousness echoed within his words. "What don't I know?"

"Nothing."

"Ronnie, what?"

"He might come back of his own volition."

"Do you know he will? Was that last text you received about Ben?"

I shook my head. "No. It was someone changing plans." I opened the kitchen door. "I want another beer, how about you?"

"Sure."

I grabbed two beers from the fridge and two stubby holders from a shelf in the pantry. Crockett picked up the bottle opener and flicked the tops off. I led the way into the lounge and sat in my favourite armchair. Romeo ambled over for a head rub then went back to his bed. Crockett stood staring out the ranchslider. A couple of minutes ticked by before he spoke. He turned around. One hand in his jeans pocket, the other holding his beer.

"You're *Genesis*, right?"

"Yeah."

"Ben is *Genesis?*"

"That's Ben's business. I can't speak for him."

"Feels like everyone's in a secret club and I didn't get the invite," Crockett said with a smile. "Maybe it's not a club I want to be in."

"I honestly thought MacKinnon was going to bring you in ... and then ..."

"Untimely death has a way of screwing things up."

"Sure does."

"Do you know who runs it now?"

I shook my head. "No clue." I could feel a smile inching closer. "I ... thought ... it might be Ginny and Tom."

Crockett managed to keep his mirth under control. "Really?"

My phone rang. I answered it.

"I was going to cook a roast," Donald said. "But it's a bit late."

"Okay. Where are you?"

"I dropped Emily home. Ran into her at the mall. I'm swinging by the supermarket and getting a cooked chicken and some buns. Kiwi dinner?"

"That's fine. I'm at home. Crockett is here."

"I'll scoop Emily back up and bring her over. We can have dinner together. Enzo is due home shortly."

"Get coleslaw and potato salad." I leapt to my feet and hurried into the kitchen. I checked the pantry for beetroot. None. "And a can of beetroot."

"Will do. Bringing Emily. See you in thirty minutes with dinner."

I hung up and joined Crockett in the lounge.

"And?"

"Donald is bringing Emily over and you're staying," I said. "We're having dinner."

I hoped wherever Ben was that he was also having dinner.

"Let me get this straight. You've gone from wanting to find Ben to staying home and having dinner."

Yeah. It did sound odd when he said it out loud like that. But I needed to step back. It was all too close and weird.

"Okay that does sound strange." I sighed. "It's too

much, Crockett. It's too much. I can't find him, and I don't know why."

Crockett strode across the room and stopped dead in front of me.

"Okay. We take a break. We have dinner. We'll see what that brute-force program of yours turns up."

"Yeah."

He shook his beer bottle. "And we have another beer."

"Yes, thank you." He took my empty with him and returned with two full bottles. "Thanks, Crockett."

"Cheers," he said clinking his bottle to mine. "Who was it who changed plans on you?"

"No one important."

"And the family thing?"

"Again, nothing important." I certainly didn't want to open the floor for more *Genesis* questions. I didn't think saying it was Kirsten Knight that changed plans on me would help our situation at all. And Crockett had never heard me talk of an *Uncle George,* but more than that, he might inadvertently mention *Uncle George* to Nana at one of their poker nights. Then there would be more questions. It would never end until everyone knew everything and that is not how this game is played.

I heard a Harley in the distance, getting louder as it cruised closer. Crockett grinned. "Enzo," he said.

"Donald will be pleased," I replied.

The only one missing from dinner was Ben.

Chapter Fifteen:
[Ronnie: Monday Monday.]

Crockett hammered on the front door just as Donald was on his way down the stairs. I knew it was Crockett because no one else knocked quite like him.

Enzo had left five minutes earlier.

"Coffee?" I asked Crockett when he emerged from the stairs.

He shook his head. "How'd that code-cracking program go?"

"It's done. We have a phrase. It's a bit odd, but it's a phrase."

"What does it say?"

I pulled my notebook from my back pocket and opened it to the relevant page.

"It says, 'small boys and their big toys create soldiers of fortune.'"

"Does it mean something? Have we deciphered something only to find another cipher?"

"No idea. But ten words is a lot to remember if it's really a passcode." A long passcode would make whatever it was for, tricky to hack.

"Wonder what it's for?"

"I'm hoping Ben will know."

"Heard anything?" Crockett held the door to the stairs open. Looked like he wanted to get on with the day.

"Not yet." I checked the kitchen and made sure everything was off and that Romeo had water.

"You ready to go see Ginny and Tom?"

"Yes."

Ten minutes later we parked on the road and walked down Tom and Ginny's driveway.

"Tom's car isn't here," Crockett said. "Probably at work."

"Let's see if Ginny is home." I unlocked the gate and walked around the house to the back door. No sign of Ginny through the dining room windows. I heard the gate close behind Crockett then his voice as he greeted a cat. I knocked on the back door before he came around the corner followed by Pierre, one of Ginny's beautiful red-pointed Birman cats.

The back door opened.

"Hellaire Ronnie, how lovely," Ginny said smiling. She looked over me from inside the kitchen. "Crockett! The day just got more interesting."

We took our shoes off at the door. I left mine in the laundry. Crockett left his on the back step and we followed Ginny into the kitchen.

"What brings you over?" Ginny asked, giving me a hug.

"I think something is going on with Ben and I don't understand what it is," I said carefully. "Have you heard from him?"

Ginny's brow creased. "Not for a wee while, Ronnie. It's only Monday and the week has barely started. Still plenty of time to catch up with Ben."

"I meant last week. Is it unusual that you didn't hear

from him?"

"No, not at all. He lives a busy life, you know that."

I nodded. "He does, and I know the filming schedule for his new television series is gruelling."

Made so much sense that no one would hear from him if he was filming. Except he wasn't, he was working for the CIA. And he was missing.

"What's going on Ronnie? Have you two had a falling out?"

I shook my head. "Not as far as I know." She didn't know about our engagement, or she was pretending she didn't know. Which was it?

Ginny looked from me to Crockett. "Why don't I put the jug on?" She waved a silver and gold bracelet clad arm at Tom's fancy coffee machine. "I'm not allowed to touch that." She laughed her comment off. "Truth is, I'd probably break it."

Crockett and I sat at the dining room table. I really didn't need more coffee.

"We've just had a coffee, Ginny. Could I have tea instead?"

"You can have anything you like, darling," she replied, putting one cup out on the bench. "Crockett, tea?"

"Yes, please."

Ginny made herself a coffee and made us a pot of tea. We'd only been guests in her home a handful of times but were always treated like friends. Crockett pulled a chair out for Ginny. I set out coasters on the beautiful Rimu table. We sat and sipped our tea and Ginny her coffee.

We were like real visitors and not a couple of people with a hidden agenda about to be laid out on the table for the world, or the clued in to see. The world? Or *Genesis*? Is Ginny one of the clued in? One and the same maybe. Thoughts rampaged trying to connect the world, the clued in, Ben's friend, and new head of *Genesis*. Crockett nudged my arm causing tea to slosh in the cup.

"What?" I asked shooting a glare in his direction.

"Your face is doing a thing," he replied.

"What thing?"

"A frowning painful looking thing." He circled his hand in front of his face.

"You're a right pair of noddies," Ginny said. "But you do look concerned Ronnie. Is that about Ben?"

"Did he tell you, our news?" If he told anyone it would be Ginny. But he only asked me on Wednesday. She said she hadn't heard from him last week.

"Yes," she replied. "Is that the ring sparkling like nobody's business on your finger?"

"It is." She indicated she wanted a closer look. I took it off and handed it to her.

Unbelievably she opened a drawer in a big wooden cabinet full of crystals and took out a loupe. Crockett and I watched as she inspected the diamonds.

"Gorgeous. He chose well," she said, while passing the ring back to me. I got the impression she saw something via the loupe but discounted it as paranoia. If there was something to see Donald would have mentioned it. He can't keep anything to himself.

"Ben did choose well," I replied with a small smile. "When did he tell you?"

She put the loupe away and settled herself back in her chair.

"He rang not sure when," she said, and took a sip of her coffee.

"I thought you hadn't heard from him."

"I did say that didn't I? Silly of me." Her bracelets jangled as she moved a hand dismissively. "How could I forget his big news?"

"I need to find him, Ginny. He's MIA."

"You are understandably concerned given your recent engagement," Ginny said. "Are you sure?"

I'd be concerned anyway, people shouldn't just vanish.

"I am sure. Radio silence is one thing, but he's missed check-ins. That's a whole different situation." I watched her.

"If that was so, people would be looking, wouldn't they?" Ginny sipped her coffee. She appeared calm. She didn't question how I knew he'd missed check-ins or that I was talking to her about it.

"It's me. I'm the people. I can't find him."

Ginny absorbed my words.

"That's your superpower isn't it? Finding people?"

"I guess so."

"And you can't find Ben?"

"I could find where he'd been, but not where he is."

"Why?"

"I don't know." My tea was almost finished. "We need

to keep moving." I sighed and looked at Crockett.

He agreed. "Direction?"

"Your guess is as good as mine." I drained the last sip from my cup. "You saw me draw a blank."

"Try again?" Crockett queried.

As tempting as it was to say there was no point, the truth was, it couldn't hurt to have another look. And there was no point throwing my toys out of the cot.

Ginny reached out and touched my hand. "Can I help you?" she asked.

I took a deep breath. She probably could. The energy from all the crystals in her home felt like an amplifier. I could feel a frown forming as I tried to figure out where the amplifier thought came from. Easier to go with it than fight it. It was what it was.

"I think you can," I said.

"What do you need, Ronnie?"

"A map?" As soon as I said it, I knew it sounded like a question.

"A map of?" Ginny asked.

"The Wellington Region." I figured I was probably pushing my luck with that. Who even used paper maps anymore, apart from me?

"Let's check Tom's office."

We followed her up the hallway to the room at the end. We'd been here before. Ginny looked in a few drawers before finding a couple of maps.

"You dowse, don't you?" She asked, handing the map to me.

"Yes."

"Do you have a pendulum with you?"

"Yep, always." I patted the neck of my hoodie, feeling the quartz point under my clothes. I hooked my fingers around the chain and pulled the pendant upwards, so it lay over my hoodie.

"Where's the best place to do the dowsing?" Ginny asked.

"Where does Ben spend the most time, when he's here?"

"Dining room," she replied. "Or the shed with Tom."

"Let's try the dining room first," I suggested.

Back we went. Crockett cleared the cups then Ginny put her mug and coasters away. She moved an ornament from the middle of the table, re-homing it on the kitchen bench.

I spread the map out and attempted to remove all non-help thoughts from my mind as I undid the necklace and refastened it in my hand. A few cleansing breaths helped move any stray worries. Silently I called the corners and protected the area and myself. Then, I asked spirit to show me yes. The pendulum swung freely in a straight line away from my body.

"Stop." The pendulum stopped dead. "Show me no." It swung back and forth across my body. "Stop." It hung still. I had two questions I wanted to ask before we started. "Are my eyes brown?" The pendulum swung across my body. "Stop." It stopped. "Are Crockett's eyes blue?" The pendulum swung out from my body. "Stop." It stopped mid swing and hung still.

"That's different," Crockett said, quietly. "No circles."

"The circles will start soon. That was me checking in and making sure things were working properly here." There was no sense trying if the place was going to interfere with what I was trying to achieve.

Ginny sat on a stool near the kitchen bench. Crockett joined her.

"It doesn't interrupt the flow if we watch or ask questions?" Ginny asked.

"Nope. Once the pendulum is ready it's all good," I replied smiling at her. "I can teach you, if you'd like."

"I would very much like that."

"Right, once we find Ben and life settles down, I'll teach you."

"And me," added Crockett. "This thing you do is fascinating."

I focused my attention on finding Ben and blocked everything else out. With my hand at the farthest corner of the map I internally asked spirit to locate Ben. Slow circles began. I moved as slowly as I could, letting the pendulum lead my hand as much as possible. As I reached the end of the map with the pendulum telling me the same as before, Crockett flipped the map over. I started again. Same. Same. Same. And then wham! The pendulum flew outward. It tugged the chain in my hand. I gripped it harder as the pendulum launched itself outward again. Then it settled into clockwise circles that became smaller and faster until it hung dead over the map.

I dropped the chain. The pendulum rolled to point at an address.

Crockett and I looked at each other. "What the hell happened there?" he asked.

My head shook. "I don't know but it felt violent." We stared at the point on the map. "Is that shaking?"

"Yeah," Crockett said. "That normal?"

"Never happened before."

"Where is it pointing?" Ginny asked, hopping off the stool and stepping closer.

"Here," I replied. "Right here."

Ginny looked as confused as we were.

Crockett dragged a sharp intake of air. "Hope you don't mind us having a look around." he said, on his way out of the room. "Inside then out."

His hand rested on the spare room door handle. I joined him. He swung it open. Last time I'd been in that room, Alex the Influencer was under guard there. Nothing looked out of place. The bed was made. Room devoid of human occupancy. Crockett opened the wardrobe and poked about inside it. Then shook his head.

I checked under the bed. There was a weekender type bag under the bed, but I didn't recognise it.

Crockett was already in the next room before I left the spare room. Ginny was following along behind.

"I think I'd know if Ben was here," she said. "He'd be quite hard to conceal."

Crockett cleared Ginny and Tom's room, then Tom's office, and the bathroom.

I spun around to face Ginny.

"Was he here?"

"Not to my knowledge," she replied.

I paused in the laundry and put my shoes on. Crockett flung the back door open and shoved his feet in his shoes on the back step. Ginny followed in her Ugg's, as we went to the shed.

"You'll need the key," Ginny said, passing a keyring to me. I handed it to Crockett. There was no one inside the shed. I walked to the far side and looked around for something, anything that said he'd been there.

Crockett called me over. He was standing in front of Tom's work bench scanning a tool board that hung on the wall. "There's a screwdriver missing," he said, pointing to an empty spot in a line of screwdrivers next to a row of chisels.

"Maybe Tom is using it," I said. Crockett arched an eyebrow at me. "Or it's the screwdriver we found."

"What does that look like?" He pointed at splashes of dark red on the surface of the bench and the ground.

"Paint I hope," I replied. I touched one of the fatter drops. It was dry on the top but tacky inside. On closure inspection of my finger, I determined it was not paint. It was blood splashes. "Ginny, where's Tom?"

"At work," she replied. "Stokes Valley."

Crockett and I traded glances. Stokes Valley wasn't a place of interest according to the pendulum. I suppose work made sense on a Monday. Monday? It was starting to feel like the weekend produced one long day that somehow mashed three days into Monday. It made me tired just thinking about it.

"Are you sure?" Crockett asked. "Could he be somewhere else?"

Ginny shook her head. "He went to work, like every other day that ends in y."

"Did he cut himself?" I asked, staring at the smudge on the pad of my index finger.

"I didn't notice any sticking plasters on him, and he didn't mention it."

"Someone bled in here," I said. "It's not super recent. Probably a couple of days ago."

"Tom left at eight this morning. I don't recall any cuts on him."

"Who else could've been in here?"

"No one that I know of." She paused. "I have a lady who does the housework, but she never comes out here. The shed is usually locked unless Tom is home."

I leaned on the bench away from the blood and watched Ginny. Her face was passive. She had one foot pointed towards the exit and the other was trying to catch up. She didn't feel comfortable with the conversation.

"No one that you know of ... that's an interesting way to put something. Bit of wriggle room allowed there. Not that you know of. So, someone could've come out here."

"Where is the key kept?" Crockett asked.

"In the kitchen drawer."

"Someone could know that?" I asked.

"I suppose," she said, her feet moved, almost a shuffle,

closer to the door. "Ronnie, what's going on?"

I laid it out for her in plain language. "Ben is missing. No one has heard from him. It looks like he was here before he went missing. There is unexplained blood on this bench and fat dried drops on the floor."

"Why would someone bleed out here?" she queried, her right foot trying to make its escape.

"Careful you don't twist yourself into a knot trying to get out of here," I said pointing to her feet.

"Don't be silly," she countered. "I'm just trying to understand what you are saying. Do you think Ben was here and his disappearance has something to do with us?"

"Maybe."

"Ronnie, Ben is our friend."

"I know. And if he was in trouble, you'd help him. I know you would."

Crockett stepped forward. "Ginny, is he in trouble?"

She threw a half-smile towards him. "Not to my knowledge." Ginny turned completely and walked back to the house leaving Crockett and me staring at each other.

"This is going well," he said. "What now?"

"What if I was right?"

He placed his hands on my shoulders and looked straight into my eyes. "Sleeper agents?"

"Yeah."

"Ronnie, I think he was here. I think he needed help. I think they've provided whatever help was required but I don't see anything more than that."

Our eyes drilled into each other until I could no longer

focus. His hands dropped to his sides.

"Okay. Benefit of the doubt. Let's go back to my office." The sound of a car easing down the driveway halted our movement.

"Wonder who this is?" Crockett said as Tom's car came into view.

We were in his parking spot, so he parked half over the shared part of the driveway. He climbed out of the car and called out a hello, then opened the car back door. A split second later the car doors were closed, and Tom was walking towards us carrying dry cleaning bags.

"Didn't expect to see you two. No doubt Ginny was pleased with the company," he said, reaching for Crockett's hand. They shook.

"I see you were on errands." I pointed at the dry-cleaning bags. It looked like a black suit in the top bag. "Ginny said you were at work."

"Thought I'd pick these up before I forgot. The dry cleaner rang to say they were ready." he replied. "You coming, or going?"

"We were going ..."

"Come on back in and I'll make us a coffee." Tom edged past us to the gate.

Just what we needed, another hot drink.

Crockett raised an eyebrow in my direction. Guess he'd had enough coffee, and tea, too.

"We're done with hot drinks" he said, holding the gate for me. "Water is fine."

I wanted to see Ginny's face when Tom walked in with

the dry cleaning and us tagging along behind. I couldn't see any sticking plasters on Tom's hands. That'd be a likely place if he cut himself working on something in the shed.

I followed Tom in and saw the look Ginny planted on him as soon as she saw me behind him. It was time to have a proper chat.

Tom carefully folded the dry-cleaning bags over a chair at the dining room table.

"Coffee, yes?"

"No thanks," I replied. "Come sit with me, Ginny." I pulled out a chair and motioned for her to use it. She tottered over and lowered herself into the seat.

"I see you found Tom after all," she said with a smile.

"We did."

Crockett sat down across from me. He turned and watched Tom at the coffee machine. "I'm good Tom, don't worry about me."

"Are you sure, I don't mind."

"Why don't you sit with us for a minute. Have a rest before you get into the whole coffee making routine," Crockett said as he pointed to an empty chair. "I'll move these bags for you. Main bedroom?"

"Yes, please," Ginny said.

Crockett stood and gathered the clothes. He returned quickly and tapped Tom on the shoulder. "Come and sit down. We need to talk."

"I don't know what's going on here, Crockett, but you seem to be forgetting this my house," Tom replied with a bit of a growl emanating from behind his words.

"No one has forgotten. We have a problem and maybe you know about it, or maybe you don't. Either way, it's a conversation we are having now."

Tom sat at the table without another word.

He was on my left and Ginny was on my right. I'd moved my chair back so I could see them both.

"Were you at a black-tie event in Lower Hutt this last week?" I asked. "Friday night actually."

Ginny's head moved in the smallest possible shake when Tom made eye contact with her. Crockett indicated he saw it too.

"No. We don't go out much," Tom said.

"So, it wasn't you and Ginny on a guest list we saw then?" I asked. "Virginia and Thomas Smith?"

"I shouldn't think so. Smith is a pretty common name."

"You shouldn't think so? Interesting. What should you think? Maybe you would like to think about why you're not telling the truth?"

"I don't know what to tell you, Ronnie. We lead a quiet life."

"Yet you just had a fancy dress and a black suit dry-cleaned." Crockett placed the dry-cleaning slip on the table in front of him. "You took the items into the cleaners on Saturday morning." He spun the piece of paper to face Tom and pushed it closer to him. "Special attention to the stain on the right sleeve of the dress."

"What stain?" I asked.

Ginny fake laughed. "You know how clumsy I can be," she said, waving a heavy bracelet encased arm. "I probably dragged my sleeve in something. That dress has flowing sleeves to accommodate my bracelets. They get into things."

I nodded in agreement. "You probably did. But what I wonder?"

Crockett produced another slip to match the first. "It says it was a biological stain and they removed it."

"Biological. That's a funny word," I said. "A lot of things are biological."

"They are, aren't they?" Crockett surmised. "I tend to think blood or spoof when I see something like that."

I shot a frown at him. "I'd definitely lean towards blood rather than anything sexual in nature. Thanks for that image, Crockett."

"We got the dry cleaning done because we are invited to a ball," Tom said with a sigh. "It's a charity ball. At the Upper Hutt town hall this coming weekend."

"On?"

"Saturday evening."

"Sounds like fun. What do you think, Crockett ... should we tag along?"

"Wouldn't that be fun." Ginny said. "All of us at the ball." Her tone implied it would not be fun.

I nodded slowly. "I bet it would be. Guess what? We'll be coming with."

Crockett looked momentarily horrified but said nothing.

"Tickets would be sold out by now," Ginny said.

"I imagine they reserve a few for last minute buyers, especially when it's a charity event." The thought of getting all gussied up and fancy appealed. Who doesn't like playing dress-up? "The ball you attended the other night, was that a charity event too?"

Ginny nodded a smidge before she could catch herself and deny going out.

"What's so special about this upcoming ball?" Crockett asked.

"It's a masked ball. It's been years since we've had a masked ball."

"That can't be all," Crockett said.

"They're raising money for Wellington Children's Hospital." Tom glanced at Ginny. "They need to buy some new equipment."

"That's a worthy cause," I said. "I'm sure we could get tickets. It'd be silly if they turned us down seeing's they're raising money for sick children."

"With a bit of luck Ben will be back from wherever he went to enjoy the ball," Ginny said with a resigned sigh.

Chapter Sixteen:
[Crockett: Where are you?]

Neither of us had much to say when we left Ginny and Tom's. Tom moved his car so we could leave. Was a quiet car ride back to Ronnie's offices. I let her go ahead up the stairs and went next door to see Emily for a minute.

"Hey, Emily!" I called, as I slid the door open and walked in.

She was shelving books at the back of the shop. She turned and smiled. "Hi, Crockett. What brings you in here?"

I strode down the back and planted a kiss on her lips. "You," I said.

"I like this type of surprise visit," she replied with a smile. "It's been a busy Monday here."

Every time she used a contraction it made me smile. Emily was slowly coming back, remembering who she was. The last few months had seen a period of rapid improvements.

"Sales good?"

"Today they are, yesterday was quiet because no one knew we were open, and I was stocktaking." She put the last book in her arms on the shelf and straightened some books up.

"Guess that would make for a quiet sales day," I said with a smile.

Emily turned to me. "How is your day?"

"Strange," I replied, honestly. "Very strange."

"Why?"

"Work things," I said dismissively, and changed the subject. "Would you like to go out for dinner with me one night this week?"

"I would like that very much," she replied. Emily stretched up and kissed me. "It is a date. Was dinner last night a date?"

"We were together so yes, it was." I wrapped my arms around her. The smell of her shampoo mixed with a dab of perfume; the result was a warm spiciness. "I'll ring you and tell you what time I'll pick you up. Any day?"

"Yes. Any day. That sounds like a good idea." She leaned back and looked up at me. "Whatever is wrong Crockett, it will work out."

I kissed her forehead. "From your mouth to the universe's ears," I said. I let her go, and left the shop, then gave her a wave as I walked past the big front window. When I got up the stairs I found Ronnie in the main office alone.

"No Steph or Jenn, that's unusual."

"I guess they're both out doing something."

"Monday business," I mumbled.

She nodded. "Jenn is on a new assignment. She wanted to get a head start so she started yesterday, and Steph is grocery shopping for the office and bookshop." She held up a square of notepaper. "They left a note."

I pulled up a chair by Ronnie's desk. "If Ben was most recently at Ginny's, and a venue in Lower Hutt and Merton Street, but there is no signal now, what does that tell us?"

A grin spread across Ronnie's lips. "I'm sorry. I think I heard a little smidge of Kentucky then." She waved a finger at me. "What in ever loving tree-lined hollers is happening here?"

I tipped my head back and laughed. "I see what you did there."

"Hard to get a signal on those holler roads."

"Bugger me. It's hard to get a signal in parts of Whitemans Valley, Mangaroa, or even Kiatoke, or Te Marua," I said. That was smart thinking.

"It's also hard to get a signal in parts of Akatarawa," Ronnie said.

"There was no Kentucky by the way. It's Virginia you hear, if anything."

"Or?"

"We've watched too much 'Justified'."

"Hush your mouth, there's no such thing." Ronnie opened a map on her computer. "Who are Ginny and Tom?"

I shrugged. "Friends of Ben's, and of ours, although we might've screwed that part up today."

"They know something. He was there. Likely he was there bleeding. Didn't seem like a gaping wound or anything."

"I agree that they need exploring. I don't think we can draw conclusions about identity based on drops of blood in a shed, Ronnie."

"It's not Ginny's or Tom's ... who else was there?"

"Good point. Alright, maybe it is Ben's blood. What do we know about Tom and Ginny?"

"We met them during Operation Hide and Seek, with little miss double-agent, or was she an actual sleeper agent, like maybe Tom and Ginny are?"

It was interesting that Ronnie was still on the sleeper agent road.

"Alex was a triple dip, I think. She was putting her very special memory to excellent use playing everyone against everyone else. Are you serious about Tom and Ginny?" I moved my legs.

"I don't think so." She shrugged. "There's something about them though."

It was good to know she wasn't serious about the whole sleeper agent thing, but I thought they were hiding something. Or perhaps not being as forthcoming as I'd like.

"If they're not, then what are they?" Ronnie leaned back in her chair and swept her fingers across the track-pad. Enlarging the map, she switched to satellite view and zoomed in on Tom and Ginny's. "What do we actually know about them?"

"I don't know what they are, but I get the feeling they're into something," I said. There were too many co-incidences in the times we'd been at their house. Too many familiar things.

"Something good or something bad?" Ronnie asked.

We watched the screen. That was when I realised it

was live. I saw a cat walk along the top of the fence. "How are you able to see their house in real time?"

Tom's car was gone. Maybe he put it in the carport or garage. Or maybe he went back to work.

Ronnie raised an eyebrow at me. "I have resources." She focused on the screen again. "Are they into something good or bad?"

"Ben thinks good."

"Ben's missing, potentially bleeding, but probably not seriously," she said.

"We know ... Ginny wears a lot of jewellery. She's gotta be quite fit to even lift her arms with that lot on. We know she breeds Birman cats. What does Tom do? Ginny said he's at work every day. What does he do?"

Ronnie frowned. "No idea. Some kind of engineering. Something to do with hills or roads."

"Let's chalk that up to something we don't know."

"Yeah."

We watched a car drive down the driveway.

"Ronnie, is that Tom's car?"

"Yep."

He executed a three-point turn and backed into his car port. We couldn't see him open the door or get out, but we saw him open the gate. He was alone. We watched for five minutes. No one else entered the house.

"We do need to dig deeper into them," I said. "He's been in and out since we were there. What's he up to?"

"Busy, busy, for a Monday. Maybe it's an errand day for him rather than a full work day." Ronnie checked her watch. "I need to ring someone." She picked up her cell phone from the desk, pushed her chair back and dialled a number while she walked around the office. When the person answered, she came back and put the phone on the desk and tapped the speaker icon.

"Kirsten, you're on speaker. It's me and Crockett in the room."

"What's up?" She asked.

"We need to meet."

I looked at my watch. The time was pushing towards the middle of the day.

"When and where?" Kirsten asked.

"There's a café in Eastbourne. Later on today?"

"Better idea." She paused. "The Green Parrot."

"That was a servicemen's haunt during World War Two. Always full of American and Kiwi military."

Random facts sometimes popped out of Ronnie's mouth. I've become used to her quirks, and I've learned a bit from her.

"Maybe you should be on our quiz team," Kirsten said with a chuckle. "I'll book a table for tonight. Meet you at eight."

"Cool. Thanks. That gives me time to walk the greyhound and make up for no beach run yesterday."

"That's right. I heard you had a retired racer."

"Maybe one day you'll meet him." Ronnie shook her head.

She gave me the impression she wasn't the world's biggest Kirsten fan. I smelt a story there. One day, I'd ask about it.

"Perhaps. I always thought I was a cat person but that could change. See you both at eight."

Ronnie hung up.

"What was that stuff about Romeo?"

"We were supposed to meet at the dog beach yesterday and she cancelled."

"Shame. I bet the ol' boy loves the beach."

"He does." Ronnie sat down in front of the screen. "Anything else happen?"

"No. Quiet as a church yard." It'd take us almost an hour to get into the city and find a park. "What time do you want to leave, and which mode of transport are we using?"

"Car. Yours if you like. Just after seven."

"Who is Kirsten?" I'd heard the name before. I'd heard Ben mention her. I got the impression he didn't like her.

"Colleague of Ben's."

"Charlie Indigo Alpha." Of course. That Kirsten. Now I knew why she wasn't a fan. "Just to clarify, Ben is missing out here, and she wants to meet in the heart of the city?"

"So, you know where The Green Parrot is then?"

"I do."

"And yes, she does want to drag me into the city. And you're coming with, and I think we should be armed."

I stood and patted myself down then flipped my jacket and revealed my sidearm and holster. "One step ahead of you."

"Look at you, being all Boy Scouty."

"Haven't the Woke brigade cancelled Scouts?"

"Do we care?"

I shook my head. The conversation Ronnie had with Kirsten rattled around my head. It felt like I'd missed something. Like they were talking in code. I leaned over Ronnie's shoulder. "What did she really say?"

"You were here. You heard the conversation."

"I heard some conversation, but I have a feeling there is more to it."

"A smidge." Ronnie held her thumb and index finger about a centimetre apart. "Nothing really."

"Then you won't mind saying." I watched her as she stared at the screen and could see a tweak of a smile in the corner of her mouth. "What?"

"Nothing really. Just girl talk."

"Girls always talk in code?"

"They do when they're talking about someone in the room."

"Me?"

"No, the other guy."

A sigh escaped. "What about me?"

"She said she's always been a cat person but that could change."

"I heard her say that, so?"

"Think about it ..."

All of a sudden it made sense. She liked women.

"Why could it change?"

"She likes you. I don't know why. I cannot fathom what would possess her to jump ship for you, but apparently, she has considered it."

"I've never met her but I'm charming. Don't know why you don't see it." I refocused on the screen when movement caught my eye. "Ronnie." I pointed. Another car crept down the driveway at Tom and Ginny's. "Can we zoom in?"

She zoomed in on the person getting out of the car. Blond, tallish, wearing a suit. The man walked to the gate and opened it.

"Ben," Ronnie said in a low whisper. "That's Ben."

"You sure?"

"I'd know that walk anywhere."

"Let's go."

I grabbed the keys off the desk and hurried down to the car with Ronnie on my heels.

Chapter Seventeen:
[Ronnie: Was that you, Ben?]

Crockett parked down the street from Tom and Ginny's and we hightailed it down the driveway on foot. The car I saw Ben alight from was still there. It wasn't Ben's car. Tom's car was still there as well. Crockett went in the back gate, and I used the front gate. He was going to the backdoor while I charged up the steps to the front door. I knocked then tried the doorknob. The door opened so I let myself in and closed it behind me.

"Hello!" I called into the house as I saw Crockett open the back door.

"Tom?" he called from the kitchen.

I went right, I knew Crockett would go into the kitchen, dining room and lounge. I took the bedrooms and bathroom. I swung the spare room door open. No one. I opened the bathroom door. No one. The master bedroom contained four cats and no people. The last room was Tom's office at the end of the hallway. Crockett was right behind me when I swung the door open and stepped inside. It was empty.

I turned to Crockett. "Where are they?"

"Shed?"

It was the only place we hadn't looked.

"Did you hear anything when you went in the back gate?"

"No."

"Cars are still there?"

"Yep."

I stood in the office and turned full circle. "This room shares a wall with the bathroom?"

"It should do, there is only one room on the left side of the hallway." Crockett backed out the door to check. "Huh. Maybe not. The bathroom door is quite a way down the hall and the shower and bath are on the laundry wall or outside wall."

I looked at the wardrobe door in Tom's office. It was really a bedroom. His desk was on the wall near the door. The wall that should be the bathroom wall. But it was too far away to be the bathroom wall.

Maybe I wasn't the only one with a bat cave in the house. I opened the wardrobe. My eyes adjusted to the dark in front of me and then I saw another door. I opened it and found stairs. Stairs? Well, that explained why the bedroom wall was so far away from the bathroom wall.

"Crockett," I said as I beckoned him closer. "Found something." I ran my hand up the wall inside the door and found a light switch. I flicked it on. Those were definitely stairs. Hidden stairs. Did Tom and Ginny have a secret life? Was I right?

A shadow fell over my shoulder from Crockett. I could feel the heat from his body as he stood behind me. "Look at that," he muttered. "Think you found something, alright."

"Shall we?"

"We shall," he replied, his voice low and soft. "Let me

go first, I'm armed."

Crockett unholstered his Glock and edged past me.

"Maybe don't shoot anyone," I whispered. "No one we know anyway until we figure this lunacy out."

I followed Crockett down the stairs. At the bottom was a short hallway and a closed door. Crockett stepped sideways towards the hinges; I moved behind him. He reached across the door and knocked.

I couldn't hear anything beyond the door. It was impossible to tell if there were people there or not.

Crockett knocked again. Louder this time. There was nothing.

He twisted the doorknob and pushed. The door opened into a small, enclosed area lit by soft lighting, spaced around the skirting. There was a blank section with no lights and no doorknob. He gave me a puzzled look then pushed on the piece of wall and it swung open. Bright white lights lit the room. I blinked several times to enable my eyes to cope with the brightness. Tom, Ginny, and Ben stood near a built-in desk containing three computer screens. I could hear the low hum of a computer working. Crockett holstered his sidearm.

"And here you are," I said, as the three of them turned to face us. "I feel like you might have something to explain."

Ben turned to face me properly. My eyes ran over him, taking in his clothes and looking for a wound. He held an ice pack in his left hand. His right hand was bandaged. Guess it was his blood in the shed. He looked a little roughed up. There was bruising on his jaw line and a small cut over his eyebrow. His left knuckles were raw.

"Are you alright?" I asked.

"Mostly," he replied. "I just got here."

"Maybe a text saying you were okay would've been a nice touch," Crockett said.

"Nice to know you care, Crockett." Ben threw a lopsided grin in his direction. "Ginny said you two want to come to the Wellington Children's Hospital Ball."

"We were looking for you," I said, making sure my voice was even and calm. "You've missed check ins and didn't answer any communications. It's been over forty-eight hours."

"I did. I'm sorry," he replied, but offered no explanation. "Are you alright?"

I nodded. I was better than he was. "And you've been what? Hanging out here in this secret underground lair like Batman? While we've been looking for you and worried that something awful had happened." I wasn't yet ready to play the fiancée card and really lay on the guilt.

"No, I just got here."

I knew that we saw him arrive. I looked at my watch. He'd gotten there fifteen minutes ago. Plenty of time to text me.

"What were you doing at the mosque?"

"You know about that ..." Ben pressed his lips together before answering. "There was a small misunderstanding."

"That got you shackled in a basement?"

"As I said, a misunderstanding."

I looked around the room. It was not that different to my own bat cave. If Ginny and Tom knew where Ben was, then they weren't *Genesis*. I was back to square one with guessing who was sending me messages. But Ginny and Tom weren't innocent bystanders. People who have secret rooms and computer systems hidden underground have reasons to hide their activity. I almost hoped they were part of an organised criminal gang. Why? Because it would amuse me. Also, because they weren't a threat to us if they were organised crime rather than spies working for someone other than the good guys.

"A misunderstanding. That's just wonderful, isn't it?" I nudged Crockett.

"It's great," he said. "I think we're all about to have a misunderstanding." Crockett's eyes hardened to match the edge in his voice. "The only way to avoid the inevitable is to have frank and honest communication. Do you think that's something you might be interested in?"

One corner of Ben's mouth twitched upward. "Could be something I'm interested in," he said.

"Perhaps it is time we put our cards on the table, so to speak," Ginny said.

"Cards and screwdrivers," I said extracting what I believed was Tom's missing screwdriver from my back pocket and handing it to Ben. "I doubt Tom would be pleased to know you lost his screwdriver."

"Thank you," Ben said to me before passing the screwdriver to Tom.

"About that coffee, Tom?" Crockett gave a verbal

nudge. "This probably isn't a beer situation and it's not quite late enough in the day to start that."

"Can I just interrupt right now and say yes to coffee, as long as it is accompanied by answers." I gave Ben a look and he knew exactly what it meant.

Ben half-smiled at me then resumed holding the ice pack to his jaw. "Coffee with conditions, nice touch, Ronnie."

"Everyone is always with the hot drinks," I grumbled. "But so far coffee has led to more coffee, sometimes tea, and no answers.

"Fair call," Crockett said.

Then Tom spoke, "We will have a drink of some sort, but for now I think we should stay down here, where we can guarantee there is no eavesdropping, and have that needed conversation."

"Are you under surveillance?" I asked.

"It's possible. It's always possible."

I looked around for chairs. I had a feeling it would take a while to get everything out in the open. I saw folding chairs on the back wall. There were two chairs at the desk. Ben turned the desk chairs to face out into the room. He and Ginny sat. Tom and Crockett grabbed folding chairs and opened them up. We sat down.

The silence was deafening.

I waited. I knew Ben was trying to find the correct starting point.

"Cell phones," Tom said, abruptly. He held his hand out to us.

I handed him mine, and Crockett handed over his. They were placed inside what looked like an ornate wooden box on the desk. He closed the lid.

"Fancy looking Faraday cage?"

"Yes," Tom said. "Our phones are in it as well."

Ginny piped up, "Tom made it. It's beautiful, isn't it?"

I nodded. I can appreciate beautiful things and still be mad at all the lies.

Ben adjusted his cuffs then spoke. I saw a rusty stain on one cuff. It looked like blood. There were more stains down his shirt front. "I've been to a ball; it was Friday night. It was a Polish Embassy ball held in Lower Hutt. We thought someone was using the ball season to hold silent auctions for weapons, or gauge interest for illegal weapon sales."

"Go on," I said.

"So, I went to the ball to see if I could get an invite into the deal. All the dancing and food and finery is a great cover for sales of black-market weapons. I think they're trading weapons for Bitcoin, but I can't say for sure yet what the currency is going to be."

"How?"

"Initially they reached out via AirDrop notes."

"That's why you had a guest list then," I commented. "Why did you toss the flash drive?"

"I didn't, but we will get to that." He adjusted the ice pack. "Let me tell my story, Ronnie."

"All right. Tell away." Far be it from me to interrupt a good tale.

"There was a terror alert, the alert was high. I had two names of wannabe terrorists, and it was possible that the Polish ball would be a soft target. So, while I was dancing and listening to people and making mental notes, I was also looking for Al-Fasil and Faheem. Two Indonesian Muslims who were believed to be here for nefarious reasons."

"By yourself ... reckless, Ben," Crockett muttered. "Thought you had more brains than that in your head."

"I wasn't entirely alone," Ben said. "Before I get to the terrorists ... at my table there were two older ladies. Nancy and Laura. I danced with both. One of them, Nancy, the oldest worked out AirDrop and sent me a photo of herself."

"Old women and tech," I grumbled. "It's been my experience that never ends well."

"It sure doesn't. Anyway, someone stole her phone and sent me a bunch of images of me dancing with Nancy. I found the guy and returned her phone. The incident pushed my strange metre into high gear."

I was making careful mental notes as Ben talked. "Why?"

"I'm backstopped by the usual people and this time the backstop is a PMC called Leviticus. The guy who had the phone said, 'Leviticus' as I got the phone back."

"So, is he also Leviticus?" I asked.

"No idea. I thought I was the only person from Leviticus involved." A frown creased his forehead. "A little later I, with Ginny's help, discovered the two men I was looking for."

I waved my hand in the air. "I'm sorry, you with whose help?"

"Ginny's," he said.

"That would be the same Ginny who didn't see you last week because you were so busy?"

I shot a questioning look at Ginny who looked suitably ashamed for the lie.

"Ronnie, let me tell the story, please."

"Carry on."

"Thank you," Ben said. "We spotted both men in the kitchen. They were working the event. That was it. They honestly looked like they were working. Except, one tried to trip me, and the other grab me, when I was leaving the bathroom. They failed. As I was going back to the venue, two women from Kentucky recognised me. I escorted them to their table."

"Are they important?"

"I don't know," he said.

"Guess the so-called terrorists learnt from their mistake," I said. "Because someone grabbed you."

"It was them. Still have story to tell ... hold your horses," Ben said. "As I was saying, they tried and failed at that point. I gave Art a call and asked him to drive us home when people started leaving. He did. All good. We got back here."

"And?"

"A little while later I got a phone call from Faheem or Al-Fasil. They had Nancy."

"They had Nancy?" Crockett asked. "Nancy Frost-Andrews, the Nancy from the ball?"

"Do you know another Nancy?" Ben asked.

"No. I don't even know that Nancy. Just random, or was it?"

"No. They thought she was important to me. I was sitting at her table, I located her lost phone, and I danced with her. They seemed to not understand people being nice to people they have just met."

"All right. Then what?" I asked.

"They wanted to trade Nancy for me."

"And you did that, didn't you." It wasn't a question. I knew Ben.

"Of course. I wound them up a bit first. They wanted me to go to Fergusson Drive and then they'd call me again."

Tom interjected, "I was against this plan of action, but I did drop Ben at the railway station so he could walk through to Fergusson Drive in time for his call."

"And?"

"They picked me up in a Transit van. Chucked a hood over my head and next thing I knew, I was in Merton Street. I did ask them why we turned down Merton Street and they refused to comment."

"They'd probably seen the hood thing done on telly and thought it would stop you knowing where they were taking you," Ginny said with a small laugh. "Plenty of silly people out there."

"What happened next?" I asked. Knowing time was

ticking. I wanted answers. And we had a meeting with Kirsten in the city for dinner.

"They cuffed me down in the basement. There was a chain attached to the wall. They clearly had some semblance of a plan. I heard a voice before they took the hood off. They had Nancy there as well."

"At least she was alive," Ginny said. "She seemed a nice lady."

Ben nodded. "She was sitting against a wall. Handcuffed with a hood over her head."

"They really liked the hood thing, the idiots," Crockett commented.

"They proceeded to ask questions about the arms deal. I was not in a position to answer any of them. They wanted to know who was involved." Ben shrugged a shoulder. "I'm an actor, how would I know anything about an arms deal?"

"And the flash drive? I have it, so?" I asked.

"The wannabe terrorists who grabbed me were more interested in my phone than whatever else was in my pocket. One of them shook my jacket because my phone wasn't in my pants pocket, so it had to be in my jacket. My phone fell out but so did the flash drive. Neither of them noticed. It bounced under the chair. When they hauled me to my feet, I shoved it to the wall with a foot," he said. "They held us for at least twenty-four hours in a basement room. Sunday morning, they moved us to a secondary location." Ben moved the position of the ice pack on his face. "They were frustrated and hadn't managed to get any information about the deal from me. How could they? I didn't really know anything. The whole time the flash drive was lying there ready to be spotted."

"The Nancy woman was still with you when they moved you?"

"Yes. She was a bit worse for wear. They'd spent hours asking questions. Demanding to know our relationship. Threatening to harm her if I didn't talk."

"Sounds like a fun time for all," Crockett said.

"They moved you both to a secondary location?" You don't ever want to be in a secondary location. If they're going to kill you, that's where they'll do it.

"Yes. Someone else arrived on Sunday morning. The hoods were put back on us. There was another male. He wasn't Indonesian. He was a British. At that point I knew I couldn't get away and free Nancy. Hoped for the best and went along with their move."

"Bloody hell," Crockett muttered. "What happened next?"

"We arrived at another location. They drove north on River Road and then a left turn and then it got windy. I figured we were in Akatarawa by the time the van stopped. I could hear sheep."

"It was a van, but you arrived here in a car," I said. "We walked past a car, not a van."

"The Brit drove the van. He may have even been there on Friday night but kept out of it. Never heard his voice or sensed another person until Sunday morning. One of the so-called terrorists must've followed us in a car."

"What next?"

"I decided I'd had enough when they tried to take us into a building on a farm. I heard the van drive away. They took the hoods off before walking us inside. No Brit just the same two idiots from earlier."

"That's when you escaped?"

"I got away when they were trying to get me into the house. Bumbling idiots is what they were, but one of them had Nancy, so it was a bit tricky getting her free." A smile rested on his lips.

"And?"

"One is dead."

"And the body?"

"You saw the car parked on the driveway."

"Really?" Crockett asked.

"Afraid so."

"And before you ask about the other guy ... There's a live prisoner in the trunk, and a dead body."

"Nancy?"

"Pretty shaken. I took her home. Not sure how alive the other guy is now, but let's say there is one dead and one alive in the trunk," Ben replied.

A Schrödinger prisoner situation. It made me smile. "You're okay?"

"Yep. That car out there is registered to a person from the Thai embassy."

"It's not an official embassy car though?" I would've remembered if I'd seen diplomatic plates.

He shook his head. "I checked the registration, it's private."

I looked at the computer screen. That's what they were doing when we came in. The Waka Kotahi: New Zealand Transport Agency database search screen was open. Not everyone could get into that particular feature.

"Did you use my login?" I asked, pointing to the screen.

"Yes."

"Okay. And you stole the car?"

"Not exactly, the owner is one of the idiots in the trunk," Ben said. "I might need a hand."

So, we had a Brit and two Indonesians causing shit. Makes a change from the Chinese, Russians, and Iranians.

"Could the Brit be Jackson Frost?"

Ben nodded. "No one used a name in reference to him, but it was a male. I expected him to be at the ball even though he's on a No-Fly list. Maybe it was him. Maybe he was there, skulking in the shadows the whole time."

"Looks like that bandage on your hand needs changing," I said. "I was pretty worried when I saw drips of blood in the shed." My eyes met Ben's.

"Why are you still driving around with the boot full of people? Why haven't you dumped them?" Crockett asked.

Akatarawa has a few likely spots for dumping bodies.

"I didn't want them showing up anywhere until I could find the person behind the trading weapons for Bitcoin. They're safer in the car. I'm safer with them in the car."

"All it takes is for you to get pulled over ..." I said.

"I can help you out of that predicament," Crockett said. "We'd better do it sooner than later."

My arm rose from the elbow, and I waved my hand. "I have a question."

"Yes, Ronnie," Ben said.

"Why are Ginny and Tom involved in your operation?"

The three of them traded looks.

"They're not," Ben said, with a shake of his head.

"Yes, they are," I said. "I know they were at the ball you attended. And they're going to the next one. Ball season seems like a lot of fun."

"They were there, but not involved, involved." He made fast eye contact with Tom.

"And you said earlier in your recounting of your weekend that Ginny helped you."

"That's not quite what I meant."

"Really? Okay. Sure. Where are we now?" I looked around for emphasis. "Looks like we're in an underground lair owned by Ginny and Tom."

"Lair?" Ben chuckled. "More a bat cave than lair."

"Tomatoes, tom-aye-toes. The point is this is quite the set up for civilians."

"They're not civilians."

"That much I guessed. Remember when I said you need to think about background checking your friends?"

"Yes, back when Alex the Influencer was in our lives." He cocked his head to one side. "The reason we were safe here ..."

"... is that they're in the intelligence community," I finished for him.

He nodded. "I didn't know then. Only worked it out recently."

"Who do they work for?" I knew they were right there and asking them would be easier.

Tom cleared his throat. "New Zealand."

"How long have you worked for us?" I asked.

"In different capacities for about thirty years," he replied. "Both of us."

"You're New Zealand Security Intelligence Service?"

Tom nodded.

"Who's the acting chief?"

He scowled. "Someone better than Chandler; Peter Piper."

I turned my attention back to Ben. "Why couldn't I locate you? Were you wearing a tinfoil helmet?"

A smile tweaked the edges of his mouth. "I don't know. What was happening?"

"Weak signal or nothing," I said. "Is this place shielded?" If it was, why put our phones in a cage?

Tom spoke, "It is, but not well. There is a foil lining but it's thin."

But maybe it was enough to stop me. And maybe Tom didn't want any of us using our phones as recording devices. I understood that.

Chapter Eighteen:
[Crockett: The things people hide.]

Ronnie was doing a great job of remaining composed in the face of the story told by Ben, Tom, and Ginny. It was impressive really. I sat back and listened. There was mounting concern about the people in Ben's boot and how long they could remain there. The expired person would eventually give the game away by the stench, and if the other was alive then noise could pose a problem.

"Ben, we need to get rid of the body, or bodies. You can't keep driving around with people in the boot of a stolen car."

"Borrowed car," Ben said. "Technically the owner is in the car."

"He won't be much help if you get pulled over," I said with a smile.

"Ideas?" Ben asked.

"Ideally we unload them in a secure location that's under cover and they're never found." I thought about it for a moment. "Art's place."

It was close. He had a massive two-car garage under the house and a secure prison cell at the back of the garage.

"Sounds good. Can you take care of that?"

"Once we're topside, I'll give him a bell."

Ben nodded. I turned my attention to the talk about dances. "What's with the balls? How many balls are we talking about, and how sure are you that they're being used as cover for arms deals?"

"Quite sure," Ben replied. "Whoever is doing this sent a coded message to my phone in a note. It's a pass phrase that I'll need once the security check is completed."

"How does it work? You can't just have twenty people in ball gowns and tuxedos glued to their phones while supposedly dancing. That would raise suspicion, wouldn't it?"

"Yes. It would," Ginny said. "We think the first ball was to garner interest in whatever is being hocked."

Tom agreed.

"The second ball is where the seller will AirDrop a link to an application, or whatever they are going to use for the bidding," Ginny said. "Well, that was my understanding."

"And how did you come by this understanding?" Ronnie asked.

"I reached out to an acquaintance within the United Kingdom Embassy. I'd heard on the grapevine that he had been in the vicinity of the disrupted deal in Poland."

"Only people cleared to receive the software will be able to move to the next stage of the process," Ben said.

"You've done a lot already then," Ronnie replied. "How'd you figure out the AirDrop?" She looked at Ben. "Ben?"

"Jonathon Tierney told me to have my Bluetooth on. Ginny and Tom let it be known to someone from an embassy that I was in the market for firepower and working for a company called Leviticus."

I stretched my right leg out. "Leviticus. Even before you mentioned them earlier, Ben, I'd heard of them. They're a private military contractor with a pretty good rep for getting shit done." They'd been around a few years. Worked in a few different theatres of operation. I glanced at Ronnie. She'd heard of them too.

"Leviticus," Ronnie said. "So, they're a Charlie Indigo Alpha company. Bloody hell. I didn't know that part."

"I think we're passed the "someone" bullshit," I said, and quietly agreed with Ronnie's take on Leviticus. "Names."

Ben, Ginny, and Tom traded glances.

"Topher Franks," Ginny replied. "He's my contact within the UK embassy. Ex-military, full-on arsehole."

Ronnie was slowly shaking her head. Disbelief on her face. "Topher Franks?"

They all nodded.

"I know Topher," she said quietly. "He was with a small military team that used to go into hotspots and pull people out. The team doesn't, and never did, exist as far as the British government was concerned. They also chased a few suitcase nukes across Europe, so the story goes."

"And now he's involved in an arms deal?" I queried, looking at Ronnie.

She shrugged. "Nothing surprises me anymore. People on that covert team weren't chosen because of their morals. But that doesn't mean he's behind this. He could just as well be working an angle. He could even be a customer."

"How do you know about them?"

"They pulled my arse out of the sandbox."

And I learnt something about Ronnie.

"Will he recognise you if you go to the ball?"

"Probably."

"Probably ... you're sitting the ball out," I said to her. "You can monitor from close by, but you cannot set foot inside."

"Seems like an overreaction," she said. "If you're all going in, then all of you will be wearing cameras. ALL of you."

"Do you have suitable concealable equipment?" I asked Ronnie.

"I do." She offered no more information. I took her at her word. She had all sorts of awesome devices in her tech room at the office.

"We need more tickets to the ball," Ginny said. "Would've been slightly easier to have another couple come in than a lone male."

Ronnie smirked. "Your wish is my command."

"Not you," I growled.

"Yeah, yeah," she said. "Emily is perfect."

I blew out a sigh. "You're determined to chuck her in the deep end at every opportunity, aren't you?"

"Not at all," Ronnie replied, grinning. "You know as well as I do that something in her switches on when she's doing things she used to do. Muscle memory or whatever.

She can do it. She'll be your date."

Not a stretch for her anyway. We were dating. At least that part was true.

"You don't need to involve her, Crockett. If it makes you uncomfortable," Ginny said. "She can be your date and have no idea what's going on, if that's best."

"Fair point."

Maybe I won't tell her what we're doing there. We're just going to a fancy dance.

"Hey, Ben, you have the app?"

"Still Phase One," he replied. "The next ball will be the decider, if I'm one of the chosen I'll get the link then to download their application."

One of the chosen. That sounded like some sort of gladiator battle. He'll be fighting lions next.

"You had a phone, but didn't check-in with me," Ronnie grumbled. "You could've texted this morning when you made your escape."

I nudged her. "Couldn't check-in, Ronnie. He's being vetted. He couldn't text. There is a good chance that one of the AirDropped images or Notes contained something else."

"I guess," she said. "That actually makes sense. But I think I can play the fiancée card now, just for a minute."

Fair call.

"And we should expect the app will have intelligence gathering capabilities. So that's going to make it interesting if Ben gets to download it."

Ben addressed her, "Thanks for worrying."

"Dick," she replied. "You're lucky I'm so easy going."

It was Ben's turn to laugh, but he did so while giving her a hug. It was probably to stop her thumping him.

"Shall we go topside?" Tom asked. "It's pretty cramped in here and I'm sure the house is clean. There could be surveillance teams in the area using directional mic type systems, but no one's called me to say anyone was lurking around over the last few days."

No one had called him?

"Who would call you about strangers in the area?" My curiosity got the better of me.

"I run the neighbourhood watch," Tom replied with a smile. "Everyone calls me the minute anything out of the ordinary happens."

"That's brilliant," I replied impressed. "The house might be clean, but his phone probably isn't," I said, indicating Ben with my thumb. No telling what was planted onto the phone via AirDrop. "Got another cage upstairs?"

Ronnie and I knew damn well he did. It was in the shed.

"Yes," Tom said. "We could always take this box up." He hefted the box off the desk. "Let's go."

Ginny led the way. Ronnie and I followed, leaving Tom and Ben to move in behind us.

Chapter Nineteen:
[Ronnie: If it's not them, then who?]

"Okay so, you two are just like the rest of us?" I said, as I sat at the dining table and puffed air out my mouth. I wanted to ask if they were *Genesis,* but I also didn't want to ask. If they were, then surely they'd know I was looking for Ben. I sat on my thoughts. Or maybe not. Maybe things were far more compartmentalised than I thought.

"I suppose we are," Ginny replied. "I've always loved a bit of intrigue and espionage."

"And I thought you got your fix from true crime drama shows," I replied.

"Well, I do, Ronnie, I didn't lie to you."

Hmmm. Perhaps.

"Crockett," I said, interrupting what I could only describe as a painful thought process. "We need to work out what the hell we're doing now."

"I need my phone," he said, motioning to the box that Tom had placed in the middle of the table.

"Go ahead," Ben said. "But leave mine in there."

I turned to Ben. "You're sure there is something on it spying?"

"I'm not, but also not certain it isn't. Better to be safe ..."

There were plenty of other things to be sorry about. Nana in the newspaper for one. Nana. Bloody hell. We don't need that right now.

Crockett shoved his phone in my face. I pushed it back a bit. "Too close."

"Read," he said.

"Don't wobble your phone then."

It was a text from my Nana: The girls and I have tickets to the Wellington Children's Hospital Ball next weekend, so we'll have to postpone poker night.

"That's just wonderful. When did they move poker night to Saturday? And do you really have nothing better to do on a Saturday night?"

"That's hardly the takeaway from that text, Ronnie."

"I don't think I can cope with the thought of Nana and the *Cronies of Doom* at the very ball you all need to be at this weekend."

"Doesn't sound like you have a choice. And I bet their next text is to Donald to get him to do their hair, pre-ball."

"What's happened," Ben asked. He'd been helping himself to some biscuits from a jar in the kitchen. "Whose hair is Donald doing?"

"Nana and the cronies," I said. "They're going to the ball."

"Not ideal," Ben said, lowering himself into a spare chair. "We're going to have to manage that."

"Yes."

"Crockett and I have dinner plans. We might have to

pick this up later." I glanced at my watch. "False alarm, we have a time."

Ben frowned. "There's a person problem to handle first. Crockett?"

Crockett was texting.

"Sorting it now, Ben. You and I are going to go visit an old friend. We're taking that car you borrowed."

"Let's go then."

They left.

I was alone with Tom and Ginny.

"We need to have a real conversation," I said. "Tom, come and sit with us."

He did. "Coffee will be ready soon."

"Not for me, thanks. Wouldn't say no to a cup of tea."

"What do you want to know, Ronnie?" Ginny asked.

"*Genesis*, are you the new heads?"

She shook her head. "No. And before you ask, we don't know who the new head is either."

"But you're part of *Genesis*?"

"We are."

"So that's what you were trying to tell me during the Alex debacle?"

"I thought you'd work it out."

"I was close, but Ben shut me down."

"Ben didn't know then either." Tom looked at me. "He didn't know."

"Okay. He didn't know. He does now?"

"Yes."

"Were you asked to find him?"

"No."

Just me then.

"Where you given any directives via *Genesis*?"

Tom nodded. "We're helping work the *Genesis* angle on the arms deals. Ben is working for the Americans and *Genesis*, this time."

"Right, so now, we're all working the same job," I said circling my finger around the table. Ginny and Tom agreed. "And the next ball is on Saturday."

"Correct."

"Guess I better go shopping," I said with little enthusiasm. "I can't sit the ball out if Nana and the *Cronies of Doom* are going to be there."

"I think I can help you out with a dress," Ginny said. "Come and have a look in my wardrobe. I'm bound to have something that will fit you."

I needed something for Emily as well. We were pretty much the same size.

"Don't suppose you could lend Emily a dress too?"

The coffee maker hissed, and coffee bubbled into the first cup under the spout. "I'll finish making the coffee." Tom rose from the table. "And I'll make you a cup of tea, Ronnie."

"Come on, Ronnie," Ginny said, as she stood slowly. "I can sort both you and Emily out."

I followed her down the hallway to the master bedroom and her magnificent walk-in wardrobe. Ginny started moving dresses, and what I could only describe as gowns, on one of the racks. "You'd be a ten, Ronnie?"

"I think so," I replied.

She glanced at me then chose three long dresses that she laid on the bed. One was pale blue, icy looking. One was yellow, sunshine yellow. And the last was red. A deep blood red.

"I think any of these will look fabulous on you with your colouring." Ginny smoothed the fabric on the deep red gown. "This might be the winner."

I picked the red gown up and held it near my face. "You think?"

She nodded. "Yes. Definitely. With your dark hair and olive skin. That is the one."

It looked like it would fit. I appreciated the simple style. Long fitted sleeves, a defined waist, enough skirt that I could move and a scooped neckline. "I should try it on," I said.

"Yes."

I shed my jeans and shirt then stepped into the dress. Ginny zipped the back up. "How is that?"

"Great," I said, swishing the skirt.

Ginny pointed me to the full-length mirror inside the wardrobe door. The dress was amazing. I stood on tiptoes to stop the dress from pooling near my feet. I'd need to wear proper heels.

"I think I have a matching tie and pocket square. Ben will be your date?"

"I hope he will be. Who did he go to the last ball with?"

"He went stag. No doubt all the single women will be dripping green poison in your direction at the next ball, especially when they catch sight of the rocks on your finger."

I quite enjoyed that image.

Ginny unzipped the dress. I stepped out of it and dressed in my regular clothes.

"Now, Emily is about your size and if I remember correctly has light brown/dark blonde hair?"

"She does."

"The icy blue?"

"Yes!"

"The Cinderellas are going to the ball," Ginny said, putting the coat hanger back into the red dress and draping it over my arm. She then picked up the blue dress and draped it over the red dress. "Take those out to the living room, so you don't forget to take them home with you later."

"Thank you, Ginny." I meant it.

"Happy to be able to share something special with you." She turned back to the remaining dress on the bed. "I'll be back down in a minute with the pocket squares and ties."

There were mugs of coffee on the table in the dining room and a cup of tea in front of the chair I'd vacated. I placed the dresses carefully over the arm of the couch and joined Tom at the table. It was safer to have the dresses away from hot drinks.

"Crockett texted. They're on their way back." He pointed to the tea placed where I'd been sitting. "That's for you."

"He say anything else?"

"No."

I sipped the tea. "This is very good. I forgot how good your tea is."

Tom gave a small smile. He wasn't big on toothy grins. Ginny tottered through the living room and placed two ties and two pocket squares on top of the dresses. She came into the dining room and took her seat.

We waited. A few minutes ticked by and then I heard a car come down the driveway. Turning my head, I saw Crockett and Ben exit the car and come in the gate. My eyes landed on the back door as it opened.

"That coffee smells good," Ben said as he walked in.

"I'll make you some," Tom replied.

Ben pulled up a spare chair motioning to Crockett to take the empty seat at the table.

"How'd it go?" I asked.

"Didn't need the cell after all," Crockett replied. "We put them in the chest freezers in Art's garage."

"Isn't someone, or many someone's, going to miss those two people?" Ginny asked.

She had a good point. Usually, people are missed.

Ben smiled a crooked smile. "The people who miss them won't be filing any missing persons reports so we don't have to worry too much."

"I beg to differ," I said. "I think we do have to worry. Not about police. More about who they worked for. Do we know who that is?"

"They're not the terror threat they were cracked up to

be. Didn't get any ID off them, but that doesn't mean much. We don't carry ID most of the time and we're not terrorists." Ben stood and took his jacket off. He hung it on the back of his chair. "They were something and they were working for someone else. Whoever the Brit was, he seemed to be in charge, or he thought he was."

"Private military perhaps," Crockett muttered. "Were those bozos working for the sellers or the enforcers for the sellers. Potentially they could be both, I suppose. Could've been part of the vetting process."

"I don't think the two who grabbed me had anything to do with the arms deal. It was a fishing expedition. They were trying to find out what I knew and who I was working for. I think they wanted in and didn't get an invite but the Brit, he was something. He really wanted to know the details about a deal. He asked me over and over about chemical weapons, bioweapons, and nukes." Ben looked thoughtful for a split second.

"I imagine he won't be thrilled when he can't contact his lackeys," I said.

"Probably not. We should expect retaliation, once he works out that they're gone." Ben moved his cup on the table. "One of them said he was Diamond Corporation."

"Seriously?" Crockett replied. "Since when do Diamond Corp hire fools?"

"They're not a company known for mistakes that's for sure," I said. "Private Military operating within New Zealand. Interesting. If they were Diamond Corp, they wouldn't be announcing it."

"I doubt they were," Ben said. "Trying to throw me off my game."

"If they'd got that bloody flash drive and gotten the data off it, it could've been bad for you, Ben."

"They didn't, Ronnie. They were idiots."

I nodded and took a breath. "That's what worries me. They were idiots. Why send idiots?"

"No idea," Ben replied. "Did you say you cracked the code?"

"I did. I plugged it into an application on the computer and let it brute-force it. There's no way in hell any of us were going to break it without computer power. Crockett and I thought it might be a Vigenère cipher to really weed out the dummies if this is something the players need to access the next step." If I was being truly honest, that cipher could've been anything. But whatever it was the computer sorted it. I thought it was a Vigenère; if that was the case then a different shift was assigned to each letter depending on how it appeared in the word. That would be a spinner for anyone's brain. That's what computers are for. The key was very short, if we were right about the key, and that would make creating the square difficult.

"Thank you."

"Also, I am coming to the ball. Nana is going to be there, so I am coming. If Topher Franks sees me then so be it." I hadn't seen him for ages. Be great to catch up. He might be a right royal arsehole, but he was good at his job.

"Do you think he'll have a problem?"

"No. Everyone knows I retired to be closer to home and spend time with Nana. Also, didn't someone say it's a masked ball?" And anyway, he liked me because I wasn't an arsehole. He'd have a problem with Frost.

"Now we have to work out if Diamond Corporation are the sellers, or the brokers, or there for the greater good," Tom said. "Or if they're involved at all. Doesn't seem likely."

He was correct. I had more questions about their potential involvement. They're a private military contractor and kidnapping isn't usually something they do. Hostage rescue, sure. But kidnapping an American and an old lady on New Zealand soil didn't sit right. So, were they really Diamond Corp or did they want us to think they were? Did they want Diamond Corp blamed?

"What about the embassy guy that expired first?" I asked Ben.

"He was with the Indonesian Mission, or so he said."

"I'm sure someone will hear about his disappearance. Do you still have the car?"

"Art has the car. We have one of his," Crockett said. "We need to get going, Ronnie."

"Dinner plans. That's right. I could cancel now that we know where Ben is."

"Or we could bring him," Crockett said. "Let's call it a field trip."

"Let's do that then." I looked at Ben. "You're going to need to change out of the penguin suit and put on something less dressy for dinner."

"Where are we going?"

"The Green Parrot."

He stood up. "Have I got clothes at yours?"

"Of course," I replied. "Would the leather weekender under the spare bed," I tipped my thumb towards the hallway, "be yours?"

"Yeah. I'll grab that."

"Let's get home, get changed, and go meet your colleague for dinner."

"My what?"

I pretended not to hear him as I gathered the dresses and extras from the couch and headed for the door. I called over my shoulder, "Thank you for your help, Ginny. We'll see you soon." I opened the door and was out the gate before Ben and Crockett caught up.

"Where are you going?" Ben asked.

"Crockett's car is up on the road. Do you want to take Art's and meet us back at mine?"

"Sure."

I hurried up the driveway holding the dresses as high as I could so no part of them dragged on the ground.

Chapter Twenty:
[Ronnie: Dinner?]

We arrived looking better than we had for most of the day. Honestly, I was over the day. It could stop at any point. Now we had to worry about retaliation from forces unknown. Yay. Kirsten looked more than surprised to see Ben walking towards the table. I made a mental note. It wasn't quite shock, but she definitely didn't expect to see him, and I wondered why.

Apart from him being missing all weekend, what would cause whatever that look was that flashed across her face? I gave an internal shrug. Maybe she didn't think I'd find him, maybe that's what it was. O ye of little faith. Technically he found himself, but I spotted him in Ginny's driveway so I'm taking some credit.

She smiled as we took our seats at the table. We each picked up a menu and read the offerings.

"No sign of any servicemen this evening," she said with a wink and a grin directed to me. "You really should join our quiz team."

It wasn't just servicemen. Cops frequented The Green Parrot Café as well. They were probably keeping an eye on the servicemen. I know I would if I was in law enforcement. I'm glad I'm not.

"Good to see you Kirsten," Ben said, his voice low and quiet.

"You too, Ben. Didn't think you'd be here."

Obviously.

Crockett nudged my foot with his. I did it back to him. He'd noticed too.

"What should you tell me?" Ben asked, leaning across the table towards Kirsten.

"That the Filet Mignon is amazing here."

A server appeared by Crockett.

"Are you all ready to order?" he asked, his phone in hand.

Kirsten nodded. "Filet Mignon," she said. He tapped on his phone.

Crockett ordered pork chops. Ben ordered a T-bone. I was not surprised in the least. He loved a steak. I quickly scanned the menu.

"Schnitzel for me please."

The server then asked about drinks. Kirsten ordered ginger beers all round. He left.

Ben leaned closer to Kirsten. "Try again. What should you tell me?"

"I don't know what you are talking about," she said, then turned her attention to Crockett. She almost purred as she asked him how he was.

"Now this bloke ..." he inclined his head towards Ben, "is back from walkabout, I'm not bad."

She smiled. "I heard you ride a Harley."

"Look, I didn't come here to fuck spiders, so if you have something to say, say it."

She peddled her friendliness back. "You don't do friendly chit-chat. Okay. Got it."

191

The server arrived with a tray of ginger beers and glasses. Conversation stopped while he handed the drinks around.

"Your meals will be about twenty minutes," he said, before he took the tray and left.

I scanned the inside of the restaurant. It was humming with voices. There weren't many empty tables. It was a busy place, and I didn't expect that on a Monday evening. It was helpful for us. Easier to blend when there were a lot of people around.

"Kirsten, what do you know about any PMC's operating within New Zealand?" I might as well just chuck it out there in the open.

"Let's get right down to it shall we?" She didn't seem happy. Perhaps she wanted to have extended flirt time with Crockett, but he'd already shut her down.

"We're on a timetable here. So, anything you can tell us would be great."

"We don't know anything officially," she replied.

"What about unofficially?"

"Perhaps there's been some water cooler talk of a PMC working here."

"Which PMC?" Crockett asked.

"Diamond Corporation, so they say."

"All of them?" I really wanted corroboration that we had one PMC to worry about and not two. "There's only one PMC currently operating inside New Zealand?"

"As far as the chit-chat goes, yes. Scuttlebutt says two of their people went missing. Don't suppose you know anything about that?"

I shook my head. "Nope."

"The two missing people were Diamond Corp?" Crockett queried.

Made me wonder if he thought like I did, that something else was going on. Who would've reported those idiots missing and said they were Diamond Corp? It wouldn't be Diamond Corp, because they were far too stupid to be any of their guys. I'd come across their people before. They were excellent.

PMC's don't carry ID saying who they are. Pretty much like the rest of us. You're not going to find a card in Ben's wallet that says CIA. And nothing in Crockett's wallet says ASIO.

"I just said that," Kirsten said. "Diamond Corp. What of it?"

The server appeared with two plates. Ben's and Kirsten's. We all made the right kind of appreciative noises at how the plates looked. He went away and came right back with mine and Crockett's. Again, the proper amount of appreciation was shown. I was hungrier than I realised, and the schnitzel was melt-in-the-mouth delicious. All conversation halted while we shovelled food into our mouths.

When the last morsel from my plate was devoured, I laid my cutlery down and smiled. "That was good."

Ben polished off his dinner. "Yes. Very good."

Kirsten eyes locked onto the sparkler on my finger. "When did that happen?"

Ben smiled at her. "Early last week."

"You didn't say anything when you came in." She sounded a little accusatory.

"Didn't realise you were interested in my personal life," Ben replied. The coolness in his voice spoke volumes.

I interrupted, "That dinner should keep us going for a bit." I smiled at Ben. "I'm glad you're back."

His eyes sparkled as he turned to face me. "How glad?"

"You know how glad."

"Gotta say, I'm quite looking forward to you in that red dress," he whispered in my ear, then planted a kiss on my cheek.

"We don't do many fancy affairs. It'll be fun," I whispered back.

We'll dance and potentially die, but we'll look bloody good doing it.

"Get a room, you two," Kirsten said. She looked straight at Ben. Her eyes narrowed to nasty slits. "You didn't use the phone I gave you. If you had, I could've found you."

"That shitty burner wasn't the type of phone I needed, Kirsten."

Crockett placed his knife and fork on his plate. "If you don't have anything else to share, then we'll head off," he said to Kirsten.

"What's the rush, big guy?"

"Told my girl I'd take her out for dessert, and I don't break promises," he replied with a small smile.

"She's a lucky woman. Hope she knows that," Kirsten said. "If you change your mind, you can reach me on this number." She passed him a card.

He didn't even look at it, just slipped it into his pocket. It'd go in the first rubbish bin he came to. I know his more subtle expressions now. He was not impressed. Something about Kirsten pissed him off.

I watched Kirsten's expression. She did know something. She hadn't relaxed the whole meal. She was good at pretending, but she wasn't relaxed and there was something brewing.

"What is it, Kirsten? What is it that you know and has you jumpy?"

"Don't know what you're talking about."

"Bullshit," I whispered with a smile on my face. "You know something. May as well spit it out."

"Jonathon Tierney is in town."

"Who?" I glanced at Ben and then Crockett. They knew who he was.

"Ask your pals, they know," she said and called for the check. "He hasn't been in New Zealand for years. And now he's here, calling the shots."

Crockett stood up. "Sounds like a *you* problem." He spun on his heels and walked to the counter. Ben and I said goodbye and followed Crockett. He turned and said to Kirsten across the room, "We got the bill. You have a good night."

He paid and we left.

It wasn't until we were on our way back to the Hutt

that Crockett spoke. "Tierney knew a friend of mine back in the day. He was her handler. He's an arsehole. Having him here is not going to be good."

"Have you met him?" Ben asked.

"No. I spoke to him once on the phone. Five years ago, when the world nearly crashed down around us." Anger bubbled through his words. "He's a dick. That is all."

"Okay," I replied.

"Crockett's right. Tierney is a dick. He's also brilliant and very good at what he does," Ben said. "He's frozen Kirsten out of the arms deal situation."

That was when Crockett and I realised Ben was working with Tierney and that was why Kirsten was unhappy.

"Well, that won't make things awkward," I said. "This guy Tierney here and working with you."

"It's fine," Ben replied. "I've already met with him. Like I said, he's good at his job. We three are a fucking good team. And Tierney is there if I need him. He's back-stopped me as Leviticus."

Ben definitely saw something different than Crockett did when it came to Tierney. History colours everything.

"At least he gave you a good solid backstop. I'm pretty sure Kirsten wouldn't have bothered and then she would've wondered why it turned to day-old custard," I said.

How much would he give this Tierney guy? Would he give *Genesis* the same intel. Would it be more or less? Would he share what he knows about Tom and Ginny?

How good was Tierney at getting information out of

his operatives? Whether I liked it or not, Ben was one of his operatives. Charlie Indigo Alpha.

Chapter Twenty-one:
[Crockett: Waste of time.]

I dropped Ben and Ronnie at her place then hightailed it to Emily's. It wasn't too late, but later than I expected to be. I didn't care that Tierney was in country; the man was slimy and didn't impact our operation. We didn't answer to him. On reflection maybe I was a little annoyed. Nothing punching him in the mouth wouldn't cure. I needed to haul that attitude back in and behave.

I knocked on the front door and waited while Emily appeared through the frosted glass panel and said, "Who is it?"

"Crockett."

The lock released and the door opened. "Hi," Emily said smiling. "What's in your hand?"

"Dessert. I realised it was a bit late to take you out." I leaned in and kissed her lips. "But I wanted to see you."

"Come in," she said.

She closed and locked the door behind us. I heard a noise in the living room as I followed her down the hallway.

"Do you have a visitor?"

Emily turned at the open doorway. "I do. Dean is here."

"Good thing I have enough dessert for three." I winked at her. She giggled.

I stepped through the doorway and saw Dean sitting in

an armchair. He smiled and greeted me warmly.

He typed on his iPad. Siri said, "Haven't seen you in a while."

"How are you?" I asked. I handed Emily the brown paper bag. "You want to dish up, or shall I?"

"I will," she said. "You catch up with Dean."

"Okay."

Dean rose from the armchair. We shook hands.

"You're looking well."

Dean typed. "You too," Siri said.

Dean sat back down, and I sat on the couch.

"What have you been up to, Dean?"

He smiled and typed; Siri spoke, "Wishing I could remember things I'm sure I always knew."

"I bet. Must be frustrating for you."

He nodded. More typing. "Yeah. Have you been busy?"

"Yes. Lots going on at the moment. Couple of new jobs."

Dean typed. "Can you tell me?"

"Not really. But there is a masked ball coming up and I was thinking I'd ask Emily to go with me."

He typed quickly. "I bet she'd love that," Siri replied. Was getting so that I forgot what Dean's voice sounded like. He didn't sound like Siri, not even the male version. But it had been a long time since I'd heard his real voice.

"Has she told you anything about herself?"

He nodded. Emily came in with two bowls of dessert with a spoon in each. She handed one to Dean and one to me.

"Thank you," Siri said. Dean tasted the ice-cream, placed the spoon in the bowl and typed. "This is good."

Emily came back with her dessert and sat next to me.

"Thanks Crockett," she said.

"Anytime, Milo."

Dean finished a mouthful of ice-cream then answered my question by typing. "Emily was telling me that she used to be a police officer here in Upper Hutt."

He was expert at typing one-handed and balancing his iPad while he ate. It was impressive.

"I was. Now I know why so many cops say hello to me. They remember me," Emily said.

"They do," I said.

Dean ate more ice-cream.

"Do you remember anything since I saw you last, Dean?"

Dean typed and Siri spoke, "I remember a woman. I see her face sometimes. Emily reminds me of her."

She reminds me of her too.

"Is it someone you were close with?"

He typed. "I think so. But it wasn't a romantic type of closeness. Not like you two." Dean grinned. "We were friends. I think." He shrugged and concentrated on his dessert.

I felt for him. In some ways his memory loss is probably a blessing, like Emily's. Having to lose everyone all over again is a lot for anyone.

Chapter Twenty-two:
[Ben: Home.]

Tuesday morning, I was feeling fine.

I rolled over and pulled my phone out of the drawer next to the bed and turned it on. It buzzed almost immediately. There was a text from Grandad asking if all was well and if I would visit. I replied, not today and hit send. Mostly I wanted to see how keen he was to meet with me after so many texts went unanswered, and if he was going to pull the boss card and demand an audience. I dropped the phone back in the drawer and closed it.

I'd bring it out again later and check for an answer.

Ronnie pushed the door open with her knee as she came in carrying two coffees.

"Morning," she said, placing one cup on the nightstand next to me.

"Morning."

Ronnie sat next on the edge of the bed close to me while I shuffled into a sitting position. "Grandad asked if I'd visit him today."

She smiled. "And you said?"

"Not today."

"Why?"

"Because the vetting is underway, and I think I should lay low for a day or two." I'm tired. Could've just said I was tired, but somehow that felt like wimping out. "You going into the office?"

"No."

Her phone jangled on the nightstand on the other side of the bed. I reached over and passed it to her. The text notification lay on the screen. I could see it was from Uncle George, but not what the text contained.

She read it and replied.

"Everything okay?"

"Yep. *Uncle George* wanted to make sure you were good and that there was nothing outstanding regarding the report I sent."

When did she send a report? I sipped my coffee. It must've been while I was asleep.

"And?"

"I told him we were fine," she said. "And that I brute-forced the cipher and we have the pass phrase."

"That's great. If all goes well, I'll need it."

"You think you'll get the invitation?"

"Yeah." I know Tierney set up my backstop. There was a damn good reason why an actor needed weapons and it had to do with who I was working for; Leviticus was the sort of company that would be in the market for weaponry. I had no doubt that if we did secure weapons, Leviticus would indeed take delivery. They'd be used for whatever job Tierney had his paramilitary arm working on. I leaned over and took my phone out of the nightstand drawer and woke it up. A few seconds later a message popped up.

Grandad: I need you to come over.

Me: Okay

Grandad: Bring your girlfriend for brunch.

Me: She might be busy Grandad.

Three dots appeared.

Grandad: Humour an old man.

I showed Ronnie the conversation.

She took a sip of coffee and put the cup down. "I'm meeting Grandad," she said slowly. "I suppose he would want to meet your *girlfriend*."

"Of course, he does. He seems quite interested in seeing you. He's not getting any younger and he's not here for long."

"Those two comments could be the one, you know."

"Are you being uncharitable towards my Grandad?"

"Not at all. Guess we are going out for brunch then," she said. "We'll take my car."

"Okay. Whatever you want, Ronnie." I opened the bedside drawer and put my phone inside it. That way nothing else could be overheard. Ronnie was the only person I knew to have her nightstands turned into Faraday cages. She's not paranoid, but she sure has a security obsession and that works in our favour.

"I wanted to stay in bed with you for the day."

I sighed. That'd be the ideal day. I checked the time. "We'll have to move to get into Grandad's by eleven and I'd like to call in on Nancy on the way."

"Jeans and tee shirt, okay?"

"That's fine. Grandad doesn't have a dress code as far

as I know. And we won't be seen in public with him. Brunch will be at his current abode."

"Which is?"

"MacKinnon's old place."

"Great. Wonder if it's haunted," she said, finishing her coffee. "Why is he staying at MacKinnon's? I thought that place was owned by the Aussies."

"So did I. I bet there's a good reason. Wasn't it originally American?"

"Maybe when MacKinnon worked for you lot. Or maybe it was always American owned, and he just got to stay there regardless of who he worked for? Or maybe it was owned by MacKinnon."

"Does it matter?"

She shook her head. "Not at all. Just musing really. At least we know where we're going and it's fairly private up there. Not a lot of traffic."

"Have you heard anything about the Brit?"

"Word is, it was Jackson Frost."

"*Genesis*?"

"Yes."

"Who ID'd him?"

"I don't know. He was incoming trouble anyway, so it looks like he made it into the country in time to have you grabbed," she said.

"You think that's what happened?"

"I do. I also think you're right about checking on Nancy this morning. A debrief. We don't want her talking about her experience. You said she was elderly?"

"I know what you're thinking. You're thinking she might know your Nana."

"Yes. I would like to avoid that scenario if possible."

And if it couldn't be avoided, we needed to minimise the outcome. "She lives in Lower Hutt. It's on our way to town which is why I thought we would visit."

"Then, you need to hit the shower and we should get moving. Your tux and shirt need dry cleaning. Or you need a new shirt as there is blood on the cuff and down the front. Not sure if it's all yours."

"Mostly not."

"Then we burn it." She picked it up off the floor by her finger and thumb and carried it carefully out of the room.

That was a good idea.

Half an hour later the shirt was burnt in the fire pit in the backyard, we had dropped the tuxedo at a dry cleaner in Wallaceville, and were on our way to Lower Hutt. I'd texted Nancy and told her I'd be calling in. She said she would be waiting. After the texts, I opened the foil lined glove compartment and put my phone in it. Ronnie had hers in the middle console. Hers wasn't potentially spying on us.

It took us fifteen minutes to arrive at Nancy's place. I parked on the road, and we walked down her long driveway hand-in-hand. When I took her home yesterday morning, I drove down the driveway. At that point I really did not want a borrowed car on the road, especially one with damaged cargo.

I knocked on the door.

We heard movement inside right before the door opened.

Ronnie stuttered a strangled hello to the unexceptional man that stood in the doorway. She recovered and said, "Where's Nancy?"

"She's inside, Ronnie. She's a lovely woman. I've just made her a cuppa."

As soon as I heard his voice, I knew who he was. I felt my fist clench.

"Jackson, why are you here?" Ronnie asked.

"I told you I was coming. Said we would grab a drink. Didn't mean this morning." He smirked when he looked at me. "I see you know Mr Reynolds."

She held up her left hand and wiggled her fingers. "He's my fiancée. How do you know Ben?"

"We had the opportunity of meeting over the weekend." He stepped aside and ushered us in. "It was a pleasure. He's charming."

"It was not a pleasure, Fuckhead," I growled.

"That's Mr Fuckhead to you."

Nancy called out from somewhere inside. "Ben! Ben! Is that you?"

We followed the voice. She was sitting at a kitchen table. She looked all right. And she did have a cup of tea.

"Are you alright?" I asked.

"Yes," she said. "And who is this?"

"My fiancée, Veronica Tracey."

Nancy put her cup down. Delight brightened her features.

"Are you related to June Tracey?"

Ronnie smiled and nodded. "I am. Do you know my Nana?" She did well to keep her voice calm considering this was nightmare territory for her.

"Not personally, dear. I saw she had a big write-up in the newspaper. She sounds like a wonderful woman."

"Oh, she is," Ronnie replied. "She's terrific."

"Is it true she is out and about solving mysteries?"

"It is. She's a regular Nancy Drew."

Nancy gave a tight smile. "Wish I was. I've the name for it." She watched Jackson for a moment. "Are you going to sit down?"

The two of us standing near her table was probably quite intimidating. I pulled a chair out and motioned to Ronnie to sit. Nancy made noises of approval.

"I take it you can get your own chair," I said to Frost, pretty tempted to hit him with a chair. I wouldn't have to lift it high. He wasn't a big man. He was a lot shorter than me. Short-assed. He was about the same height as Tom Cruise. If you can call that height. I know Ronnie had opinions on short men. In my experience she was correct.

"Yes, let's sit. Let's sit, and chat," Frost said.

"Let's talk about how you got into the country," Ronnie said.

His brow furrowed. "I don't know what you mean?"

"I mean, I know you're not MI6. I know you were disavowed and put on a No-Fly list. So, I ask again ... how did you get into the country?"

His smirk came back. "Oh, that's precious, you didn't

think a little thing like a No-Fly would stop me, did you?"

"I hoped," Ronnie said.

She didn't like him. He probably put himself in a box and air freighted it.

"We were going to have a beer," he said. "Remember?"

"I remember. That was your idea not mine. I'm not the one with a memory problem, Jackson."

"What does that mean?"

"Think about it."

I enjoyed Ronnie's short conversation with Frost. It sounded like she had something on him.

"You're not talking about Iran, surely? That was eons ago. Should be over that by now. I am."

"It was Egypt you piece of crap. And of course, *you're* over it. You weren't the one abandoned in the desert."

"They sent in a rescue team, what's your problem?"

"You, Jackson. You are the problem. You left me in a compromised position and fucked off with some Bedouin tribe, promising weapons and cash to whomever got you out."

Nancy gasped. "Oh, you poor girl," she said, reaching out and patting Ronnie's hand. "That must've been terrifying." She glared at Frost. "What a vile creature you are, Jackson."

"That's not nice, Nancy. I've been nothing but kind to you today," Frost said, his voice almost oozed smooth.

"Why are you here?" Ronnie asked. "I don't mean New Zealand. I mean here." She pointed to the floor to hammer home her point. "What are you doing at this lovely woman's house?"

"Visiting."

I looked at Nancy. "He's visiting you? After the weekend he subjected you to?"

"That wasn't Jackson," she said. "I'd have recognised his voice, if it was Jackson."

She would've recognised his voice? It was him.

"Who is Jackson Frost to you?" I asked, feeling Ronnie's eyes on me.

"He's my nephew. My sister's boy."

Shit. And he had his aunt kidnapped. What an asshole. Nancy Frost-Andrews. I should've seen that coming. Why didn't she recognise his voice?

"That's interesting," Ronnie said. "So, you haven't changed at all then over the years. Still a champion arsehole."

Nancy clamped her lips together as if she was stopping herself from commenting. She didn't look horrified at Ronnie's comment. Maybe she knew what he was. Maybe she'd always known. It's hard to hide your true self when you're a prize-winning dickhead.

"Ronnie, you need to let it go. Egypt was a long time ago. You made it out."

"I did, no thanks to you." She smiled at him. "Can't say I was surprised to find you'd been disavowed."

"And you retired, or did you? Are you not so bloody perfect, yourself?"

"I retired. You know that. You know I am a private investigator. You rang me at work."

"And engaged to an actor. How wonderful for you both."

His smarmy voice was getting on my nerves.

"What is it you want?" I asked. "What will make this ..." I swirled my finger in the air. "End?"

"What's your rush?"

"My grandfather is waiting for us."

"Is he?" He looked at Ronnie. "Is he?"

"Yes," Ronnie replied. "We're not the ones who have issues with the truth."

Jackson cackled until his aunt said, "That's enough Jackson. You need to be nicer to my guests."

"They're not nice to me."

"Oh, diddums, did the nasty lady and man say mean things to you?" Ronnie replied. "Gee I wonder why."

"See, Aunty? See, she's not nice."

"It seems to me that she has reason to be cross with you. Be the bigger person, Jackson. For once in your life, be the bigger person," Nancy said with a long sigh.

I bit my lip. Ronnie covered her mouth with her hand.

"Why are you so horrible to your own flesh and blood, Aunt Nancy?" The look on his face was best described as a sulk. "You're nothing like mummy."

Nancy drew in a breath and said, "She coddled you when you should've been smacked."

Ronnie's eyes grew wider. Her hand clamped tightly across her mouth again. Nancy wasn't finished. "I had a delightful evening with Mr Reynolds on Friday. We danced and danced. He retrieved my phone after it was misplaced. He was charming and congenial. Not at all like you." Nancy smiled. Old lips stretched taut. "If I could've chosen a nephew, it would've been someone like Ben. Someone with stature that can dance with a woman without giving the appearance of a child standing on their mother's feet and being waltzed around the room." Nancy looked across to me. "What a wonderful evening I had."

Ronnie and I made eye contact. I could see the laughter in her eyes.

I cleared my throat. "What is it you want, Frost?"

"We had such a lovely visit over the weekend, didn't we? I thought we could do it again." He smirked. "You've dropped in at the perfect time. I have questions."

"I don't have answers. We have brunch waiting." I stood and took Ronnie's hand in mine. "I'll call in another day, Nancy. When your nephew isn't here."

Nancy lifted her cup from the saucer. "That would be lovely." She nodded at Ronnie. "What a treat to meet you, Veronica."

Ronnie stood next to me.

Jackson Frost stayed seated. He shoved a piece of cake into his mouth.

"We'll let ourselves out," Ronnie said. She addressed Frost. "Hope you choke."

On that note we left.

And now I knew who was supposedly behind the kidnapping. A little man with a big-chip. It still didn't feel right. He was a nasty little man, but was he the brains behind the deal? That was doubtful.

I opened the car door for Ronnie. She smiled and sat in her seat, and by the time I got into the driver's seat, she was buckled up and laughing.

We laughed all the way into the city, barely getting ourselves under control before climbing the many steps through the bush to meet Tierney for brunch. We were only ten minutes late.

"I forgot how far up the house is," Ronnie said, as I pressed the bell next to the massive front door. We could see someone walking towards the door. It didn't look like Tierney.

The door swung open. It wasn't Tierney. The man held an ornate wooden box. He opened the lid. I put my phone inside and so did Ronnie. It was another Faraday cage.

"I am Jonathon's assistant. You may call me Adam. Please come in."

"Good morning, Adam," I said. "Where's Jonathon?"

"Brunch will be served in the main dining room, Sir. He's waiting for you. Follow me."

Ronnie whispered in my ear as we followed Adam. "Not fancy you said, jeans and tee shirt were okay, you said. Adam is full on Alfred."

"You're okay. Trust me."

Chapter Twenty-three:
[Ronnie: The man, the mountain.]

"Come, come, dear boy," Tierney said with obvious pleasure when we entered the dining room behind Adam or Alfred.

Tierney was standing and grasped my hand in a firm shake. His hand was sinews and bone - an old hand belonging to an old man. His dark eyes were recessed by bushy grey eyebrows. I doubted he missed anything.

"Delighted to meet you, Ronnie," he said. "I can call you, Ronnie?"

"Yes, Sir. I prefer it to Veronica."

He smiled. "You do suit Ronnie. That's a compliment by the way."

"Now sit." He gestured to the table laden with food. "We have a selection. Not knowing what you would like, Adam here opted for a bit of everything. A smorgasbord if you will"

"Thank you." Ben pulled a chair out for me.

Tierney sat at the head of the table, and Ben and I were opposite each other.

"Ronnie, you were New Zealand Security Intelligence Service?" Tierney asked, passing pancakes to me.

I forked two onto the plate in front of me, then handed the plate over to Ben.

"Yes, I was," I replied, pouring syrup.

"And what do you do now?"

I had a feeling he knew exactly what I did. Don't ask questions if you don't already know the answer.

"Private investigator. I have my own agency."

"Wonderful," he said with a smile. "I thought it was time we met. Ben is quite serious about you."

He should be; we're engaged. Didn't seem like he knew that wee nugget of info.

Ben winked at me from across the table. Oh, right, he was about to tell him.

"Jonathon," Ben spoke to get his attention. "Ronnie is my fiancée."

Tierney smiled at us. "That is good news." He raised his glass of orange juice. "To the happy couple."

We clinked glasses. So far Jonathon Tierney wasn't living up to his arsehole brand.

The rest of the brunch followed the same vein. It was pleasant. He could've been Ben's grandfather; it was that level of pleasant. Once we'd finished eating and had fresh coffees, Tierney asked us to accompany him into his study. He sat in an armchair. We sat on a Chesterfield sofa. Between us and Tierney was a large coffee table. I expected the business end of this meeting to begin, and I wasn't disappointed.

It felt a bit weird seeing Tierney sitting in the same armchair MacKinnon favoured.

Tierney placed his cup on the table and sat back.

"Ronnie," he said.

"Yes, Sir."

"You have on occasion worked for us ..."

I waited.

He watched me.

"I would like you to consider doing so again."

"What are you offering?"

"A very nice payday on us," he replied.

"That goes without saying. My accountant is always happy when I pick up extracurricular hours."

He considered my comment. "You run it through your business."

"I do."

He smiled. "I would like you to work with Ben."

From the corner of my eye, I spotted movement. Ben clenched his jaw.

"With Ben," I repeated.

He nodded. "We will read you in, of course."

"Wouldn't it be easier to put Kirsten Knight in with Ben?"

Ben clenched so hard I thought he'd crack teeth.

"Ronnie, dear woman, if I wanted Kirsten or thought she was capable, she would already be included."

Interesting.

Ben's jaw relaxed.

"What do you say Ronnie, will you join us?" Tierney asked, picking up his cup.

I turned to Ben. "Are you okay with this?" I pointed between him and myself. "You have to be absolutely sure."

"Of course, I'm okay with it." I believed him.

My attention reverted to Tierney. "I'm in."

"Let's get down to business ..." Tierney produced a file from behind him and laid it on the table. He opened the cover and picked up the first sheet of paper. "INTERPOL are after Jackson Frost. He's wanted in Poland in connection to the deaths of two Polish civilians. They also think he was behind an arms deal that was disrupted."

"Jackson whingy-pants Frost is the arms dealer we're after?" We had him. We could've taken him this morning.

Tierney passed me the piece of paper he held. "Not exactly," he said. "Read."

I scanned the paper quickly. Jackson Frost was named as one of the people behind the arms deal in Poland. He was believed to be working with someone else. Someone was directing him, giving him orders. An Unknown Subject. The civilians killed were shot by Frost as he made his escape after armed operatives crashed the party. There was one witness who made a statement and was murdered two days later in Germany while visiting family.

It was time to share something and see what Tierney knew because there was nothing on the paper that said two MI6 officers were killed in Poland. Crockett knew about it so it wasn't a *Genesis* secret.

"I heard Frost was responsible for the deaths of two MI6 officers. I hadn't heard about the civilian deaths."

A small smile tweaked the corner of Tierney's mouth. "Where did you hear that?"

"A friend in ASIO."

"Ah, of course, Mr Crocker." Tierney's dark beady eyes met mine. "That's correct."

My eyes flicked over the paper in my hand. "There's nothing about who the disruptive operatives were?"

He shook his head. "Some say it was an international strike team. Some say it was GSG-9."

"If it were GSG-9 then Frost would not have escaped," I said. GSG-9 were German special forces, a paramilitary unit within the German police, and the most lethal counterterrorism squad in the world. "Have they ever missed a target?"

"Not that I know of," he said and picked up another sheet of paper. "Bearing that in mind, it's more likely that it was a strike team of some sort. No country has claimed responsibility for the disruption of the arms deal. No faction has stepped forward to take credit."

Genesis. It was *Genesis.*

He handed me the second sheet of paper. It was an intelligence report on the arms deal in Poland. I passed it to Ben. He read it and handed it back to Tierney.

"Interesting that they think there is a worldwide top-secret agency gathering intelligence and sending in strike teams," I said. "Who would run such a thing?"

"I'm sure I don't know," Tierney said. "Just like I don't know who would work for such a secret organisation."

"And the point?" Ben asked.

"Not only are INTERPOL champing at the bit to get their hands on Frost, but I believe there is another agency or organisation wanting him for similar reasons we do. And that is not to stand trial for murder."

I knew very well what the final outcome of the CIA's

217

mission regarding Frost was and did not need to hear it. Frost would disappear off the face of the earth. *Genesis* probably had a fairly similar goal.

"How sure are you that Frost is directly involved in the arms deal?" I asked. "We suspect he was behind Ben's kidnapping and also the kidnapping of Nancy Frost-Andrews."

Tierney leaned back and tapped his fingers on his chin. "When did you come to this conclusion?"

"This morning," Ben said. "The reason we were late. We checked on Nancy and found Frost there. They're related."

"You sure he was behind the kidnapping?"

Ben nodded. "He was there. I had a hood on the whole time, but it was him asking the questions on the second day."

"We haven't discussed the questions ..."

"What was I doing at the Polish ball? Why was I sitting with the people I sat with? What did I want? Why was an actor so interested in old women? Why was I really at the ball? And it continued in that vein. At no point did he ask anything about arms deals or espionage. He seemed to be fixated on why I'd danced with his aunt. At the time I didn't know Nancy was his aunt. I found that out this morning."

"Nonsense questions," Tierney said. "Busy work. Someone wanted him occupied."

"Exactly. It was almost as if he didn't know what he should be asking."

Tierney nodded. "Maybe whoever controls him thought he was capable of coming up with some interrogation questions without help."

"Possibly," Ben said. "They were wrong."

"And the two men working for him?"

"Not a problem."

"Who were they attached to?"

"They wanted me to believe they were Diamond Corporation, much like whoever went and screwed that Polish deal up wanted the world to think it was GSG-9."

"False flag operations."

I sat back listening and taking it all in. The Polish situation was *Genesis*, I was sure of that. But the two so-called terrorists were not. Maybe someone is looking to get *Genesis* blamed for a bunch of things. How convenient to have a super-secret scapegoat.

I pushed the Polish situation away. I knew who that was. But the two men here working with Frost: why did they want everyone to think they were Diamond Corp? Why?

All of a sudden, I could feel eyes on me. I looked up and found Ben and Tierney watching me.

"Hello?" I said with a smile. "Did you want something?"

"What were you thinking about just then?" Ben asked. "Because it looked intense."

"Frost. Why is he trying to throw Diamond Corp under the bus?"

"Discredit and destroy," Ben said.

"But why? They're world renowned private military contractors. Apart from the O'Hare Group there is no one else I'd prefer when it comes to hostage rescue and personal protection in shitty places."

"Have either of you come across dirt on Diamond Corp?" Tierney asked.

"No," I said.

"No," Ben said. "There was a male at the ball, the person who took Nancy's phone. When I retrieved the phone he said, 'Leviticus' to me."

"Describe him," Tierney said.

"My height, short dark hair - military cut, green eyes, clean shaven, no obvious scars or tattoos, wearing a tux. There were a lot of tuxedos."

Tierney picked up his phone and tapped at the screen for a few seconds. He then turned it to face Ben. "Is this him?"

"Yes. Who is he?"

"He is with Leviticus."

"Who is he?"

"No one you need to worry about, Ben. He's with us."

Ben didn't appear thrilled at the lack of information surrounding the male.

I changed the subject. "Do you see why it's so strange that those bargain basement so-called terrorists declared they were Diamond Corp?" I asked. "They could've said Wagner Group and no one would've been as suspicious."

Ben chuckled. My ploy worked.

"Do you think Frost is trying to set up a PMC to take

the fall for him if the deal falls over?" Tierney asked.

"Maybe." I didn't know. I was just voicing a thought - something we would be wise to consider. I rummaged around in my mind trying to find anything from *Genesis* that would help. Nothing popped up.

"We will take that under advisement. As more information comes to light, we can make better decisions." Tierney made eye contact with Ben. "Now, Ben, please keep in touch. I am aware that your phone is more than likely compromised, so let's have Ronnie keep in touch for those times when you can't have your phone out in the open."

"Yes. I'll copy the number over when we leave."

"That's settled then. Do you have everything you need for the next ball?"

"I do. We have the passcode. I still have no idea why Nancy and I would be grabbed by Frost if Frost is behind the sale. Unless ..."

"It was part of the process," I said. "Is there any way to find out if other patrons disappeared over the weekend?"

"We have the guest list. Would you like to call them all and ask?" Ben asked.

"No," I replied.

Tierney tapped the table. "Get me the guest list, and I will have a survey created and everyone contacted."

I pulled the flash drive from my pocket and handed it to him. "It's on this."

I'd already copied it and sent it to *Genesis* to see if any names were of interest.

"Thank you, I'll have results by Thursday."

Impressive. There were three hundred and forty-seven people on the list.

He didn't look like he'd finished. Ben and I waited. From the folder he took another piece of paper.

"This is something I would like you to keep in mind while you are working," he said. His beady old eyes darted back and forth across the page. "A colleague has reached out to me, personally. He saw a warning flag and ..." Tierney paused for a beat. "And we need to be aware that an alias has surfaced."

"What does that mean?" I asked. I could feel the frown burrowing into my brow and forced it away. I don't need deep wrinkles before I get married.

"There is a protocol for FBI agents who for whatever reason, never a good one, have to disappear. They're given a new identity and helped to start a new life. And one of those aliases has surfaced."

"Is it like WitSec?" Ben queried.

Tierney nodded his head slowly. "It is, but this is within the FBI. So, we're talking about former agents rather than someone who has given evidence against dangerous criminals. There are three people at any one time who can see the flags generated by this protocol. The Director and two assigned special agents." He looked at Ben, then me. "The problem here is that one agent is dead, and the other is supposedly dead as well."

The frown was back.

"And it's something we need to look into?" Ben asked.

He too wore a frown. By the time we set a wedding date our faces would look like road maps.

"Yes, and no."

Tierney passed the paper in his hand to Ben. Ben read it then handed it to me. I saw names I'd only heard of in fictional retelling of stories from the FBI - stuff Crockett assured me was true.

Good grief.

Tierney shot me a warning glance. Don't say the name out loud. My eyes lingered on the final paragraph and the name Dane Wesson.

"And the Director thinks he's alive?" Ben asked. "Then can't he just send someone to pick him up?"

"If it were that easy my boy, I wouldn't know about it."

"Why isn't it that easy?" I asked handing him back the piece of paper. "Why did you tell us?"

"Dave Crocker," he said.

A rock formed in my throat and dropped with a splash into my stomach. Shit. Crockett. What the hell?

"What about him," Ben asked. "We work with him, more often than not."

Tierney nodded. "I am aware. Mr Crocker may know where our person of interest is."

"He may know ..." I echoed. "He might know?"

Well shit. Then everyone didn't die like Crockett said. Secrets. One day they all come unstuck. Mud just got deeper. I circled back to what the paper told us. If he really was alive then he had to have been seriously injured. His injuries could be way worse than Emily's. If Wesson was alive, why wouldn't he reach out to the FBI? Maybe he didn't have the means, maybe he didn't have anything he used to have. That smacked of Emily and her brain injury. If Wesson was alive but had no memories, or if he was incapable of thinking, then how was he any use? Well, that went dark fast.

Ben touched my hand. "Thoughts?" he asked.

I guess my face was giving me away.

"If he is so broken that he can offer nothing, then what is the point of even looking for him? Why find a dead man? Is this about the red flag?" I took a breath. I could find them, but I needed more than I had. "Do we at least get a photo of the alias? Are they using the alias or have they reverted to their real name. Are they confirmed as within New Zealand?"

"All good questions, Ronnie. Unfortunately, the one person who can ID the alias is presumed dead. The new Director could only see a warning flag, and the name of the agent who investigates *The Wayward Son Protocol* triggers. On further attempts to access the protocol the Director managed to find an alias assigned to a former agent but not their real name." He paused. "The alias that was seen was assigned when that agent entered the program and was set up with a new life." I knew Tierney wasn't finished speaking. "There was a safeguard built into the protocol. It should've reverted to the new Director and have had new agents assigned but the program that runs it refused to accept the final death certificate to enable that to happen."

"So, the Director is locked out?"

He nodded.

"Do they know why the death certificate wasn't accepted?"

"No. They thought it was a glitch when the flag popped up. It seems it was not a glitch. Now, the Director wants to know if our target survived."

"What is it you want us to do?" Ben asked.

"I want you to find the person of interest and confirm he is unable to operate under the protocol."

Okay.

"Time would be better spent locating the person who has surfaced," I said. "I can do that, but I need a little bit more information."

Tierney's eyes were laser focused on mine. I returned the intensity of the stare.

"I do believe you can," he said.

"What is it you want exactly?" Ben asked.

Tierney pulled a pen out of his pocket and wrote on the back of a piece of paper then handed it to Ben. He read it and gave it to me.

Find Wesson. Confirm his condition. Find the former-agent whose alias has surfaced, remove them from the equation. The alias is linked to the arms deal. Intelligence came across from the FBI.

I nodded and gave the paper back. That looked like something *Genesis* needed to know.

Tierney took a Zippo lighter from his pocket, pulled a copper rubbish bin close then lifted it onto the table. He lit the papers one at a time and dropped them into the bin. Plumes of smoke rose. I hurriedly looked for smoke alarms. There were none in the study. That was smart.

"I will need as much information as you can get me, Sir," I said.

He nodded. The smoke dwindled. He placed the bin back on the floor. "Unfortunately, Ronnie, that was all the information we have. If he is alive, then someone is harbouring Mr Wesson. Someone must be paying his medical expenses, and they would be considerable. Enough to bankrupt a person of normal means."

He wasn't a New Zealander, so ACC wasn't available to him, or was it?

"Sir, would he have gotten ACC help when he was injured?" Could we track him through the system, was what I was really asking. "If he stayed here ACC would continue helping him?"

"I think he would have qualified for some medical assistance but as far as we know there was no request for help beyond the emergency room. A death certificate was issued."

"If he's dead there will be no finding the person." But he didn't believe he was and for whatever reason his buddy in the FBI didn't believe he was either and the *Wayward Son Protocol* wouldn't accept the death certificate. It could be a glitch. "Why does anyone think he may not be dead?"

"We do not officially know that he is alive. We do not know what condition he would be in if he is."

That didn't answer my question.

"Why would anyone think he survived? From what I know of the incident, Crockett is the lone survivor. He's certainly never mentioned another survivor."

Tierney's thin lips rounded in the corners into a small smile.

"Would he tell you?"

I shrugged. "Probably not. But you know something, don't you?"

"I know that Mr Crocker became a close friend of Mitch Iverson's. I also know that Mr Crocker visits Miss Jones regularly." He blinked. "Mr Crocker spends time with rehab patients."

I let that sink in and wallow about. I knew Crockett was friends with Mitch Iverson. He'd rung him for help on various things while I was with him. He also went fishing with him. I didn't know why that would interest the Charlie Indigo Alphas of the world or even the Foxtrot Beta Indigos. I wished I could stop thinking in the phonetic alphabet whenever initialisms arose. I also wasn't aware that Crockett spent time with rehab patients. I knew about Emily. They were an item. Why would he spend time with rehab patients? Was he just a really good guy who liked to help? He came across as a nice guy. Maybe that's all there was to it.

"I see you are considering all the information." Tierney smiled at me. "I have the utmost faith in your abilities, Ronnie."

"Give me the alias name, please."

"Cassidy Tailor."

Good to know he has faith. He wants me to find someone who uses an alias, and we have no information about the person. The alias is generic. We don't even know if it's a male or female, non-binary, or Martian.

"One last question," I said. "Gender of the alias is?"

"Female," he replied. "Last known gender is female."

"Thank you. And one more question. Why is Crockett's friendship with Mitch Iverson of interest?"

"My dear, Mr Iverson has the means to pay the sort of medical bills that would come from a dreadful incident like the drone strike on the laboratory in Upper Hutt."

That was the first time I had absolute confirmation that it was a drone strike. Up until then it was a fairy story. Urban legend. Because why on earth would anyone use a drone to hit a target within the Upper Hutt City limits? Within a suburb? Up until then, I'd believed what everyone else believed, that it was an explosion from within the lab. And the conspiracy nuts who declared there was a trail in the night sky beforehand were just that, nuts.

Crockett had told me it was a drone strike, but even then, I didn't really believe it. It's Upper Hutt, plenty happens there, but a drone strike from friendly forces really pushed the dingy into deep water.

"We will look into it," Ben said. "You'll hear from us as soon as we have something."

"Happy hunting," Tierney replied. "Adam will see you out."

A bell rang and Adam arrived in the room.

"It was a pleasure to meet you, Ronnie," Tierney said. "Stay in touch, won't you?"

"Of course."

"That makes an old man happy. Thank you my dear."

Ben and I followed Adam to the front door. He handed our phones back and we walked in silence down the many steps to the car.

Chapter Twenty-four.
[Crockett: Questions?]

Ronnie and Ben rang me and asked me to meet with them in the morning.

Perfect.

I planned on spending this afternoon at the rehab group checking on an old friend. Even if he didn't know he was an old friend. I picked Emily up from the book-shop to take her to the group meeting. She took the after-noon off when it was her fortnightly group day.

Emily waved to her friend Melanie on the footpath as I parked the car. Melanie waited and walked in with us. She was a few years older than Emily, but like her, she'd suffered a traumatic brain injury and was recovering. Her recovery was going well, and I had no idea she'd had a stroke a year earlier. Brains were interesting. I found the group interesting. Everyone had a different story, but they all had a traumatic brain injury of some kind. Some were well-recovered, or on the road to recovery, while others were struggling to form words and sentences, and others seemed perfectly normal until nonsense came out of their mouths. Then there was Dean who couldn't speak, but he could write. For whatever reason the words wouldn't come out of his mouth, but they sure flowed from his fingertips. He had an iPad with him all the time. He was a really special bloke, and he still is, but all he sees is broken pieces and his own frustration at not being able to speak or think as fast as he once could. He was still my mate even if he didn't know how we met or what happened to him. We told him it was a car accident. Just like they told Emily.

Melanie held the door for Emily. Then I took the door and waited for the next few people to arrive. I didn't join in with the group. I made the coffee and tea and put the snacks out. I hung around and tried not to get in the way. It was good to see Emily with the friends she'd made here, and it was good to see Dean trying. Anger got the best of him some days. I got him an industrial iPad case the same type he would've used in the field back in the day. It was dear but cheaper than replacing the iPad when he threw it at a wall or onto the ground. Anger was a common theme in the group. Lack of impulse control and anger together were a potentially lethal combination.

Dean looked up when I walked closer to the group sitting in a circle.

"Hello," I said, making sure everyone felt as if I'd spoken to them.

A chorus of hellos returned. Dean turned his iPad so I could see it. He'd replied with a hello. Today was a good day. Some days he sat and scowled at everyone. Mostly Emily could get through to him on those days.

"Thanks for lending a hand, Crockett," the coordinator said as she took her seat.

"You're welcome, Janet."

I left them to it and manned my refreshment station.

There was chatter and laughter followed by a discussion about someone's current concern or issue. The most common issue was about regular people being unthinking and rude. Brain injury isn't always obvious. Dean carried scars like Emily. But even then, it was hard to tell there was anything wrong until someone spoke to him and then demanded to know why he didn't reply. If he didn't have the iPad, he always had his phone. I knew of at least two people who thought he was ignoring them and being rude, because they'd said something to him, and he immediately pulled out his phone.

He wasn't.

One bloke hit him when he was out one night with Emily a week or so ago. Dean popped him back and knocked the bloke out. That was a tricky situation to navigate. Police were involved. Emily was there. I wanted to smack the idiot myself, but Dean did a pretty good job of it. It took some finessing to get the bloke to drop the assault charge and to accept that he was in the wrong. Dean wasn't exactly in the right, but no one blamed him, not after I got through with them.

My biggest concern was that someone would talk about it and describe Dean, or worse someone had videoed it and the internet would trawl up a photo attached to his real name. I didn't want to move him. He was happy where he was, for the most part. Maybe he was more settled, than happy.

I made coffee and tea. Eventually the chatter died away and people gravitated towards me to get a drink and a biscuit. Dean came over and pointed at the coffee pot and then used American sign language to sign 'coffee please'. I passed him a mug of coffee without milk or sugar. I knew how he drank his coffee. I handed Emily a NATO coffee. She loved to ask for NATO coffee. It was fun. I remembered when she first recalled how she drank her coffee. It felt like a breakthrough. She'd moved ahead a lot since I'd first met her. I knew a lot more about her now and she knew a lot more about herself. She no longer needed a constant reminder of her name. She knew she was a cop once and a private eye. She was awesome at surveillance. I believe she worked for, or with, Americans within the intelligence community at some point in her life. Little things that she said were familiar to me from that community, but as yet she couldn't draw on that memory set.

Dean tapped my arm.

"What do you need?" I asked.

He signed: To talk to you.

Signing was new.

"Okay?" I signed: You alright? Is here, okay?

He signed: I'm okay, then shook his head.

"Privately?"

He nodded.

"Come on then," I said and pointed to a door at the back of the room. "That way."

Dean started walking.

I spun around to find Janet. She was on the other side of the room talking to Melanie.

I strode across the room and waved. She acknowledged me. "Sorry, don't mean to interrupt but Dean wants a word with me. Okay if I use your office?"

"Absolutely." She took a key from her pocket and handed it to me. "Lock up when you're finished in there."

"Sure thing."

I caught up with Dean and unlocked the office door.

Janet's office was simple yet comfortable. There were a couple of armchairs, a desk, and a desk chair. Filing cabinets lined one wall and there was a high window above them.

Dean pointed to them and signed: Not many people use paper files now.

"Yeah. She must have a lot."

He smiled.

"Sit down and tell me what's going on." I pointed to an armchair.

We sat down. Dean put the iPad next to him on the seat.

He signed: Don't need that with you.

"True," I replied. "You don't. How did you know I could sign?"

His hand and fingers moved: You are different to others.

"Not that different." I chuckled.

His hand moved again: When did you learn?

"A long time ago. Another life. I did undercover work. I learnt then."

He nodded and smiled, then signed: You are different.

"When did you realise you could sign?"

He signed: Some words came back over the last two years. Long time. Two days ago, I knew.

He'd kept the signing quiet. If he'd remembered some words over the last two years he did not let on.

"How?"

Dean's hands moved: person signing on TV. Understood most of what they were saying. But different. I looked it up. I sign in ASL. Kiwi's use NZSL.

I nodded. "NZSL is based on BSL, I think."

He nodded and signed: You know ASL.

"I do. I worked with a lot of Americans. ASL was better for me to learn."

Dean: I am American?

"You are American."

Dean: This is not America.

"It is New Zealand."

He nodded.

Dean: Why am I here?

"This is where you had the accident."

He shook his head. A nnnn sound came out of his mouth. He signed quickly.

"Do it slower for me."

He repeated: No accident. No accident. No accident.

"You remember?"

He shook his head.

Dean: No. No accident.

"You don't remember?"

He nodded.

But he knew it wasn't an accident. So, something had

changed. He could sign. That was a change and a big one.

Dean pointed to himself then signed: Who am I?

"Dean Worcester."

He shook his head again.

Dean: Who am I? Different name.

Ah, crap. I needed to talk to Mitch. If he knew he had a different name, then things were changing rapidly, and suddenly. I'd seen Emily switch gears like that, so I knew it could happen, but no one expected Dean to recall anything at all from his life.

Dean: Different name

I looked into his eyes and for a split second I saw Dane Wesson. Then he vanished. I knew he wasn't going to let the name thing go.

"Dean. If I tell you. Don't tell anyone else. Not even Emily. It's not safe."

Dean: Why?

"Because it's not safe. Tell no one."

I watched him process that information.

He nodded and signed okay.

"You are Dane Wesson."

He stared at me. Just stared. He didn't blink. He didn't seem to be breathing. He stared.

"Dean?" It was hard to break a habit and call him anything but Dean. He suited Dean. El used to call him Squirrel. He suited that too. Bright eyed and bushy tailed, ready for anything, always hungry.

His head moved. He signed: Stewart Smith

That was his brother's name.

"Stewart died a long time ago."

He stared again, this time into space. His hand moved: Brother. Different name to me.

"Yeah. I don't know why."

He stared into space again.

Someone knocked lightly on the door.

Dean turned his attention towards the door and signed: Emily.

I hauled myself to my feet and opened the door. Emily stood there smiling. I glanced back at Dean. He smiled.

Not something I'd seen a lot of on his face. It was a real smile and he looked like his old self.

"Do you need something Emily?"

"Everyone is leaving."

"Okay, we'll be there in a minute." I fished the car keys from my pocket and gave them to her. "Wait for me in the car?"

"Okay." She took the keys and left.

"Dean, do you want to go home?"

He shook his head.

Dean signed: With you.

"Okay, come on then. I need to lock this door and give the key to Janet." Dean picked up his iPad and walked past me. "Emily has opened the car. Go wait with her."

He gave me the okay sign.

I locked up and then found Janet doing dishes in the kitchen. I gave her the office key.

"Everything all right?"

"Yes. I think it is."

"Anything I need to know about Dean?"

"No, man talk, you know ..."

She nodded. "Of course. Have a good rest of your afternoon."

"Will do. See you next time."

Emily waved as I walked towards the car. I winked at her and eased into the driver's seat.

"All good in here?"

"Yes. Dean is coming with us to my place."

"All right then. Let's go."

I adjusted the rear-view mirror to see Dean. He signed: okay. I moved the mirror so I could see through the back window.

Ten minutes later we were all sitting in Emily's lounge. Dean was using his iPad to tell Emily he could use ASL and that he remembered how by himself.

"That's really good, Dean. Isn't it Crockett?"

"Sure is. A major breakthrough."

I wondered how much more he'd say, but not for long. He told Emily he remembered his brother and that he had died a long time ago.

All I wanted to do was give Mitch a ring and let him know what had happened. "Emily, have you got any beers in that fridge of yours?"

"Yes. Coronas."

"Do you have limes?"

"Of course."

"Dean, want a beer?"

He nodded. Emily started to stand. "I'll do it. You talk

238

to Dean. I'll be right back. You want one, Emily?"

"Yes, please."

Once in the kitchen I grabbed three beers from the fridge while ringing Mitch.

"Hey, Crockett," he said. I laid the phone on the bench and hit the speaker button.

"Hey. Things have changed," I said, taking a lime from the fruit bowl and slicing it into wedges.

"What things?"

"He remembers his brother; he remembers how to use ASL."

"That's good. And?" I popped the tops off the beers.

"I told him his name."

"Why?"

"He knew it wasn't Worcester." Even though that was his real name, it was not the name he used. It was complicated. Life is fucking complicated.

"How'd that go?"

"That was when he asked about Stewart."

"Okay. Keep me posted."

Emily called out, "Where are the beers?"

"Call you later if I have anything more."

I hung up, pocketed my phone and took all three beers into the lounge. I'm a champion beer wrangler.

Chapter Twenty-five.
[Ronnie: Why did I say yes?]

"Office or home?" Ben asked when we finally got onto Fergusson Drive.

"Some place quiet."

"Neither of the proffered choices ... where would you like to go?"

"Try the office."

"You won't be disturbed in your room, will you?"

"No. Steph and Jenn don't go in there." His eyes met mine for a split second. "Eyes on the road."

"Why don't they go in there?"

"I think they find my skill set as creepy as you do."

"For the record, I have never said it was creepy," he replied. "All the idiots are on the road today." He threw the bird at an offending driver of a silver Outlander. "Did you get your license from a box of Fruit Loops, pal."

"You or him?"

Ben grinned. I could see the dimple in his left cheek. The car crawled through the Countdown carpark, and into Geange Street, then left onto Princes and left into Leader Lane. He parked at the end of the lane.

"Come on then, let's go see who's in the office," I said, clambering out of the car. He caught up to me at the stairs and held the door for me. "Thank you."

I am polite. Most of the time.

I swung the main office door open and saw Steph at

her desk. "Hi!"

She looked over at me and pointed accusingly. I steeled myself.

"You!" she said.

Oh, God.

"Nana?" A knot tightened. I tried to lighten my voice. "How is she?"

"She's honky dory. Just bloody wonderful. Full of the joys of her newfound fame."

"I thought our engagement might distract her for a wee while."

Steph shook her head. "You left your run too late if you hoped to distract an old woman on a mission."

"Oh, man, what did she do?"

"She's arthritic knee-deep in new cases. And that is more exciting than your engagement." She smiled at Ben. "Sorry Ben, but your news and those big rocks are not big enough for Nana."

Buggery bollocks.

"But wait there's more," Steph said. It sounded like she was enjoying herself now. "She needs your help!"

"With?"

Steph produced a memo pad. "There is a missing person, a potential theft, and many ..." she counted. "Five people are wanting the ancient Scooby gang to locate long lost relatives, and one wants to reconnect with a love interest. I think the love interest might've been a soldier in the proper Great War. Good luck with that."

"And she phoned?"

Steph chortled maniacally. "Did she hell. She came in."

"I'm sorry." I was sorry, mostly because if she came in, she could come back. "Why do they let them out?"

"I have no idea. Perhaps take that up with the Crypt Keeper."

"He's doing a piss poor job so far."

Steph cackled.

"By the way, congratulations Ben. Are you aware what you're signing up for with this one?"

"I am."

"Brave or stupid, jury is still out," Steph said as she waved the memo pad at us. "Do not forget that Nana wants help. I cannot deal with those women again this week."

"We might have to wait a bit to help Nana. I've just been pulled into an extracurricular job."

"The pay better be worth me potentially warding off those crones again."

"It is. I'll be back ... in other words I am not in."

Ben had his phone in his hand. If it was transmitting info whoever was listening just found out I was invited into a job and that my Nana was *investigating* many things. Bugger. Hope they enjoyed that particular nonsense. But seeing the phone reminded me to have Ben put it somewhere safe for the next step, which was locating two people without a lot of information around them. Best of luck to me.

Was Tierney right about Crockett? I briefly wondered if I should just ask him point blank. How would I say it?

Oi, Crockett, what about this crazy notion that not everyone died five years ago? Or, were you really the last man standing? He was meeting us tomorrow, maybe I would ask.

Our Intel came straight from Charlie Indigo, so it's gotta be good. I caught myself before laughter exploded from my mouth. Would *Genesis* know?

A hand on my arm caught my attention. Ben's brow creased. "Hey, you with me?"

"Yep." My focus returned.

"I think she was lost in Nana land," Steph said. "Probably planning an escape route."

I nodded. Sure, that's where I was.

"Right, it's time to get going on this thing." I led the way. We stopped at the tech room and put Ben's phone in the cage.

At the door of my calm place, I turned to Ben. "Are you sure you are comfortable with this next step?"

"No."

"At least you're honest." I opened the door. "Come on then. Sit somewhere and keep quiet."

I locked the door behind us. "Last chance."

"You don't scare me," Ben said smiling his famous smile.

"I'd hate you to be scared of me."

His eyes sparkled. "That door's locked?"

"You know it is ... there will be plenty of time for shenanigans when I find these people."

"Down to business then."

"Hold those thoughts."

"Consider them held, ma'am." His smile was killer.

I turned my attention to business. "Hey Siri, play *Ghost Story* by Carrie Underwood."

The HomePod Mini in the bookcase said, "Playing *Ghost Story*."

Music filled the room. I chose a starting point and a person. Ben watched as I spread out a map of New Zealand. It seemed like a good idea to go big. I took the smoke alarm down and shut it in a drawer. Then I lit a few candles. From the bookcase I picked up a pendulum. I wasn't using the one I wore for this. These were complete strangers. Then I needed to tune the obsidian pendulum into the vibration. It didn't take long to get a good swing away from me for yes and across my body for no.

"Who first?" Ben asked in a stilted whisper.

"Dane."

I'm glad he didn't ask why. There was no earthly reason.

I started in the deep south and let the pendulum swing however it wanted as I moved slowly north. It got through the entire South Island without incident. He wasn't south.

I placed the pendulum in my pocket and changed the map to a Wellington Region map. With the pendulum back in my hand, I started at Wellington's south coast and let the pendulum guide me. There was a long pause over Newtown at the hospital. Okay, I could be on the right track then. If someone survived, they would definitely be in hospital and Wellington was the base hospital for the region. The swing changed over the western hills, not enough to say someone was there, but enough for me to be sure they were there once. I acknowledged the change, and we moved on following the motorway into Petone and Lower Hutt. Another hospital. That made sense. Further north we went. A strong signal almost pulled the pendulum from my hand over what was the Wallaceville Centre for Disease Control, otherwise known as the site of a major explosion. Ground Zero. I gripped the chain tighter as it tried to pull free.

"What's happening?" Ben whispered.

"It's telling me there is a very strong pull there."

Ben stood up and came closer. "That's where the explosion was."

"Yeah." Lots of people died. A lot of energy roamed free.

The pendulum moved again into Upper Hutt City. It showed me Dane had been into the city, to the supermarkets, to the mall. It was time to ask a question.

I took a big breath in and let it out slowly. "Where is he?"

We moved back to Heretaunga then moved towards Wallaceville again. Tight circles spun over an address then the pendulum stopped dead and hung. I let it go. It pointed directly at an address in Wallaceville/Trentham. If there was an actual suburb border, it would be on it.

The music changed to The Rolling Stones: *Sympathy for the Devil.*

"What does that mean?" Ben said from beside me.

"That's where he is. He's not dead."

"Wow. Okay, you're sure?"

"Yes. He's there." I pointed. "Right there." At Emily's. Buggery bollocks. That's a bit close to home for comfort.

I rolled my shoulders to relieve the tension then took a notebook and pen from the bookcase. I wrote the address down.

"It's Emily's place," Ben said as he read it.

Our eyes locked.

What could that mean?

I picked the pendulum up again and asked it to find his home. Where does Dane Wesson live?

Then it moved towards Heretaunga and dropped on an address in Heretaunga Square.

I thanked the spirit and let the pendulum go. My head was starting to ache.

I wrote Dane Wesson's address under Emily's.

"You okay to look for the alias now?"

I put the obsidian pendulum away and picked up a lapis lazuli pendulum.

"I think so. If I don't get anything, I'll give it a rest and try again later."

Ben smiled and sat back in his chair.

I went back to the big map.

After tuning the pendulum, I started in Stewart Island and followed the pendulum to Marlborough without any alerts.

When I got to Wellington things started to heat up a

bit. I switched maps again and concentrated on the name: Cassidy Tailor.

Wellington CBD was a hot spot, but not as hot as an old hotel down near the railway station on Maginnity Street. The Wellesley. I knew the hotel. It was a boutique hotel. A historic building and I loved its magnificent staircase. There were thirteen bedrooms. I think that was part of its charm for me. Such a historically unlucky number.

Maybe it was unlucky for Cassidy Tailor and whoever she used to be.

I let the pendulum take me out to the Hutt. It spun in tight circles over the Event Centre.

"That's where you were?" I asked Ben.

He stood and checked. "Yes."

"Okay. She was there too."

No other alerts so I let the pendulum take me back to the hotel.

"Here," I said. "The person is staying at The Wellesley Hotel."

"Okay." He said nothing else and watched as I added the hotel address to the notebook. Ben remained silent and watchful as I closed everything down, blew out the candles, and flapped my arms around to move the plumes of smoke so I could put the smoke alarm back where it belonged.

With everything returned to normal, I sat down and took a few cleansing breaths.

"We don't know who the person used to be, but we

know where the person is staying. We don't know what she looks like either. Do you think Dane would be able to ID the person?"

"Do you remember seeing Cassidy Tailor on the guest list?" Ben asked.

I shook my head. "Nope, I think that name would've stood out."

"So, she didn't use the alias, maybe she used her original name."

"Or something else entirely." Ben looked tired too. "How many American women do you think were at the ball?"

"No idea. I came across two. Sisters from Eastern Kentucky."

"Maybe it's one of them we're looking for?" Funny that they were from the same place *Justified* was set. Crockett and I loved that show. Life is strange at the best of times. Often life was both entertaining and strange.

"Ronnie, there were three hundred and forty plus guests. Bound to be other Americans there."

"We won't know if Dane can ID the woman until we speak with him." I paused for a beat. "Can we speak with him tomorrow?"

Ben smiled; his eyes lit with gold fleck within light blue. "Sure. Do you want to blow this popsicle stand and head back to your place?"

I nodded. "I do."

He stood, took my hands and pulled me to my feet and into his arms. "It doesn't scare me, you know. I just don't understand how it works." His breath ruffled my hair as he spoke.

"You're not the only one. I don't know how it works either. I only know that Dad used to use willow sticks to find underground water and I thought I'd try the technique to find lost things." His arms tightened around me. "It's magic."

"It does seem that way."

I leaned back a smidge and kissed him. "Let's go." I ripped the page from the notebook and shoved it in my pocket.

With the door locked and Ben's phone returned to him, we said goodbye to Steph who shook her fist in my direction then yelled, "She rang twice. She is on a roll!"

I closed the door and hurried down the stairs in case Nana rang back. She didn't ring my phone. That was odd. Usually, she tried every avenue known to her to get hold of me. Email, text messages, voice mail, phone calls, calls to work, popping in unannounced, and eventually summoning Donald. I didn't ponder too long on the whys and got in the car.

"Do you need anything while we are near the supermarket?"

"Don't think so," I replied. "I could do with a beer."

"Is there beer in the fridge at home?"

"Yes. And limes."

"Home then."

We couldn't talk in the car with Ben's phone in his pocket. So, I said nothing else.

It took two rude gestures and ten minutes to get home.

Ben grabbed the stubby holders while I sliced lime. What a team.

We were sitting in the lounge enjoying our beers when a Harley roared up the street.

"Wonder if that's Enzo or Crockett," I said, and took another deep drink from my beer bottle.

Chapter Twenty-six:
[Mitch: Back in the deep.]

A cell phone rang. Its trill disturbed the girls as they coloured at the dining room table. Grace looked up, her eyes searching the area in front of her. I could see her mother in those eyes. "Daddy!"

"Daddy!" Echoed Isabella. Always the echo.

"I'm coming," I said, as I levered myself out of the window seat in the living room. I crossed the room and smiled at the girls as I passed the table. "Nice job on the colouring."

I picked up my cell phone. Looked at the name on the screen then showed the girls. It rang on, in my hand.

Grace squealed, "Crockett!"

I answered the call as Grace asked if they could talk too. I held my index finger up to let them know they had to wait. Isabella smiled up at me.

"Crockett is nice," she said.

"Hey, Crockett. How's things?"

His voice crackled then came through crystal clear. "Good mate. How's it going with you three?"

"Same as always." I moved into the kitchen. "The girls would like to talk when we are done."

"I'd hoped they'd want to say hello."

"And you called me for?" I shifted a glass of water from the edge of the bench.

Grace looked up and said, "Sorry Daddy." I smiled at

her. I knew she was sorry. We'd broken enough glasses for all of us to be sorry.

"Just wanted to touch base mate. You reckon it's time yet?"

"Could be. What's your opinion?"

"I think we should immerse him in the whole shit-show and see what happens," Crockett said.

"That seems counterintuitive."

"The sooner the better, Mitch," Crockett said. "Why can't we just dump everything on him at once, and see what happens?"

"Because we've been playing within the guidelines provided by his psychologist and neurologist. They gave us a plan, remember?"

"I know. But we need to do something. We need to help him."

"How much does he know now?"

"A little more than before, but not much. He's got a name. He knows he's American. He thinks he might've been a cop. He knows, and now uses, ASL."

"Does he know we got him dual citizenship?"

"Not yet."

"He hasn't asked questions? Not even after my last visit?"

"He asked about his name. That's it. He remembered his brother. As far as I know he doesn't recognise me at all as someone from a previous life." Crockett paused. "But then, I didn't have a long relationship with him and Delta A. And I didn't have the crazy psychic bond that he had with Ellie, and she had with you."

That was true. We had a medically fascinating bond, or so SSA Dr Kurt Henderson and Dr Leon Kapowski told me once upon a time. I shut my eyes and leaned against the fridge.

"Show him some more pictures and let's see what happens?"

I wasn't sure if that was good or bad, as ideas went. Thinking positive thoughts hadn't got me very far this go-round. Of all the people to have survived hell, it was him. We could use him. If he could remember who he truly was and if his incredible brain still worked like it used to work. Too many ifs.

"Could you hop into his head like you could Ellie's?"

"No. Ellie, Dane, and Stewart all shared that ability with each other."

"Bet that made things interesting," Crockett said. "Pictures it is then."

"Have you shown him pictures of the girls?"

"Not yet. I've stuck to adults. I've alternated between photos of his brother and Delta A."

"And now he remembers his brother, maybe photos do make a difference."

"I've been throwing a few in of Caine Grafton and Director O'Hare as well."

"Should I be there this time?" My eyes pinged open. I visited every eight weeks. I noted that Dean didn't look much like a member of Delta A anymore. He was thinner and not himself. The guy I used to know was larger than life and enthusiastic about almost everything.

Thinking of the last visit to Dean pulled someone else into view. She had long dark blonde hair. There was a fine scar that ran from under her hair line down her temple and jaw and ended under her chin. There was another fine scar, which now looked more like a crease, under her left eye. She had half a leg missing. When I met Emily, all I could think was how much she reminded me of Ellie. She had familiar scars: one on her forehead and a big one inside her right forearm. She didn't hide them. Ellie always did. I thought that it was good that Emily didn't hide her scars. I considered why I felt that way and decided it meant they no longer meant anything to her, and she wasn't covering them to stop people staring or asking questions. The sacrifice was that people she once knew no longer meant anything to her either. It was a double-edged sword situation. The world was full of things that could slice you and spill your guts far and wide.

"Mitch? You still with me?"

"Yeah. Just thinking. Unhelpful thoughts."

"Share them?"

"No." Emily limped into view. Her blue eyes once held infinite knowledge and love, but now reflected very little of the woman she used to be. That was an understatement. They reflected what amounted to a blank slate. Just like Dean. Blank. But she was beginning to fill in the blanks. Emily's progress was incredible.

"Stay with the conversation, Mitch."

"Yep."

"You're due to come up in a couple of weeks, aren't you?"

"Yeah." I thought about what Ronnie had told me in the *Genesis* message system. I had to pass it on to Crockett. "Crockett we might have a problem."

"What?"

I couldn't exactly say Ronnie and Ben relayed intelligence via *Genesis* to me. "A report came to light. I've been asked about it. Someone is looking for Dane Wesson."

"Why?"

"I'm not sure. But I bet it has something to do with *The Wayward Son Protocol.* I just don't know what."

"That was Ellie's domain, yeah?"

"Not really, she was read into some of it when she first met Dane and Stewart. Back when O'Hare was the Director."

"How do you know?"

"You've forgotten I was married to her? She confided in me about various agency things with O'Hare's blessing because of my security clearance. I acted on Ellie's behalf a few times when she was incapacitated."

"I didn't know that." Crockett replied. "I didn't know her long enough to know that. I wish I had known her longer."

I wish she'd retired when I first suggested it. We all have wishes.

Chapter Twenty-seven:
[Ronnie: The visit.]

Wednesday rolled around far too quickly. After breakfast with Donald and Enzo, Ben and I disappeared into my bat cave.

I wanted to plug the address the pendulum gave us into a database or two. The idea was to find out who owned the house. I wanted to know if Dane owned it or if someone else did. I'm nosy like that. Didn't take long for a result to ping. The house was owned by a trust. We had a name for the trust, and a postcode, but not much else. It was a family trust, and we wouldn't be able to get much more information than we already had.

I typed the postcode into another database. 7281. It came back as Linkwater.

"That's the second time Linkwater has cropped up in the last week," I said, pointing to the screen.

Two seconds later a chat window opened.

Genesis: Anything that requires reporting?
Me: ...

I looked at Ben. "I have to tell them about Tierney."

He nodded. "We probably should have done that last night."

Me: Tierney is in town and Ben is working with him.

Tierney asked me to join.

Genesis: Anything else?

Me: The so-called terrorists tried to say they were Diamond Corp. Suspect false flag op. Made contact with Jackson Frost. He's still a dickhead. And he's still short.

Genesis: Leopards don't change their spots, Ronnie. Have you come across Sandra King or Steve Sadler?

Me: Not yet.

Genesis: Anything from Tierney?

Me: Not since he said he wanted us to look into the possibility that Dane Wesson survived. *The Wayward Son Protocol* is locked down and Wesson may be the only person who can ID an alias Tierney suspects is involved in the arms deal.

"That's either going to rock the boat, or sink it," Ben said.

We waited. No dots moved on the screen. The chat window swirled into a mosaic of pixels then vanished. We looked at each other and shrugged.

"That's weird, right?" Ben finally said.

"I don't know. Guess if my phone starts blowing with messages from *Uncle George,* we'll know how weird it was or not."

I shut everything down. Closed the door and returned my wardrobe to its usual state. I scanned Ben for signs he had his phone with him.

He didn't.

"Where is your phone?"

"Nightstand."

Good to know.

"I think I should've mentioned the Linkwater thing," I said, as we walked down the hall to the kitchen.

"We don't know what that means yet."

"True. Might be nothing."

We laughed.

Nothing is ever nothing.

"I'm not carrying my phone today. You'll have to keep in touch with Grandad for me, okay?"

"Absolutely."

I texted Grandad and told him we were going out and that we thought we would visit someone who might become a friend.

Grandad: Have fun you two. Don't forget about the old man.

Me: We won't forget you. Thank you for brunch yesterday.

Grandad: We should do dinner. I'd like to meet your grandmother.

Me: I'll consult her diary secretary (smiley face)

Ben had watched the text exchange over my shoulder. "Him and Nana in the same room ..."

"Worse, at the same table." I pocketed my phone. "They'll be skiing in Tahiti before that happens."

Ben chuckled but didn't refute my comment.

It didn't take long to get to Heretaunga Square and

find the house we were looking for. We walked up the path to the front door. There weren't any outward signs of life. I stepped up two steps to a small porch and knocked on the glass-panelled front door. Ben looked out into the street.

"Maybe he's out," I said, and rapped my knuckles on the glass again. No bell.

"Camera," Ben said, "In the eaves."

No one came to the door. "Shall we have a look around back? Maybe he's in the backyard." It wasn't really a question; I was already off the porch and walking around the side of the house. We found another three cameras. "He'll probably know we've been here. I'll leave one of my cards." I pulled a card from my bag and slipped it under the backdoor. "He might give us a call."

"We'll try back later," Ben said. He took my hand, and we went back to the car. We sat for a few minutes watching the house. Maybe he didn't like to answer the door. I could understand that. Maybe he was hiding.

We drove away.

"City?" Ben asked.

"Not much point. We can't ID her without knowing what she looks like. Unless, I guess, you recognise someone at the hotel. Or we ask at the front desk for Cassidy Tailor and get her to come down to the reception."

"Now, that's an idea."

"Is it a good one?"

"Let's go find out," Ben said. "We can swing back this way later. If he's still not home, we can set up surveillance and catch him that way."

Twinges of something were firing in my gut, possibly because if anyone tried that with Emily, I'd be livid, and someone would pay.

"What?" Ben said, catching my eye for a millisecond.

"Should we even be looking for him. He hasn't done anything wrong. He's not wanted. He's not a spy. He's someone who was hurt." I took a breath. "What if he's like Emily? Then us turning up and telling him he's an FBI agent, and they need him to open a program and find an alias, pushes him too far and he lashes out, or he falls through the injuries into a place no one can reach him?"

"Okay. Grandad said ..."

"Crockett might know more than we think."

Ben indicated, turned around and headed for Crockett's place. "If he knows. If he's been taking care of him, then we need to talk to him first," he said.

I agreed wholeheartedly. The last thing I wanted was to cause harm to someone like Dane Wesson or stomp all over Crockett's toes. He wore steel caps, and he would be harder on ours.

"I feel like we should've given him a heads up right away."

"All the more reason to talk to him now," Ben replied. "What is with the traffic?"

"No idea. Maybe we should've gone the back way?"

Bumper to bumper on Fergusson Drive was unusual during the day.

Chapter Twenty-eight:
[Mitch: Now what?]

Crockett called back after a disconnect.

"Everything all right?"

"Yep. Just a bad line I think."

"Gave me time to think. Perhaps the photos are a good idea."

"Okay. I'll start bringing out the photos before you arrive," Crockett said. His voice loud and clear in my ear. "Maybe a couple of days before."

Sunlight played upon the water catching my eye as I tried to concentrate on the call and Crockett's voice.

"Did you talk to his occupational therapist?" I asked.

"Yes. I thought you got the last report too," Crockett replied.

"I did."

"He might remember ..."

"And he might not."

"Have you thought about bringing the girls?"

"No. They weren't quite two last time they saw him. I don't want to risk it."

God, what if they recognised him like some form of imprinting even though he looks different to the photos we have? What would that do to them?

"They could be a powerful trigger. Might be time to consider it."

"I thought that too until the neurologist warned me

that the twins could be sensory overload and undo the little progress he's made." That was a very good reason to not subject my daughters to that situation. That was better than me saying I didn't want them to remember someone who was a big part of their lives before their second birthday.

"That's the guy from the States, right?"

"Yeah. Leon Kapowski."

"When's he back next?"

I opened my diary on the kitchen table and flicked through some pages. "Next week."

"That's earlier than I thought. I'll set everything up. Maybe bring your visit forward, Mitch. Once you and Kapowski are here we can crank the memory triggers. See what happens."

I sighed. I didn't mean to, but life happens.

"Mitch?" Crockett's voice echoed his sigh. "I know this has been a process. Mate, I feel for you."

"In case you don't know, I appreciate your role and the burden you took on." And the lies he's had to tell to keep him safe. Above all else, we had to protect Worcester/Wesson. It was better if the world thought that Crockett was the last man standing, because he wasn't Delta A. Dane meant a lot to Ellie and to our family. He was always there for her. For us. I remembered how awful it was when Dane's brother died. I remembered everything. Some days I wished I didn't. Dane was the last link to my wife and our former life.

"Jesus, Mitch. It's Dane Wesson. He's a fucking legend. It's a privilege. He survived the fucking impossible."

"Was. And now he's Dean Worcester."

"Come on. We don't know if this is definitely a *was* situation. And a far as I'm concerned, he still is a legend."

"Crockett, realism suggests otherwise."

Grace's voice rose, "Daddy! We want to talk to Crockett."

"Of course, Gracie."

Crockett's voice came in fast. "Before I talk to the girls … Why don't I bring him to you this time? Change of scenery might help."

I froze.

Isabella tugged my arm. "Our turn! You said, Daddy." Sometimes I heard her mother in her voice. It came through the most when she felt there was an injustice.

I stared at the phone. I had no answer. Would the girls wonder why he was here, and their mommy wasn't? Would they remember? Did I want to remember all the painful details?

"Give Daddy the phone when you are finished talking to Crockett, please."

"Yes, Daddy!" She squealed into the phone as I passed it to her. The girls ran back to the table giggling and talking at speed to Crockett. I almost felt sorry for him. Almost. They would be seven in a few days. Seven. Where did that time go?

While the girls talked, I went into the hallway and sat on the stairs. My thoughts wandered to a fictitious scenario. I thought about what it would be like to bring Ellie home if she was in limbo like Dane. She'd be blindsided, completely out of her comfort zone such as it was. All progress could be lost. It was dangerous.

Would Ellie tolerate 'could'?

A loud crack resounded in my head. It's not Ellie. It's Dane. It could've been Ellie, but it's not, it's Dane. If Ellie were here, she'd go with her gut.

My gut was wrapped up in keeping our daughters safe. It hadn't had an opinion on Ellie in three years, when hope abandoned me. Why start now? She was gone. Our connection was lost. She disappeared in a drone strike. They all did, apart from Crockett and Dane Wesson and he may as well have. Because it was not him, I'd been visiting all these years. It was the person he'd become and that was a far cry from the Dane Wesson I knew. It was the hope I visited, hope that maybe Ellie was out there somewhere. Alive. I knew in my heart that was unhelpful and impossible.

I listened to the girls telling Crockett about their drawings and that they caught a fish last week. It brought a smile to my lips. It wasn't last week; it was last month. They were still a bit young for a sense of time and days. Everything was last week. I sat back on the stairs. Yesterday was gone. Should I be letting memories of El go too?

I rubbed my face and ran my hands through my short hair. If I had her back, I'd be dropping her into the operation I'm running. I corrected myself, *Genesis* was running. The only reason I didn't hook Crockett into *Genesis* was Dane Wesson. I needed Crockett there for Dane.

Ronnie and Ben were good, they'd find a take-down and stop the deal. They'd also find Dane if I didn't do something about it. I'd authorised them to bring in anyone required. And I knew that meant Crockett would be involved at some stage, and if he was, he could run interference and keep Dane hidden, maybe. My knuckles cracked as I flexed them. Once Ben went missing, I knew Crockett would step up and help Ronnie. Enzo would, too. They worked well together. They were a team, just not an official one. Even so they reminded me a little of Ellie's team.

Welcome to this crazy world, where a relative nobody like me became the new head of *Genesis*. I was aware that Ronnie suspected Tom and Ginny as being the top tier of the organisation. That was purposeful. It was better to have nothing that came back to me. I was an unknown - a wild card. It was safer to stay that way.

In some ways, bringing Dean here would be a better option than me going up there again. It would mean I could still monitor communications and keep an eye on the current operation, and the other ops that were simultaneously running across SE Asia and Oceania. It was a smart move to keep the head of this branch of the organisation within New Zealand and tucked away in the Marlborough Sounds. MacKinnon set it all up well before his untimely death. My name was never to hit the airways or even make it to interagency gossip. I was not an intelligence officer, but I did have a current very high security clearance. I'd maintained that since moving to New Zealand. I also still co-owned a US tech company. The company still had US government contracts. I was still designing drones and other devices. Apart from *Genesis,* I had zero ties to any sort of intelligence gathering agency.

As far as my world, and the rest of the world knew, everyone from Delta A was killed executing a mission on New Zealand soil, along with a Russian, an American civilian, and some Kiwi detectives. There were a lot of dead heroes that night and a lot of pain.

Tragic didn't even begin to describe it. I remembered it as if it were yesterday. I felt it happen. The panic as she slipped away from me. All of a sudden, I was there again. Smoke, destruction, and fire filled my mind. Through a veil of mist, I saw Sam reach for her and hold her close. She'd died doing what she loved: being a fucking hero. She knew more than anyone that death was preferable to a vegetative state. So, when Dane opened his eyes and started responding it was miraculous. He was up and living as best he could as a blank slate. He was a man that was hard to kill. He just refused to die. Ellie was a wife and mother who couldn't hold on because the end was too violent and destructive.

Isabella appeared in front of me and held out the phone.

"Bye Daddy," she said, and ran back to join Grace.

I looked at the screen. Crockett was still there. I put the phone to my ear and walked into my bedroom.

"Bring him down."

"You sure?"

"Yes. I'll let Leon know. He can adjust his travel accordingly. I pay him enough that that shouldn't be a problem."

"You alright?"

"Yes." No.

"Bring him to the house?"

"No. I'll book a motel in Picton. I know a place. It'll be perfect."

And the girls will have their nanny taking care of them. I was not exposing them to the shell that used to be their mother's colleague and friend, to the memory of the person who would play with them for hours. A person they loved.

"I'll see you then. Send me details. When is Leon due to arrive again?"

"Next Friday."

"Good. We should have this situation here wrapped up by then."

I had a thought. "Have you taken him to ground zero?"

"Yeah. We walked past it a few weeks ago. He asked what they were building, but didn't react at all to the place."

"How's Emily?" I thought I'd better ask. Crockett was waist deep in special people.

"She's doing a lot better."

"Does she know?" I was curious as to how much of Emily was coming back.

"No. She's friends with Dean, but she doesn't know who he was. I told him he can't tell her his real name."

"Good thinking. And she has no idea what he used to do?"

"No. Dane doesn't know who he was and what he did, so that's not a surprise."

"That's what I don't get. She was on the premises when the strike hit. And she's doing so much better than Dean."

"Different people. And she was in a car. It was indirect whereas Dean was right in the thick of it," Crockett said, I heard him swallow. "I'm sorry. This must be hard on you. Re-living that night non-stop."

"I guess." Not as hard as it would be for Crockett. He was there. His life was on the line. He had to deal with survivor guilt every day. "How much does Emily know?"

"No memory of the strike at all. The story holds. Everyone who knows her believed she was in a car crash and lost her leg in the field," he said.

"Good that she can't remember. Thanks for everything, Crockett. See you soon."

I hung up and threw the phone onto my bed. My mind was made up. We'd try one more time to trigger something that I hoped Dean could grasp and build on. If it didn't happen then he could live out his life in anonymity doing whatever it was that brought him joy. I would continue taking very good care of him but move on with my life. Perhaps the time had come to put that night, and the huge loss of my wife and her entire team, to bed.

Chapter Twenty-nine:
[Ronnie: Will he tell the truth?]

We let ourselves through the back gate. I knocked on the door. The door swung open. Crockett had an iPad in his hand.

"Thought you'd show up sooner or later," he said, darkening the screen before I could see what he was looking at. "Come in, take a pew. Looks like we need to have a conversation."

Ben closed the door behind us. We sat on his couch and Crockett pulled up an armchair, so we were closer. There was no need for talking loudly across the room. "Start talking."

"We know Dane Wesson is alive," I said. "We need to talk to him."

Crockett shook his head slowly. "There'll be no talking."

"He is alive?" I asked.

He gave the smallest nod.

"Can we see him?" Ben asked. "We need to talk to him."

"You really do not," he said.

"I left him a card. He might ring me without telling you," I said, with a smile.

"He won't ring."

"It's important Crockett," I said. "Really important. He can ID someone who could be behind the arms deal."

"Trust me when I say Dane Wesson cannot ID anyone and will not call you."

That was when I realised, I was right, and Dane was damaged beyond Emily. And I did not relish the prospect of tipping his precarious world upside down for the sake of an ID.

"We might have another way," I said. "Might be able to use Ben, if we can clap eyes on the person. She might look familiar enough for him to at least say that's someone he saw at the ball." I took a beat. "That's not going to give a positive ID, but it's better than nothing."

"Do you want a hand?" Crockett asked.

"That would be good," I replied. "I still want to meet Dane Wesson."

"You can meet him. You can't run back to Tierney with this and say he's alive."

Ben and I gave Crockett a look.

"All right," Ben said. "We can say he was wrong. That there was no sign of Wesson."

"How sure was he that Wesson was alive?"

"There was something about a protocol that refused to accept his death certificate. I don't know what that was really about. Sounded like a glitch to me," Ben said. "Do you know anything about a protocol that involved Dane Wesson?"

Crockett shook his head. "I know someone who might. If you really want to find out. But you can't take it back to Tierney. This is need to know, and he doesn't. All he needs to know is you can't find any evidence of him being alive."

I nodded. "We can do that."

"How'd you find him?" Crockett asked. Then he smiled, touched his thumb and index finger together and circled in the air. "That's how, right?"

"Yep," Ben said. "She did her thing."

"And you were there?"

I nudged Ben. "Not just me that thought you were scared of dowsing."

"I'm not scared of it." Ben attempted a scowl but failed.

"Wesson isn't home, or did you tell him not to answer the door?" I asked Crockett.

"I told him not to answer the door."

"The cameras. You monitor them."

"I do."

"You love a camera, don't you?"

"I do. The more the merrier."

"He might ring me anyway, you know," I said. "Curiosity is a powerful thing."

"He won't ring you, Ronnie."

Okay then. He won't ring.

"Are you one-hundred percent sure that he can't ID the person for us?" Ben asked. "One-hundred percent."

"I am."

"Do you know what *The Wayward Son Protocol* is?"

He shook his head. "I wasn't FBI, so if it was something to do with anyone in the FBI, I wouldn't know about it."

"You never heard anyone mention it?"

"Ronnie, I don't know what it is." Crockett shook his head. "The sort of people we are talking about did not share readily, nor did they gossip."

Fair enough.

"Can we at least meet Dane?"

"If I say yes, do not upset him."

"All right."

Twenty-minutes flew by and involved a small lecture from Crockett on how we were to behave. He texted Dane and said he was bringing friends over to meet him. And we left.

Chapter Thirty:
[Crockett: Here's Dane!]

Dean, because he had been Dean to me for too long to flip back to Dane overnight, was waiting inside his open front door. He waved in an understated way like blokes do.

"Hi ya, Dean. You good?"

He nodded and signed okay.

He beckoned us to follow him, and we did. He walked into the dining room and sat at the table while motioning us to do the same.

"Introductions," I said. "This is Ronnie Tracey and Ben Reynolds. Ronnie and Ben, this is Dean."

Dean signed: Famous actor.

Ben smiled and replied, "Only sometimes."

Dean looked at Ronnie then signed: Famous grandmother.

She shook her head. "Not famous," she said as she signed. "Nana is a troublemaker."

Dean laughed.

"Everyone knows sign," I said. "Well, that makes life easier."

Ronnie cocked her head to one side. "Dean, why sign language?"

I imagine she worked out quickly that he's not deaf.

Dean signed: Speech is hard.

Now there's an understatement.

"Fair enough," Ben said. "But you don't need to talk to get your point across." He signed while he spoke.

Dane had watched his hands then replied: American like me.

"Yes, I am."

"Did you know me?"

"No, I didn't," Ben replied. "It's a big country."

They both laughed. "New Zealand is small. I know you from TV."

"Don't believe everything you see, Dean. TV is much more exciting than real life."

It was nice seeing Dean chatting (even in sign) and enjoying himself.

Ronnie smiled at Dean, and I could see the question before she spoke.

"Do you remember coming to New Zealand?"

Dean shook his head while signing: Long time ago. Memory not good.

He picked up his iPad from a dresser behind him and typed. Siri said, "I don't remember coming here or not being here."

"That must be annoying," Ronnie said.

Dean typed, Siri spoke, "Sometimes. Less annoying now. I have friends and can do some stuff without help."

"What about family?" Ronnie asked. "Do you have family."

He typed quickly, Siri spoke, "No. Had a brother once."

I watched for signs that Dean was tired or getting irritated with the questions. He was handling it okay. That was new. Usually on about question three, he was done.

He typed, Siri said, "What do you do Ronnie? I know Ben is an actor."

"I'm a private investigator. Used to work for our government before that."

More typing led to Siri asking, "Work for the government, what sort of work?"

"I gathered intelligence."

"Spy," Siri said.

Ronnie nodded. "I was an officer with the New Zealand Security Intelligence Service."

"Good job?"

"Yes, most of the time. Travelled a lot. Saw a great deal of the world." Ronnie smiled. "What did you do before ... before you came here?"

Dean looked straight into her eyes and froze. Everything went quiet. We waited. He finally blinked and typed. "I am not Dean," Siri said. He looked at me and shook his head then tapped the screen again. "I am not Dean."

"You are Dean to me," I said, while watching to see where this was going.

He typed, then stopped, then typed again. Then deleted whatever he'd typed and started again. "I am Dane Wesson. I am Dane Wesson. I am a special agent with the Federal Bureau of Investigation. My name is Dane Wesson. I am broken," Siri said.

Bugger me days, he knows who he is.

Ronnie stuck her hand out towards Dean. "I am very

pleased to meet you, Dane," she said, and he shook her hand.

Ben did the same, then said, "It is a pleasure to meet you, Special Agent Wesson."

Dane face brightened like a light flicked on. He smiled then typed fast on the iPad.

"I am Dane Wesson. My brother was Stewart Smith. There was something special about us, but I don't know what it was. I wish to know, but I can't remember," Siri said.

Ronnie looked at me. I shook my head. She stared at me and nodded. I shook my head. No. Don't do it. She was going to do it.

"Dane," Ronnie said. "I am going to tell you something that I know about you."

He didn't type. He didn't move.

"Not wise," I said to Ronnie, softly. "Not wise."

Dean's head swung my way. He typed. "Crockett, you know?" Siri asked. "You know?"

"I don't know much," I said. "Not much, Dean, not much."

He was tapping on the iPad, frustration flying from his fingers. "You know more than me. I am Dane."

Ronnie interrupted us, "Dane, if I tell you what I know, will you listen?"

He nodded. Then typed. "Yes, I will listen, and Crockett will listen, then talk," Siri said.

"You were an agent assigned to something called *The Wayward Son Protocol*. You were in a danger close situation with your team, here in New Zealand. You were with Delta A. They were an elite team within the criminal investigation department of the FBI," Ronnie said quietly. "Well, look at that, I knew more than I thought." she smiled.

Dane remained silent. He kept his attention on Ronnie, until I spoke.

"Looks like we're just going to rip the band-aid right off. No finesse, no building up to it."

Ronnie looked at me. "You've had a while to do that, and haven't?"

"We've been following the guidelines set by a neurologist."

"We?" Ronnie asked.

"Me," I corrected.

I hadn't noticed Dane typing until Siri started talking. "Danger close. Danger close. All for one."

All for one was what Dane, Lee, and Kurt said right before the explosion. Ellie had whispered *Danger Close* into our comms. And the last thing I heard was her team saying, 'All for one.' All of a sudden, I was right there in the smoke and flames, choking, gurgling, death and destruction. I felt a hand on my arm - firm pressure. Then I heard Ben's calm voice, "Crockett, you with us?"

I took a few deep breaths. "I'm good." My vision cleared. No more smoke. "Dane? You okay?"

Colour had drained from his face. It was too much. We'd gone too far. This was a disaster. He looked shattered. There was nothing for what felt like minutes but was probably seconds. Time gets screwy when memories like that surface. They were all good people. All of them. Now it was just me and Dane. That was marginally better than when it was just me who remembered the night when the gates of hell opened and sucked the life from good people. I'd done a pretty good job of burying that shit.

"What's happening?" Ben asked. The question was directed to me.

"Things that should stay buried are now free ranging."

"I'm sorry," Ronnie said. I could tell she meant it, but it didn't help.

Pandora's fucking box was open, and it was going to take a lot to get the lid back on it, and maybe some big chains and an anchor to weigh the fucker down.

Dane typed, Siri said, "Did we win?"

"Yes. We won," I said. "That's why the rest of us are still standing."

Dane smiled. "Worth it," Siri said.

Was it?

Was it really?

The price we paid was steep.

Siri spoke again, "You should have told me before."

"I couldn't tell you before, Dane. I didn't want to talk about it, and I couldn't tell you because you weren't well enough to hear."

I'd weighed it all up over the years. Trying to find a hint of the real Dane Wesson, or enough of him so I could talk to him about it all. But until today, he was Dean

Worcester. Ironically, that was his given name. But he'd gone by Dane Wesson since he was first hooked into *The Wayward Son Protocol*. His brother, too, had his name changed for the protocol. It was an attempt at humour, I think, on someone's part. Smith and Wesson. It never sat right with me, the FBI having a sense of humour. I knew a lot more than I was willing to share with Ronnie and Ben, thanks to long days fishing with Mitch.

I had no idea where we were going from here. I guessed there was no point pretending Dane was dead now. I pulled my phone out and made a call.

Mitch answered on the third ring. "What's up?"

"We can stop hiding him now," I said, not caring that Ben, Ronnie, and Dane were listening. "He knows. I don't know how okay he is, but he knows who he is."

Siri spoke, "Who is on the phone?"

"Mitch," I said. "I'm talking to Mitch. Remember him?"

Dane nodded then typed. "Mitch visits me," Siri said. I watched Dane's face. Something happened. It went from something I'd seen a hundred times - a sort of blankness to life and animation. He typed. "Mitch was married to Ellie," Siri said.

And the world stopped turning.

Mitch's voice thickened when he said, "I heard that."

"Yeah, he's back. I've gotta go. I wanted you to know. Maybe talk to Leon and see what he has to say about this rapid change."

"I'll give him a call. Do the math, find the right time,

and give him a call. Pass the phone to Dane."

I did.

He listened and gave it back. Then he typed for Siri. "Mitch said, welcome home."

I hung up. My head was spinning, and I could only imagine what Dane's was doing. Cartwheels would probably be close.

"Hey, about the alias," Ben said, his eyebrows rising as he looked in my direction. "Is this a 'strike while the memories are surfacing' situation, or a 'we should wait a bit' situation?"

"I've got no fucking idea. This is all new territory. I guess we'll have to play it by ear, unless Mitch gets hold of Leon and he has other ideas. Maybe a road trip is in order?"

Chapter Thirty-one:
[Ronnie: Roady.]

"We have to go. There is someone else we need to find. Someone we hoped Dane could ID," Ben said.

Dane typed. "I don't know if I can," Siri said.

"You didn't think today would happen either," Crockett replied.

"That's for sure," Siri said.

I was starting to think of Siri as Dane.

"Do you want to try?" I asked.

Dane nodded and pointed to Crockett.

"Probably a good idea for him to come." Just in case. "Okay, Crockett?"

Crockett hadn't looked okay since Dane had said 'All for one'. He looked spooked, shaken, a bit iffy, and not his usual confident (some would say cocky) self.

"Sure. Let's get this clown show on the road," Crockett said.

"Circus," Ben replied. "It's a circus."

"My oath it is," Crockett said with zero humour.

Dane laughed.

A thought surfaced and I voiced it. "How careful do we need to be with Dane as far as recognition goes?"

"He hasn't been far. Moderately, I'd say."

"What are you trying to avoid?"

"People taking photos or video destined for the internet. He doesn't look exactly like he used to, but his biometrics haven't changed. And they don't lie."

"Do you think anyone who knew him would recognise him?" I asked. I wanted to know how careful we needed to be.

"I think they would do a double take then dismiss it because he's dead," he replied. "Dead, remember that. We've resurrected the dead. And that's going to have challenges."

"Got it."

"So, we go and see what happens?" Ben asked.

"Let's do it," Siri said from the table. Dane was already on his feet. He vanished down the hallway. We followed and found him at the front door, pulling on a leather jacket.

"One car?" Ben asked. "No one with objections?"

None of us objected. Dane had his hand on the front door handle.

"Wait please," Crockett said as he checked his phone.

"Camera check?" I asked with a smile. I knew what he was like.

"Pays to be cautious," he said. "It's all clear. Carry on."

I guessed Dane was also used to Crockett's caution. I knew Crockett set up alerts for cameras he had installed at the bookshop and at Emily's place, and I'd bet all the afternoon teas in the world that he'd done the same for Dane's house. So, him checking, was a 'just in case' move. Enzo did the same thing at our place with cameras and alerts set that pinged on his phone and mine. He too was serious about security and keeping his family safe. It meant I could spend less time worrying about Donald and Nana when she was visiting him unsupervised.

Ben drove. Crockett called shotgun. Dean and I were happy in the back. Dean had left his iPad on the table, so he asked to use my phone to talk. I opened Notes.

Me: What do you remember about *The Wayward Son Protocol*?
Dane: It's classified. Director's eyes only.

That was good. He remembered the security clearance required.

Me: What if I said the new Director cannot access it because it wouldn't accept your death certificate?

I handed Dane the phone and looked out the window at the traffic, not really taking anything in, just looking.
Dane tapped my arm and gave me the phone.

Dane: That shouldn't happen.
Me: Humour me

I handed my response to him.
We'd crossed Silverstream bridge, and the scenery changed on my side, to a golf course and the river.
Dane passed the phone back.

Dane: I don't know why that would happen.

Did he not remember or not want to say?

I nodded and went back to watching the scenery. Seemed a smart idea to stop pushing and just look out the window. The ever-changing view held appeal.

"Alright back there?" Ben asked.

"Yep," I replied.

My thoughts occupied me until we were in the city and the hunt for a parking spot began. They were as scarce as hen's teeth, as Nana would say. It was a weekday. I was less than thrilled at the prospect of being stuck in rush hour traffic trying to make our way back to the Hutt. It is what it is. I doubted this next part of the equation would be quick.

"If there isn't a parking space on our next go-around the block, I'll park up by the embassy and we'll walk down," Ben said.

"Let's hope you find a park. Taking our passenger anywhere near the embassy could be a disaster," Crockett said.

No one wanted a disaster.

Ben found a park. Two abreast we made our way to Maginnity Street and the old-time beauty that was The Wellesley Hotel. I felt safer off the street and in the hotel lobby. I approached the reception desk manned by a well-dressed, well-presented man.

"Hello," I said. "We are supposed to meet with one of your guests." I scanned the man for a name tag but couldn't see one.

"What is the guest's name? I can look it up for you."

"Cassidy Tailor," I said, then checked my watch. "We're a few minutes late."

"That's not a name I recognise. We're a very small hotel and have thirteen rooms. Six are occupied.

"Could you check anyway?"

He nodded and consulted his computer then looked up at me. "Sorry ma'am, Cassidy Tailor is not registered."

Dane stepped up beside me and signed that he needed my phone. I glanced at it to unlock it for him. He wrote then handed the phone to me.

Dane: Try Caroline Tilson

"Could you try Caroline Tilson, please?"

He did as he was asked, with a smile. "I can tell you without checking that Caroline Tilson checked out two hours ago. You are quite late for that meeting."

"Thank you," I said. Dane nodded at the man.

I turned to walk away, then had a different thought. "Excuse me. Would you describe Ms Tilson for me? Just in case it's not the right person?"

"That's a little out of the ordinary, but yes. Mid-fifties, greying brown hair - she wears her hair in a ponytail."

"Height?"

"Shorter than you. I'd say around the one-hundred-and-sixty-centimetre mark. I wouldn't say she was large, but she wasn't slim. Average middle-aged woman. I suppose."

"Glasses?"

"To read, I think."

"Thank you." I turned to Dane. "Does that sound like your Aunt?"

He shrugged. As you'd expect, it wasn't the best description ever.

Turning back to the man at the reception desk, I said, "You don't know where she was going? She's becoming forgetful. Could well put herself in harm's way." I turned to Ben. "Can you believe she's forgotten all about us?"

Crockett piped up, "And she's forgotten her name."

Ben chuckled. "One big crazy family. Good thing we are here to take care of her."

The concierge smiled at us. "Will that be all, ma'am?"

"You don't know where she was going?" Ben asked.

He smiled at Ben. "Another American, how delightful," he said, his voice flattening. "Of course, you would be American, wouldn't you."

He didn't appear to recognise Ben from the telly, so that was a bonus.

"Aunt Caroline is American," Ben replied.

"Yes, sir, she certainly is. I'm very sorry. I do not know where Ms Tilson was going from here."

And with that, we hurried back to the relative safety of the car with nothing lost and something gained. We had another name, and confirmation that she was American. I chose to sit in the back again, I wanted to make notes. Dane remembered a name. Was it her real name?

That was a question for Dane.

"Dane, is Caroline Tilson her real name?"

He nodded, smiled, and gestured for my phone. I handed it over and signed the passcode. Easier if he could unlock it himself.

"Everyone good back there?" Ben asked.

Thumbs up from Dane. "All good," I said.

"Time to high-tail it out of dodge," Crockett said.

"Ben, do you think Tilson slash Tailor will be at the ball on Saturday?"

"I hope so," Ben replied. "We stand a chance of finding out if she's involved if we can get close to her."

"If not?" Siri said.

"Then we need a new plan," Ben said.

"Did you tell me what you think she is involved in?" Siri asked.

"Arms deal," I said. "We think she might have an involvement in an illegal arms deal."

Crockett twisted in his seat so he could see us. "We have intelligence that says an arms deal that was scuppered in Poland and Thailand, has moved to New Zealand."

Dane typed. Siri spoke, "And you think Caroline Tilson aka Cassidy Tailor is behind it, or somehow involved?"

"Yes," we all answered at once.

Dane typed again. "Why her?" Siri asked.

"That's what we don't know," Ben replied. "We would like to know."

"I don't remember seeing either name on the guest list," I said. "She may have a second alias."

My phone alerted. Dane handed it to me.

Ben's Grandad: You were in the city and didn't visit.
Me: We were checking an engagement venue.
Ben's Grandad: Did you have joy?
Me: No. We will try a different venue.

"What's happening?" Ben asked. "You're suddenly quiet and texting."

"Grandad knew we were in the city," I said.

"Then we were seen," Ben replied. "That's not good."

"How not good?" Crockett asked.

"About as not-good as it gets," Ben replied. "Let's get Dane home."

"Let's ditch my car," I said. "Go to Naenae. We're garaging this car and picking up another one. He'll have my plates and be using traffic cams to keep an eye on where we go."

"We'll get off the highway at Petone and head towards Woburn; stick to the back roads on the Eastern side of the valley," Ben said.

"Good thinking," I replied.

Dane tapped my arm, I handed him my phone and watched as he used the passcode and opened Notes. I watched traffic while he typed. I noticed Ben checking the rearview mirror more often than he usually did.

"Have we picked up a tail?" I asked.

"Not sure. We'll know when we exit," he replied. "There's a grey SUV three cars back."

I knew not to turn around and look no matter how much I wanted to see who it could be. Crockett used the wing mirror.

"Could be right," he said.

Dane handed me the phone. An entire screen of questions met my eyes.

Dane: Who is Ben's Grandad?

Why are you worried enough to change cars?

Who would be following us?

Why would someone be following us?

Is this about me or about Tilson?

What is going on?

This is frustrating. I want to talk. I want to be part of this. I want to go home.

Who is Ben's grandad? Did he know Tierney, before?

"Crockett, Dane wants me to answer some questions. They include who Ben's grandad is." Figured he needed a heads up.

"Go easy, Ronnie," Crockett said.

"I will."

I moved in my seat so I could see Dane easier. "It's been a big day for you and your brain. I am going to answer your questions, but you need to be honest. If it's too much tell me to stop."

He nodded.

"Ben's Grandad is a codename. It's a codename we use for a man called Jonathon Tierney."

Dane stared unblinking at me. Had I broken him with the first answer? It felt like it took forever for him to respond. Second ticked over into minutes.

"Are you alright?" I asked.

His stare continued, but in his eyes I could see processing. He wasn't blank. He was processing the name and trying to make sense of what was happening. His hand shot out and took my phone. He took a deep breath, unlocked the phone, and typed. Then gave me the phone.

Dane: Jonathon Tierney is CIA. He helped us. He helped Ellie. He sent Cooper. Cooper had eyes in the sky. When Ellie called danger close it was a CIA drone that both killed everyone and saved everyone.

I reached out and squeezed Dane's hand.

"That's a lot you need to process. A lot that for you is still fresh," I said. "Take all the time you need."

That's the thing with shit like this. If it's a buried memory or a locked memory and it suddenly hits the air, it makes it a fresh wound all over again. He didn't have five years to work through it like Crockett. If Crockett did work through it. Maybe he pushed it away and tried to man it out.

"You ready for me to answer more questions, or is that enough for now?"

Dane reached for my phone and wrote.

I could see what he said: Tell me more, please.

So, I did.

I told him everything I knew about the current situation, and all I knew about the situation that landed him in New Zealand, which was not much. I'd had the official line. An explosion at the research facility in Wallaceville and I'd heard Crockett's abridged version.

Chapter Thirty-two
[Crockett: When it rains.]

I stayed with Dane. My car was there anyway. Dane wanted to talk, he wanted to know details. The last thing I wanted to talk about was the day Delta A and so many other people lost their lives. It didn't matter that we won. It didn't matter at all. Not when I've watched Mitch, and the girls, try to move past devastation. Not when I've lived it. Not now, when Dane needs to know, and have a chance to process it all for himself.

"We're gonna need beer," I said, lowering myself into an armchair in his lounge.

I'd seen the look on his face before, but this time it was different. This time it was Dane not Dean.

He signed: Beer on the way.

He handed me a beer and sat opposite me in an armchair. He had his iPad. I guess he didn't want to put his beer down to sign. I couldn't blame him.

And it began. Straight back into hell without any preamble.

Dane typed.

"How did Ellie die?" Siri asked. "Were you with her? Why didn't you and I die? What happened to Kurt and Lee?"

"Hold your horses, pal. Let's ask one question at a time." I took another swig of beer to soften the blow. "Ellie died in a drone strike. It was almost instant, so they told me."

Dane was typing. "Almost?" Siri asked.

"That's as good as it gets, Dane. I'm moving to your second question." I took another swig of beer and gave a new answer. "I wasn't with her, nor were you. We were on our way to her position. She was with Kurt and maybe Cooper. I'm not sure." I don't want to think about this too much, or too long. It would help no one.

"Cooper?"

"Remember him the CIA dude? Tierney sent him to us. He got us the eyes in the sky and strike capability."

He nodded. "I remember. He killed Ellie," Siri said.

I shook my head. "No, Dane, Ellie made the call. Ellie called in the strike fully aware of what would happen. We signed up to be danger close. There was no other way in the end."

And the afternoon drifted into evening, and beersies went down one after the other, until we made dinner.

The more we talked the more Dane sounded like Dane, well, a robotic AI version of himself. I couldn't remember what his voice sounded like, but it didn't sound like the American male Siri.

"Who is Mitch?" Siri asked.

It took a while for that question to surface. I could tell Dane was tired. He knew who Mitch was earlier just like he knew who Cooper was. I told him anyway. "Mitch Iverson, he was Ellie's husband."

Dane smiled. "Kids," Siri said. He typed some more. "Two. Don't know names."

"Grace and Isabella," I said. "I met them after the strike."

Dane typed some more. "Now? Where do I go from here?"

I shrugged. "Dunno. Where do you want to go?"

Dane typed for Siri. "Don't know."

"How about we take a break, get some sleep, and worry about what could be next, another day?"

He nodded, then shook his head. He typed.

"What if this is gone tomorrow? What if I can't remember again?"

"Do you think that could happen?" I had no idea. I never expected to be answering questions about the fucking night that changed our worlds. I didn't expect anything like that to ever happen.

Dane shrugged then typed. I waited for Siri to speak.

"How did it happen today? It just did, right?"

I shook my head. "No, first you remembered you knew ASL. I think this memory return was on the cards we just didn't know it."

Dane plugged the iPad in to charge. He signed: Stay tonight. Too much beer to drive.

I agreed.

He grabbed me a couple of blankets and a pillow, then said goodnight.

His couch was comfy. I'd be fine.

Chapter Thirty-three:
[Mitch: Coming home.]

"We need him operational." Assistant Director Thomas's voice grated through the airways and pissed me off. Who did that dick think he was? He's FBI. He's not CIA. He's not *Genesis*. He's not calling the shots. He's got no right to give me orders. "Did you think I wouldn't find out he was alive?"

"How did you find out?" I wanted to see if Thomas would say Tierney passed the intel to him.

"It doesn't matter. He was seen. Alive."

"I think it does matter. Doppelgängers and all that. They say everyone has one."

"Mitch, you know damn well it was Dane Wesson, and he was seen alive in Wellington, New Zealand. Yesterday. Wasn't he?" He took a beat. "We need him operational."

"It's not going to happen."

"It has to," he said.

"No. I'm sure it's being handled by more suitable people." This was a *Genesis* operation not the FBI's. But also, it was a CIA operation. Sometimes those FBI suits think they're the only people in the world who can do anything. They're wrong. They're idiots.

"He's our ace. He walks into that ball and our resurrected former agent will lose her head."

"You're assuming she knows who he was?" That's dangerous. "He doesn't know who he was/is so how will that help?" I decided that denial could work. Deny Dean knew he was Dane Wesson. Deny he was partially operational. I'd stopped denying he was alive. But alive and living a full life are two different things. It would not be in Dean/ Dane's best interests to be thrown into a high-intensity situation.

"All we need is for them to realise he's alive. Doesn't matter if he knows anything or not. It will be enough."

"You can't un-play that card. There's no walking him back. And you seriously think that the threat of him will halt whatever is happening?"

"I do."

"That's a lot to put on the memory of an agent."

"He isn't just an agent, Iverson."

"Brain dead legend, that work better for you?"

"I didn't expect callousness."

"It's true. Not callous."

"Technology is only as good as the person using it."

"He's not tech, Thomas, he is a human being."

"Isn't he? How much of him did our government re-build?"

"I don't know. What are you saying? That he's the bionic fucking man to be used as you see fit?"

"I don't understand the reference."

"Of course, you don't, you fucking millennial." Thomas was the youngest director yet, and it showed.

"You don't have to use that type of language."

"I think you should consult the accounts department. You'll find I paid for ninety percent of his care and rehab.

So, fuck off with your 'we rebuilt him' mentality."

"He is still ours, there was no resignation, and we want him deployed to a combined FBI and CIA operation."

"No resignation? Medically he is unfit for duty. I don't think *no resignation* comes into it."

"There's no paperwork discharging him from duty."

"Seriously? There was no paperwork? That's the biggest load of bullshit I've ever heard."

"It is not a request. We want him deployed. He's the only one who can do this."

"You must be confusing me with one of your employees."

"That's not what I meant."

"Neither of us work for you. If you've somehow lost the paperwork, I will resend it."

"Why are you so resistant to letting Wesson do his job?"

"It's not his job anymore. He doesn't even know he was FBI."

"I find that hard to believe. He was a brilliant agent and huge asset. And you are telling me he doesn't *know* that?" There was a sharp intake of breath. "You're telling me that the only surviving member of Delta A, and the person who was last assigned to *The Wayward Son Protocol* because of his brilliant mind, doesn't know anything?"

"You saw the medical reports. You know that's true."

"What I know, Mitch, is that I was sent a death certificate for an agent who is very much alive. Do you know what that means?"

I did know, but denial was now the only way forward.

"That someone made an error?"

A callous laugh echoed down the line. "An error. More like kidnapping a federal employee and holding him against his will, manufacturing his death. I sincerely hope you didn't collect any death benefits."

"He was never held against his will, Thomas. He doesn't know who he is. And was never expected to live past day three." I was trying to remain calm and not let Thomas rile me; it was not easy.

"And the medical reports? I'm sure they were true at the time," Thomas said. "Are they true now?"

All I could think about was how pissed Ellie would be at this asshole wanting to force one of her team into a job he couldn't possibly do.

"Of course, they were true. And still are."

"It's been sometime since the *accident*. Things must have changed."

"They haven't changed. I'm out. Dane Wesson no longer exists. You are not going anywhere near the man he now is." I tapped a key and woke my laptop from its slumber. "You'll be hearing from my lawyers."

I hit the end call button and placed the phone on the desk. I gave the situation and Dane a few seconds thought; I didn't need more than that to know what I needed to do. I picked the phone up and called Crockett. We had to get Dane somewhere safe. It was our job to take care of him the way Ellie would have. *The Wayward*

Son Protocol was no longer Dane's problem.

He answered on the third ring. "Hey, what's up?"

"I need you to move him now. He can't remain where he is. FBI want to use him in a joint op. We can't let that happen."

"Shit. Okay. I'm at his house. Where am I taking him?"

"Somewhere they won't find him."

"I've still got friends," Crockett said. "I can hide him up here unless ... if I get him to you, will he be safe?"

"Yes. We have security personal onsite because of the twins. They're O'Hare Security."

"Excellent. I'm bringing him to you. Today. Be ready."

"We will be."

I hung up and made one more call to O'Hare Security and asked for two more teams for a protective detail. It still felt strange calling O'Hare's and not hearing Sean O'Hare's voice. Diego Juarez was in charge of close protection detail assignments, and he'd been trained well by Sean. I had no concerns. They had a New Zealand branch of the company. The once small Virginia company was global now. It wouldn't take long for extra personnel to be deployed to me. And two minutes on the phone with Juarez netted me two more teams and a highly trained occupational therapist, with a high security clearance within the O'Hare organisation, to help with Dean's potential recovery.

Chimes rang out from my computer. The nice thing about being way out in the Sounds was that I didn't have to keep everything locked away in a secure room. I used the mezzanine upstairs as an open plan office. I was right between the guest bedroom and the twins' bedroom. When the weather was good, I opened up the deck doors and worked enveloped in sea air, and the best view imaginable. Looking over the water of Mahau Sound while listening to bellbirds and the many Tui. The occasional Weka looking for trouble near the potting shed always entertained the girls. As did the quail.

I scanned the screen in front of me.

Isabella's head popped up on the other side of my desk.

"Boo! Where's your sister?"

She giggled. "Are you grumpy Daddy?"

"No Pumpkin, Daddy is not grumpy." No doubt she'd heard my tone while I was speaking with Thomas. I pulled a face at her. She giggled some more. I ducked down and looked under my desk then back at Isabella. "Where's your sister?"

Another alert pinged on the computer screen.

"Not here," Isabella said, with way too much enthusiasm for two words. I glanced around the room. Small feet poked out from under the drapes in the nearest corner of the room. In the interests of the game, I pretended not to see them.

"I wonder where she is?" I crossed the floor and checked the other drapes, avoiding the ones harbouring the giggling child. I opened the cabinets. "No Grace."

I spun around, with a frown on my face. "Where could she be?" I tapped my index finger on my chin.

One more check under the desk again and then I peered into the guest bedroom. Isabella laughed harder. "I better check under the bed." I made a big show of checking the whole room then sat back at my desk. I shrugged my shoulders. "I guess Grace doesn't want to see Crockett later today."

All of a sudden, a squeal let loose from behind the curtains.

"Who said that?" I asked, looking at Isabella.

She held her hands palms up. "Mr Nobody."

"That's what I thought." I stood up. "We'd better get ready for visitors."

The curtains in the corner rustled, then out popped Grace.

"I'm here Daddy!"

I clutched my chest and staggered backwards. "You scared me!"

She giggled and bounced on the balls of her feet. "I tricked you!"

"You sure did. Do you want visitors today?"

Isabella bounced up and down on the balls of her feet. "Crockett is coming!"

Grace nodded. "We can show him our pictures. We like it when Crockett visits."

"I know," I said with a big smile. "I think he likes visiting us too."

Another chime from the computer grabbed my attention. "How about you two go tidy your room for a few minutes. I'll answer these emails then we'll get everything ready for Crockett."

"Okay," Grace replied, and grabbed Isabella's hand to drag her into their bedroom.

I sat back at my desk and read all the incoming notifications.

An intelligence report arrived from an analyst. There was a private military contractor operating out of the Indonesian Embassy in Wellington. Two operatives were missing. It appeared they were taking a close interest in Ben Reynolds prior to their disappearance. It was confirmed as a false flag situation. The missing operatives were carrying Diamond Corporation ID cards. Ben had already questioned their validity and Ronnie suggested they were a false flag operation as well.

I leaned back in my chair. If they were the ones who grabbed Ben, then no one was going to find them. I couldn't muster any sympathy.

The next report beckoned. There were another two operatives missing. Their last known location was Upper Hutt. I read on. Intelligence suggested they were looking for a spy not for arms dealers. They were legitimately from Diamond Corporation. I opened another report that contained full identity information on the missing people. One was female and the other was male. They weren't from different organisations, but different branches of the same company, except I knew they weren't. The first two missing people were working as drivers at the Indonesian Mission, and they were identified as potential terrorists: Al-Fasil and Faheem. Their corporate ID cards said Diamond Corp, and it was a lie. The female and other male were Diamond Corp, Black Watch, and were based in Auckland, and that was true.

I opened *Genesis* and sent a text message to Ronnie. Sometimes I couldn't wait for her to access the system. I told her to add my *Genesis* phone number to her contacts when Reynolds vanished. She'd checked in every three hours until she found him. Ronnie told me she'd added my number under Uncle George. Guess it's time to drag out good old *Uncle George* and see how he was.

Uncle George: Let's get a drink soon.

I re-read the Intel reports while I waited for a response.

Three dots emerged in the text field on my phone.

Ronnie was typing.

Ronnie: How about wine this time, Uncle George?
Uncle George: Wine does sound better than beer.

Let's get a drink means check messages.
Wine meant she needed thirty minutes.
Beer means it's all good.

As far as the rest of the world was concerned, Ronnie got a text from good old Uncle George and was arranging to meet him for a glass of wine. She was very family orientated. No one could say otherwise. I let myself think about the article I saw in the newspaper the other day. Ronnie's Nana and her friends made the front page of the *Canterbury Times* newspaper for solving mysteries. I had never met Ronnie's family, nor had I met Ronnie. It sounded like they were a tight-knit family and that was a good thing. MacKinnon said Ronnie retired to be closer to her family, so I imagined she was enjoying the time. Her Nana sounded like a very interesting woman.

Chapter Thirty-four:
[Ronnie: Hiding in plain sight.]

Morning whipped around faster than any other. I awoke thinking about Dane, and how Tierney knew we were in the city. I didn't think that would be good for Dane. I rolled over. No Ben. Wonder where he went? The bedroom door opened and there he was, carrying two mugs of coffee. It smelt great. Just what I needed.

"I could get used to this," I said, taking a mug from him. "Coffee in bed."

"I better check my phone," he said, placing his coffee on the bedside table and opening the drawer. He put the phone on the bed. We waited for it to realise it was out in the open. A flurry of messages popped up on the lock screen. They were all from Grandad.

I glanced at my phone. There were several messages from Grandad. One was from Crockett and one was from Steph.

Ben read his messages. We knew we couldn't discuss them until his phone was safely in the drawer. I read my messages.

Grandad wanted us to meet him at a venue he'd found and thought we'd approve of for the engagement party. That we could talk about.

"Did you get a message from your Grandad about a venue for our engagement party?"

"I did. He doesn't say where. Let's hope it's better than the last venue."

We drank coffee and continued reading our messages. Crockett's was an interesting one, and I knew I couldn't talk about it out loud. The last thing we wanted was anyone thinking Dane Wesson was alive and well. And by the sound of Crockett's message, he was exactly that. I looked at the time stamp. It had been sent half an hour ago. Crockett must've stayed. That was a good idea. Steph wanted me to stop the harassment by Nana. That was a much harder thing to solve. The only way I could do it was by putting everything aside and helping her and that wasn't ideal. I considered phoning her and saying that I'd be able to help after the ball this weekend.

What day was it?

"Nana is annoying Steph," I said. "That woman is incorrigible."

"Are you talking about your Nana or Steph?"

"Yes."

He chuckled. "Finish your coffee before you phone Nana," Ben said. "You'll need to be fully caffeinated for that conversation."

He wasn't wrong.

I vaguely remembered getting texts and replying to texts late the night before. I looked in iMessage and sure enough there was a conversation with Uncle George. I needed to go check for a report in the bat cave.

"Has Donald left for work?" I asked absently, while re-reading the conversation from last night.

"Yes. Enzo has gone too. Before you ask, I let Romeo out, and he's now back on his bed."

"Thank you."

"What's next?"

"I'll hit the shower," I said, pointing to my wardrobe and signing 'bat cave.'

"I might join you," he replied. A drawer opened. Ben put his phone back in the drawer.

I jumped out of bed and opened the wardrobe. A few seconds later we were both seated at the desk inside my bat cave, ready to read a report.

The chat window activated.

Three dots appeared.

"*Genesis* is typing," I said, mimicking a robotic voice.

A chime told us that the report was downloaded and ready. I clicked on it because Genesis was still typing.

It was confirmation that the two idiots who kidnapped Ben were using a false flag. They were not, nor had they ever been Diamond Corp. They weren't any other PMC either. They were idiots, hired hands, unknowns, until the fake chatter started.

"Why?" Ben said. "Why create a fake terror situation? That's a lot of work for nothing."

"I don't get it either. What did it achieve?"

Our eyes met.

"*Genesis* distributed the threat assessment, but we don't think anyone picked it up, right?" Ben said. "The point could've been to out us. To have *Genesis* intelligence people looking for something, that whoever was behind it, could control."

I looked at the screen. *Genesis* was still typing. Either

there was a lot coming in a single chat or whoever did the typing was interrupted.

"Whatever it was for, they're dead, and not our problem," I said. "Is this taking forever or what?"

"Impatient this morning, Ronnie."

Yeah. I was.

Finally, a message popped up on the screen.

Genesis: The false flag operation is over. There are two legitimate Diamond Corp operatives in play. No doubt you will meet them. Right now, you are required to keep Dane Wesson out of CIA hands. *Genesis* is aware that Wesson has returned memories. He is valuable. Confirmation of his live status reached the FBI. They want him operational and involved in the arms deal situation. That is not a good idea. He is to be protected and kept out of the intelligence sphere. He is not to be put into play. It is too dangerous. *Genesis* is aware that Dave Crocker is handling the Wesson situation and has been for quite some time. It is imperative that Wesson remain safe. He may have to be moved to ensure his ongoing safety.

Ben and I looked at each other. "Wow," I said. "So, Tierney has already told the FBI that Wesson is alive. Fast work."

"He would've told them before he told us he'd seen us in the city. I know him. What I don't know is why he cares what the FBI want."

"I'm sure he has a reason."

"No doubt," Ben said.

"So, do we tell Crockett that Wesson needs moving, or does he already know?"

I typed a reply in the chat window.

Me: Message understood.

Genesis: If you have contact with Diamond Corp let me know. There is reason to believe that they are spy hunting, and they are not involved with the arms deal.

Me: Spy hunting. Not fake terrorist hunting?

Genesis: Intel says spy hunting.

The chat window dissolved into sparkly pixels then vanished.

"That's interesting. Spy hunting by Diamond Corp," Ben said. "Can't wait to find out who they're looking for."

"My money is on Jackson Frost," I said with a sneer.

"You might be right."

"We haven't come across the Canadian or the other Brit yet. Might be one of them?"

"It could be your Nana for all we know," Ben replied.

We laughed, but not too much, because Nana had a way of getting involved in all manner of things.

We exited my bat cave and put everything back the way it was supposed to be. This time we really did have a shower and get proper clothes on. Ben left his phone on the bedside table. It was probably better if it wasn't locked safely away all the time. It'd be too suspicious if nothing registered on the GPS or whatever bug it held.

"Let's go see Crockett?" Ben said and jangled car keys.

"Good idea. I've got some reports to write later. So many wayward spouse cases at the moment," I said. It was lies. I had no reports to write.

"Do we both need a phone?" Ben asked.

"Nah, not when we're together. Who would we text?"

"Grandad ..."

"He'll figure it out and text me if he needs you," I said. And with that we left.

Crockett's car was still at Dane's. I knocked on the door. He would've gotten a phone alert from the camera when we got close to the house anyway. Footsteps inside came closer. Dane swung the door open.

"Come in," he signed, "Crockett is making bacon and eggs, if you're hungry."

"I think we might be," I said.

Ben shut the door and we followed Dane to the kitchen.

"You smell the bacon cooking from your place, did you?" Crockett asked. Dane busied himself making toast.

"It blew in on the wind," Ben replied.

"What's up?"

"Dane needs to be moved."

Crockett stopped pushing the bacon around the pan. "Now how would you two know that?"

I shrugged. "Couldn't tell you. Just do."

"What else do you just know?"

"The so-called 'terrorists' situation was a false flag. Confirmed. There are two Diamond Corp people spy hunting. Water is wet. The sky is blue. Dane needs moving because the CIA know he's alive."

"How do the CIA know he's alive?"

"Someone saw him yesterday in the city, with us."

"That's not good."

"Not at all."

"I was planning on taking him down south for a week. Bit of a break. It's a lot with all this memory shit."

Dane piled toast on a plate and left the room. He returned with his iPad.

He typed.

"Dane can make his own decisions," Siri said.

"Yes. You can. This is about protection," I said. "Not making decisions for you but protecting you while you are returning."

Dane typed.

"Crockett and I were going fishing," Siri said. "I don't know if I like fishing. I want to find out."

"No problem," I said. "Go fishing with Crockett."

Crockett lifted the bacon out of the pan and placed it on paper towels to drain.

"Fishing," Crockett said. "It's good for the soul. If you need me up here with this arms deal situation, tell me."

"We can manage," Ben said. "We can manage while you are gone. When are you planning on leaving?"

"Today."

"All right then," Ben said. "Over easy for my egg, please."

"Done," Crockett replied. "Be useful and set the table."

Dane pointed to the correct drawer and left Ben to rummage through it gathering knives and forks. I used my intuition and found plates, exactly where I thought they would be. Two minutes later we were all sitting at the table eating breakfast and wondering what the day would hold.

"Are you flying?" I asked Crockett.

"Yeah. Charter."

"Good thinking." That way they could leave from a smaller airport with less cameras and less risk. "Paraparaumu airport?"

"Yes. We've got a midday flight to Picton."

"Are you headed down to your mates?" I knew he had a mate in Marlborough. Mitch Iverson was his mate in Marlborough. Tierney knew him too. What a small world.

"Yeah, the weather looks good so here's hoping we catch some snapper."

Breakfast was good and appreciated. I offered to do the dishes. Ben helped. I washed. He dried. Once we were done, we said our farewells and wished them a safe trip.

Next stop was Nana's. I needed to make sure everything was going smoothly there and that she wasn't going to annoy Steph all day. It's one thing to annoy me; we're blood. Donald and I are well used to Nana and her ways. It wasn't fair to inflict that on other people. Not fair at all.

All was quiet at Nana's. She was having a cup of tea.

The Cronies weren't with her.

I kissed her papery cheek. "Morning Nana."

"Good morning, Veronica. Ben, how are you?"

"Good, thank you," he said, kissing the proffered cheek. He was family now; there was no escape. He had to take his chances with creeping death like the rest of us.

"Did Stephanie tell you I popped into the office, and that I require some help?" Nana asked.

"Yes, Nana. That is why we are here, to help. What do you need?"

"Some help finding a few people, really," she said, her voice changing to include extra feeble. Manipulation was her superpower. She'd practised hard all my life.

"None of that Nana. I'm here to help. You don't have put the feeble act on. I don't want to hear anything suggesting you won't be here this Christmas. We all know that's bollocks and you'll outlive the lot of us."

Nana tutted. "We know nothing of the sort," she said, but the extra sprinkling of feeble was gone.

I chalked that up as a small win.

"Give me names, I'll look them up for you," I replied.

She produced a notebook and handed it to me.

"Do bring it back when you're done, Veronica."

"Yes, Nana. I'll be back as soon as I have something for you."

"What a good girl you are."

We left.

Chapter Thirty-five:
[Ronnie: Cinderella.]

And just like that, it was ball day.

"Zip, please," I asked, turning my back to Ben. I felt his fingers grasp the zip pull and slide the zip closed. The red dress fit like a glove. I turned slowly in front of the mirror. "What do you think?"

He whistled. "Very nice, babe."

I handed him the matching tie and pocket square from the dressing table. "Matchy-matchy."

"For you, always," he replied.

That was the right answer. Tonight was going to be fun. As long as nothing bad happened. Ben wrapped his arms around my waist from behind and kissed the side of my neck.

"It's a very nice dress," he whispered.

I turned in his arms and looked into his pale blue eyes. "We ready to go dancing and romancing? The perfect couple on show?"

Ben's eyes lit from within. "Always." He took my hand and twirled me. "The car is waiting."

I picked up our masks from the dressing table and handed his to him. Mine was secured with hair clips into the sides of my hair do. Donald is clever. He'd swept my long hair up into a creation held in place by clips and hairspray. I was pretty sure I was flammable. I attached my mask, adjusted it slightly across the bridge of my nose, picked up my fur coat from the bed, and declared myself ready to go.

Ben's mask had an invisible elastic to secure around his head. It seemed to melt into his hair. I watched Ben send a text, then slide his phone into his inside tuxedo pocket.

"How is Grandad?" I asked, as we walked down the stairs together.

"He's good. Sends his best."

No doubt he did send his best. I'd heard the hype surrounding Jonathon Tierney, but in person he played a grandfather figure to perfection.

Ben took my coat and held it while I slipped my arms into the sleeves. If nothing else our last mission gained us access to phenomenal fur coats. Baranov furs were remarkable.

Ben opened the front door. A black town car was parked at the curb. The driver exited the vehicle and opened the back passenger door. Ben helped me into the car and closed the door. The driver opened the driver's side passenger door for Ben. We were very fancy tonight.

It was a short drive to the venue, just eight minutes door-to-door.

We met up with Tom and Ginny in the foyer, or what was being used as a foyer. It was all part of the arts and entertainment centre, Whirinaki Whare Taonga. Ginny and I checked in our coats. The coat check tickets were handed to our escorts. It was very old school.

Ben produced the ball tickets and handed them to a woman by the main entrance doors. She smiled and wished us a wonderful evening. I took Ben's arm, and we entered the town hall. Tables were down at one end and a dance floor at the other. We entered at about the middle of the room. It looked nothing like the town hall. Whoever was in charge of decorations and atmosphere, did a bang-up job. There were a lot of people. Music played, but in an unobtrusive way. There was a microphone stand on a small stage to our left. I didn't know who the compere was until I saw a slightly familiar man standing to the side of the small stage. I dragged his image into my mind and placed it in context. It was Bunty from Bunty in the morning on Magic radio. That was a good choice.

I suddenly thought a weapon would've been handy. Not practical. There were no pockets in my beautiful dress and my tiny evening purse had barely enough room for my phone. Not much chance of concealing a weapon on me or in my purse.

I squeezed Ben's arm. He looked at me. "Shall we find our table?" he asked.

"Good idea." It would be nice to have a base to return to once the dancing started.

He tapped Tom's shoulder. Tom and Ginny were a few steps in front of us. "Table," Ben said.

As we approached the tables, a young woman asked our names. She carried a tablet and wore a smart black dress. She looked at her tablet and asked us to follow her.

Thankfully, we were seated together and not at the back either. We were three tables in, on the row closest to the wall, opposite the main door. We faced the main room, and no one was seated behind us. There was more than enough room for us to move around and for servers to get by. It was a perfect place to sit. I glanced along the tables in our row and smiled when anyone looked up.

A thought bubbled up.

Had someone organised the seating to account for the deal? Surely not. We'd got last minute tickets. But Ben, Ginny, and Tom were at the last ball. So maybe?

I leaned close to Ben and whispered, "Recognise anyone from the last one?"

"I do. And they're seated like us, backs to the walls. Both sides of the room and I think there are two people seated on the back wall," he whispered in my ear.

I turned my face towards him. His lips brushed mine. We were good at this relationship thing. I had high hopes that we'd be good at marriage too. I heard another thought this time in Nana's voice: They won't buy the cow if you give the milk away for free. I never did appreciate being likened to a cow. And she was wrong. Didn't happen often, but it did happen.

"What's going on?" Ben asked, his voice still a husky whisper.

"Nana encroached," I replied.

He squeezed my hand and smiled. "She's not here yet. Let's enjoy the night."

"Yes, let's do that. Or at least until she arrives."

"How did I forget they had tickets?"

Let's enjoy a glorious dance and a big old arms deal. All chatter about an impending terror attack died with Al-

Fasil and Faheem. It was staged. Someone went to some trouble to create a falsified mock terror situation. I guessed it served a purpose, but I didn't know what it was. Maybe the point was to flush out a *Genesis* operative? If that was the case, it was clever, but I don't think anyone gave their hand away.

There was one more ball and then the season was over. This was the night the software would be offered to those who passed the vetting process. The last time was a feeler. The dealer or dealers, trying to gauge interest, then verify the buyers and have them download a special app. We thought Ben passed the vetting. If an invitation to download the application arrived tonight, we would know for sure. We suspected the first deal would be open for bids later tonight.

It felt nuts to me that they verified an actor. Everyone knows he's an actor. It's not a secret. Why would an actor need to buy arms? Tierney had convinced them that he did, that he was working for Leviticus. His backstop held. It was rock solid. Ben was no longer just an actor. He was a crucial part of the PMC. And everyone knew PMC's needed arms.

I was watching people come in and mill about. I recognised quite a few people because I knew them from life. The mayor and his wife entered. I'd find a moment to say hello later. Our glasses were filled with bubbly by a server dressed in black, then the bottle was put into a clear champagne bucket full of ice. Ben clinked his champagne glass to mine before we each took a sip.

The room hummed. There were voices, glasses clinking, chairs moving, heels on the polished wooden floor, and music underlying everything. Then Nana and the *Cronies of Doom* arrived followed by Crockett and Emily. The gang was all here. Crockett got back from his brief fishing sojourn in the nick of time. He left Dane down south with his mate, Mitch. Mitch was married to Ellie and she was Delta A so was Dane Wesson. They had to know each other in that other life. I wouldn't be surprised if Mitch had paid for all Dane's care like Tierney suggested.

I watched as the same woman in a black dress escorted Nana and her entourage to their table and placed Crockett and Emily nearby.

Ben whispered in my ear, "Nancy and her friend Laura have arrived."

My eyes left Nana to see where Nancy would be seated. I watched as the woman in black guided them towards Nana's table. "It's the same table," I whispered. "This is not good."

"Not at all good," Ben replied.

Ginny leaned towards me, "What are you looking at?"

"Nana, she's the one in the peacock blue gown with ..."

"The peacock feather mask," Ginny finished.

"Yes."

"So, the two women with her, are her friends?"

"Yes."

"And why is your voice strained?"

"Because they just sat Nancy Frost-Andrews and her

friend at the same table."

"Oh dear." Ginny understood. She'd heard the stories about my Nana and no doubt Ben had filled her in about Nancy Frost-Andrews. "How will we manage that situation?"

"I'm not sure yet."

"Let me know how I can help," Ginny said, picking up her glass. "Chin-chin."

Nancy waved at us, probably Ben rather than me. He did a small, understated wave back. It was barely a 'wa' really.

"Ronnie, incoming. That woman by the door."

I looked over. "I see two women, which one do you recognise."

"Both. Didn't see the second one at first."

"And they are?"

"Willa and her sister Hazel. From Eastern Kentucky."

"American," I said. "And they look it. Which one is Willa?"

"The one with brown hair."

"She would fit the description of Caroline Tilson."

"She would, but so would Laura, Nancy's friend," he said.

"Laura isn't American, is she?"

"No."

"Back to Willa then."

"Be handy if we had Dane with us," Ben said with a raspy whisper.

"Probably better he isn't, but yes, his eyes would be

handy."

"What's that look?" Ben asked waving a finger near my face.

"Be handy if we had his eyes ..."

"You're wearing a camera ... can we get him to log into the feed?"

"Crockett might be able to get hold of him or his mate that he deposited Dane with down south." I was already on my feet, my chair pushed back into the wall. "Coming?" I reached for Ben's hand as he stood.

"Yes."

We floated past tables nodding and smiling and made a stop at the table with Willa and Hazel. Ben didn't introduce me. So I didn't offer my name. They were delightful. I hoped it wasn't either of them. Up close I could see how Willa fitted the description we had. From the people I'd seen so far, at least forty women fitted the description and that was with their masks on. Some of the masks were incredible. People had gone all out to match their masks to their dresses, and most of the partners also matched. It was quite the affair to remember. I saw a photographer moving around the hall taking pictures. That made sense. I recalled a sign in the foyer saying there was a photographer and to let them know if you didn't want your picture taken. We didn't care, but I bet some did.

Emily smiled up at me when I tapped her on the shoulder. "Hello, Ronnie. Hello Ben," she said. "Isn't this fun?"

"Sure is," Ben replied. The band started the first dance number. "May I have the pleasure of the first dance?"

Emily beamed. "Yes."

Ben kissed my hand and let it go to take Emily's. Off they went, with him leading her around the dance floor like a pro. I slid into her seat.

"You need something?" Crockett asked.

"I need you to enable Dane to log into my camera so I can use his eyes to ID the Caroline Tilson woman."

"That's clever. I'll send the link and passcode to Mitch. He can set it up their end. You'll get a text from one of them when it's done." Crockett smiled. "I need a minute."

"I knew you were the man to ask."

He sent a longish text message. "Done."

"Shall we dance?"

For a second, I thought Crockett was going to say no. With a sigh he took my hand and stood. "It's not going to be pretty," he said. "Hope you are wearing decent shoes so, when I stomp all over your feet, it doesn't hurt too much."

"I'm feeling quite confident about keeping my feet out of the way. Come on."

He dipped his head to bring his mouth near my ear as we danced. "Where is your phone?"

"At our table, in my bag. Ginny is watching it."

"Okay. I'm sure Dane is loving the view of my suit jacket."

"It's done already?"

"It is."

"How do you know?"

"I'm wearing an earpiece. Mitch rang and told me."

"Sneaky."

"Smart," he replied and twirled me.

Crockett can't dance? Really? The music wound down and we went back to our respective partners. Ben and I rejoined Tom and Ginny at our table.

"I've been watching your Nana," Ginny said. "She and Nancy have been in bow-headed conversation."

"That can't be good," I replied. "Guess I'm going over to break it up."

Ginny winked at me. "I'll come."

I was about to say no. The last thing I wanted was Nana getting her arthritic claws into another of our friends, but better Ginny than Nancy.

Ben's phone buzzed. He checked it out of view by holding it below the table. His face gave nothing away. I gazed around the room hoping to spot other people sneakily checking their phones. On the back wall, I saw one person looking at something in his lap. He could just be that impressed with himself, but I somehow doubted that was it.

"Excuse me a moment," I said to everyone at the table. "I'm going to see Nana, with Ginny."

I hoped Dane was getting good clear images from my necklace as I made my way past people. It was a beautiful necklace; a black diamond encrusted yellow gold leopard with a sapphire eye. The eye was a tiny camera lens. I wasn't sure how hard Dane would have to work to imagine people without masks, but most of the masks covered eyes and not entire faces. However, there were a few very creepy completely blank white full-face masks. I wanted him to get a good look at Nancy, Laura, Hazel, and Willa.

"Hello, are we having fun?" I asked, kissing Nana's cheek. "This is our friend Ginny, Nana."

Nana's thin lips parted, and pure joy shone from her elderly features. I knew how much she'd wanted to meet Ginny. This was perfect for her. Not for me or Ben, but it's all about Nana and keeping her the hell away from Nancy and that arsehole nephew of hers.

"Sit down, Ginny," Nana said, making no attempt to hide her delight. "Nancy was sitting there, but she's off mingling."

Was she indeed. "I'll leave you to your chat," I said. I couldn't see Nancy anywhere and that concerned me. Laura was still at the table. Hazel was at her table, but Willa was gone. I scanned the dancers to see if she was dancing with someone. Crockett appeared beside me as I stood on the edge of the dance floor.

"What's going on?" he asked.

"Thought I'd find that lady Ben came across at the last ball. The one from East Kentucky."

"I think we better dance," Crockett said, taking my hand.

"Lead on," I said.

He dipped his head ever so slightly and said, "Caroline is not from Kentucky."

"Might not be her then," I replied. We danced into the

middle of the floor and there she was, dancing with a familiar short man. Masks don't add height. "Spin me."

"Are you sure?" Crockett asked.

I whispered, "Yes and look over my shoulder."

"Ah, I see," he replied.

"Slow spin." I hoped their faces were on camera during the controlled twirl. Crockett twirled me twice. That should do it.

"Where are we going now?"

"Back to my table," I said, "My feet don't like these heels." I wondered how Emily was getting on in heels with her prosthetic leg.

"Not surprised," Crockett said with a smile in his voice. "You're at least five centimetres taller than usual. I'm always amazed how people can walk, let alone dance, in heels like yours."

"Not well is the answer. Not as well as Emily."

"I think she practised," he said smiling.

Crockett escorted me to Ben, then joined us.

"Dane isn't one hundred percent sure that the woman is Caroline Tilson."

"Okay. I'll go for a walk and see if I can get closer and maybe get her talking."

"Be careful," Ben said.

"I will. I need to check on Nana anyway."

Tom smiled from his seat. "Ginny has Nana. They'll be having a good old chin-wag. Don't worry about her."

"Be easier to let go of the worry if Jackson Frost wasn't here."

Crockett touched my arm. Ben was checking his phone again.

"He's here?"

"He's dancing with Willa."

"That little bloke?"

"Yep."

"Thought he'd be taller."

"Bet he hears that a lot."

Crockett's expression changed from easy going dance partner, to murderous arsehole. That wasn't something I saw often on his face, but every now and then someone causes that response. Last time it was someone who threatened Emily. And that ended very badly for that person. And now, it was back. I guessed he knew about Jackson Frost.

"He's wanted by INTERPOL on a Red Notice."

Tierney said he was wanted but didn't mention the Red Notice. "And you know that how?"

He sighed. "I keep an eye on Red Notices."

"Of course, you do," I said with a smile. "Who is it you're hoping to see on a Red Notice?"

He shrugged. "An old friend."

"A friend? And you think there will be a Red Notice issued by INTERPOL for a friend?"

"I'm surprised it hasn't happened yet. But I do know they issued a Red Notice on Jackson Frost for his part in the homicide of two Polish nationals. It went out this morning."

That's why Tierney didn't tell us about the Red Notice.

It'd just happened. Before Frost was wanted in connection to two murders. Now he was suspect number one.

"Do you think there are any law enforcement here tonight?"

"Bound to be, but do they know about the Red Notice, that is the question," Crockett said. "We can't do much, but we can point him out."

"How about we get photo evidence of him in the country then pass it to someone at NCB."

"Okay, you know someone on the team?"

"Do you remember meeting my cop mate, Liam?"

"Yes. He's with INTERPOL now?"

"He sure is. He's with NCB at Police Headquarters."

Crockett nodded. "Good to know."

"He's a good guy. I can provide the address for Frost's Aunt in Lower Hutt."

"That'd be handy."

"Let's get him locked up after we've finished with him," I said. "I want to know how the little shit got into New Zealand. He's on a 'No-Fly'."

I picked up my glass and took a sip of the cool champagne. Ben put his phone face down on the table and rejoined the party.

He topped up my glass. "Thank you," I said. "Everything okay? Heard from your Grandad?"

"Everything is good. I did get a text from Grandad; he hopes we are having fun."

"Are we?" I asked.

"We are," he replied. "More fun to come yet."

I looked around at the tables nearest us. It didn't appear that anyone cared about what we were doing. Maybe Ben's mask was just enough to confuse or befuddle fans. Emily caught my eye. She made her way towards us, with a smile on her face, and a glass in her hand. She looked spectacular in the dress Ginny loaned her.

I heard Crockett suck in a sharp breath. He was watching her too. He was smitten all right.

"She's …"

"Everything," I finished for him.

"Yeah." Murder was erased from his features and replaced with calm. "You joining us, Milo?"

"I am," she replied.

Crockett stood, pushed his chair back, and offered it to her. She sat. He took the vacant seat next to her. For a split second I wondered why he'd done that, then it made sense. I watched Frost slime his way through the tables. Crockett wanted Emily safe between him and me. That meant I was also safe because Ben was on the other side of me. Emily and I were sandwiched between Ben and Crockett.

Ah, men, so adorable. I chuckled internally. He meant well.

"Dance with me, Ronnie," Ben whispered. He slipped his phone in the top inside pocket of his tux.

"I would love to dance with you," I said. "You can show off with your fancy moves."

Ben led me to the dance floor. "Quick Step, hope you can keep up."

"Don't worry about me," I replied. It'd been a while since Donald and I took ballroom dancing lessons, but some things you don't forget.

By the time we rounded the floor for the third time, I was nearly breathless and couldn't stop smiling if my life depended on it. That's when I realised, we had the floor, and everyone else had stepped back. People clapped as the music wound down.

I curtsied to Ben at the end of the dance; he replied with a bow.

Over the hum of the room, I heard Nana's voice. "That's my granddaughter and her fiancé. Aren't they magnificent together?"

Ben escorted me to our table. Once seated, he checked his phone again.

"I didn't know you could dance like that, Ronnie," Emily said. "You two were so good."

I sipped my drink. "Nana sent Donald and me to ballroom dancing when we were teenagers. The real surprise is how good Ben is."

Ben nudged me. "It always feels like I'm learning something about you, Ronnie. Just when I think I know you, there's another surprise."

I leaned against his shoulder. "Could say the same about you."

"Can you Tango?"

"Yes. But we are not doing that here." Bad enough with the Quick Step clearing the floor.

"At our wedding?"

"Perfect."

His phone buzzed again.

He checked it and I chatted to Emily. Crockett was watching the room, nodding hello to people and smiling at others. Tom wandered off. I wasn't sure where he'd gone. Ginny was still talking to Nana. Nancy was in conversation with her friend Laura. Willa and Hazel left the ballroom together. I saw them disappear into the foyer. Bathroom break perhaps.

"Excuse me," I said to Ben. He stood and pushed his chair in so I could get past. I picked up my sparkling evening purse. "I won't be long. Bathroom break."

"Be careful," he said, kissing me. His phone buzzed again.

"I will. Enjoy that alert on your phone."

I waved at Nana and the *Cronies of Doom* on my way out. Once in the foyer I looked for the bathroom symbols. They were easy to find. I didn't see Willa or Hazel in the foyer. There was a good chance they were in the bathroom. I swung the big door open to reveal a mirrored wall and a row of basins. Opposite them was a row of cubicles. Hazel was fixing her lipstick. She smiled at me via the mirror. I hoped Dane could get a clear picture.

"You and Ben Reynolds cut a fine picture on the dance floor," she said. It was definitely an American accent, but it didn't sound Southern.

"Thank you," I replied, and opened my purse. I pulled out my lipstick and reapplied it. The diamonds on my finger sparkled in the light. I still couldn't ignore them or pretend they'd been there forever.

"That's beautiful," she said, pointing at the ring.

"It is."

"Engaged?"

"Yes." I wasn't volunteering much. I dropped the lipstick into my purse and closed it.

"We had the pleasure of dancing with Ben at the last ball. He's charming and the man can dance."

"He is," I said, washing my hands with masses of foaming soap and water. "Who's we?"

"My sister. She's outside having a cigarette. Who are you engaged to?"

It couldn't be Ben, I guessed, not a Kiwi marrying a semi-famous Yank. Saints preserve us.

"Ben Reynolds," I said, smiling at her attempt to show how pleased she was for us.

She was not pleased. Her mouth was all over the place and nothing on it said pleased.

"How lovely. When's the wedding?"

"We haven't set a date yet."

"Haven't heard anything from the magazines regarding Ben's engagement."

"We haven't let his agent send out the press releases yet," I replied, grabbing a bunch of paper towels and drying my hands.

"Are you waiting for something?" she asked, touching up her chin with some loose powder.

"We've been busy with work. And we are newly engaged." Not that it's anyone's business.

"The elderly woman with her two friends. Is she related to you?"

I shook my head. "Never seen her before in my life."

I left the room just as Willa, the missing sister, walked in. Or I thought it was the sister.

"You and Ben put on quite a show," she said. "I'm Willa. We met Ben at the last ball."

"Pleased to meet you, I'm on my way out."

I walked past her just as her sister called out. "She's Ben Reynolds betrothed."

Willa grabbed my arm. "Don't think we've met." That wasn't a Kentucky accent either. It was more generic West Coast than anything. Like it'd been polished until you couldn't place it in a state.

I shook my arm free. "We have now."

She tried again, I excused myself. Letting the door close as I walked away. It wouldn't take me long to get back to Ben. Streamers, balloons, flowers, people in finery and having a wonderful time. I ignored it all and made a bee line for Ben and safety.

"What's the matter?" Crockett asked, when he saw me duck around someone and tap Ben on the shoulder to get him to let me in.

"Willa and Hazel."

Crockett nodded and looked like he was listening. Dane was probably talking in his ear.

"You met both of them?" Ben asked.

"Yes. No hint of Kentucky in their voices by the way. They like you, but don't seem so thrilled with me." I watched the diamonds twinkle as my fingers moved. "Could be this that's pissed them off."

"Not a bad thought, women fighting over me."

"Trust me, Ben, no one is fighting. Although that Willa chick grabbed my arm. So good chance she'll need a punch in the nose later." She was a bit old to be throwing a green-eyed fit over Ben.

Ben chuckled. Crockett leaned behind Emily to get my attention.

I leaned back. "What? Because I'll be the one punching Willa in the nose."

"Dane is as sure as he can be that Willa is Caroline Tilson," he said. "Get this, Tilson has a sister called Hazel, so good chance she is the *actual* sister."

"Good to know. So now what? What is she selling? Arms?"

"He didn't know that, but he does know she was involved in illegal arms deals within America to gangs, while she was supposedly seconded to the DEA."

"Why supposedly?"

"I was DEA undercover with a major gang during the time period she was supposedly working undercover. We did arms deals. Never came across a woman."

"And that means what?"

"Either Dane is remembering it wrong, or she wasn't seconded to the DEA. Maybe she remained with the FBI, or maybe she was involved in extracurricular deals and had a choice ... disappear or go to prison."

"Why would anyone in the FBI grant her a choice?"

"I don't know, Ronnie, seems insane, but she might've rolled over on her comrades." He smiled. An attempt at loosening his frown which failed.

"You need to relax. You're way too intense for a dance. If that woman walks back in here and sees you looking daggers and talking to me, she might get antsy."

Ben put his arm around me and whispered in my ear, "They just walked back in. Tell Crockett to fix his face."

"I don't think he can. I think he's had it since birth."

Crockett commented, "Laugh it up, Cary Grant, you'll keep."

Amusement settled on Ben's face. He waved to someone. I looked over and saw it was Willa. She and her sister were incoming.

"I forbid you from dancing with either of those women," I said, trying to sound like I meant it, but the thought of forbidding him was far too funny for me. I crack myself up some days. Almost as funny as Ben trying to forbid me from something.

"As you wish," Ben said, kissing me just as they stopped in front of our table.

"Congratulations," Willa said. "We didn't get your fiancée's name when we met her."

"Because I didn't give it to you," I said.

None of us offered a name.

"Perhaps we could have a dance. Next waltz?" Willa asked, looking directly at Ben.

"Unfortunately, my dance card is full."

"I'm sure your lovely fiancée wouldn't mind giving up

one dance."

"I'm afraid I do mind," I said.

Crockett and Emily stood. "We're dancing," Emily said.

"Have fun. We're resting," I replied.

Tom stood and asked, "Would one of you lovely ladies like this dance?"

Hazel beamed. "I would," she said. "Who are you?" She was the more pleasant sister.

"I'm Tom, and you are?"

"Hazel," she said, and off they went to the dance floor.

Ben's phone was buzzing in his pocket, or he had a bumblebee hidden in there. Willa stood awkwardly by the table.

"I suppose I shall go back to our table."

"I'm sure there are plenty of people looking for a dance partner. Didn't I see you with a little man earlier?" I asked.

She huffed loudly and spun on her expensive heels. Over her shoulder she said, "I'm not at all sure you know what you are doing, Ben, marrying that one."

The audacity. I waved her off. Then looked up and realised Nana was waving me over. This is not the most fun I've ever had.

"Nana wants me," I said.

"We're in the running," Ben whispered to me.

"What are we interested in?"

"Anti-aircraft missile system."

"Buggery bollocks," I said half under my breath. "Do

you get to see it in action?"

"Yes. Tonight."

"Which system?"

He whispered in my ear, "The S-400."

"What the actual? That's Russian." I mumbled in his ear pretending we were whispering sweet nothings to each other. "How are they going to test it?"

"Indeed, it is Russian, and I don't know how they're going to test it. Now smile and go see Nana."

My brain spun around the S-400 and what I knew about it. Technically it had an operational range of up to four-hundred kilometres and a surveillance range of up to six-hundred kilometres. It could engage targets to an altitude of thirty kilometres, flying at a speed of 17,000 kilometres per hour. That was Mach thirteen. Thirteen times the speed of sound. Thirteen times. This was so bad. If they were going to test it for their bidders, then something disastrous was going to happen. It had to be in Europe or maybe Africa. Those systems were mounted on fecking big trucks. It boggled my mind to think someone stole an S-400 from the Russians. Where have they been hiding those trucks? Who, and where, did they steal it from? Has Russia handed over a multi-billion-dollar weapons system for fun? I doubted that. They like to annoy but I doubted they'd go that far. Putin isn't going to take a hit of billions to annoy the US, is he?

"Veronica dear, are you having fun?" Nana asked as I slipped into an empty chair near her.

"Of course, Nana. Are you three enjoying yourselves?"

"It is fabulous," Ester said. "Isn't it, Frankie?"

"Been a long time since we wore gowns," Frankie said. An elderly man attracted her attention. He asked her to dance. She giggled like a teenager and off she went.

I was pleased they were having a good time.

Nancy was deep in conversation with Ginny.

Interesting.

They barely acknowledged me, and I was fine with that. My mind was still spinning over the Russian toys that were for sale. My purse buzzed. I had a quick look at my phone. It was a text from *Uncle George*. It'd have to wait. I wasn't in a place where I could read that. Nana is very aware that I don't have an *Uncle George* and she's nosy enough to peer at the screen. Could she see the text with the privacy shielded impact resistant glass I had on my phone? If anyone could, it would be Nana. That's how my luck runs when it comes to Nana.

The missile thing would not get out of my head. I don't know what I thought was going to be for sale. I mean, it was never going to be rifles. I just never thought it would be a huge thing like an S-400 system. That was pricey as hell. The missiles alone were spendy. It was comparable to the US Patriot system. Plenty of those were stationed around the world protecting airspace.

What did the bidders want with a system designed to protect air space? I thought that was the question I needed to answer.

But this was someone selling an entire S-400 system to anyone with billions to chuck around. There is always money for weapons and terrorism. Imagine taking the billions and instead of buying a weapons system to kill people, they invested it into education, health care, and feeding the hungry.

Sometimes I tell myself fairy tales to make life bearable.

"Veronica." Nana's voice jolted me back to the moment.

"Yes," I said, pushing a smile in her direction.

"You were miles away."

True.

"I best get back to Ben before someone tries to dance with him," I said. I don't feel like sharing.

"The evening will be drawing to a close before long. Hopefully we will see you and Ben on the dance floor before it ends. It's such a treat seeing you dance again."

"Fingers crossed," I said, and made my way back to Ben.

He smiled at me and stood so I could access my chair. Emily and Crockett were still dancing, and I'd lost sight of Tom. No doubt he was keeping the sister occupied. Scanning the dance floor didn't net Frost. I turned my attention to the tables. It's easy to miss him so I adjusted my view accordingly. Like trying to find a child in a sea of adults.

I didn't see him. Ben's phone had a lot of activity. There were constant buzzes. Every time his phone buzzed, I looked around to see who else could be getting alerts. I never saw Frost when the phone buzzed. I wondered where he was. He was possibly hiding somewhere so he could keep an eye on the application and whatever the app was doing. I hadn't even seen it yet. No doubt I'd get to see it later when we were back home to safety.

Willa was gone.

I'd seen her move towards the table she was sitting at, but she wasn't there or on the dance floor. Perhaps she was with Frost somewhere. Perhaps they were in it together.

Crockett and Emily bustled back from the dance floor as the music drifted away. Emily was clearly enjoying herself. Crockett was all smiles. It was nice seeing them out together having fun.

I nudged Ben. "One last dance?" I asked, as I heard the band strike up another song. I listened and counted beats. "Viennese waltz?"

"Perfect," Ben said as he rose to his feet, tucked his phone in his pocket, and escorted me to the dance floor.

We stood on the floor as the music played. Ben took me in his arms. I watched his face. He counted and off we went. I enjoyed the Viennese Waltz far more than the slow waltz. Less up and down. Up and down gets tiring in five-centimetre heels.

There is nothing that compares to dancing with someone you truly enjoy. Ben's eyes stayed with mine for the entire dance. There was no way anyone was going to tap in. This was our dance, and we were well matched. As the music drew to an end, we moved to the edge of the floor. Bunty picked up a microphone and announced how much money was raised during the evening from tickets sold and a silent auction. New equipment would be purchased for Wellington Children's Hospital and McDonalds pledged to match funds raised dollar-for-dollar. There was a round of applause from the room. Ben placed his hand in the small of my back and guided me to the table. Ginny joined us at the table and Tom was back.

Nana waved as she and the *Cronies of Doom* vacated their table and headed out the door. Enzo was picking them up. No doubt he'd texted and told Nana to go out to the car. We'd decided because of the mishap after the last ball, that everyone we were responsible for would be leaving safely. No nonsense.

Tom helped Ginny to her seat. "The car service texted me," he said. "They will be out front in ten minutes. We will wait at the table until they text saying they're there."

"Sound good to me."

Crockett and Emily were coming with us. Safe. That's how we needed to be.

I was itching to get a look at the application and the bidding.

And to dob Frost into INTERPOL.

Chapter Thirty-six:
[Ben: FML.]

My phone was going ballistic by the time we got to Ronnie's. We were last to be dropped home. I wanted to make sure everyone else got home safely. The house was dark and silent as we made our way up the stairs. Romeo barely thumped his tail on his bed when we crept into the kitchen doing our best to keep from waking anyone. Moonlight bathed the kitchen.

Ronnie was dying to ask questions. I could see the struggle on her face.

"Nightcap?" I asked, opening the booze cupboard. "Brandy?"

"Yes. Why not." She smiled. "I'll go change."

I poured us a drink each and followed her carrying the brandy glasses. Ronnie had left the door open for me. I placed the glasses on her nightstand next to her phone and sat on the bed. Ronnie wasn't in her room.

My phone was still buzzing away. I pulled it from my pocket and watched alerts popping up, one of top of the other, all from the new app. I'd seen something like the app I'd downloaded before. A Paramilitary app used by the CIA. It also looked like it could be related to 'Teamwire', which was a secure European communication application for military and police.

I started reading the alerts.

Ronnie came back wearing a long tee shirt.

"Thank you," she said, climbing up on the bed and picking up a glass. She sat cross-legged with her back against the pillows.

"You're welcome," I said, smiling. "Pass me my drink?"

She held the glass out to me. I watched another set of alerts, ping.

"That's going to be annoying if it carries on," Ronnie said, and took a sip of brandy.

"Yes, it is." I turned the phone so she could see the messages. We couldn't talk about it out loud. She picked up her phone and opened Notes. She typed then showed me the screen.

Ronnie: When's the demonstration?"

I took her phone and typed: 1650 tomorrow NZDT.

Ronnie took the phone from me and typed: Well, we know the system is not in New Zealand. Where could it be?

I held my hand out for the phone. She placed it in my hand and smiled.

Me: Someone wanted it earlier in the day, but the response was it would still be dark. Sunrise is after 0540 wherever they are. And for whatever reason, they want daylight.

Ronnie sipped her brandy and shot me a smile. She took her phone then opened her closet and pushed aside the clothes to get to the hidden door and biometric pad.

342

She waved and disappeared into her bat cave, closing the door behind her. No doubt she'd be looking up timezones and trying to rule out various places.

I watched two bidders try and get the demo time changed. The number of messages from the app increased as two more bidders queried several things about the price. They were shut down fast. I read everything that appeared on my screen but made no comments. I knew what I wanted and was happy to wait until the demonstration before I finalised my bid. Let them try and outdo each other. There was no sense driving the price up. They were idiots. I dropped the phone on the bed and considered joining Ronnie.

I drained my glass and stood up.

Ronnie appeared from her secret room with a smile on her face and no brandy in her glass.

"Pleased with yourself?"

"Yes," she replied and placed the glass on the nightstand.

I wrapped my arms around her. "You smell good."

"I'm guessing that's a compliment," she replied as a laugh vibrated through her.

"It is."

Her breath tickled my neck as she whispered, "I think I know where they're going to test it."

"You do, do you," I whispered back. She unwrapped one of my arms from around her and pulled me towards her closet.

I got the hint. She almost dragged me into the closet in

her haste to show me whatever it was she found. She closed the door behind us.

"Your phone isn't in here, right?"

"Correct," I said, as I sat next to her and looked at computer screens full of information.

"Using the sunrise time you gave me, I started searching different time zones and likely places. They're hardly going to test a system like that in Monaco, are they?"

"Probably not."

"I started ruling out countries and time zones and was pretty much left with Bravo time. So, I worked that idea and I think Sudan might be the place, or it's inside Russia, because they're telling porkies. I think it's in Bravo time, but they didn't move something as big as the S-400 to Sudan or out to sea on a ship. Someone would've seen those massive trucks moving. It's not something that would go unnoticed by all the eyes on Russian arms and troop movement."

I nodded. She pointed to the middle screen.

"Kaliningrad. It does look most likely. Or it's something completely different."

"Different like what Ronnie?"

"Like a nuclear warhead fired from Belarus to wherever the hell they can reach whatever target they choose, and with that begins World War Three. Or maybe an Iskander missile firing on Warsaw from Minsk and dragging NATO into war. It doesn't have to be a nuke to do that."

"You've gone to a dark place," I said, smiling at her. "I

wish none of that was possible."

A chat window appeared.

"Incoming *Genesis* communication," Ronnie said.

Genesis: Progress?

Ronnie: Yes. There's a demonstration of the system tomorrow at 1650. Ben is here.

She looked at me. "How do you see it?"

"The app has live video feed capability."

Genesis: Ben, I need everything you have. Is it possible to download all the chat from the app?

Ronnie pushed the keyboard in my direction. "It's for you."

Ronnie's name popped up on the screen as I began to write: Ben here. Everything is destroyed within seconds of it being read. I can't do screen shots because it announces you've taken a screen shot. Thought I'd try and pretend it was an accident.

Genesis: We'll have to rely on your memory.

Ronnie: It's Ronnie. Were any reports filed about movement of large trucks headed from Russia to a ship anywhere? Any troop movements around Sudan?

Genesis: I'll check with my counterpart over that way. I'll find out. What are you thinking?

Ronnie: That the system is still within Russia because the movement of an S-400 would be noticed. Russia isn't going to sit idly by and let one be stolen. This test is coming from Russia. I doubt there is any way of disguising any missile firing from those massive systems. We're going to know when it's fired, but we won't know what the target is.

Genesis: What are you thinking Ben?"

Ronnie: Ben here. We need more intel.

I was thinking Ronnie wasn't completely out of left field with her observation. We had nothing to indicate there was movement of weapons like the S-400 or Iskander since Russia lined up air defence along the Belarus Poland border, and then announced they were giving them nukes. Lukashenko took delivery of nuclear warheads, but Russia maintained control of them.

Ronnie held her hands poised over the keyboard for a second before committing herself. She looked at me. And another message popped up on her screen but not from *Genesis*. It was in Signal.

"What's that?" I asked, and pointed at the new chat window.

"A friend in Eastern Europe," she replied and opened the message.

We read it together.

Alina: Broken Arrow

Cold washed over me as the words hit like a lump of ice. Broken arrow is a nuclear incident.

Ronnie: What!

Alina: It's chaos. Channels are locking down. No one is talking.

Ronnie: Is it an incident or has something been lost?

Alinia: Lost

Ronnie: How?

Alina: Lida Air Base, Belarus. There is a nuclear warhead missing.

The entire conversation vanished.

"It's not a weapon, it's a war," she said.

Ronnie: It's Ronnie. I think the bidding is not for the weapon, it's for an act of war.

Genesis: More information required.

Ronnie: I was warned moments ago by a friend that a Broken Arrow incident has occurred at Lida Air Base in Belarus. We need confirmation.

Genesis: I'll get what I can.

"Everything in the application suggests that nine bidders are bidding on a weapon system. Two have asked how the system would be delivered in the open chat environment," I said.

"And the answer?"

"It was a fob off. Whoever it is behind this told them that it was a logistics issue for later. Do you think it could be right?" I leaned back in my chair and swiveled to face Ronnie. "Is it possible?"

She nodded. "Anything is possible. What we need to know is if it's probable or not."

The conversation on the screen warped and fell apart then vanished.

We remained in the office.

"I think you probably are right. It could be the missing nuclear warhead and the target could be Warsaw," I said.

"If the warhead is fired from Kaliningrad?"

"It might be easier to hit Warsaw," I said.

"What about Copenhagen?"

"Maybe."

Neither of us believed the weapon was still in Belarus.

"Different question," Ronnie said. "How many bidders were at the ball?"

Good question.

"I was led to believe it would be all of them. But that would've required them to be in New Zealand prior to the first ball. I don't know where the bidders have come from, but I'm picking they're not all American or Kiwi."

"Is Frost bidding? He's a Brit?"

I shrugged. "No one uses names. They assigned code-names."

"If we take Frost out of the equation then we'd see if anyone goes quiet?"

"That would tell us something," I said. "There are ten counting me according to the app."

"What about Caroline Tilson?"

"Don't know what she has to do with it. Could be bidding on behalf of someone."

"You hear any other accents at the ball?" Ronnie asked.

"Lots but none that stood out."

Ronnie's phone rang.

Chapter Thirty-seven:
[Ronnie: I don't want to be right.]

I picked my phone up and swiped my finger across the screen to answer the call. I knew who it was: good old *Uncle George*.

"Do you have something?" I asked, putting the call on speaker.

"I'm going over all the reports over the last four months. It was three months ago we first heard about an arms deal happening." The voice was distorted. Couldn't tell if it was male or female, or if there was an accent.

"Thanks. Soonish would be good. We need to pinpoint the target."

"Do you know anything?"

Ben spoke, "According to the program, the target is over the horizon. Seven bidders asked for the target to be OTH. But no one mentioned nukes. So now we suspect a broken arrow, it's probably not OTH. As far as I am aware, the warhead in question is a battlefield nuke."

"It depends where they try and fire it from. I'll put the word out, and everyone will start looking for an Over The Horizon target from Sudan and Kaliningrad, and closer targets from anywhere in the vicinity of Lida Air Base."

"Check ships," Ben said. "Could be at sea. Moving something as big as the S-400 would cause ripples, someone would've picked it up. Iskander missiles systems are on the prohibited from export list, but the S-400 has been sold to India and Turkey, which makes it almost feasible as a black-market item."

"Are you thinking this is not an auction for the S-400?" The line started to crackle.

"That's what we both think," I said. "But if someone is going to take control of an S-400 system there are only so many places that can happen. And we don't know if the broken arrow can be fired from an S-400. That's a game changer."

"I'll reach out to my counterpart in Europe and see what intelligence they have around movement and potential targets."

"If it's an Iskander missile armed with a nuclear warhead, it might not be an OTH target despite what the bidders were calling for."

The line crackled again, and the call dropped. I checked the call was gone.

"Every now and then the calls from *Uncle George* drop," I said.

"And?" Ben asked.

"Makes me wonder where our little *Genesis* operation has its HQ."

"Okay Sherlock, you pinged Sudan and Kaliningrad and now you want to go after the boss?"

"Aren't you curious?"

"A little, maybe." He spun his chair to face me. "We have bigger issues with this 'deal that might not be a deal' situation, Frost flaunting himself despite the Red Notice, and Nancy - there's something about her."

"Yes. I would agree with that."

"And then there's Willa and Hazel," Ben said.

"Who seem to have lost their 'Justified' accents," I added. "And Willa is Caroline Tilson aka Cassidy Tailor."

"That's what Dane said. You think he's right?"

"No reason not to think so," I replied.

"Okay," Ben said. "She's the missing alias the FBI lost with a connection to *The Wayward Son Protocol*."

"Not like we can check; no one else can access it."

"And she's somehow tied up with this arms deal. This roving deal that started in Poland, traveled to Thailand, and landed here," Ben said.

"That about sums it up."

"What happened to Sandra King and Steven Sadler?" Ben asked.

"I have no clue. Could be bad."

"Frost might've got them." Ben shook his head, not believing his own words. "Someone is pulling his strings. He is not behind any of this; he's a puppet, and not a very good one."

"No doubt. And he's a gross little man."

"Topher Franks?"

"He's not gross or little," I replied grinning.

"Not what I meant."

"He's hunting whoever he came to get. It's not Frost," I said.

"You're sure?"

"He clocked him at the ball."

"How did I miss that?"

"You were downloading software and bidding on supposedly stolen Russian weaponry."

"And cutting a rug with you."

"Cutting a rug? Are you Nana now?"

He shrugged. "Maybe, she's one helluva woman. It said so in the newspaper."

A groan popped out of my mouth before I could stop it. "I still have to help her with something."

"Because we don't have enough going on ..."

My turn to shrug. "We've got the Dane Wesson situation under control. We can tick that off."

Ben ticked the air. "Done."

"He's safe right?"

Ben nodded. "Crockett made sure he was safe."

"Do you know where he took him?"

"To his buddy Mitch's place."

"Where does he live, again?" I thought I might be onto something, but only time would tell.

"Marlborough somewhere."

"You don't know? Don't you boys talk about fishing and shit?"

"We do. I haven't grilled him on the particulars of his buddy's address." He looked deep into my eyes. "Is it important?"

"Probably not. It's just, Linkwater is in Marlborough, and I wondered if he was close."

"Why?"

"It's a place that's cropped up a couple of times recently," I said.

"Good or bad?"

"Curious," I replied. "I find it curious."

"If it was more, you'd tell me?"

"Yes. Once upon a time I might not have ..."

"That's fair," Ben replied with a grin.

"Now what?"

"We need to do something about Frost. We can keep an eye on him or get him scooped up." Ben smiled. "I vote for the latter."

"Me too. I'll give Liam a call in the morning." I glanced at my phone screen. "It's almost morning."

"Why Liam?"

"He's with INTERPOL now."

"Then he's the perfect person to deal with Mr Red Notice," Ben said. "Is there any point getting any sleep?"

"Nope. What's right in front of us now?" I stretched.

"The auction."

"And?" I was twisting in my chair.

"Let's get rid of Frost first thing. We did our job by getting an ID on Caroline, flick that to the FBI via Grandad, and that problem is solved."

"Let's see if we can locate Sandra King and Steven Sadler. I thought they would've been in touch by now," I said.

"Hopefully we'll find them alive. You could do your thing?"

"I could." A thought wouldn't leave me alone, so I voiced it. "What if there is only one auction. That was it.

The final auction doesn't happen?"

"Because?"

"Because all they needed was an audience when they fired a nuke and started a war." I chewed my lip. "What happens if they start a nuclear war?"

Ben spun my chair, so I faced him. "Everything I've read, every report, every single one, Ronnie ..."

"All of them, Ben?" I smiled.

"Smartass. But yes. All of them say that Australia and New Zealand are the safest countries to be in if a country in the Northern Hemisphere fires a nuclear warhead."

"A country?"

"Okay Russia, if Russia fires a nuke, at say, the Ukraine, or even an American base in Europe."

"Will ... would the US retaliate with a nuclear strike?"

"No. That's not the mandated response. Escalation to point of annihilation is not in anyone's best interests. No one wants a scorched earth situation."

"And if the second auction goes ahead and it's a second nuke?"

"You're jumping ahead. We need to deal with now. Let's do that, okay?"

The computer pinged with an incoming communication. We waited for the words to appear.

Genesis: Locate Steven Sadler and Sandra King. Last seen together at Wellington Railway Station boarding a train to the Hutt Valley twenty minutes ago.

That's got to be the first train out of the city for the morning.

Ronnie: Any clue where they were headed? There are seventeen stations on the Hutt Valley line. The trip out to Upper Hutt takes an average of forty-three minutes. There are cameras on board the trains and at all the stations. Can we confirm they're still on board?

Genesis: Working on gaining access to the cameras on the train.

Ronnie: Going mobile.

Genesis: Stay Frosty.

I stood and took Ben's hand, holding my phone in the other. "Come on fiancé, we need to get dressed into pursuit clothing." Something other than a long tee-shirt would be smart. Underwear would help.

After checking I'd shut everything down, I locked the bat cave door behind us. *Genesis* would move communication to text message as *Uncle George,* or a voice call, depending on the situation.

We dressed in jeans, tee shirts, and sweatshirts. It was chilly in the early morning.

"Where's the best place for coffee?" Ben asked, looking at his watch. "At zero six hundred."

"Petrol station."

"Great, gas station coffee. A true gastronomic delight," he said, looking at the messages on his phone. He showed me the screen. Forty messages. All the bidders were out doing each other, and then there were four messages asking why he was so quiet. He replied: I was sleeping.

Then, he shoved the phone into his pocket, and it rang.

He hauled it out and showed me the screen.

It was an incoming call via the app.

He answered it and put it on speaker. "Reynolds speaking."

"Why are you the only person who slept last night?"

"I was tired."

"You didn't bid after midnight."

I listened and decided the voice was distorted somehow, probably in a similar way that *Genesis* distorts voices.

"As I said, I was tired."

"Or you don't want this missile system and you're wasting our time."

"If you think that, then kick me out of the program," Ben said.

"If we think you're a time waster Reynolds, we won't just kick you out of the program."

"Ah, right, a threat. Of course, how else would you operate if not threateningly?"

"What is that supposed to mean?"

"Exactly what I said." He paused. He smiled at me then said, "You're prepared to threaten customers. That's good business."

"I'm sure the people you're buying for won't be happy if we pull you from the bidding." There was a pause. "I heard Leviticus wants this system at all costs."

"They'll get over it."

Ben hung up. We waited to see what would happen next. There was nothing immediately, so we took my car to the closest petrol station for coffee.

And his phone rang.

I pointed to the door of the petrol station, signed the word coffee, and exited the car with my phone in my pocket.

Warm lights bathed the shop. I stepped through the automatic doors. A voice called out from behind the counter. I looked over and smiled.

"Hey there, two long blacks please."

"Coming right up," the woman said from behind a coffee machine at the end of the counter and started grinding beans.

My phone buzzed. A quick check revealed a text from *Uncle George*. He'd found an asset working on the trains and was in the process of getting into the security cameras. I told him we'd lurk near Silverstream Station. I had a feeling they were headed our way. If they wanted to be close and head in a specific direction, but not make it look like they were together, then they'd split up. Silverstream would be an okay first stop. One would be there, then one would be at Trentham or Wallaceville. Then they'd take alternative transport, a bus, a cab, Shanks's pony. I asked for photos, and they arrived.

King was an attractive blonde. Sadler was tall and dark haired. He'd be easy to spot. He was hit-his-head-on-a-door-frame tall. Judging by the photo taken. I studied the image. It was from a surveillance camera. Airport maybe.

Uncle George: Confirming one exit at Silverstream. Sandra King.

Me: Thanks

The coffee machine hissed and spat.

So, King got off the train at Silverstream and we weren't there yet. Where would be a likely place for Sadler to leave the train, I wondered. It would probably be Trentham or Wallaceville. What would I do? I'd get off at Trentham then walk. King was probably going to bus or walk.

Me: Check buses from Silverstream, they have cameras.

Uncle George: On it

More hissing and spitting from the coffee machine and then the woman asked if I wanted sugar. I opted yes, for both, and asked for a little bit of cold water in the top of the black coffees.

"Would you like ice instead of water?"

"Yes, thanks, that would be great."

The coffees were lidded and placed on the counter. I paid with cash and took the coffees back to the car. Ben was smiling when he leaned over and opened my door for me. I had a quick look to see where his phone was. He pointed to the glove box.

"You look pleased," I said, and handed him a coffee.

"Probably did too much messing with whoever is behind this deal. Not that I think whoever is behind it, is the person calling from the app. But you know, no name, so ..."

"King disembarked the train in Silverstream. I'm waiting to hear if she got a bus from there."

"That's something. And Sadler?"

"He might jump off in Trentham or Wallaceville."

I passed him my phone. "Photos."

"We shouldn't have too much trouble," Ben replied handing my phone back.

We both sipped our coffees. Ben pulled his phone from the glovebox. Two seconds later the screen lit with messages. Ben watched the screen, and I watched him.

If we had kids.

I stopped that thought. We weren't parent material, no matter how cute his dimples were. And they were ridiculously cute. We were dog parent material. It's way less messy.

An incoming text on my phone made me jump.

"All right?" Ben asked.

"Yep."

A quick read of the long message told me they'd bought tickets on the train. Both tickets were to Upper Hutt. *Genesis* must've gotten hold of the crew member that sold them. That was something to file away in case we ever decided to take the train again as a semi-safe escape route. *Genesis* now had assets inside Metlink.

That was important information.

Ben put his phone safely back into the glovebox.

Another incoming text buzzed on mine.

"Trentham it is."

"Where are they headed?"

"I don't know. Somewhere in Upper Hutt."

Another text came through.

King was on a bus heading north to Upper Hutt.

"Bus stop?" Ben queried.

"If I were her, I wouldn't get off at the railway station, but the stop before it. That's over on Wilson Street near Bradley Lane."

"Opposite Beaurepaires?"

"Yep. Just around the corner from there."

"Isn't Beaurepaires on the corner?"

"Yes. But you knew what I meant."

Ben smiled. "Let's go."

He put his coffee in the cup holder in the middle console and started the engine. We weren't far away. Two minutes at most.

Main Street was quiet. Shops didn't open until nine, so traffic and people were scarce. In the wing mirror I saw a bus coming up behind us.

"Could be her bus," I said, as Ben checked the rearview mirror.

He indicated and parked outside a row of shops opposite the Wilson Street intersection. We could watch the bus go around the corner and see if anyone got off at the bus stop. The bus indicated and pulled into the bus stop. When it pulled away, a lone woman stood on the footpath looking up and down the street, as if deciding which way to go. She started walking towards Main Street instead of towards the library. She was coming our way.

"This is me," I said to Ben, and swung the car door open. "I'll be back."

Chapter Thirty-eight:
[Ronnie: Friends?]

The woman strode purposefully towards the intersection. She wore a black jacket, dark blue jeans, and dark-coloured sneakers. I crossed Main Street and strode towards her equally as purposefully.

I waved. Kiwis are friendly. Everyone says so.

She slowed and looked over her shoulder, then back at me.

"Hi, Sandra King?" I asked when I was a metre away.

She stopped walking. Suspicion blossomed in her eyes. "Who are you?"

"A friend."

"I don't have friends in New Zealand," she said.

"You do now." I thrust my hand out. "Ronnie Tracey. Pleased to meet you. We've been expecting you."

"Ronnie Tracey," she echoed. "Surprised we didn't meet while you were stationed overseas."

"So am I." I pointed back to where I'd come from and waved to Ben. "Ben Reynolds is bringing the car over."

"Ben Reynolds," she repeated. "How did you know I'd be here?"

"Oh, you know, spycraft," I said with a grin. "Do you want a ride? Shall we go find Sadler?"

"Yeah, why not," she replied. She didn't sound altogether sure, but I was trying to appear friendly and not at all dodgy. "What's been going on?"

"We have a lot to discuss," I said, as the car pulled up beside the curb. I opened the front passenger door. "In you go. I'll take the back."

She sat the front passenger seat. I sat in the back.

"Ben Reynolds meet Sandra King," I said as I leaned forward between the seats. I didn't give either of them time to reply. "Did Sadler get off in Trentham?"

"Yes," she said. "He's walking."

"Do you know which streets? Or can you contact him?"

"I can." She pulled a phone from a pocket and made a call. When the call was answered she said, "I've met Ronnie Tracey and Ben Reynolds. Which way are you walking?"

I couldn't hear what his response was, but I'm sure it was interesting.

"What street are you on?"

She hung up.

"He's going to wait at Trentham Station on the racecourse side. I presume that means something to you?"

"It does," Ben replied. "Buckle up."

I leaned back in my seat and clicked my seat belt. King's seatbelt clicked into place. Ben drove towards Trentham Railway Station. Five minutes later we saw a tall male standing by the entrance to the station on Racecourse Road. Ben pulled up next to him and zapped his window down.

"Steven Sadler?"

"Ben Reynolds?" Came the reply.

"Jump in," Ben said.

I opened the passenger door from the inside. Steven Sadler folded himself into the car.

"Do you have enough leg room?" Ben asked.

"It'll do," he replied.

"I'm Ronnie Tracey," I said, offering my hand.

He shook it.

"Nicer than walking," Sadler said. "Thanks for the lift. Where are we going?"

"My offices," I said. Ben nodded.

"We heard Frost was in Upper Hutt," King said. She scrunched around in her seat so she could see us in the back.

"He was," Ben said. "We found a family member of his in Lower Hutt. Don't know if he was staying there, but we did see him there."

"Do you want him?" I enquired. My plans involved getting him scooped up by INTERPOL.

"We want him out of the way," Sadler said.

"About that," I said. "Any objections if I call INTERPOL and have him picked up?"

Sadler gave a small head shake. "Is he worth talking to beforehand?"

Ben fielded that question. "Short answer, no."

"Is there a longer answer?" Sadler asked.

"He came on like he was in charge but couldn't formulate a question to save his life. I had the distinct displeasure of him and two goons after the first ball. He used a couple of wannabe Bin Ladens to kidnap his own aunt and get me to trade her life for mine. At that point I did not know she was his aunt, or I would've stayed home and gone to sleep."

"He sounds like a charmer," Sadler said.

"Yep, he is that. He's a little man with a big ideas." Ben said.

"What happened to his goons?" Sadler asked. "Do I want to know?"

I screwed up my nose and shook my head. "Don't ask."

Sadler smiled.

Ben drove past the office, turned into the Woolworths carpark, then turned into Geange Street; left on Princes and straight into Leader Lane which ran behind the shops where Donald had his salon, and the café on the corner, and my offices. It was too early for anyone to be at work, so the few parks that were down the lane were empty. If we used the back door instead of the Fergusson drive one, we could get up the second set of stairs and run zero risk of being spotted. I led the way. Ben came last with our coffees and his phone. No one spoke until we were inside the main office. Ben grabbed my keys and disappeared.

"Have a seat," I said to King and Sadler, pointing to the big leather sofa under the window. "Can I get you anything? Coffee?"

"Tea, if you have it," Sadler said.

"Tea would be welcome," King agreed.

"I do have tea. When Ben gets back, I'll go make a pot."

"Where is he?" Sadler asked.

"Just putting something away."

366

He was putting his phone in the Faraday cage. He came back in, fairly quickly, and I left them in his capable hands to make a pot of tea. We're nice. We're hospitable. Can't fault our manners. Nana would be pleased.

Five minutes later, I carried a tray into the room and placed it on the coffee table. I went back and shut the door. Sadler helped himself to the tea, pouring them both a steaming mug full. We waited for them to settle.

"You're here because of the arms deal, right?" Ben asked.

"We are," Sadler confirmed.

"Working together or just travelling together?" I asked.

"Both," King said. "You were expecting us?"

"Indeed," I said. "Got word over a week ago that you were travelling this way. Did you get waylaid?"

"Something like that," King replied. "There was, and still is, a situation in Eastern Europe," Sadler said. "It's sticky."

"Broken arrow sticky?" Ben asked.

"That's next level black tar sticky," Sadler replied with a nod.

"It's true then," I said. "How come no one's talking. There's zero chatter. Zip."

"Russians have lost a nuclear warhead. That's about as humiliating as it gets. They're scrambling. Cover story is the Ukraine war."

"Handy. So, it's not lost, it's been misplaced?"

"Something like that."

"Handy they have a war to blame it on," I said.

King smiled. "Everything is blamed on the war."

Ben nodded. "Even here. We couldn't get a canister of helium because of the war."

Everyone laughed and just like that the ice melted away.

"Now what?" King asked.

"So far this mission has been a lot more Keystone cop than I'd like," I said, picking up a wine biscuit from the plate on the tray.

Sadler frowned. "In what way?"

"Frost is about as useless as you could get. As for the wannabe Bin Ladens he, or someone employed, those idiots wouldn't have been able to find dog shit in a dog park."

"Two of my mates were killed because of that little turd Frost," Sadler said.

"How do we get invited into the arms deal. We nearly didn't come because we knew we'd be late," King asked.

"You came all the way down here, knowing you would be too late for the bidding on the first round, and knowing there was a broken arrow in Europe." Ben placed his coffee on the table. "All this way ..."

Sadler wiped his mouth with the back of his hand. "Heard Frost was here."

"And you lost two mates," I said quietly. "He's not my favourite person either."

"What's he done to you?" Sadler asked, shaking his head. "The guy's been a fucking dickhead from day one."

"Left me in a desert and buggered off."

King looked at Sadler. "It was Ronnie," she said.

He nodded. "We were swapping stories about the wanker on our travels. She told me someone was left in the desert while he swanned off with Bedouins and made deals."

"That was me," I said waving my hand. "I hoped to never see his short arse again."

"People like that, they're cockroaches; never seem to die," Sadler said.

"Of course, Australia and New Zealand have another attraction," Ben said. "Safest place to be in case of a broken arrow in Europe. But that wouldn't have figured into your plans."

"Maybe a little bit," Sadler said.

Self-preservation, there was nothing wrong with that. With what I knew as sure as Nana loved shortbread, I would not be heading offshore any time soon. Whether the broken arrow was really what the bidding was about or not.

"You know what's weird?" I asked. No one responded. "The arms deal that bounced around the world and landed here is happening via a piece of software meaning they could've been anywhere in the world, and it wouldn't matter."

"I see what you mean. There's got to be a reason they insisted the interested parties front up when they're using software for the bidding, surely?" Sadler said. "And the two losers that you mentioned, there's got to be something behind that?"

"I'd like to think they weren't just time wasters, but maybe they were," I said. "What do you think Ben?"

"Definitely time wasters. But they wasted more than my time. Those idiots interfered with other people over the course of the weekend following the first ball."

That was the first I'd heard about that.

"When did you find that out?"

Ben picked up a biscuit. "I couldn't tell you without checking. My phone fair explodes with bullshit the minute it hits open air. But I definitely saw that in a text message from Grandad."

I decided I liked Grandad as a name for Tierney. It seemed friendlier than his real name. And for us, Ben and me, he was friendly.

"We should've followed up. Who else was grabbed?" I took my phone out of my pocket. "I'll text him and get a list." I stopped moving. "Interfered with? That sounds disgusting."

"Yeah. Don't think anyone else was abducted like I was, but would anyone say that when it could open up a line of questioning, they wouldn't want?"

"Were they with you the whole time?" I was aware of Sadler and King's interest in the conversation.

"I don't think they were with us the whole time. Some-one was, but was it those bozos or was it Frost? There were long periods of time when no one spoke. Could've been anyone in the room. They really liked keeping the black hood on me."

I glanced at my watch. It was time to make a phone

call. I chose Liam from my contacts and rang him.

He answered fairly quickly. "Ronnie?"

"Yep. Got a hot tip for you."

"Shoot."

"I've got an address for Jackson Frost. He's definitely in New Zealand and I believe you have a Red Notice with his mug on it."

"I do. Text me the address. How did ... never mind, I don't want to know."

"Texting it to you now. Have fun!" I hung up and handed the phone to Ben. "Can you text Liam with Nancy's address please?"

He took the phone, sent the text, and passed it back with a smile.

"First job of the day done," I said, biting my biscuit.

"What's next?" Ben asked.

"Grandad," I replied. Texting Grandad to ask for a list of people who were accosted over that first weekend. I didn't want to know what sort of survey he put together to get that information. I just wanted names.

"Grandad?" King asked. "Not your real-life Grandad, Ronnie?"

"No, nope, not at all."

"We read an article in the paper about an elderly woman, June Tracey, any relation?"

"My Nana," I replied. "Don't let her catch you calling her elderly." She's happy to tell the world she's ninety-four, but she doesn't want to be called elderly.

"I put two and two together when you told me your

name. Just wondered if it was a family business and your Grandad was getting intel for you."

I shook my head. "Definitely not a family business."

They heard. And they weren't in New Zealand at the time. Don't tell me she was international now.

"Can I ask how you read the article?"

"The Guardian ran the story," King said. "It was online."

Of course, it was. I hoped Nana did not know she'd reached international audiences with her troublemaking.

"It's my Grandad, Ronnie is referring to," Ben said. "No relation to her."

Neither of us was keen to say who he was. We hardly knew the people in front of us. *Genesis* said they were friendly, but we hardly knew them.

My phone buzzed.

Grandad: Shane Mansilla, Daniel Henry, Robert Jackson, Brendon Cullen, Luke Nash, Tim Morgan, Madison Blake, Neve O'Reilly, Leah Addison.

I read the list out loud. And waited to see if anyone recognised a name or two.

I didn't. Ben didn't.

"Either of you heard those names before?" King asked us. King looked at Sadler. If I hadn't turned my head at the right time, I would've missed the subtle nod.

I shook my head. I scrabbled over the guest list I'd read from the first ball in my mind and none of the names were familiar in an 'I've seen them before' kind of way. But they had to be on the list we gave Grandad. That was strange. In my brain's defence, there were over three hundred names. Memorising them all wasn't in my wheelhouse.

"Does that list have gender?" Sadler asked.

"Nope, just names," I said. "None of them are familiar."

"How'd you get the names?"

Ben spoke, "I got my hands on a guest list from the first ball. We asked someone to survey all the guests and find out if they'd been approached by anyone after the ball."

"And the names you read out are the people who responded with confirmation that someone approached them?" King asked.

"Yes," I said.

"Why would they say?"

"Guess the questions were worded in a way that didn't seem like anyone was interrogating them," I said. "We just knew it was happening, not who was doing it, and how it would be achieved."

"So, you think those people would have been at the second ball ..."

"You'd think," I replied. "We need the guest list to confirm." I looked at Ben. "Where would that be? Who was running the ball for the charity event?"

"A woman ..."

I could see him thinking and waited for steam to rush

out his ears.

"We might need more than that, Ben," I said with a smile.

"Karen Rendel."

"Good work." I went and grabbed my laptop from my desk. "Let's find her." I typed her name into the usual white pages database. "Good news, she isn't hiding. She lives in Golf Road. Even better news, she's a wedding planner."

"Let's have a look at the house first, before we go wherever your mind just went," Ben said.

It was too late I was already there. "We could just go and ask her if she'd plan our wedding ..."

"House first, then field trip," Ben replied. "She might not be receptive to drop-ins on a Sunday."

I opened the address in Maps and zoomed in. "Big house set on impressive grounds. Looks like the perimeter fencing is concrete block and over six feet high." I spun my laptop to face him, and he lifted it off my knee to get it closer.

"Dogs?" Ben asked.

"Probably," I replied. "We can go for a walk and suss it."

Sadler leaned closer to see the image on the screen. "What kind of gates? Will they have a gate code?"

"Depends on how security conscious they are," I said. "I would if I were them, but then not everyone sees the world like we do."

"We could go knock on the door and ask for the list,"

King said. "Or ask for a contact number of someone on the list."

"Pick a name then," I said. "We'll rock up and ask. At least she might get the laptop with the list on it if we've got a good enough reason to contact someone."

"We've got a bit of expertise. I'm sure between us all we can come up with a reason that would cause her to bring that list up. Or at least show us where it is," Sadler said.

"Ben should ask," I said.

The other two nodded.

"He's the pretty boy and the famous one," Sadler said.

"He's good at getting people to talk," I replied.

"Field trip then," King said. "How far away is it?"

"Seven minutes," I said.

I could've said we could go grab Romeo and walk down from home. We know people find it hard to refuse him entry to places. But I had a feeling Ben would be fine. He could turn on his famous charm, and dazzle Mrs Rendel with his sparkling personality.

"Before we go ..." Ben passed the computer back to me. "How sure are you two about the Europe situation?"

"As sure as we can be given the extremely fast shut-down of all channels. And we noticed a few people looking for flights to anywhere but another European city."

"People like who?"

"Like us. Like you. Spooks are running."

That observation felt like a big fat lie. I had nothing to challenge it with, but it didn't feel right.

"What's the word from official channels. What are MI6 saying?" Ben asked. I guessed he didn't like what Sadler said either.

"I can't tell you that."

"King, can you tell us what you heard from CSIS." I asked. We were told King was Canadian and an intelligence officer with see-sis.

She shrugged. "Same as Sadler. Can't tell you."

"So, sharing," I replied. "Right, this is what we're doing ..." I took a breath and outlined my plan. "Ben and I are going in to see Karen Rendel, on our own. We will ask her to plan our wedding. I will ask her to give me the contact details for Neve O'Reilly because of the gown she wore. I liked it enough to want to use the same designer for my wedding dress. Of course, I would have to talk to Neve O'Reilly to find out who designed the gown."

"I have a good feeling about this."

Sadler and King sat silently.

"I need to make a phone call, I'll be right back," I said, and excused myself. I went down the hall and into my private room, locking the door behind me. I rang Enzo.

"Hiya," I said when he answered.

"How was the ball?"

"Great fun," I replied. "I need a hand."

"Name it," he said. I could hear the calm in his voice. Enzo was a calm, chilled guy until he wasn't.

"Two people have turned up, both from the intelligence community. I need them babysat while Ben and I go confirm something."

"What don't you like about them, Ronnie?"

"Pretty much everything. They're too late to be here for our operation so I'm not sure why they are here. Made noises that they were here to grab someone. I've already had him scooped up. I don't know, Enzo, just something off."

"Where are they?"

"My office," I said. "We probably want them out of there in case Steph and Jenn call into work for something." Then I had an idea. "Unless you want to put them in my lock-up?"

"Let's keep it friendly until we know more," Enzo said. "Crockett's office. Take them there, I'll clear it with him and then meet you at his office."

"Ten minutes, Enzo."

"Done."

"Thank you."

"Family does for family, Ronnie."

It is a family business, but the loudest part of the family isn't involved. Did I just lump Donald in with Nana? Yes, I did. I hung up, pocketed my phone, let myself out, and locked up behind me.

Sadler and King looked up when I opened the main office door. I shot them a friendly smile. I'm friendly. Look at me being friendly. Nana would be proud. She liked my smile.

Ben stood. "All okay out there?" he asked.

"Yes. Enzo is meeting us at Crockett's office in ten. So, we best get going."

King scowled. "I thought we were going to see that woman?"

"We are. You aren't."

They animated and blustered. "That's not what we talked about," King said.

"We're going with you," Sadler affirmed.

I didn't like either of their tones.

"You'll go where we take you," I replied. "And if that isn't what you want, we're happy to cuff you and leave you in the lock-up for the day. After all that tea I'm sure that would become uncomfortable pretty quick." Some days I am pleased with my past self who decided we needed a jail cell built into one of our under-used rooms here. It was known as the lock-up.

"Why? You know who we are?"

"Do we?"

"Of course, you do," Sadler snapped.

"What's this about?" King asked. She wasn't any happier than her friend. "We're on the same side."

Yeah, I'm not convinced.

"Let's go," Ben said. "Quicker we get there, the quicker we get back."

Ben opened the main door and ushered them out. I followed behind. Once at the car, Ben encouraged Sadler to sit in the front and King in the back with me. No one resisted. They complained a lot.

Chapter Thirty-nine:
[Ben: The wedding planner.]

We left the complaining couple to Enzo. He would find out who they were just in case they weren't who they said they were. I know Ronnie had suspicions. They were too late if they were supposed to be involved in the deal. That was a major red flag.

I parked on the road. We approached the gates hand-in-hand.

It was just after nine and by the look of it we were going to have a clear sky and warm day.

The big wooden gates were shut. There was a smaller wooden gate from the street by the letterbox. There was no buzzer and no warning about dogs. I opened the latch and held the gate for Ronnie.

We made sure the gate was shut behind us. If you open it, you close it. Life has rules.

Hand-in-hand we walked up a rosebush-lined, stone path to the house. A large verandah ran the length of the front. It looked like it could be closed if required; the wall was stone with a wooden cap. I saw a porch swing. The house reminded me of houses I'd seen in the South back home. We climbed the four steps to the verandah. There was a proper bell by the front door. It was made of brass and hung from a wrought iron bracket. I rang it twice.

Ronnie smiled at me. "This is a cool house."

I smiled back and nodded.

It didn't take too long before the front door swung open revealing a woman in her fifties, wearing jeans and a loose-fitting pin-striped, pink shirt.

"Good morning," she said. "How can I help?"

That was when I saw the recognition flick in her eyes.

"We have a request," Ronnie said, while making sure her engagement ring came into view. "Karen Rendel, wedding planner?"

Karen smiled. "Yes, that's me."

"We're sorry to call in on a Sunday," I said. "Hope you don't mind."

"Not at all. Come in."

We followed her inside to a comfortable den.

"And you are?" she said, sitting in a large red leather armchair, and gesturing to a sofa.

"I'm Ronnie Tracey," Ronnie replied, and sat on the sofa.

"I'm Ben Reynolds," I said, and sat next to Ronnie.

"Of course, Mr Reynolds. We watch your programme."

There you go.

"That's a beautiful ring, Ms Tracey," she said, then turned to me. "Well done, Mr Reynolds. You have exquisite taste."

"Thank you," we said.

"We were hoping you would take us on as clients," Ronnie said, with a friendly smile on her lips. "Could you tell us a bit about what we can expect with a wedding planner and how we go about all this?"

I could see Karen Rendel was pleased at the prospect

of taking charge of our wedding. She nodded. "I can do that. Shall we have a chat about the wedding?"

"That would be great. Again, we're sorry to encroach on your Sunday," Ronnie said.

Karen smiled. Her expression changed. She wanted our business.

"Now, as for wedding planning, what have you discussed so far?"

"Not much," I said. "We are newly engaged and would like to do this together." I squeezed Ronnie's hand.

"Excellent," she said. "Did you have any themes in mind?"

Our blank faces probably suggested we did not.

"That's fine," she continued. "It's not necessary to have a theme. What about a colour palette?"

"Definitely not tangerine and purple," Ronnie said.

Karen smiled. "Bad experience?"

"You could say that."

I watched a thought form on Karen's face. "Of course, you're Ronnie Tracey. Your cousin is Donald Henere-Tracey."

"You know Donald?"

"Yes. Oh, my goodness. He is my preferred hair designer for the weddings my company plans."

Already we had a way in. I'd never thought about Donald as being the conduit. If anything was going to cement our relationship with Karen Rendel, it would be Donald.

Karen smiled at us.

"I know why you don't want a garish colour scheme,"

Karen said. "But you must admit that it certainly worked for Donald and Enzo."

"It did," we agreed.

"Could you show us sample colours?" I asked.

"Of course, I have a palette book that will give you a good idea." She stood and went to shelves behind her desk. "Hopefully you'll see something you like. Of course, we can put any colour combination together. Have a look. Might give us a starting point." She handed the binder to me.

We flicked through the first few pages together. A lot of golds and beiges in the beginning. "What do you think?" I whispered to Ronnie and pointed to a page with soft yellows and silver.

"It's quite nice." She leaned close. "How about you choose the colour scheme and I choose my frock?"

"Perfect."

Karen lifted her eyes from a pad of paper on her knee. "Did you have a style of dress in mind, Ronnie?" She smiled. "I'm finely tuned to dress discussion," she said. "Didn't mean to eavesdrop."

Ronnie nodded and smiled. "We're dividing up the tasks," she said. "If it's okay with you. Could you and I discuss frocks?"

"Come over to my desk Ronnie. I have designs we can look through."

"Great."

Ronnie stood and followed Karen. I kept an ear out and looked at the colour samples and suggested use of colour. It wasn't the worst job. But I was under no illusion as to who would really be planning our wedding. That would be Ronnie's Nana.

Ronnie and Karen chatted as Karen showed her designs from various designers. The chatter went on for about half an hour and then Ronnie asked if she'd seen a particular gown from the masked ball.

"I think her name was Neve," Ronnie said. "I couldn't be sure. But I remember thinking her gown would be a spectacular wedding dress."

"Can you describe it?"

I listened, because she could not, and I wanted to see how far she'd take it. Not far. Ronnie flapped her hands around and tried a few descriptive words then gave up.

"Honestly, I remember thinking at the time I should find out who she was wearing."

And Karen kicked in. "We can do that," she said. "I have a list of everyone at the ball because of course, we like to send thank you cards for donations, and keep in touch."

She moved papers around on the desk, then opened a white ring binder. We thought it would be on her computer. I watched without watching.

"Let's see if we can find her," Karen said. "Most women love talking gowns, so, I'm sure it wouldn't be a problem. But of course, I will ask discreetly before putting you in touch."

"That's wonderful, thank you," Ronnie said.

"While you're looking, how about a nice pot of coffee?"

Karen asked.

"Please," I said from the sofa. "I would love a coffee."

"Right, you as well, Ronnie?"

"Yes, thank you."

"I'll get the coffee underway and be back shortly. You look through that and hopefully you can find her."

"Thank you," Ronnie said smiling.

As soon as Karen left the room, Ronnie pulled her phone from her pocket and photographed every page of the guest list.

I joined her at the desk with the colour binder open at a brown palette, it was more gold than brown.

"What do you think?" I asked.

"I got all the pages. Neve O'Reilly is on the list."

"We'll go through with the designer query and see what happens?" I kissed her cheek. Karen came into view with a tray holding a French Press, small coffee cups, and pastries.

She set the tray on the coffee table and turned to us. "Any luck?"

Ronnie gave a slight smile. "I think so."

"And, I we have a colour palette," I said. "Deep golds and cream. Do you mind if we photograph the page? I was just getting Ronnie's approval."

"Not at all."

Ronnie whipped her phone out and took a photo of the open page then put it back in her pocket.

"Come and have coffee," Karen said. "I think you two are going to be my dream couple. Already chosen a colour palette and no arguing."

Ronnie beamed. I wondered if we could use Karen.

And Ronnie answered the question for me, "We would like to hire you. Do you have venues you prefer?"

I nudged her with my elbow. "Nana," I mumbled.

"Oh yes, Ronnie, your famous Nana. How could I forget?" Karen said smiling. "I would be happy to include your Nana in the planning."

"That's very kind," Ronnie said. "Nana is a handful. I wouldn't wish her on anyone."

"Don't be silly. It'll be fine. I saw the photos, so I know what she did for Donald. He was adamant that Nana plan his wedding. And I am happy to include her."

"Thank you," Ronnie said. "She has opinions."

Karen smiled. "I come across many people with strong opinions in this job. I am well used to managing them."

"Good. You'll need to bring your A-game to wrangle my Nana."

"Did you say you found the owner of the gown you liked?" Karen asked Ronnie while pouring the coffee. I laid the open colour book on an end table and sat with Ronnie on the sofa.

"I did," Ronnie said. "There was only one Neve, so I hope it's her."

"We'll have our coffee and then I'll reach out and ask her about her dress." Karen held out a cup to her.

"Thank you," Ronnie said and took the offered cup.

We had what we needed. I glanced at my watch, trying not to be obvious. We'd been there over an hour. And it was a Sunday. Karen really went over and above to get clients.

"Thank you for seeing us today. Sorry to drop in unannounced," I said. "We were feeling impulsive."

"I'm happy to be able to help. Usually Sundays are quiet. Saturdays are wedding days and Sundays are recovery days. But yesterday I'd planned for the masked ball and had no wedding."

"It must've taken quite a while to plan the ball," I said.

"About as long as it takes to plan a wedding," she replied with a laugh. "But it was good fun, and I didn't have to consult brides for theme, colours, or anything else."

"Sounds like you enjoyed it," I said.

"You were there. It was a wonderful night. We raised a lot of money."

I finished my coffee.

Karen took a sip of hers. "Dancing," she said. "A venue with a large dance floor?"

I nodded. "Yes."

"Have you discussed your first dance?"

"Tango," Ronnie said with a grin. "Our first dance will be a tango."

Karen's eyes widened. "I don't believe anyone has chosen a tango as their first dance at any of my weddings. I shall enjoy the planning of this wedding," she said, smiling. "I shall enjoy this very much."

"Good," Ronnie said.

"I'll make enquiries and get a venue booked. That's

usually the hardest part. Give me the month and I will work with it," she said.

Ronnie and I looked at each other. "Next winter; June," I said. Ronnie smiled her agreement.

Chapter Forty:
[Ronnie: Tango baby.]

Crockett was in his office when we arrived. He and Enzo were talking in the outer office. There was no sign of Sadler and King. His private office door was closed.

"How'd it go?" Crockett asked.

"Pretty good. We have a wedding planner. Karen Rendel is a professional and she's doing our wedding." I said with a big smile at them both. "June wedding."

Enzo's face crumpled. "No. You can't. Nana will ..." Words failed Enzo.

"... Crack a shit!" Crockett finished the sentence for him.

"Hear us out," Ben said. "It's not all bad. Our planner is happy to include Ronnie's Nana, but she and her cronies won't be able to override our wishes."

They stood there flapping their mouths like they were catching flies for at least five seconds before Enzo's voice kicked in. "She has no idea what she's agreed to do."

"She must have some clue," I said. "Donald is her preferred hair designer."

Enzo wasn't convinced. "My darling husband is blinkered when it comes to Nana, even after all the shenanigans she's dragged him into."

I shrugged. "She's a professional. She should be able to manage Nana."

"I hope she charges like a wounded bull," Crockett said

with a chuckle. "She might need a nice holiday to recover."

"Moving on," I said, and tipped my thumb towards his closed office. "The guests?"

"They're interesting," Crockett said. "Why are they in New Zealand?"

"We were told they were coming, expected them over a week ago, and they're supposedly here for the bidding," I said.

"I'm calling bullshit on that. No one arrives a good week late for an arms deal," Crockett muttered. "What the hell are they playing at?"

"Have you spoken to them?" I said to Enzo.

"I have."

"And?"

"I don't think they are who they say they are."

Whoa. What?

"We asked for pictures and got them."

"Who from?"

"Can't say, but a trusted source."

"And you've never come across them before?" Enzo asked.

"Correct. It's a big world."

"Not that big, Ronnie. Not that big."

That was an interesting comment from Enzo. I hadn't come across any of the three men standing in front of me before they dropped into my life, and we were all in the same field.

"Who are they? I was expecting a female Canadian intelligence officer named Sandra King, and a male with MI6 named Steven Sadler. These two fit the bill," I said. "So, if they're not Sadler and King, who are they?"

"The woman is Kallie Duncan. She isn't Canadian, she's American."

"Okay, and?"

"Her pal is Kevin Jones."

"Why are they pretending to be intelligence officers?"

"They're Diamond Corporation PMC's," Enzo said. "What they're here for is to find all the people involved in the deal and remove them from the land of the living."

"They're piggybacking on our intelligence," Ben said carefully. "They're late because they wanted the people identified. Then they can just pop them off."

"And Frost?"

"Apparently having him here was a bonus. An actual monetary bonus."

"It was only a matter of time before there was bounty on him," I said. "Does that mean we can collect for having him picked up?"

"You can try."

"The idiots that grabbed Ben wanted him to believe they were PMC's with Diamond Corp," I said. "Strange isn't it."

We all agreed.

"What do we know about Diamond Corp?" Crockett asked.

"We know that there are two Diamond Corp operatives spy hunting in New Zealand," I said. "Are they them?"

"Maybe, but these two have just arrived in the last twenty-four hours."

"Then not them. We were told earlier than the last twenty-four hours," Ben said.

"Where are the real Sandra King and Steven Sadler?"

"They say they don't know," Enzo said. "I find that difficult to believe because they are travelling as them."

"You got ID?"

"Crockett pulled some strings. They arrived yesterday morning on a flight from Sydney. The names they used were Steven Sadler and Sandra King."

"I did pull strings. And I also pulled passport verification. The photos of King and Sadler are the people in there ... but the photos CSIS and MI6 have, are definitely not."

"Fake passports," I mumbled. "You've gotta be good to make that work with the chips in them now."

"Tech gets better, forgeries get better. It's the way of the world."

"What do we do with them?" I asked. "We can't let them run around killing people, or can we?"

"We probably shouldn't," Crockett replied.

"They want the people bidding on an arms deal ... maybe we can turn a blind eye?" I said questioning myself as I said it. I couldn't let them go knowing they were going to commit murders in New Zealand. No. That's a step too far.

"It would end the deal. Think about it. The people bidding, are buying weapons to kill other people with,"

Crockett said. "When's the trial?"

Ben said, "This evening."

"If they find them all, and kill them before hand?"

"We won't get whoever is behind the entire deal. They'll set up again and maybe it will go ahead, and no one will be able to stop it," Ben said.

"Does anyone have intelligence suggesting that the head honcho is in New Zealand?" Crockett asked.

"No," I replied.

"So, the chances of getting whoever it is are slim," he said.

I gave it thought. We all seemed to be thinking. There we were standing in the outer office of Crockett's tradie company, trying to decide if we were happy to let some hired guns loose in New Zealand, to kill a bunch of people.

"There is something else you should know," I said. "We suspect a broken arrow. They, in Crockett's office, confirmed a broken arrow situation in Europe, but is that true?"

"What does that have to do with the arms sale?" Enzo said with care. "What are you saying, Ronnie?"

"I'm saying we don't know what will be fired from the S-400 this evening."

"Do we know what's happening with the sale?"

Ben shook his head. "I had to leave my phone in the Faraday cage in Ronnie's office. Can't afford that software to be listening to our conversations."

"I say, we go get it and find out what's going on,"

Crockett said. "There's one more ball, right? The last ball of the season, are they going to use that?"

"Right, there is another ball, but if Ronnie's correct it will all come to a head this evening and that last ball won't be involved."

"How close do you think you are, Ronnie?" Enzo asked.

"Very, couldn't tell you why. I have this feeling I can't shake that the whole point of the fucking bidding is to get an audience, then whoever it is fires a missile from that S-400, and we all find out it's a nuke that was fired."

"And the point?" Crockett asked. "Because if you're right, then we have a bigger problem than those two in there." He tipped his thumb towards his office door.

"It's hunch, that's all. But I think someone is going to fire a nuclear warhead from Kaliningrad, at a NATO target to force NATO into the Ukraine-Russian war."

"And the arms deal?" he asked.

"It's a way of having witnesses to his destruction. Bitcoin will fall into the nominated account and a full-scale war will begin. War is profitable."

"It is," Crockett agreed. "And your gut is telling you someone is going to make it look like Russia fired a nuke at a NATO target."

"Thing is, Putin hasn't ruled out battlefield nuclear warheads and he moved some into Belarus. Do you think Lukashenko took delivery of them because they're pretty, or because he's willing to fire them?" I said.

Crockett rolled his eyes. "He's trustworthy, you know

he is."

"If his pal says fire, he will do it," I said. "Think back to 2018. Russia moved Iskander missiles to Kaliningrad which are nuclear capable, and the rumour mill had Russia upgrading a nuclear storage site in Kaliningrad. Why would you do that unless you planned on moving some nukes into the nice home Putin built for them?"

"Alright. Belarus has battlefield nukes belonging to Russia. Kaliningrad is Russian and has battlefield nukes. Someone has purloined a nuke and is going to fire it at a NATO target this evening our time ... that is what you're saying?" Crockett asked.

"That's what I'm saying." And I would very much like to be wrong.

"Right, let's turn our guests free, and let them mop up the bidders in New Zealand?"

I wasn't opposed to that idea. It worried me that I wasn't opposed to that idea.

"Any chance of locating the person, or organisation, behind this?" Enzo asked.

"I don't know. We're not the only ones working on this, but we're the only ones with inside access in New Zealand. Everyone is trying to find the organisation behind this mess," I said. "Or maybe not everyone."

"We were told Diamond Corp was spy hunting," Ben said.

"I doubt anyone would come out and say it was a kill-mission," I replied. "Guess they figured we'd probably keep out of their way if they were spy hunting. But assuming the identities of actual spies and trying to find a way into our job that way? Not very nice. I'd also like to know where King and Sadler really are."

"I'll go ask," Enzo said, throwing a smile at me and walking into the other room. He closed the door behind him.

Ben, Crockett, and I waited.

I leaned on the wall and jammed my hands in my jeans pockets. Sunlight streamed in through the unshaded window. It really was a nice day. It was a shame we weren't out enjoying it. Complications. Always complications.

Enzo opened the door then closed it as he stepped out.

"They would like to toddle off and kill people," he said. "King and Sadler are still in Europe. Apparently."

I pulled my phone from my pocket and called *Uncle George*.

I waited as the phone rang and rang.

The call dropped.

Okay.

I looked at my phone screen as a call popped up. *Uncle George*.

Maybe he was indisposed a second ago?

I answered.

"Ronnie, how can I help?" This time it was a slightly more feminine voice on the line.

"Locate Sandra King and Steven Sadler, please."

"I was under the impression you had them."

"So were we. They are not them, but they might be Diamond Corp: Kallie Duncan and Kevin Jones."

"I'll see what I can do. What have they told you about Sadler and King?"

"That they are still in Europe."

"Do they know anything about the mission?"

"Yep. They're well aware of the arms deal and wanted the list of names. They're here to stop their intake of oxygen." And we gave them the bloody names, I thought but kept it to myself.

"I'll get back to you, as soon as I can."

"Thanks *Uncle George*."

I hung up.

"Are we having fun yet?" Crockett asked.

"Yeah, truck loads," I said.

"Are we turning them loose?"

"Not yet. *Uncle George* is getting back to me first. I want to know the real Sadler and King aren't in a ditch somewhere."

"Jones has a real beef with Jackson Frost," Enzo said. "I didn't know Frost was in New Zealand."

"He's a horrible little man," I said. "Had him picked up by INTERPOL this morning. I hope I did anyway."

"Jones mentioned the two MI6 intelligence officers that were killed in Poland and said Frost was behind it."

"That's what we heard too," Ben said. "It was an arms deal gone bad. That's why we suspected Frost had something to do with this deal, but I don't believe he does. Chances are whoever is calling the shots keeps him around as a fall guy."

That made sense. He wasn't smart enough to bring the whole deal together, but he would have enough connections. It'd look good on paper. It would make him the person everyone sees in various locations and who pops up like a bad smell every time an arms deal is in the wind. Then they'd hang him out to dry if anything went south. Like Poland. Did I feel sorry for him being the scape goat? No. Couldn't happen to a nicer guy.

"That's an evil looking smile, Ronnie," Enzo commented pointing to my face. "What were you thinking about?"

"Frost getting his comeuppance," I replied with a shrug. "I hope he gets everything he so richly deserves."

"Pretty sure our guests feel the same way."

"Anyone that's met him feels the same way." I turned and looked out the window. There wasn't much traffic on the street. It was such a nice day people were out walking. Crockett's office wasn't in Upper Hutt city. He'd moved offices and was now in Camp Street, Trentham. He was near a bakery. They weren't open on Sundays. I watched a couple walk down the street with a child on a scooter. Across the road there was a panel beater workshop. They weren't open either. It was fairly peaceful on a Sunday in Camp Street. During the week the bakery was a favourite place for armed forces to grab lunch. The only place that seemed to be bustling today was the laundrette. Army towns have a lot of laundrettes. And Upper Hutt is an Army town. It was also home to Joint Forces Command. We regularly saw Army, Navy, and Airforce uniforms about town.

I faced the room again.

"What?" Crockett said when I made eye contact with him.

"Put them in the cell at Art's?" At least at Art's place no one would come across them by accident. I really didn't want to explain to Steph or Jenn why I had two people in our lock-up at work. Not today anyway.

"They'll have to be shackled," Enzo replied. "And frisked prior."

"Can you two handle that?" I asked.

"Of course," Crockett replied. "What are you two going to do?"

"Wait for confirmation that the real Sadler and King are alive. And see if we can find any of the people on the list."

"Sing out if you need help. Once they're locked up," Crockett said, "I'll leave Art and Plunger as the security detail. We'll head to your office?"

"Okay, that works," I replied.

Crockett already had Art on the phone and was making plans.

I waved. We left.

Chapter Forty-one:
[Crockett: Crazy times.]

Ronnie sat at her desk. I sat in front of her, listening to her on the phone. She was trying to get Diamond Corp to admit they were head-hunting, not spy-hunting. It didn't sound like anyone was playing ball. She was persistent, I'll give her that. She changed tactics. She was calm, reasonable, giving nothing away, but pushing gently. All of a sudden, she shot me a grin and beckoned me closer as she wrote on a lined pad in all caps.

Confirmation. Head-hunt. Sadler and King turned up in Prague. Bound and gagged. No ID.

"Jesus," I hissed, "Alive?"

She shook her head. Diamond Corp just tossed their own under the bus.

"That'll be coming down the pipeline," I said as she hung up.

"No doubt," Ronnie said rocking back in her chair. "I'm going to tap into some sources and see what's being said."

"Are they another job for your mate, Liam?"

"I suppose they will be sooner or later," she said. "For now, we have them, right?"

"Yep. Art and Plunger are security. They're shackled in his cells."

"Does Art know about his freezer?"

"No doubt he's looked. The car was in his garage for a

few days."

"Was?"

"Gone. It'll be in pieces at Pick a Part by now."

"Good."

"Where'd Ben go?"

"He's out the back with his phone. Checking, bidding, trying to blend in and not look suspicious. He gave them a bit of flack earlier this morning."

"Fair enough."

"Sources ...," Ronnie said and righted her chair. "Come with?"

"Sure, where are we going?"

"Tom and Ginny's. I want to make sure they're okay, and Tom might be the source we need."

"I can see that. Go tell Ben we're out."

She stood, turned her laptop off, and grabbed her backpack from the back of her chair. She tossed her phone in the front pocket and zipped it shut. I picked up my keys from her desk.

Ronnie and I made sure Ben was all right, then locked up and left. He'd meet us in an hour or so. We would let him know where. There were quite a few cars on the road. People were out to do their groceries and living their lives. There was a steady stream of cars both north and south on Fergusson Drive. Even so, the drive to Elmslie Road took only ten minutes. I parked on the road. We walked down. One of the cats saw us and followed, walking on the top of the fence to the front gate. Ginny was sitting on the deck having a smoke.

"Helliare, Ronnie. Morning, Crockett," she called. "Nice day."

"Beautiful day," Ronnie replied. "Everything quiet and normal here?"

"It is," she replied. "Recovering from last night's festivities. What a night. You and Ben are magic on the dance floor."

"The things we find out, huh?" I said, with a grin at Ginny and Ronnie. "Dark horses those two."

"You weren't too shabby yourself, Crockett," Ginny said. "What brings you out this way today?"

I looked at Ronnie and she took over. "We have a list of names and I suspect they are aliases. Was hoping I could run them by you and Tom. Maybe they would trigger something that's helpful."

"Let's go inside and find Tom," Ginny said, stubbing her cigarette out and picking up the butt. She stood and tottered across the deck to the open ranch slider. "Come on in."

We followed her in, and she called for Tom. He poked his head around the hallway door.

"I'm right here." He clocked us and said, "Ronnie and Crockett, good to see you."

"And you," I said. "Looked like you enjoyed yourself last night."

Tom entered the lounge. "I think we all did," he said. "What can we do for you? Ben's okay?"

"He's fine," Ronnie said. "We have a list of names and we matched them to the guest list from last night."

"Fast work," Tom said. "How'd you do that?"

"Oh, you know, called in on the organiser and had the perfect excuse to see the guest list."

"I bet there's more to that story."

"Later," Ronnie replied. She pulled a notebook from her pocket. "Names." Ronnie read them out. Neither Tom nor Ginny appeared to recognise any bar a first name.

"Shane is our mechanic. Certainly, didn't see him at the ball," Ginny said.

"The rest aren't ringing any bells, sorry about that," Tom said. "But let's go downstairs and plug them into the system." He led the way up the hall.

Ginny linked her arm with Ronnie's. "You haven't tried *Genesis*?"

I followed behind.

"Not yet."

"Well, we can send them if we have no joy in Tom's databases."

"Cool," Ronnie replied, and tried to stifle a yawn.

"No yawning," I said. "It's contagious and we've got a day to get through."

"Some of us haven't slept," she replied and yawned. "I bet Ben's having a nap."

We all followed Tom down the stairs, hidden in the wardrobe of his home office, and into a small room which led to another room, large enough for us all to be semi-comfortable.

A computer fired up. A screen came to life. Tom sat at his large desk. I grabbed the stacked folding chairs from the back wall, and set them in a semi-circle behind Tom.

Ronnie handed him the notebook with the list of names. He typed slowly, using the time-honoured hunt and peck method. It would've been simpler to offer to type for him, but sometimes blokes can get a bit prickly. So, I said nothing and waited.

Shane Mansilla came back as a mechanic in Upper Hutt. There was absolutely nothing to suggest he wasn't a mechanic. He'd been a business owner for over twenty years.

"Probably not that Shane," Ronnie said.

"I shouldn't think so," Ginny replied. "He's our mechanic. And I think we would've seen him, or he would've seen us, last night, and said hello."

"Next," I said.

Tom painstakingly typed 'David Henry' into his search bar.

We all watched to see what would happen.

The words 'person deceased' popped up on the screen. Under that was an obituary.

One at a time he plugged each of the remaining names into the search bar.

One came back as a teacher at Trentham School. Further investigation showed the person died two years ago. The rest of the names were also dead people.

He searched cemeteries and discovered that all the names were from Akatarawa Cemetery.

"Is that helpful?" I asked.

"No," Tom said. "It's a big place. There is no requirement to sign in. It's a cemetery. A good place to find names that are no longer in use."

"Names are all bogus," Ronnie said. "Can we find out anything else? Like for example the first time those names were used by live people?"

"We can," Tom said. He opened a programme. "I'll send them to *Genesis* and get that system to search for them. Might have more luck. Bigger databases. These people, they're not New Zealanders, right?"

"We don't know for sure, but suspect not," I said.

"They had to enter the country somewhere."

I nodded. "It wouldn't be under those names."

Tom swivelled his chair so he faced us. "They're all in the app that Ben has, yes? They're bidding?"

Ronnie nodded. "Names don't match the app. Everyone was assigned a code name."

"Get Ben on the phone or get him here," Tom said. "The code names might give us something we can use."

"Why didn't I think of that?" Ronnie mumbled as she stood up and opened the door.

"Because you are exhausted," Ginny told her. "Don't be long."

She closed the door behind her.

"What happened this morning?" Ginny asked me.

"Two people who we knew were coming into the country arrived, but it's not them."

"Run that by me again," Tom asked.

"Sadler and King, they're dead. Their bodies were found in Prague. Two Diamond Corp operatives murdered them and took their places."

"Shit," Tom said. "Sadler was a good guy."

"You knew them?"

"Him, I knew. We'd worked a job together a few years ago."

I pulled my phone out and showed Tom the photo I took of King.

"Bugger me," Tom mumbled. "You know, he looks a little like him. Enough to fool someone in the distance."

"Or people who'd never come across him like us," I said.

"Yes."

"This is not the first time we've heard the name Diamond Corp. What's going on there?" Ginny asked.

"Ronnie got the hierarchy to admit they've got people here head-hunting, not spy-hunting. Bloody rude if you ask me. Diamond Corp are wankers."

"Maybe those two idiots Ben dealt with were trying to let us all know that Diamond Corp were up to no good," Ginny said. "Or they were just arseholes trying to blame shit on a company they knew was working inside our borders."

Ronnie opened the door.

"Ben is coming over. He said there was a ruckus in the middle of town."

"Ben used the word ruckus?"

"No not quite, I might've used that word." She sat in her chair. "Something happened. Shots fired. Police everywhere."

"Shots fired?" Tom queried.

"That's a little unusual," Ginny said. "Not to say it doesn't happen, but it is a little unusual. Don't tell me it was outside Maccas again."

Ronnie chuckled. "Apparently it was Logan Street by the Mall entrance."

Tom opened another programme and typed. When he'd finished, he sat back and watched the screen. CCTV images sprang to life. He navigated to where he wanted to be and sure enough there were police everywhere around the Logan Street Mall entrance.

"Does anyone *not* know how to tap into CCTV in this city." I said, more to myself than anyone.

Ronnie said, "Nah, probably not."

Tom rolled back the footage to before the police arrived. There was a body on the ground. He rolled back a little further and stopped. He zoomed in. That shouldn't even be possible with city owned CCTV. But he did it and the image was clear enough to be useful.

"Two males," Tom said. He moved the mouse pointer and zoomed in on one male. He had a weapon in his hand. The other guy was a few metres in front of him; closer to the door of the Mall.

"Any chance of getting a face?"

"Doing my best," Tom said, moving the image and hoping the gunman turned towards the camera. "Nearly. Side profile is the best I can do for him. But the victim, he's standing more angled towards the camera."

We all watched as Tom pulled the bloke's face into focus.

"I've seen him before," I said. "He was at the ball last night. Sitting across from your table, Ronnie, he was on the far wall."

"Ben thought people involved in the arms deal were seated along the walls, giving them shelter. People couldn't get behind them. But that would mean someone working there knew who they were."

"Yes, it would," Tom replied. "Who organised the ball?"

"Karen Rendel," Ronnie replied. "She's a wedding planner."

Ronnie's expression changed from curious to a frown.

"You went to see her this morning," I said. "And now someone is dead."

"I don't think the two things are related," Ronnie said. "Are they?"

"Do the math, Ronnie. It's a bit of a coincidence," I said.

"Rendel?"

"Who the fuck knows, makes as much sense as anything else," Ginny said. "We need to get names on those two. The dead guy and the shooter." She gestured at the screen with a rattling bracelet clad forearm.

"I'll plug the dead guy into a bio-recognition database. Time to send everything to *Genesis* and see what comes back," Tom said, and tapped away at his keyboard. "Sounds like things are coming unglued for the dealer."

Chapter Forty-two:
[Ronnie: Where to from here?]

I sat on the couch in Ginny's lounge and waited for Ben. Everyone else was downstairs. Waiting for facial recognition and information regarding our wedding planner. It didn't seem possible that she would be involved. Why would a wedding planner be dealing in arms? Why would a wedding planner with a lucrative business be dealing in arms? Was she at the first ball? Does she know Frost the lunatic? Does she know Nancy? What about my theory on the nuke? It seemed like every minute the questions grew. What the hell was up with Diamond Corp? I struggled to see how killing two espionage officers was good for business. I guess Diamond Corp operatives are already working on the fringe of society. They're already hired guns, so murder is not such a big stretch.

Who was behind the shooting?

I heard the gate, but not a car. Footsteps moved across the deck. The ranch-slider opened, and Ben walked in.

"You okay?" I asked as he slumped onto the couch next to me.

"Tired. We're not as young as we used to be."

"Speak for yourself."

He planted a kiss on my lips. "What's happening here? Where is everyone?"

"I was waiting for you and trying to make sense out of everything. They're all downstairs."

"Ah, I see." He slung an arm around my shoulders. "Any ID on the dead guy yet?"

"Not as far as I know," I said, resting my head on his shoulder. That was dangerous. It would be far too easy to fall asleep like that. "Did you see the shooting?"

"No. I heard the report from the gun. It echoed. It made me think it was right in front of the Mall."

"And?"

"I ran over and had a quick look."

"Cops there by then?"

"They were arriving. I left."

"You didn't see the shooter leave?"

"No. No one else around. The shooter would've left down Logan or gone into the Mall."

"Not the Mall. It'd be too easy to be spotted. Down Logan. A car waiting on Queen Street. Then back roads away from town."

"Makes sense. Shall we go find everyone before we both fall asleep?"

"Where's your phone?"

"Car," he replied, standing and pulling me to my feet. "Come on, they might have something by now."

Or not. I followed Ben along the hall and down the secret staircase.

"Knock, knock," he said outside the hidden office, then swung the door open. "Howdy."

Crockett grabbed another chair. Ben and I joined the fray.

"Anything?" I asked.

Tom spun his chair around to face us. "Plenty," he replied. "The dead man is on your list. We think he was Mansilla, which we know is not his real name. His real name is Santiago Sanchez. Spanish national."

"How did you drill down to his real name?"

"Facial recognition," Tom said. "Who killed him, however, is a mystery."

"Nothing from the image?" I asked.

"Side profile. I've printed it out for us to look at. Who knows? It might mean something. So far, not to Ginny and me, nor Crockett." He picked up a photo from his desk and passed it to Ben. "Seen him before?"

Ben shuffled his chair closer to mine. We both looked at the photograph. There was something slightly familiar about the man.

"He was at the ball," I said. "Sitting down from us. I could only see his profile under the mask."

"He was at the first ball," Ben said. "This is the idiot who took Nancy's phone. I'm almost certain. If it's that guy, then he said Leviticus when I challenged him and took the phone back."

"Leviticus," Crockett said. "A PMC."

Ben's eyebrow arched. "Yes. The one I'm backstopped to."

"Good to know," Crockett said. "Was he the one who sent photos to you?"

"I thought so. He had the phone, and the photos came up as from Nancy's phone," Ben replied. "Need a name, then we can find the prick."

"Need a better photo," I said. Or we could ask Grandad who he is.

Tom smiled. "I tried other cameras hoping to see him on his way to the mall, or on his way from, but he didn't appear on any. Probably means he arrived and left via Logan and Queen Street."

Ben nudged me. "You called it."

"Wish it was helpful information."

Ginny tapped Ben on the shoulder. "Darling, when is the weapon trial?"

"In three hours."

"Where do you need to be for that?"

"Anywhere. Doesn't really matter as long as my phone is in my hand."

"What's the bidding like?" Tom asked.

"It hit almost seven hundred thousand in bitcoin before I arrived here."

"What's that in real money?" Ginny asked. "You know, US dollars."

"Twenty-five million give or take, in today's market," Ben replied. "I've been keeping an eye on it."

"Who is leading the bidding?" Tom asked.

"Someone called Ashen was leading," Ben said.

"Was?"

"I haven't checked since I got here, so, they might not be leading now."

"I think you should check. If someone is missing or has stopped bidding, then we might know who they are in relation to the app," Tom said.

"That was a long-winded way of saying we could ID them," I said. "I thought Ben and I were tired and struggling, but it seems to be contagious."

"I'm going to go grab my phone."

"Good thinking, Batman," I said. "Have we had a look at the codenames used?"

"Not yet," Ben said. "I'll be right back."

He left.

We all trudged up after him because the shielding in Tom's cave would prevent the phone from receiving data.

I claimed a position on the couch, Ginny sat next to me, and one of the Birmans came over for a pat.

"Who is this one?" I asked.

"Meg," she replied. "She's not really a knee cat."

And without any bidding, Meg jumped onto my knee and curled up.

"Typical, and she makes a liar of me."

The ranch slider opened, and Ben came in. Our chattering would now be about cats and the weather, not bidding or weapons.

He showed me the bid screen. He hadn't placed a bid, nor had someone called Ashen.

I showed Ginny. She motioned for a pen and paper. I gave her my notebook and pen. She looked at the name again and wrote 'Shane' on a page.

It's an anagram.

Ben showed us another screen. It showed all the names. He pointed out his was 'Binman'. Ginny wrote all the names down, then ran through the list converting them to actual names. They were all anagrams.

Ashen = Shane
Nailed = Daniel
Orbite = Robert
Branned = Brendan
Leku = Luke
Mit = Tim
Diamonds = Maddison
Even = Neve
Hale = Leah

And the final one was Binman. She wrote Benjamin next to it. We knew it was correct even though it wasn't an accurate anagram because it was used every time Ben commented or bid.

She crossed Shane off the list. Dead people don't matter.

I took the notebook and pen while Ginny told Ben about the cat that was asleep on my lap, and what a liar she had made her. On a clean page I wrote: Do you think the killer is involved in the bidding? I handed it to Ben.

He nodded.

That made sense. How else would anyone know who to kill.

Ben's phone blew up with alerts. He handed me the notebook and scrolled on his phone screen, then showed me. Everyone was asking where Ashen was. He'd been leading and now his phone was inactive. No one mentioned the shooting.

I needed to move the subject to regular things.

"We should probably go home and see what Donald is doing for dinner tonight," I said. "Don't know if they'll be home or not. Might have a roast if they are?"

"Good idea. I could murder a roast dinner," Ben said.

"If it's a chook, I'm in," Crockett said.

"It'll be a chook," I replied. "See if Emily wants to come over for dinner. Ginny, Tom, do you want to have dinner with us all?"

Tom and Ginny looked at each other. "Great idea," Ginny said. "We'll bring dessert."

"Now you're talking," Crockett said. "What time?"

"Let's say dinner at six," I said. "We'll see you all at four thirty for pre-dinner nibbles and drinks?"

The weapons trial was at four fifty. Ten to five.

"Sounds good," Tom said, and everyone agreed.

Chapter Forty-three:
[Ben: Bang!]

Ronnie and I stopped off at the New World in Silver-stream for a fresh whole chicken and assorted vegetables. I have learned from my time in New Zealand, and especially with Ronnie and her family, that a roast of any description is not a roast without kumara. Other vegetables are also required to be roasted alongside the meat and they are pumpkin, parsnips, carrots, and potatoes. But it is not a proper roast without kumara. I also know that Ronnie likes purple kumara, Donald likes red, and Nana prefers the orange type. I'm an American. As far as I'm concerned, it's all sweet potato.

I carried the basket, Ronnie chose the kumara, three varieties, and then the parsnips.

"Have you got everything else at home?" I asked, as we made our way to the meat section.

"Yeah, Donald did the last grocery shop and he's veggie mad."

Ronnie chose a large fresh chicken.

"Are you going to dress that bird?" I asked as she placed it next to the kumara in the basket I carried.

"In a tux?" she enquired with a cheeky grin.

"You know that's not what I meant."

"It's stuffing. I intend to stuff it with sage and onion *stuffing*." She looked up at the signs that hung at the end of every row. "Where do you think the sage would be?"

I knew she wasn't talking to me. She was talking to herself. And all of a sudden, she said, "Ah, there!" And strode down an aisle. I caught up in time for a box of dried sage to be dropped into the basket.

"Wine?" I asked.

"Yes," she said.

We grabbed two bottles of a Marlborough Sauvignon Blanc and two bottles of a Marlborough Cabernet Sauvignon.

"Beer?" I asked.

"Pretty sure there are Coronas in the fridge, aren't there?"

"Yeah, I thought so."

She pulled out her phone and rang Donald.

"Hey, check the fridge for me. Is there beer?"

I couldn't hear his response, but it satisfied Ronnie, and I imagined the answer was yes. She hung up. My phone buzzed on our way to the checkout. I placed the items on the conveyor belt and scooted past Ronnie to put the basket back. I stayed by the window on the other side of the checkout and checked my phone. Busy. Busy. More bids had landed. I had another look to see who was leading. It wasn't the dead guy. It was the person they called Branned. I placed a bid. For a whole second I led the bidding. Then Mit outbid me. This was not as much fun as Trademe. There was no auto bid feature. And Ronnie didn't believe we were bidding on anything tangible. It's not like I'm going to have an S-400 shipped to me. I imagine the shipping on that would be out of most people's price range, even the multi-billionaire club would think twice about that shipping invoice.

Ronnie interrupted my thoughts when she passed me a shopping bag.

"Everything okay?"

"Yep. Let's go make dinner for our friends." I pocketed my phone. If anyone was listening, I'm sure whoever was on the other end was enjoying our shopping for items for dinner.

Fifteen minutes later, Ronnie was crumbing slices of bread in the blender while Donald cut an onion into tiny pieces. I cracked a couple of beers and handed one to Enzo. He and I went through to the lounge and out onto the balcony that overlooked the street. I left my phone on the dining room table. It was far enough away that it couldn't overhear me, but not stashed away anywhere. I wanted to know when the launch took place. We all wanted to watch that.

Enzo leaned his hip against the railing and looked into the house.

"Big dinner for a particular reason?" he asked.

"Ronnie thought it would be a good idea," I said.

"Isn't that trial this evening?"

"Yep. Ten to five. Everyone is supposed to arrive at four-thirty so we're all here for the show."

"Any idea what the target is?"

"It depends on what is being fired." I wanted to measure my response, not be overly dramatic, but not intentionally downplay what could be a world altering event.

"Initially the target was supposed to be OTH, but other factors have come into play. It might be a city in Europe."

Ronnie's voice rang out from the kitchen. "Ben, I think your phone is having some sort of meltdown."

"Guess that's for me," I said, and went to see what my phone had to say.

Two texts.

Grandad: Another murder in Upper Hutt. This time Brendan Cullen.

Crockett: Someone else was shot in UH.

If we locked up the two people who were going to clean up the bidders, then who was doing the killing? Maybe it was Leviticus.

I replied to Grandad: Do we have anything else?

I replied to Crockett: See you soon, Amigo.

I checked the app and the bidding while I had my phone. It didn't pay to lead the bidding for long. Diamonds now led the bidding. I sighed. Someone inside had to be doing the killing. I had a few people to choose from, but I guess when the killing stops there won't be many of us left, hopefully me and the killer, unless I'm unlucky, and whoever it is, gets to me.

I added a new bid. This time I lifted it a cool thirty thousand bitcoin. Let's see if that weeds the field out.

"Okay?" Ronnie said poking her head into the dining

room.

"Yep." I picked up my beer. It was empty. I took the bottle through to the laundry and added it to the recycling bin in the corner. I grabbed myself another and went back to the dining room. I was still leading, so I left my phone there and rejoined Enzo on the balcony. He was still going on his beer. Time seemed to fly. It wasn't long before I could smell a chicken starting to roast, and our guests arrived.

Donald took drink orders. He loved playing host. It was one-hundred percent in his wheelhouse.

Ronnie came out with my phone in her hand. "It's making noises again."

I checked my watch. She checked hers. We nodded at each other.

I was no longer leading the bidding. Hale was the leader. I watched as the amount on the screen dropped to zero.

A pop-up read "All bids are final". Another pop-up read "Hale won the bid".

Ronnie and I watched the screen. I wished I had the software on my iPad so we could all easily see the screen, but it wasn't iPad compatible.

The next best thing was me holding my phone sideways and everyone crowding around me, so that's what we did.

A new screen opened. It was a live video feed. We watched in silence. A voice gave a countdown from five. Five. Four. Three. Two. One. Fire.

A huge cloud of smoke and crap flew into the air as the missile launched. We still didn't know the target. I couldn't take my eyes off the screen. I sensed movement around me.

"Confirm target," Tom said. I looked at him quickly. He was on his phone.

Nothing on the screen showed a target. The missile shot straight up or that's what it looked like.

Seconds ticked over into minutes. No one spoke.

Then the voice we'd heard counting down said, "Mission success. Target reached."

Another video window opened. That one showed a missile hitting a building in a city.

All of a sudden, the video feeds stopped. The application closed.

I looked back at the faces looking at me, and held up my finger. I hurried into the kitchen and put my phone on the bench then returned.

Tom's phone was ringing. Crockett's phone was ringing. Ronnie took hers from her pocket and looked at the screen then showed me. *Uncle George* was ringing.

She answered. Crockett answered. Tom answered. Enzo, Donald, Ginny, Emily, and I witnessed the world change.

Ronnie listened but didn't speak. Then she hung up. So did Crockett. Tom spoke. He walked out onto the balcony talking on his phone.

"And?" I said to Ronnie. "Where did it hit?"

"Copenhagen."

"Shit."

"Were you right?" Crockett asked.

She nodded. Crockett moved closer to Emily and put an arm around her shoulders. And shook his head at me. It was bad.

Tom came back in with his phone hanging in his hand. "Confirmation that Copenhagen was hit by a nuclear warhead, fired from Kaliningrad. NATO states are scrambling. Russia is in denial mode."

"Christ," Crockett said. "There should be a fucking phone tree for these events. Word would get out quicker if everyone rang the next person on their list."

"Who called you?" I asked him.

"My A's-E-O case officer," he replied.

"Who are you going to call?"

"My team." He walked away and made a call.

Ronnie sat in an armchair and closed her eyes. I knelt next to her. "You, okay?"

"I didn't want to be right, Ben. I didn't want to be right."

"I know."

Chapter Forty-four:
[Ronnie: Who are you?]

Morning came with declarations of annoyance from NATO. Denial from Russia. Bluster and bullshit from everywhere. No war, yet. My phone rang red-hot all night. Ben's wasn't exactly quiet either. Mostly my phone was *Genesis* related. How did I know before anyone else? Who have I talked to? It was a fecking guess. It made sense to me. I tried to make it make sense to everyone.

Then I looked at my screen, and Siri said, "Ben's Grandad is calling."

I swiped my finger across the bottom of the screen and walked down the hallway in search of coffee and Ben.

"Can we talk?" Tierney asked.

"Yes."

"I've heard there is someone trying to find you."

"I'm not difficult to find. They can't be trying very hard," I said, and walked through the kitchen, smiled at Ben who was making coffee, then went into the lounge.

"No, you're not. That could be a problem."

Great. What we need is another problem. I grabbed the TV remote and flicked on the television in the lounge to the news. There was a banner running under the news presenter on the screen. Breaking news: The city of Copenhagen hit with a missile yesterday evening, New Zealand time. No one accepting responsibility. NATO called an emergency meeting. Breaking: Missile was a nuclear warhead; satellite imaging shows an s-400 in Kaliningrad fired within the time frame required for the strike against Copenhagen.

"Ronnie, are you there?"

"Yeah. The news is saying it was a nuke. Who is looking for me?"

"That was bound to happen. We can't keep it quiet. Everyone has a camera and access to social media. Word spreads faster than ever."

"And Russia?"

"Denying it was them. Promising a full investigation. They're saying that no s-400 fired. Screaming that the footage was photoshopped. There will be certain people who will believe them."

"Footage?"

"The terrorists behind the bidding released footage of the weapon system targeting and firing, followed by footage of the strike."

"Of course, they did."

"Where's Ben?"

"On his phone. The bidding has started again, but now everyone knows they're bidding on a missile firing and they're not getting their hands on the system. The people behind this made a lot of money last night. I half expected them to cut and run."

"If they have access to another nuclear warhead, and a different missile launch system, they're going to keep going."

"Shouldn't Russia have tightened security immediately?"

"Yes."

"The people behind this are Russian, aren't they?"

"Potentially."

"I have to go. Where are these people who want to find me, and who are they?"

"Diamond Corp."

"Again? Awesome. We've run out of cell space for Diamond Corp operatives."

"Ronnie?" That was a please explain tone, and I ignored the bejesus out of it, and hung up.

Ben half-smiled and handed me a cup of coffee.

"Thank you."

"Who was it?" He nodded towards my phone.

"Your Grandad. Someone is looking for me."

"Awesome."

"How's everything on your end?"

"Two more dead, or at least two more silent on the app."

"Who?"

"Leku and Even. So, Luke Nash and Neve O'Reilly."

"Leaves six, including you."

"They're not going to get as much money for the next launch."

"Have they come clean and said everyone's bidding on war?"

He nodded. "We have the opportunity to provide a target."

"It just gets better and better." I sipped my coffee.

"Grandad said someone is trying to find me."

"Who?"

"He thought it was someone from Diamond Corp." I drank more coffee and stared at the television. "Where's Donald?"

"Work."

"I thought he'd be hiding under his bed," I said with a smile.

"Enzo worked his magic. Donald went to work. Enzo said he'd have lunch with him to make sure he was okay."

"I'll shower and find clothes, then go check on Nana," I said. "You staying here?"

"I think so. I need to keep an eye on things."

I kissed him and got ready to visit Nana.

On my way, I made a hands-free phone call to Crockett.

"Just me, what's happening your end?"

"All quiet. Emily is going to open up. I'll join you. Where are you going?"

"Nana's place."

"See you there in ten." I touched the screen and hung up the call. Business as normal. Welcome to Monday. We may or may not have an escalation of the Ukraine-Russian war. If they were planning a major attack, it'd be all on.

I shoved those thoughts aside and parked on the street near Nana's retirement home. The doors opened as I approached. Margot's head bobbed behind the desk, then popped up.

"Ronnie, nice to see you," she said, and pointed to the hand sanitiser and the visitor book. There was no box of masks. That was interesting.

"Are we not masking now?"

"Only in the common rooms. Your Nana is in her apartment. If she was out mingling, I'd throw a mask your way."

"Anyone been in to see her?" I signed the visitor book and scanned the morning visitor names.

"She's popular since that article." Margot pointed to a name. "Did you know the story went international?"

"I did. Who would've thought it?"

"Probably needed some happy news to report," Margot said with a sigh.

"This person, Kallie Duncan, when did she see Nana?" There was a name, but no time.

"She's still there unless she went out the garden door." Margot spun the book and looked at the entry. "I see she forgot to write the time." Margot picked up a pen and wrote it for her after checking the clock on the wall. "There, twenty minutes ago. Early for a visit I thought, but she said she had urgent business for June."

Of course, she did.

I took a photo of the entry and sent it to Uncle George with a question mark.

"I'll go see Nana," I said. "Have a good morning."

"You too," she said as I walked away.

The next doors opened automatically. I avoided walking frames and cane wielding old folk. When I passed the common lounge, the familiar smell of boiled sweets, lavender, and creeping death, wafted out the open double door.

Someone inside called out, "Hello, Veronica!" I didn't see who it was.

I made my way to the interior door of Nana's apartment without further incident. I didn't knock. Instead, I swung the door wide open. Nana was in her sitting room area. There was a woman with her back to the door. She didn't move. I couldn't tell from the back of her head if she was old, or the Kallie Duncan woman.

"Hi, Nana," I said.

Nana looked up and said, "Is that you Virginia? Come closer dear, I can't see you way over there."

I'll play.

"It's me," I replied, and joined her.

The woman sat in my chair. Rude. Nana seemed fine. I kissed her papery cheek.

"You haven't seen Veronica, have you?" Nana asked with a tight smile.

"Not today. Bit early for her to be out and about." I gave the woman in my chair my attention. "And you are? You look a bit young to be an inmate here."

"Kallie," she said. "Who is Veronica to you?" Her accent was interesting. She wasn't from New Zealand. I couldn't quite place it, but it was European. German? What were the chances of two people called Kallie turning up in Upper Hutt?

"That's none of your business," I said with a smile. You clearly don't know what I look like which is interesting. There are photos on our website. Or there were. Maybe Jenn got rid of them. I made a mental note to ask. "Where are you from?"

The woman bristled but didn't answer my question. "Where is Veronica?"

"Again, not your business. Who are you? Why are you visiting my Nana?" I asked and glanced at the clock, and knew Crockett would be walking through the door any minute. "Perhaps we should go outside and have a chat," I said. "Are you German?"

"I'm quite comfortable. Your Nana is famous. She's gone worldwide with her mystery solving," the woman said. "Now, where is Veronica? I'm not here to talk about myself."

I shrugged. "No idea. I'm not her keeper."

I had my right hand in my pocket wrapped around my phone. I'd talked to Crockett last. Could I pocket dial him? It was worth a shot except my phone was locked and I couldn't exactly pull it out and look at it to unlock it. Perhaps no call then.

"We might be here a long time," Kallie said. "I'm looking for Veronica. Who is she to you?"

I shook my head. "Not your business. Why do you want her?"

"Are you her secretary or her keeper?" The woman asked. "I need to speak to Veronica, Ronnie, whatever people call her."

"If you wait here, she will eventually show up," I said. Then addressed Nana, "Where are Frankie and Ester. I thought you three were joined at the arthritic hip."

"The ladies are organising our cases. I do hope Veronica hurries up. I don't suppose you know if she managed to locate the person we are looking for?"

I shook my head. "Haven't spoken to her since Friday."

The corridor door swung open. Crockett filled the door frame, motorbike helmet in his hand. Kallie's attention moved from me, and I grabbed my wrist with my right hand. Making sure he saw. It was a signal that told him someone was holding me against my will or there's an arsehole in the room. It was open to interpretation.

Without saying a word Crockett was behind Kallie. He placed his motorbike helmet on the side table, leaned down, and grabbed her arms, pinning them to her sides. He then lifted her clean off the chair and over the back. It was impressive. Guess all the weight training paid off.

I rose to my feet and hurried to the kitchen. Nana had plastic cable ties in the junk drawer, and duct tape. I removed one of the bigger ties and fastened one of Kallie's wrists then looped the second tie through it and tightened it onto her free wrist. Done. I patted her down and found a curved blade. It wasn't very big. It looked like a claw. Crockett saw it and raised an eyebrow.

"Everyone carries curved blades as a matter of course," I said and put it on the kitchen bench. "Do you want duct tape?"

"Might look a bit suspicious if we duct tape her

mouth."

"Garden door?"

"Definitely, Ronnie."

Kallie, or whoever she was, growled. "I should've known."

"How could you? You clearly didn't have a photo. Strange. Under prepared. Bloody hopeless as far as I can tell."

Crockett pushed her towards the ranch slider to the garden. "Where's your car?" he asked me.

"On the road."

"Then let's go."

"You want to leave your Harley here?"

"It'll be fine," Nana said. "We'll take good care of it."

I shot a warning look. "You will not attempt to ride that motorbike."

Nana smiled.

"I have the key Ronnie," Crockett said.

Good.

Crockett exited through the sliding door with the captive. I gave Nana a quick peck on the cheek. "That was clever, Nana, calling me Virginia."

"I learnt a thing or two from your grandfather, you know," she replied. "Now go and find out what that woman wants."

"Yes, Nana."

I hurried after Crockett.

Chapter Forty-five:
[Crockett: Disaster.]

"Who are you?" Ronnie leaned on the wall, her hands in her jeans pockets. She watched the woman in the chair in my living room, waiting and patient. My patience was wearing thin.

Time ticked by in painful seconds. Each felt longer than the last. We'd been at the questioning stage for nearly three hours. She was either wasting our time, or plain annoying.

The woman cleared her throat and opened her mouth to speak.

Donald burst through the front door. He was flapping and shaken.

A rush of emotions hit Ronnie's face at once. The woman closed her mouth. I threw a smile at Ronnie. She nodded.

"Problem Donald?" I enquired.

Donald gaped at the woman sitting on a dining chair in the middle of my living room.

"Shut your mouth, Donald. You look special. Not in a good way," Ronnie said.

Donald clamped his teeth together.

"You burst into my house so I'm going out on a fairly thick limb and say you want me," I said to him.

Donald made a squeaking noise and nodded.

"Come on," I said, taking him by the arm.

"Where to?" Donald said quietly.

"To wherever the problem is."

He took a deep breath and pointed out the now open front door.

"Right, lead the way."

I shrugged at Ronnie. She nodded. I followed Donald out the door, then through the side gate to the driveway. Donald's car was parked in front of my garage.

"Enzo's in the back," Donald said, brushing moisture from his eyes.

I opened the passenger side door. Enzo was slouched. His hands were hard against his abdomen, dark red staining his fingers and shirt, as it leaked onto the car seat.

"What happened?" I asked, leaning into the car and lifting Enzo's hands so I could get a better look at the wound.

"Got jumped," Enzo replied. "It was a knife."

"And the person who did this?"

"No longer needs medical attention," he said slowly.

"You need an ambulance, but someone will report a knife wound. How do you feel about outpatient care?"

"As long as it's not a vet," he replied.

"Come on, I'll help you inside."

I helped him out of the car, and to stand. Donald stood back out of the way. I motioned to him to come closer.

"Go inside, tell Ronnie to relocate the guest to the spare room."

He nodded and hurried away.

I had one arm around Enzo. We walked slowly and carefully. I had no idea how bad the wound was, and I didn't want to aggravate anything. Once we were inside, I shut the front door and got Enzo to the couch. It crossed my mind that leather was a good choice in furnishing fabric. It was easier to clean than cloth. Donald fussed around not really doing anything.

"You good?" I stood up straight and pulled my phone from my pocket. Enzo nodded. I hurried into the kitchen and grabbed some clean tea-towels from a drawer. Back in the lounge I pressed a folded tea-towel to the leaking wound and got Enzo to apply pressure again. Ronnie appeared. She took charge of Donald, and I made a call in the kitchen.

Technically I wasn't calling a vet, more a vet nurse. Enzo didn't need to know. No one needed to know.

"Sarah, it's Crockett. I need a favour."

"You're in luck, I'm off today. What's up?"

"Knife wound, abdominal."

"Hospital," she replied.

"Not ideal in this case."

"Why not?"

"For reasons."

She sighed loudly. "Where are you?"

"Home. It's not me, by the way."

"I gathered that. I'll be there in ten." She sounded a little snippy. "Don't give him anything to eat or drink."

"Might be a her."

"Is it?"

"No."

Sarah's crankiness broke with a laugh. "Ten," she said and hung up.

I poked my head around the dividing wall. Enzo hadn't moved. Donald was sitting with him and calmer. Ronnie saw me and came over.

"Bit bleedy," she said.

"He'll be fine. Got a ... a ... nurse friend coming over."

She gave me a look. "Did you have trouble finding the words nurse and friend?"

I shook my head at her.

"What's our guest doing?"

"She's handcuffed and sitting on the same chair she was before, but in the spare room."

"Good. Get anything out of her?"

"Not yet. I'd suggest letting Enzo have a go, but that's probably not wise considering his current condition."

"I have faith in you. See what you can get out of her before my friend arrives. It's getting pretty crowded in this house."

"I know, right? When did you last have this many people in your house?"

I grimaced. It was during the Alex the Terrible weekend.

"I don't like it."

She reached up and patted my shoulder. "There, there, Crockett. It'll be all right."

"Smart arse," I grumbled, but I felt a smile tweaking the edges of my mouth. "Go get something from that woman. Even her name would be good. How many Kallie Duncans are there in the world?"

She half-arse saluted with two fingers and vanished towards the hallway, avoiding the lounge by going through the kitchen. I couldn't say I blamed her. I took a breath and returned to Enzo.

"Help is on the way," I said when Donald made eye contact with me. He nodded. "How's the patient?"

"Leaking," Enzo replied.

"I need you to tell me what happened," I said, jamming my hands in my jeans pockets and rocking back on my heels.

"I went to meet Donald at work. Someone jumped me."

"In the middle of Upper Hutt, in broad daylight. That took some balls." And I'd bet there is a body somewhere.

Before I could ask Enzo said, "I dropped him in the alley ... it's got a name." He was struggling a bit.

Donald piped up, "Leader Lane."

"That's where Ronnie parks, right?"

"Yes," Donald replied.

"I'll get it dealt with." I pulled my phone from my pocket and rang Art. He's the best man for tight spots. "Yo, mate, I need a body disposal. Leader Lane, Upper Hutt." I looked at Enzo.

He said, "Twenty minutes ago."

I spoke into the phone. "Might be too late. Do what you can."

"I'll grab Plunger. We'll see what's what and get back

435

to you."

"Cheers."

I pressed the red end button and shoved my phone back into my pocket. There was a knock on the door. Donald almost sprung out of his skin.

"Who is it? Is it police? I don't want to go to jail!"

"Relax, Donald. No one is going to jail. It'll be my friend. Sarah."

Or the police, but they tended to knock louder.

I walked around the couch and swung the door open. Sarah smiled up at me. She carried a dark blue messenger bag with a white cross on it over her shoulder.

"Come on in," I said. I waited until she was across the threshold, had a quick squizz around the back yard, and closed the door. All was quiet. That's how it should be.

Sarah was already kneeling in front of Enzo. She wasted no time getting gloves on and getting down to business.

"Do you need my help?" I asked.

"Nope. I'll be fine." She smiled at Enzo. "I'm Sarah and I'll be your cabin crew for this trip."

Donald laughed. Enzo smiled.

"I feel better already," Enzo said, after a sharp intake of breath caused by Sarah's probing fingers.

"How long was the blade?" She opened a sterile dressing pack on the floor. "Was it straight?"

"Yeah, and small. Ten centimetres or close enough."

"Good," she said, then clarified her comment. "Better than a hunting knife. Not good, good."

"That's encouraging."

"It's a tidy wound. Nothing serious nicked as far as I can tell. I do advise keeping away from knives in the future."

She cleaned the wound. "I might need to pack it," she said. "So, you are going to have to change the packing and take it easy."

Donald paled. "You mean you are going to shove something into the wound?"

"Maybe, but not necessarily. I'll scan it and see."

She fished a box from her bag and opened it. "Portable scanner," she said, noticing my interest.

It looked like one our vet used on mum's bitch to see how many pups there were. I kept that to myself. Sarah used the wand to view the wound and surrounding tissue. I had no idea what she could see, because it looked like nothing from where I stood.

"I think we're good," she said and packed the scanner away. "I'll suture. You're still going to have to be careful. No messing with armed persons."

She injected something around the two-centimetre wound. It was two centimetres on the outside, ten deep. Could it be a pocketknife? I peered over Sarah's shoulder at the wound. If it was a small knife like a pocketknife, the assailant must've jammed it to the hilt. The discolouration around the wound would be bruising from the hilt. I stepped back.

"Right there, Crockett?" Sarah asked, tying off the suture thread.

"It's illegal to carry any kind of knife in New Zealand, but plenty of people carry Swiss Army pocket knives on key chains."

Sarah snipped the thread. "You can carry a hunting knife or a butcher's knife ... if you are going hunting or about to butcher an animal."

"Enzo was very lucky then."

"What are you saying, I'm prey or an animal that was about to be butchered?" Enzo infected his voice with a good deal of mock outrage. Sarah stuck a waterproof dressing over the tidily sutured wound. He was probably lucky she didn't put an Elizabethan collar around his neck to stop him licking.

"You're good," she said to him. "I'll leave you with a bunch of dressings and sterile dressing packs so you can keep it nice and clean."

"Thank you." Enzo smiled as Donald took his hand.

"Thank you very much Sarah," Donald said, kissing Enzo's hand. "He's the most wonderful husband."

Enzo winked at Donald. "Only the best for you, Lover."

I retched.

Sarah chuckled. She wrapped all the blood-soaked gauze pads and the other rubbish in the sheet from the dressing pack and handed it to me.

"Rubbish bin," she said. "He's going to need antibiotics. Can you organise that?"

"Yeah, got a friend who is a pharmacist."

"Get on to it. Don't wait for infection to set in."

"Will do."

I removed the rubbish to the kitchen bin while she finished packing up. Once back in the lounge, I saw Sarah was by the door waiting to leave. "Call me anytime, Crockett."

"Thanks Sarah."

"We still on for the movies next month? You and Emily still good to come?"

"Absolutely. Say hey to Josh for me."

And with that she was gone.

Chapter Forty-six:
[Ronnie: PMC.]

I leaned on the wall. It had become a habit. Same as having my hands jammed into my jeans pockets. I'd noticed Crockett did that a lot too. I did it to stop myself waving my hands around when I spoke. It made me look far too approachable and friendly. There was nothing friendly about my demeanour today. Nana was in the line of fire. I blame the article in the newspaper for that nonsense. And now Enzo was stabbed and bleeding. Any chance at a good mood vanished with both those things. And now we had another Kallie Duncan? What the actual?

I let the woman sitting in the chair wonder what I was going to ask, or do, next. She was probably thirty, or thereabouts, and fit. She looked quite capable of taking care of herself. And yet, we'd grabbed her, and now she was properly handcuffed and shackled. Sitting in a chair.

She wasn't so much sitting as restrained in the chair.

She looked up at me slowly. "I'll be missed by now."

I nodded. "I'd expect you to be."

"Planning on keeping me here long?" She tried to move a little bit. "My legs are going to sleep."

"Bugger," I said. "Sucks to be you."

"How long are you going to keep me here?"

"Don't know. Guess that depends on you." I adjusted my footing, but remained leaning against the wall. Never ask a question if you don't already know the answer, was looping around in my mind. "Diamond Corporation - why are they interested in me?"

"They're not."

"Okay." Liar. "Then why were you haranguing my Nana?" I stepped forward making her look up to see my face. As soon as she did, I snapped a picture with my phone and sent it to Steph at the office with a text that asked her to run the face through everything. She'd have to use my computer and log in as me for the task.

"What do you think you're going to find with a photo of me?"

I didn't much like the scoffing tone she used. "I'm pretty sure I'll get an ID. Maybe not immediately, but I will."

"I could save you the trouble."

"But would you tell the truth?"

"Kallie Duncan."

At least she was sticking to her fake name. That's just great.

"And I suppose that's your real name and you know who I am ... but you didn't recognise me earlier. I feel like your prep needs work."

Kallie smiled. "Veronica Tracey."

"Now we have some names. What is it you hoped to achieve this morning?"

"Exactly what we did achieve."

I left the room. Crockett was in the lounge talking to Enzo. He seemed in a better state. I heard noises in the kitchen and rightly assumed Donald was in there making coffee. His head poked around the dividing wall. "Coffee,

Ronnie?"

"Sure, thanks."

"What's happening in there?" Crockett asked, tipping his thumb towards the hallway. "Got a name?"

"She offered one. Kallie Duncan."

"Say that again?" Enzo said as a frown creased his brow.

I did.

"Will the real Kallie Duncan please stand up. I dug into her when we came across the Sandra King/Kallie Duncan business. She's definitely with Diamond Corporation, or more specifically Blue Watch."

"And?" I prodded, hoping he had more for me.

"They did this, or they want me to think they did this." Enzo lifted his bloody shirt. "The guy who stabbed me carried a Diamond Corporation ID card in his wallet." Enzo leaned over and removed a wallet from his own back pocket. He handed it to Crockett. "Take a look; it's interesting."

Crockett opened the wallet and pulled out several cards. One was a black corporate ID card. The type that was swiped to gain access to buildings. Crockett handed it to me. I inspected it and gave it back. Kevin Jones. It was sloppy of him to carry anything that identified him. So why was he carrying something like that? And who was he? Because Kevin Jones was the guy we'd come across with Kallie Duncan, aka Sandra King. Kevin Jones posed as Steven Sadler. They were locked up at Art's.

"So, who are they really?" I knew I was frowning and

had to work quite hard to relax my brow muscles. "We confirmed that Sadler and King were Jones and Duncan. Didn't we?"

"Yeah, we did," Enzo said. "They were head-hunting."

"Now there's two people pretending to be Jones and Duncan. I'm not confused, how about you?"

"Not at all," Enzo said. "Makes perfect sense."

"They could be up to anything, Ronnie," Crockett replied. "What are the odds of Duncan and Jones being aliases? We think we ID'd them before we locked them up, but did we?"

"I'd imagine the chances of them being aliases is quite high."

"We need to know who this Kallie Duncan chick really is?" Enzo said. "There are getting to be too many spies in this city."

"My question is why carry something that could lead back to the parent body?" I looked from Enzo to Crockett. "Anyone?"

"Because then we'll think that it's really them," Crockett said. "They clearly don't know about the real Duncan and Jones being here. Except now they may not be the real Duncan and Jones."

"We thought King and Sadler were coming. Or at least Ben and I did," I replied. "We didn't know names of any Diamond Corp employees. That was Secret Squirrel bizzo. But we got intel saying they were spy-hunting here. And it turned out they were head-hunting, looking for the people who bid on the first arms deal."

"But why do we need to know they're here?" Enzo asked. "Is the whole thing a false flag operation?"

"Good question, isn't it?" I looked at Crockett hoping he had something enlightening to share. "I'd hazard a guess and say that everything we've come across is bullshit. But I'd like to think what was behind it all was a desire to prevent what happened yesterday from happening?"

"They failed. That nuke flew into Copenhagen and killed civilians," Crockett said. "They could be around trying to get us to back off ..."

"The only reason I can think of is that the Pride Ball is coming up fast," I said. It's the last ball of the season. There was supposed to be the biggest arms haul up for sale during the final ball. "Maybe they think it's still going to go ahead." What if they're behind the supposed sale? "Are they wanting to blame Diamond Corp for the arms deals?"

"Maybe. But why stab Enzo?" Crockett asked.

"Is the deal still going to go ahead despite the attack? Do they want anyone linked to us to keep away from the Pride Ball?" I asked.

"That makes about as much sense as anything else." Enzo agreed.

"And you and Donald have tickets?" Crockett asked.

"Yes."

"I think we can deduce that Diamond Corporation know something about the arms deals going down at various balls. Or Diamond Corp are behind the arms deals and are onto us as disruptors. Or they're here hunting a spy, and this is all incidental," I said.

"Shit," Enzo mumbled. "They thought I was involved in some way?"

"Well ... probably. That means you need to keep Donald close," I said. "Especially as you dispatched one of their own. We need to get infallible IDs on these people."

"I'm picking that Diamond Corp were asked to make contact with us and get our help. And that whoever they are after has something to do with the Pride Ball. Is it the arms deal? That's something I'll ask the new Kallie Duncan," Crockett said.

"Are you saying I overreacted and now someone is dead?" Enzo queried with an attempt at looking horrified at the supposed allegation.

"Nope. You saw a threat and you were stabbed, so nope. Perhaps whatshisface could've chosen a better way to ask for help, or perhaps they wanted to take you out, like Ronnie thought." Crockett smiled.

"All right, so, that wasn't the best, but we have to move forward. Supposedly the second arms deal will happen at the next ball. It looks like they're going to offer long range missiles. And ..." Crockett paused for effect. "The thought of some crackpot, bloody, shit-arsed little terror group getting hold of them, is not a good one. But nor is a long-range nuclear warhead launching at an innocent target."

"How did they know we'd have tickets?" Enzo asked.

"Either it was a guess, or it's irrelevant, or someone, like your beloved husband has been talking about it all over his socials ... which do you think is more likely?"

Enzo shot me a half a smile. "We quite innocently purchased our tickets well before you alerted us to the trading going on using balls to get everyone together in one venue without suspicion."

"I know. Donald has been raving about it for months." I looked towards the kitchen. "They could be making sure you don't trip over something at the ball."

Enzo nodded.

"Would Diamond Corp send people in without telling them who else is operating here?" Enzo asked.

"I don't know. But, if they knew about you - as in - your profession and thought there was a chance you and Donald would be going to the ball, they might've wanted to reach out and see if you could work together."

"That doesn't make me feel stink at all," Enzo grumbled.

"If he wanted to talk, he shouldn't have surprised you, or stabbed you." I smiled at him. "Buck up, Enzo, he brought it on himself."

It was a shitty situation. Sometimes people go about things the wrong way and cause more shit than ever. We were knee-deep. Crockett would be making comments about putting our waders on if this kept up.

"We won't be going to the ball now, so who is going to use our legitimate tickets?"

"Donald will be going with a new date," I replied. Ben texted me. I read the text. The next deal was happening today, they brought it forward. The Pride Ball was out.

Did I want to share that when I saw an opportunity to wind Crockett up? No. I didn't. I deserved some fun. It'd been a stressful few weeks.

Enzo shook his head. "No, Ronnie, that's too dangerous."

Crockett agreed with Enzo.

"It'll be fine. Crockett can keep him safe."

I watched the colour drain from Crockett's face. His mouth opened and shut like a goldfish for a few seconds before words flowed. "You're dreaming if you think I'm taking Donald to the Pride Ball."

"It is not like I'm suggesting you go in drag or anything," I said, trying hard to keep the amusement out of my voice, but that would be hilarious.

He narrowed his eyes at me. "You are a nasty bit of gear."

All I could do was smile. I finally found something that got to him.

"You'd look fantastic in heels, fishnets, a corset ... I'm seeing some kind of Frankenfurter get up. Rocky Horror Picture Show. Perfect for you."

Enzo grabbed his side as laughter flowed. Donald rushed into the room.

"Calm, he's supposed to be calm," Donald squawked. He looked from Enzo to Crockett. Crockett had taken up residence in his favourite chair across the room from me and Enzo.

"He'll be fine," I said to Donald. "Chill out. Just go finish making the coffee."

He planted his hands on his hips and glared at me. "Leave my husband alone, and what have you done to Crockett?"

"Nothing." I shrugged. "I was giving him some fashion advice."

Everyone's a critic.

Donald huffed and left. Enzo reined in the hilarity. Crockett sprang to his feet.

"I'm too tall for heels," he snapped.

"Yeah, you are a bit," I replied. "Do you want to go chat with Ms Duncan?"

He nodded and left. At the doorway he looked back at me and said, "You need to come up with a new plan."

I sank to the couch next to Enzo and gave up trying to keep my composure. Laughter welled up and chortled from my mouth. There was no containing it, not while my brain threw up images of Crockett superimposed over the "Time Warp" scene from the Rocky Horror Picture Show. It was all too much.

"Where would we get a corset to fit Crockett?" Enzo asked quietly.

That was the end for me. Laughter, tears, and snot. I could barely breathe. When I glanced at Enzo, he wasn't far behind. It was too much.

"You'll break your stitches ...," I garbled between breaths and laughter.

"It's worth it." He gasped choking breaths. "It's at Te Papa."

"What kind of music?"

Enzo struggled to breathe and talk, "Lady Gaga, Cher, Madonna, Shania Twain, Dolly Parton, Celine Dion, Barbara Streisand."

More laughter bubbled up. Donald swung into the room. "The theme is Leather and Spice."

That was it. I was dead.

Straight to hell.

Chapter Forty-seven:
[Ronnie: Oh, Nana!]

When Nana called, I left Enzo and Donald in Crockett's care. He was also having a friendly chat with the second Kallie Duncan.

I sat heavily into a chair in Nana's apartment and eyed the three crones with suspicion. They were fussing over a dress. It was a very nice dress. One could say it was a ball gown. But they were at the last ball. Surely, they weren't going to the Pride Ball? A knot tightened in my stomach.

"Why did you need to see me, Nana?" I eventually asked, and unfortunately punctuated the sentence with a sigh. No sigh ever escaped my Nana.

"What are you sighing about, young lady? Are you too busy for your poor old Nana?" She attached a generous helping of frailty to her voice. "Goodness after this morning, I'd think you'd want to make sure I was all right."

It was all an act.

All of it.

"I'm sure I would never be too busy for you, Nana." I smiled sweetly. "Now, what's going on here?" I waved a hand at the deep blue dress draped over a chair.

"We have tickets to the next ball. I told you that Veronica. This is my dress."

"Which ball Nana?" She couldn't mean the Pride Ball. "You were just at a ball. Not tired yet?"

"Veronica, there are only so many balls in our futures.

We're not getting any younger."

"I suppose you aren't, although you're well-preserved Nana." I mustered a kind smile. "Which ball?"

"Why, the one Donald and Enzo are going to of course." Oh no. Nope. She did not mean the Pride Ball. "We're allies you know."

They were something all right. Allies? Sure, why not? She definitely meant the Pride Ball.

"Of course, you are. Frankie, do you have a dress too?"

"Yes, dear," she replied. "It's not as fancy as June's."

Of course, it isn't. It's always better not to upstage Nana.

"And you Ester?"

"I do," she said, and then stretched her thin lips into a smile. "It's going to be a wonderful night."

Magical. I wouldn't miss it.

Enzo isn't going. Crockett thinks he is going, unless Enzo told him the truth about the deal being moved up to today. I told him he could tell him. Oh man. It was getting complicated. But really, no one was going. We didn't need to attend another ball. Another attempt at creating a war suitable for NATO to fight, was already underway.

"Have you heard from Donald today?" I asked.

"Not today. He said he'll be over tomorrow."

"I don't think Enzo can go to the ball," I said trying to come up with a reason that wasn't 'someone stabbed him'. "So, Donald might be taking Crockett." I really am going to hell.

The three elderly troublemakers stopped what they

were doing and slowly turned to face me. Nana tutted. Ester and Frankie followed suit. A trio of elderly tutters was worse than stereo.

"Why?" Nana asked.

"Because he has to work," I said. There, excuse found.

"They've been looking forward to this all year." Nana sounded disappointed.

"Such a shame," Ester said softly.

Frankie echoed the sentiment.

"I'm sure it will still be a fun night for Donald. Especially with you three in attendance."

"That's right," Ester said. "We shall have to step up and make sure Donald has a wonderful night."

Yes. That doesn't sound troublemakery at all.

"And I still don't know why you wanted to see me, Nana?"

"Just to catch up dear. We've been so busy with new cases, I feel like I haven't seen you at all since our writeup in the paper."

And there it was. The real reason.

"You were in the newspaper?" I attempted delight and surprise all at once. Judging by the narrowed eyes on Nana, I had failed.

"You did see the story. Oh, Veronica, you didn't even congratulate us."

"I've been a bit busy with work Nana and, you know, getting engaged. But congratulations." Then my mind circled back to the new cases comment. "Lots of new cases Nana?"

"Four," Ester said. "Four since yesterday. It's marvellous fun."

"Good. Now, I'm here because?"

"Well," said Nana, as Frankie pulled out a notebook. "We've been looking for Mildred's grandson. He's vanished without a trace."

"I see. What can I do to help?"

"You have those database things on your computer. Don't you?" Ester asked.

"I do."

"Do you think you could put his name in and see if there's something about him?" Frankie passed me the notebook with a page open. I took it and read the name. I knew the name. I'd seen it quite recently, a few times, and I wondered who the real one was. Kevin Jones. What were the odds? I snapped a picture of the notebook page with my phone. It was typical that Kevin Jones would be someone one of the Cronies of Dooms associates would miss. Two degrees of separation makes life tricky again. I conceded that New Zealand might be half a degree of separation. But Kevin Jones was an import. It shouldn't hold true for him.

"I'll do it when I get back to the office," I said. "Have you met this man?"

They all shook their blue rinsed heads. Excellent. Neither had we. Or maybe the real one is the dead one?

Nana patted my shoulder with her boney hand. "I knew you'd be able to help, Veronica. We do appreciate it."

I stood up and kissed Nana's aged cheek. "I'll do my best."

I handed the notebook back to Frankie and let myself out. The journey back to my offices didn't take long. Traffic was light, and everyone remembered how to use roundabouts and indicators. Amazing. I hurried up the stairs and into the main office.

"Didn't expect to see you," Steph said, her eyes peering over her computer screen.

"I was just summoned to Nana's," I replied, dropping my bag on my chair. "Jenn working the new job?"

"Yes. She's loving it. And Nana wanted?"

"To tell me how many new cases they had ..." I air quoted the word 'cases'. "It's all go with the decrepit Nancy Drew brigade."

"Who knew the newspaper story would result in more old people with mysteries," Steph replied.

"I know! Colour me shocked."

That wasn't the bit that worried me. It was the Pride Ball. At that point I realised I hadn't asked Steph if she and Jenn were going. It was the last ball of the season, and I was pleased to be sitting it out. I was also pleased that no more bodies had dropped since earlier today. That app Ben had was dynamite.

I sat at my desk and switched my computer on, then fished my notebook out of my bag. Not that I needed it to add Kevin Jones to a search protocol in the first database. That was futile really, but if I did it, then I could tell Nana I found nothing. I knew I would find nothing. Not only is he dead but he's a shadow. Or he's alive and a shadow. Or he never existed. People like him are not in databases.

"Hey Steph?"

"Yes?"

"Are you and Jenn going to the Pride Ball?"

"We are. Don't usually, but we thought we'd go. Since COVID we haven't been out much. We're still being cautious, but Jenn came up with a crafty way of wearing surgical masks, and still keeping to the Leather and Spice theme. How could I say no?"

I liked the mask idea. I did enjoy the masked ball. I fired off a text to Donald. At the last ball there was a huge array of sparkly, feathery, gorgeous masks, and plenty of the Zorro or Lone Ranger type on men. Maybe I could convince Nana and the *Cronies of Doom* to wear masks. Just in case someone nasty was at the Pride Ball. Now they were famous, it didn't pay to take chances.

Me: Is the Pride Ball a masked ball?

Donald: Not technically, but there is no reason why masks couldn't be worn. Have you an idea?"

Me: Nana and the gang are going. I thought we could have them wear masks.

Donald: That's a good idea.

And just like that I had an idea. I didn't want them at the Pride Ball because they could be recognised. It's doubtful anyone would recognise them behind plague masks. I think I saw plague masks and other leathery masks somewhere. None of them would be recognisable with masks. Oh, yeah, this was an idea and a half. I'm not fond of that whole plague mask scene, but I won't be there. It might just provide some security for Nana and *the Cronies*.

My computer pinged with a 'no result' alert.

I rang Nana and let her know that he wasn't in my databases. She thanked me but sounded disappointed. She'd be a lot more disappointed with the truth. I floated the idea of amazing leather masks for her and the *Cronies of Doom*. She wasn't against the idea until she realised no one would be able to recognise her. Bugger.

My next call was to Donald. He answered quickly. "I need you to convince Nana that a plague mask is perfect and that everyone will be masked at the Pride Ball."

"I thought you were?"

"She doesn't like the idea, because no one will recognise her!"

"Leave it with me. You obviously didn't sell it the right way. Let's remove the plague mask idea and go with something sparkly with feathers and an opportunity to craft the masks with my help."

Brilliant.

"Thank you, Donald. How's Enzo?"

"He's fine, enjoying being waited on."

"I bet. Bye."

With Donald on the job, Nana and her pals would be masked, and loving it.

I thought about what we were doing. What were the

chances that there weren't any players left by Friday night's ball? I thought the odds were quite high. But then again we furnished the imposters with a list of names, and they were locked up. It had to be someone who was part of the bidding who was killing everyone else. We needed to look into the Karen Rendel thing. Someone had to make sure everyone was seated in the correct places. Was that her job? I didn't see seating charts, but then I was focused on the guest lists.

I rang Ben. He answered quickly.

"Question," I said. "Seating ..."

"You're right. I'll pick you up in fifteen."

I hung up and dropped my phone in my bag.

"I'm off out again," I said to Steph. "Need to check something. You heard any local news today?"

"You mean the four murders in the last twenty-four hours, that kind of news?"

"Yes."

"Increased police presence in the CBD. A few taped off areas, but apart from that, not much."

"Good."

"Is it secret squirrel stuff?"

"Yes."

"What about that nuclear missile? Jenn is worried there will be an all-out nuclear war."

"Jenn has little to worry about in that regard. Ben doesn't think it's likely." I smiled at Steph. "I'd tell you if I thought otherwise."

"I know. Just Jenn is worried. She said she was flying

off to the pharmacy to buy iodine."

"If that keeps her happy and calm, then she should buy iodine."

"Does it work?" she asked.

"Drinking potassium Iodide or taking the pills? The pills used to be in emergency kits, they absolutely work."

"Good," Steph replied with a smile.

I just lied to my best friend. Potassium Iodide is used for nuclear power station emergencies. It protects the thyroid against damage from radioidoine, not from the fallout from nuclear warheads.

"We'll all be fine."

"Be safe," Steph said as I headed for the door.

"Always."

I ran down the stairs and out the door just as Ben pulled up at the curb. Seconds later we were on our way to speak with Karen Rendel. I very much hoped we didn't need to disengage her as our wedding planner. The thought of someone who could wrangle Nana, and stop us being steamrolled into Nana's vision for our nuptials, was glorious.

Chapter Forty-eight:
[Mitch: It's all on.]

Dane sat at the table with the girls. They were colouring; he was writing in a journal. They were thrilled to have him here. They liked visitors and I think they recognised something in Dane. He wasn't a stranger in their eyes. It was shame Crockett couldn't stay.

I went up to my computer happy in the knowledge that everyone downstairs was safe.

Reports were flooding in from Europe. The world was scrambling to understand how a nuclear warhead hit innocent people. There was no understanding acts of war. Men make war. They've done that since the dawn of time. It's the answer to a tanking economy. It's the answer to a country turning on itself. Nothing brings people together faster than a common enemy. Anti-Russia sentiment was louder than ever.

I read the last report of the morning then texted Ronnie. It wasn't getting any better.

Uncle George: Reports of a second broken arrow

I could tell Ronnie had read the message and three dots appeared as she typed. They stopped and started a number of times.

Ronnie: They've canned the Pride Ball. We have four dead from the list of names. Need verification on Kallie Duncan and Kevin Jones.

She'd attached photos of two different women and of one male.

I plugged the photos into a database.

Dane came upstairs. He paused on the first step of the staircase that led to the mezzanine. Siri said, "Okay if I come up?"

"Yes," I said. He climbed the rest of the stairs. "Grab a chair." I pointed to a chair near the wicker couch. "Bring it over here."

He did. "What are you doing?" Siri asked.

"Trying to get an identity on this woman and the man." I passed him my phone with the photos open.

He typed on his iPad. Then Siri spoke, "The second woman is Johanna Klein. She's German."

"And you know this?"

Siri said, "I do. Don't know why, but I do."

About two seconds later, the database I was using spat out a name to match the second photograph. "Johanna Klein, German National. Works for Weber Group."

Uncle George: Second woman is Johanna Klein. Weber Group.

Ronnie: Thanks. Weber Group PMC's?

Uncle George: Affirmative

I looked at Dane. "You're really back, aren't you?"

He nodded then typed. "I think I am," Siri said. "Can I look at the footage from the last ball?"

"Of course." I loaded it up and moved the monitor so Dane could see it. He motioned for the mouse. I pushed it towards him.

I leaned back and watched him work. After such a long absence, seeing him as he used to be, minus his voice, was awesome. That used to be Dane's favourite word. He was always awesome. Ellie was always okay.

Dane paused the video and zoomed in on a person seated near a wall.

"Is the person important?" I asked.

He nodded. He picked up my phone, held it towards me to unlock it, then took a photo of the screen and sent it to Ronnie.

Uncle George: this person from the last ball is Sebastian Fellows.

He handed me the phone.

"Who is he?"

Dane typed on his iPad, and Siri said, "Bad guy."

"Do you recognise anyone else?"

He typed. Siri said, "Not yet."

He went back to watching the footage. There was three hours of footage to go over.

My phone buzzed.

Ronnie: Sebastian Fellows is not on our list.

I showed Dane. He nodded. Then took my phone. He typed. When I got my phone back, he'd sent a text to Ronnie that said: Daniel Henry; is that name on your list? Same person.

Ronnie: Thank you. Now we know what he looks like we might have a chance at grabbing someone from the deal.

"You need anything?" I asked Dane.
He shook his head.
"I'll check on the girls."
He nodded. His eyes never left the screen. I went downstairs.

Chapter Forty-nine:
[Ronnie: The Wayward Son.]

I leaned into Ben and whispered, "Sebastian Fellows is Daniel Henry's name."

Ben turned his head and whispered back. "Excellent."

We were waiting for Karen to bring coffee. She wasn't at all put out by our second sudden appearance. Or at least that was the impression she gave.

I heard cups rattling and they drew closer.

Karen stepped through the doorway with a bright smile and a laden tray. She sat the tray on the coffee table.

"Now, how can I help?" she asked, pouring the coffees.

"I wondered if you'd managed to get hold of Neve?" I said, matching her bright smile with one of my own. Ben and I knew she was dead, but did Karen?

"I did try this morning, but the call rang out." She passed me a cup. "I left a voice message."

"Hopefully she'll call soon then," I said and took a sip of coffee. It was bitter compared to the coffee she'd made us the day before. I placed the cup on the small end table next to me.

"Is there anything else I can help you with?"

"Just a question about the ball. Who did the seating plan?"

She raised her cup to her lips, then put it down without drinking. "Why would you ask that?"

"Curious. Was it you or do you have someone who sorts out seating and handles guests' preferences?"

"Oh, I see," she said. She still looked guarded. "Usually, it's a joint effort. Especially for a wedding. I would take into account family issues and so forth. It can be tricky with some families."

I nodded. I'm sure it could. Mine would be no exception.

Ben placed his cup back on the tray, grabbing Karen's attention. "Did you get a list of people who wanted to sit with their backs to the walls for the ball?"

This time deep lines appeared in her forehead. "Why are we talking about the ball and not your wedding?"

"Because Karen, someone had certain people seated with their backs to the wall," I said. My tongue felt odd. I ignored it and pressed on with my questions. "I would like to know who made the seating plan for the masked ball."

"I made the seating chart myself. There was no input by others," she said, her voice haughty. "Let's enjoy our coffee."

An alarm rang in my brain. The coffee was bitter. My tongue no longer felt strange. I looked at Ben. He went to pick his cup up and I shook my head just enough to tell him not to.

"I'm not inclined to believe that. Something else that might interest you ..." I said and paused. "Four of the people at your masked ball are now dead."

Her mouth opened then closed. Then opened. "How

would that have anything to do with me?"

"It probably doesn't, but it might have something to do with the person who suggested the seating plan."

"I don't know what you are talking about."

I sighed. "No one ever does until they do."

Ben smiled at the woman. "Do you know a Sebastian Fellows?"

She froze. Proper froze.

"Breathe, Karen," I said.

She blinked and took a breath. "I don't know that person."

Liar, liar, pants of fire.

I stood up and walked to her desk. I wanted to know if the binder associated with the ball was still around.

"What are you doing?" she asked, struggling to her feet.

"Wait there, I'll be back," I said as I spotted it on the floor and lifted it into my arms. It was substantial and I was curious as to what else was in it besides the guest lists. We hadn't come across any Sebastians in the lists. Names like that stand out. It's not the most common name in New Zealand. I sat next to Ben. "Look what I found," I said to him, and flipped the cover open. It was an indexed binder. How wonderful. I imagined that wedding planning required precision timing and indexes, as well as flags and notes. It'd be a hard habit to break all that indexing and organising. I ran my finger down the index until I found the floor plans and seating plans. I flipped entire sections over to get to the plans.

Ben and I took careful note of the names of people around the edge of the hall.

They were all there. All the people from the app.

I turned another page. Karen drew in a sharp breath. I looked up and smiled at her. "I must be getting close."

I turned another page.

Ben pointed to the name Sebastian Fellows with a phone number next to it and a note that said he wanted people seated around the walls and there was a list.

"Sebastian Fellows is Daniel Henry," Ben said. "He was at the ball, he is bidding, he is behind it, and he is here in New Zealand."

"And she put something in our coffee," I whispered, and snapped a photo of the page, then added the phone number to my phone.

"Now what?" Karen said.

"Now, we go to work, and you start planning our wedding. We'll take this binder with us."

"You can't take that, I will need it to contact the winners of the silent auction," she said, holding her hand out for the book.

"We'll bring it back, I promise," I said. "Today, don't answer the phone, don't answer the door. Maybe go somewhere no one can find you. Everything will be fine and tomorrow all will be normal."

My phone alerted. I glanced at it. "Bomb threat at Auckland Airport," I said.

"That can't be real," Karen said.

"It can," I replied. "People have no idea how many

466

times it never gets to the public announcement stage. Most of the time people like us stop threats before they become something that can't be walked back."

I tucked the book under my arm. "Nice try with the poison or whatever it was in the coffee. If I were you, I'd get rid of that evidence. Just in case the police turn up."

Her mouth opened then closed. I hope she bit her tongue.

We left.

"Your office. Can you do your thing and find this guy before the next missile?"

I grimaced at Ben. "Phone?"

"Glove compartment," he replied.

"Let's hope I can find him," I said. While Ben drove, I sent as much as I could to *Uncle George,* and then to Crockett, and Enzo. Enzo might be down, but he wasn't out. I asked him to take Donald and go to Nana. Someone had to be with her. Told him to arm himself.

I texted Art and told him to arm up and protect Kallie and Kevin. I believed they were the real PMCs, but I wouldn't swear to it on Nana's life.

Crockett: What do I do with our guest?
Me: Whatever you need to do, to keep everyone safe.
Crockett: Did you hear about the bomb threat?
Me: Yes. They're getting desperate.

I ran up the stairs with Ben matching my speed. I didn't go to the main office. I went straight to my room. I took the pendulum from around my neck, grabbed a map of the region and spread it out. Ben kicked the door shut and sat in the chair he used last time. I took several cleansing breaths and spoke to the pendulum. Once I had a base, yes and no, and confirmation that spirit would show me what I asked to see and not mess around, I got busy.

I could feel my heart thumping in my chest. We were close. My hand was dragged all over the region, pausing at times, then moving on until there was a giant pull to the mosque in Trentham.

"You have got to be kidding," Ben said, when he saw the pendulum drop, shake, and roll, then stop pointing at the mosque.

"Nope. He's there."

Ben nodded, jumped to his feet, sending the chair back into the wall, then grabbed the door handle. I was right behind him as he went into the tech room. At the back of the room was a walk-in safe. I leaned around him and pressed my thumb on the lock. It clunked. Ben pulled the door. Inside were rifles, pistols, smoke grenades, pretty much everything you'd want or need when hunting bad people. He handed me a kevlar vest from the back wall of the safe and dropped another over his head. He passed me a handgun, paddle holster, and ammunition. Then he took the same for himself. A couple of smoke grenades each went into a black messenger bag he took from a shelf outside the safe.

We nodded at each other, satisfied with what we had.

I texted Crocket: Meet us at the first place we looked for Ben.

We left.

It was a Monday. We were going to be right next to a school. I rang Tierney from my phone as Ben drove.

"We found the person behind this shit. He's at the mosque in Trentham. We are going in. Alert police that we are armed and will be next door to Fergusson Intermediate. We need the area locked down. We are not waiting. We have one chance to get him before the next launch."

"Be safe, my dear. I've got everything else covered."

He hung up. Ben pulled up outside the dairy. There were teenagers lurking. We left the car carrying weapons and wearing Kevlar.

They stopped talking and stared. "Go into the shop," I said. "Stay there."

A few started to argue. Joe came out of the fish and chip shop. "Ronnie?"

"Get those kids inside. Keep the door locked."

I ran into the café. "Lock up," I said to the proprietor. The woman glowered but followed me to the door.

Ben came out of the dairy as I exited the café. Doors closed.

Sirens screamed from Fergusson Drive.

Ben and I jogged to the edge of the mosque property. No cars.

I hoped Mohammad wasn't there. He was a nice guy. I

469

didn't want anyone good caught in this mess.

I heard a voice a little way behind me. Crockett.

He ran up. "Front," Crockett said.

"Back," Ben said. "You're with me, Ronnie."

No one said another word. I saw blue and red flashing lights racing towards us. Crockett signalled he was moving. I followed Ben. We hit the back door as I heard Crockett kick in the front door.

I squeezed Ben's shoulder. He moved. I stayed on his shoulder. We saw Crockett coming towards us. There was no sign of Mohammad. Ben pointed to the door that led to stairs; there was light coming from under it. I looked over my shoulder when I heard another voice.

Police.

"Armed police coming in," a voice said. I recognised him as Jerry as he joined me behind Ben.

Crockett shoved the door wide.

Jerry motioned to me to step back.

Great, he can have all the fun then. We do the all the work; he has all the fun.

I let him in. I moved back to the outer door. Down the hallway I saw two more police officers. By the back door was another.

There was a muffled bang.

Then there was silence.

Then the sound of gunfire rang out.

Two minutes ticked by. We heard nothing.

Ben called out, "Coming up!"

Then I saw movement.

Ben came out first. He looked okay.

"Got him," he said.

An officer behind me spoke into his radio and said the situation was under control.

A handcuffed man was pushed up the stairs by Crockett. He followed Ben out. Ben grabbed his arm and pushed him against the kitchen cabinets.

"Sebastian Fellows aka Daniel Henry aka Nailed," he said, pointing to the man who sneered.

Two plain clothed people hustled down the hall towards us.

One spoke, "Bill sent us."

I nodded. "Tierney must've called him," I said to Ben.

"Makes sense." Ben shook hands with the first man. "Ben Reynolds, this is Daniel Henry," he said.

"We'll take him off your hands," the man said.

"Not so fast," Ben replied. "ID."

I rang Bill at Army Intelligence.

"Did you send us help?"

"I did. You should have Simon Conner and Chris Conner in front of you."

"Related?"

"Can't you tell?"

"I can now." I hung up.

Ben and Crockett smiled at me. I nodded.

"Can we go for a beer?" I asked, as Simon and Chris removed the target from our presence."

"Yes," Ben replied. He faced the police officers who were waiting to see what would happen next. "Thank you," Ben said. "You don't know it, but the world should be thanking you."

Jerry shook his head. "Always dramatic, Reynolds."

"It's in my genes," Ben said laughing.

The End.

I know some of you quite enjoy a code:

Rczi mzvyzmn wmzvocz gdaz dioj xcvmvxozmn
oczmz dn ij gdhdo ji ocz gziboc ja ocjnz g
dqzn. Mjiidz, Wzi, Xmjxfzoo, Iviv, Ziuj, Y
jivgy, viy ocz Xmjidzn ja Yjjh ocvif tjp a
jm bdqdib oczh gdaz.

Acknowledgments:

Nicky Hurle - thank you!

Chrissy - Because life is by far more fun with someone who really knows you, has your back no matter what, and will bring a shovel without question. 40/45?

Big thanks to *Robyn and Duigald* for returning for another round with Ronnie and Ben!

Margot Kinberg - for making sure Ben and Mitch are still American and being a golden grammar hammer and much trusted first reader. https://margot-kin-berg.com/

Pete Turner - for being an awesome go-to espionage guy and for his unwavering encouragement. Everyone need a friend like Pete. https://www.breakitdownshow.-com/

Geoff Inwood - for listening when I rabbited on about scenes or the premise of the story, for your patient and thoughtful answers to my questions.

My children and my father - for being amazing humans and for always being super supportive: Caleb (&Lizzie), Rebekah (& Joshua Luke), Patricia (& Tim),

Josephine (& Matt), Joshua (& Jenna), Caoilfhionn (& Matt), & Brianna.

My grandchildren: Isaac, Deaglán, Caeden, Connaire, Benjamin, Dylan, Cayde, David, Corey, Lily, Xanthy, Violet, Aspyn and the newest addition!

Pip - It was great having you back in NZ for 7 months. Cheers for the laughs, tequila, and encouragement.

Readers - without readers a story exists in the dark so thank you for providing light.

About the author:

Cat Connor is a prolific crime thriller author hailing from New Zealand. Her expertise in the genre is reflected in her engaging and suspenseful narratives, which have garnered a loyal following. Her work is known for its intricate plots, dynamic characters, and relentless pace, keeping readers on the edge of their seats until the very end. She has authored multiple books, including the popular Ellie Conway FBI-Byte" series, which follows the exploits of an FBI unit that investigates serial crime.

Cat's passion for crime and espionage is evident in her writing, as she strives to create a world that is both authentic and thrilling. Her meticulous attention to detail and extensive research have won her critical acclaim and accolades from readers and peers alike. In addition to writing, Cat enjoys speaking on topics related to writing and publishing. Her talks are known for their candidness, humour, and practical advice. With her unique blend of talent, expertise, and passion, Cat Connor has established herself as one of the most exciting and accomplished authors in the crime thriller genre.

Her other passions include music, reading, tequila, red wine, coffee, and chocolate. When she's not writing she can be found binge watching TV shows and spending time with her much adored animals; Diesel the Mastador, Patrick the Tuxedo cat, Dallas the seal-point tortie Birman, and Jimmy the thug.

You can follow and contact Cat at the following places:

Website: www.catconnor.com
X: @catconnor (Not there much anymore)
Facebook: @cat.connor
Instagram: @catconnorauthor
Bluesky: @catconnor.bsky.social
Threads: @catconnorauthor

Also by Cat Connor:

The Kiwi set Veronica Tracey Spy/PI series:
[Nothing happens here] -2020
[Lure the lie] - 2021
[Leave a message] - 2022
[Whiskey Tango Foxtrot] - 2023
[Xray Mike Alpha Sierra] - 2023 (Christmas short story)
[Foxtrot Mike Lima] - 2024
[India Romeo Lima] - WIP

The FBI based Byte Series:
Killerbyte - 2009
Terrorbyte - 2010
Exacerbyte - 2011
Flashbyte - 2012
Soundbyte - 2013
Snakebyte - 2013 (novella)
Databyte - 2014
Eraserbyte - 2015
Psychobyte - 2016
Metabyte - 2017
Qubyte - 2018
Cryptobyte - 2019
Vaporbyte - 2020 (red)
Vaporbyte -2020 (purple)
Raidbyte - 2021 (collection of longer short bytes)
Cachebyte - 2024 (collection of short bytes)

Milton Keynes UK
Ingram Content Group UK Ltd.
UKHW012251110624
443988UK00005B/338